MY LAST STORY UNFOLDED

THE LAST STORY

BY GAURAV MAHESHWARI

BLUEROSE PUBLISHERS
India | U.K.

Copyright © Gaurav Maheshwari 2024

All rights reserved by author. No part of this publication may be reproduced, stored in a retrieval system or transmitted in any form or by any means, electronic, mechanical, photocopying, recording or otherwise, without the prior permission of the author. Although every precaution has been taken to verify the accuracy of the information contained herein, the publisher assumes no responsibility for any errors or omissions. No liability is assumed for damages that may result from the use of information contained within.

BlueRose Publishers takes no responsibility for any damages, losses, or liabilities that may arise from the use or misuse of the information, products, or services provided in this publication.

For permissions requests or inquiries regarding this publication, please contact:

BLUEROSE PUBLISHERS
www.BlueRoseONE.com
info@bluerosepublishers.com
+91 8882 898 898
+4407342408967

ISBN: 978-93-6452-493-3

Cover Design: Shivani
Typesetting: Sagar

First Edition: December 2024

Preface

Friends, I'm not writing this book just for any one person, I'm writing it for all the friends who've supported me through thick and thin. I thought of writing it in English, but then I realized that doing so would probably make me lose all the emotion in the process. So instead, this book will be a mix of humor, rawness, and a whole lot of "bakchodi" (nonsense). You'll laugh, and maybe even shed a tear or two. What can I say, life's like that, isn't it? At some point, you realize that no matter what happens, peace seems to be something you'll never truly find.

But hey, let's begin this crazy, wild, Titanic-like journey of mine.

Before anything else, I want to start with a massive "thank you" to the one up there. Yes, you heard me right. Despite everything—whatever happened, whatever kept happening—he gave me the best people. My family, my friends, my brothers, and colleagues—each one of them, the best I could ever have. So, from the bottom of my heart, a huge thank you to all of you. Without you, I wouldn't be who I am today.

Now, let's get into the real drama of life. It hasn't always been conventional, you know. Every day brought something new, and at times it felt like I was living in some absurd comedy show—where people are serious but also joking around at the same time. But the truth is, in life, it's the small things that turn into the biggest struggles, and often, the same small things bring the most joy too.

But there's one thing I've learned through all of this, something that I'll always hold close to my heart... and that is to keep laughing at yourself, no matter what. That's where the real joy of life lies. If you take life too seriously, it will never end. So, the key is to just be yourself, and enjoy each moment as it comes. Because once you understand yourself, no external problem can truly shake you.

Thank you, friends. Thank you, everyone. Without all of you, none of this would have been possible.

Contents

Chapter 1
Rage Unleashed 1

Chapter 2
The Beginning of the Sweetest Chapter 7

Chapter 3
A New Beginning 10

Chapter 4
Heartstring woven 15

Chapter 5
Where Dream embrace 23

Chapter 6
"I Love You" and the Long-Distance Relationship Begins 40

Chapter 7
Fortune Double edge 47

Chapter 8
She is the Best 50

Chapter 9
Aggressive Garv was back 60

Chapter 10
Change in the Life of The Fire 69

Chapter 11
The First Date and the Best Date of Garv's Life 80

Chapter 12
Did Their First Date End? 89

Chapter 13
Failure's Taste 103

Chapter 14
'Things Started Changing for Both
Betterment, We Guess' 107

Chapter 15
Challenges are there, but apologies and
compromises work through everything 114

Chapter 16
Love is in the Air 123

Chapter 17
Never break Trust 143

Chapter 18
Poker Face Works and Misunderstandings 150

Chapter 19
Office Fights and Buddy in Trouble 169

Chapter 20
A Boon Amidst a Crisis 173

Chapter 21
Playing the Role of Catalyst and Keeping Patience 183

Chapter 23
The Best Trip of Their Lives Begins 237

Chapter 24
Even Rocks Get Cracks 254

Chapter 25
   Good Old Times Are Back 304
Chapter 26
   Stars Are Really Farther Than They Appear 318
Chapter 27
   Love sometimes make people extraordinary Blind 327

Chapter 1

Rage Unleashed

Let me introduce you to this guy, a bit of a character. Don't judge him too harshly, friends, but I swear, I've never met a bigger fool in my life than him.

Life was moving along just fine for him, but even from childhood, his anger, attitude, and energy were something else. He would fight anyone, anywhere, for his friends and family. Now, you must be wondering how aggressive he could really be. Well, he had quite the temper, and everyone knew it—on the field or in school, people believed it was always better to be on his team because he played with such intensity. But at the same time, when it came to girls, he was an introvert from the start.

As he grew older, his temper only grew with him. It was nearly impossible for him to go a week without some sort of mess. He was the type of guy whose fists always seemed ready for action, so someone or the other ended up with bruises every week—be it at school, in tuition, or in his society.

So let's formally introduce him. The guy who's swung everything from bats, belts, stumps, and pens to whatever else he could find at people—but somehow, he could never quite lose the habit of crying afterward. Meet Garv Maheshwari.

And it all started back in eighth grade.

Diwali vacation, early morning:

"Hey, get up, man! If you don't wake up now, someone else will grab the spot!" Garv nudged his friend. "Get up, or you're gonna get it from me."

Devik grunted, half-asleep, "Bro, I'm getting up. It's only 5:45, geez."

"Look, I'm telling you, if we lose the middle pitch, you'll regret it. I've got better things to plant my stakes in."

Devik muttered, "Fine, fine, I'll come along. Let me take a quick dump, alright?"

After rounding up the rest of their friends, Garv and Devik—childhood buddies, always seen together after school—mounted their bikes and pedaled their way to the ground.

"Man, you're a fool," Garv grumbled. "Now those local goons are probably gonna come around and mess with us again. Look, it's already 6:30."

Devik laughed, "Don't worry, man, no one's probably there yet."

Once they reached the ground, their friend Hitesh greeted them, smirking, "Bro, you woke us all up just to be the last one here yourself?"

"Got us out here to get messed up, huh?" teased Chinoy, affectionately.

Garv rolled his eyes. "What can I do? This guy here spends half an hour just going to the bathroom."

And then came Chapri, the usual troublemaker. As soon as he spotted Garv, he grabbed the collar of one of Garv's friends and sneered, "Get out of here, or else..."

That was all it took. Garv and Chinoy launched themselves at him, bat in hand, ready to let him have it. But when they started playing, Chapri threw a rock at Chinoy, adding a few choice words before storming off.

"Next time," Garv muttered under his breath, "I'm bringing a screwdriver and a hammer. Let's see him try anything then."

The next morning, they arrived at the ground, and there was Chapri again, that little pest.

"If you try anything today," Garv warned, "we'll bury you six feet under."

With that, Garv pulled out his hammer and screwdriver, while his friends grabbed their bats, and anyone left empty-handed armed themselves with stones. In the middle of all this, one of them snatched the ball.

"Bro, we just pooled our money for this ball," Chinoy groaned. "Put it back in your pocket, okay?"

And after that day, Chapri never dared to show his face again. But Devik, wise as he was, had already jumped over the wall to hide in the neighboring society.

After Diwali vacations, as revision tests began:

That's when Anshika Saxena made her grand entrance. Her arrival sent waves through all three sections; it was as if the entire crowd of top rankers had met their match. With the FA (the 25-mark exams) coming up in just a week, the atmosphere was tense.

Mahesh announced his score: a solid 94, as usual. Harsha followed with 93.5, and Daga, still cheerful and unaffected by the competition, reported 91.

Then there was Kajol, a close friend of Harsha, who scored 93. But the talk of the class was Anshika herself, who had managed a whopping 97.

The entire class of toppers was stunned. They were left wondering how someone could manage that in just a week. Tension started brewing among the two best friends, Harsha and Kajol, as they eyed Anshika with newfound rivalry.

Amidst all this, you might be wondering where Garv was. Well, he was perfectly content with his own score of 82, entirely unbothered by any sense of competition. He was just waiting for the next period—sports.

Anshika shot Garv a few looks, which he chose to ignore completely.

A few days later, during the revision tests:

"Mam, Garv is cheating from a textbook," Anshika reported out loud.

Garv's eyes went wide in shock. He took it personally; science was his favorite subject, and he prided himself on scoring well in it. Today, however, he had forgotten one diagram and decided to take a quick peek at his book—only to be called out in front of everyone.

"Garv, your paper will not be checked," the teacher declared, disapprovingly.

Once the period ended, Garv approached Anshika at her desk.

"Have I ever bothered you? Then what was the need to complain?" he asked, frustrated.

"You were cheating, and I saw it," Anshika replied matter-of-factly. "If I hadn't spoken up, they'd think I was a cheater too."

From that day forward, Garv never missed a chance to tease her. He started calling her "Aunty," "Complaint Box," and even "Chapli." But did Anshika care? Not one bit. She stayed engrossed in her books, hardly paying any attention to his taunts.

Eventually, the exams ended, and Anshika topped the class. That gave Garv a new nickname for her: "Rattu Total."

One day, Garv confided in his friend Rajat, whom he'd known since kindergarten. "Man, I wish they'd just change her section. She's got it out for me."

Rajat chuckled. "Relax, bro. She's not going to eat you alive."

"Dude, I've never met someone like her in my life. It's like her only goal is to be number one in everything," Garv muttered.

When their bus finally arrived at school, they expected the classroom to be empty since they always reached early. But as they entered, they were surprised to see The Ace—Anshika—already there.

Garv and Rajat exchanged a glance, set their bags down, and headed straight for the ground.

"God, please help me survive this year," Garv prayed out loud. "If they make her the monitor, I swear she'll chew me up and spit me out."

"Are we really going to make Mahesh or Harsha the monitor? Why are you even worried about that?" Rajat said with a laugh.

In the first period, the class teacher announced that Anshika would be the new monitor. To keep Garv from causing too much trouble, she seated him next to a new student, Karthik.

Garv actually felt good about it—Karthik was a lot like him, mischievous but also a top student. They quickly became partners in creating havoc in the classroom. However, since Karthik was a scholar, Anshika overlooked his antics and never mentioned his name.

But for Garv, things were different. He kept getting in trouble:

"Garv was disturbing the class."

"Garv didn't complete his homework."

"Garv hasn't cut his nails."

"Garv was fighting with classmates"—though he thought, *fighting involves two people; why is it always my fault?*

"Garv left the class without asking."

Garv's frustration grew as Anshika's big, bold handwriting filled the remarks section in his notebooks and reports, which his teachers, parents, and even the principal saw. That year, he got scolded a lot at home.

One day, the classroom was especially noisy.

"Garv, stop making noise, or I'll complain to ma'am again," Anshika warned.

But this time, Garv had had enough. He hadn't done anything; he was quietly resting with his head down. He snapped, "Hey, 'Chakki'! First check what I'm doing—I'm sitting peacefully here!"

Unfortunately, Deepika ma'am overheard that and called him out of the class.

"Are you out of your mind, Garv? Who talks like that? And do you know the principal was just here?"

"But ma'am, I was doing nothing. She just complains for no reason! I was peacefully sitting with my head down, but she only seems to see me," Garv explained in frustration.

Deepika ma'am asked Garv's friends, and his desk partner confirmed he had been quiet. Reluctantly, Anshika muttered, "Sorry…"

Garv responded, "You're the one who needs to say sorry."

Though he apologized, Garv's bitterness lingered. The nickname "Chakki" caught on, and the rivalry between their groups only intensified.

By the end of ninth grade, it was announced that Garv's class would be changed for tenth grade, since board exams were coming up.

"Finally, I'll get some peace," Garv sighed with relief.

But Rajat chuckled, "Brother, the heavens heard you. Let's celebrate this evening."

Chapter 2

The Beginning of the Sweetest Chapter

Garv was enjoying his new class, feeling the comfort of unity and freedom. But as fate would have it, peace was short-lived.

After summer vacation, during roll call in his new class, the teacher of XC announced, "Garv, you're moving back to XA."

"What did I do now?" Garv exclaimed in disbelief. "Ma'am, why is my class changing again?"

"The girl assigned to your class had her parents request a switch, and the principal approved," the teacher explained.

Back in XA, Deepika ma'am immediately reminded him, "Garv, you're in tenth grade now. No more messing around." But she realized she'd have to take extra measures to keep him in line.

And so, she made him sit with Anshika.

"Ma'am, please, anywhere but next to her," Garv pleaded.

"It's either that, or you sit outside," she responded firmly.

The whole class laughed, even his friends, flashing him sympathetic but amused smiles as he settled into his seat next to Anshika, feeling like he was trapped.

Before the storm unfolds, let's step back to understand Garv a little more.

Garv's mother was a Delhi University BA and B.Ed. graduate and had been tutoring students ever since they moved to Surat. Garv had a younger brother, Dhruv, whom he loved dearly, though they shared the typical sibling rivalry, complete with WWE-style fights. Garv's dad, an Accounts Head at Essar Steel, was strict with him, as he was frustrated by Garv's growing disinterest in studies in favor of mischief and games. Despite the frequent scoldings, Garv knew deep down that his father loved him.

Garv's friends—Devik, Nishant, Mahesh, Vishal, Ronak, Rajat, Karthik, and Ruchi—were central to his life, and they'll continue to shape his story as we move forward. Although he didn't fear losing much, he only prayed never to hurt his mother. Garv had an emotional side, often crying alone whenever he felt he had disappointed her.

There was a time, back in first grade, when he ran to his mom after scoring good marks, hugging her tightly. Unbeknownst to him, that hug had caused her to lose a pregnancy due to its suddenness. No one blamed him, but Garv silently carried the guilt, which perhaps hardened him from the outside while softening him within.

～

Ready for the roller-coaster ride? Fasten up, because this journey's going to be one you'll remember.

The bell rang, signaling the start of the sports period.

"Kya bhai, khelna nahi hai kya?" Garv's friends called out, hoping he'd join them.

"Arre, khelne ka toh bilkul mann nahi hai yaar. Soch raha hoon uske saath ek din bitana mushkil hai, aur poori 10th uske saath kaise nikaalunga?" Garv muttered in frustration.

"Dikkat kya hai, bhai? Baithna hi toh hai, shaadi toh nahi karni!" Nishant laughed, trying to lighten his mood. "Aur hum tere aas paas hi baithte hain na? Chal, tension mat le!"

For the next seven days, Garv somehow kept his calm, although they were his quietest days in school. He barely spoke to his friends, no usual jokes or loud laughter. He simply sat in silence next to Anshika, avoiding eye contact and quietly putting up with the awkwardness. But on the eighth day, his patience finally broke.

"Anshika, please, mujhe us taraf baithne do," he requested with a hopeful smile.

Anshika glanced at him, considering. "Thik hai, alternate days mein swap karte hain. Ek din tu wahan baith ja, ek din main."

"Thank you," Garv said, relieved. "Aaj main baith sakta hoon na?"

She nodded, adding, "Bas, Garv, mujhe disturb mat karna, please."

Garv promised with a grin, "Bilkul nahi hoga, Anshika."

The next morning, Garv made sure to arrive early, feeling a small thrill as he got to sit with his friends again.

"Arey, aaj jaldi aa gaya kya, bhai?" Mahesh teased, grinning.

"Arre, ghanta! Yeh toh compromise kiya hai—ek din, ek din ka!" Garv muttered under his breath.

Anshika heard his words, and Garv saw her giving him a warning look. He whispered to his friends, "Bhai, ab ek baar tum log mere paas aana. Main gali deta hoon toh tum mujhe mukka maar dena, warna phir se nikal jayegi!"

For the first time, Garv was trying to change his behavior. Little did he know, this was just the beginning.

Chapter 3

A New Beginning

One rainy day, Garv noticed that Anshika seemed to be shivering slightly from the cold breeze entering the classroom. He hesitated, then got up quietly, switched off the fan above them, and closed the door to block out the chilly wind.

His classmates noticed. "Bhai, yeh kya kar raha hai? Fan kyon band kar diya?"

"Arre bhai, thoda fever jaisa lag raha hai," he said, using the excuse to avoid explaining his real reason. Anshika caught his eye, giving him a soft smile.

"Thanks, Garv," she said quietly.

Garv felt a strange, unfamiliar warmth at her gratitude and just gave her a quick smile before slipping out to the washroom to compose himself.

In the last period, math class began—Garv's least favorite subject. He struggled with the sums, and Anshika noticed his frustration.

"Kya hua, Garv? Main samjha doon?" she offered, a touch of concern in her voice.

Garv was taken aback but nodded, and she started explaining the tricky trigonometry problem to him.

Just as he was beginning to understand, the math teacher's voice boomed. "Garv! Stand up!"

"Sir... kuch hua?" he stammered, caught off guard.

"Bas tumhe padhai mein mann nahi lagta, aur dusron ko bhi tang karte ho. Get out!" the teacher barked, sending Garv out of the classroom.

Garv left without a word, finding Nishant already outside, grinning. "Bhai, tu bhi? Kya kiya tune?"

Garv explained the situation, shrugging it off, though he couldn't deny that Anshika's attempt to help had touched him. He knew she hadn't meant any harm.

"Vaise, tu kuch bhi keh, pehle baat tak nahi hoti thi, ab toh samjhane bhi lagi hai," Nishant teased.

Garv just rolled his eyes but couldn't hide a small smile.

As they waited for the bell to ring, Garv noticed a familiar face near the school gate—Anshika's mom. He remembered Nishant telling him she often came to pick up Anshika's younger brother.

When the bell finally rang, Garv avoided any eye contact with Anshika, quietly gathering his things and hurrying toward the bus.

The next morning, Garv arrived early and chose a seat on the opposite side, away from the fan, knowing Anshika would appreciate the warmer spot. He left his bag there to reserve the place and quickly went to the washroom.

When he returned, Rajat came up to him. "Bhai, Anshika tujhe dhoond rahi thi."

Puzzled, Garv walked over to her. "Kya hua, Anshika?"

She looked up, surprised but appreciative, and smiled.

The school bell rang, and it was time for the sports period.

"Kya bhai, khelna nahi hai kya?" asked Garv's friends.

"Arey bhai, bilkul nahi. Samajh nahi aa raha, iskae saath ek din bitana mushkil hai; poori 10th class saath mein bitha diya hai toh kya hoga mera," Garv grumbled.

"Bhai, dikkat kya hai? Baithna hi toh hai, shaadi thodi na karni hai! Hum bhi toh aage-peeche baithe hain tere, chal, khelte hain," Nishant and Mahesh tried to cheer him up.

For the next seven days, Garv followed the same routine. He'd walk into class every morning to find Anshika already sitting on the side where his friends usually sat. Garv felt helpless, but he kept his cool, staying unusually silent. His friends noticed that these were probably the quietest days of Garv's school life.

Eventually, Garv's patience broke.

"Anshika, please, mujhe us side baithne do," Garv requested one morning.

"Jaldi aao aur baith jao," she replied nonchalantly. "Mere bhi dost us side baithte hain, so why should I sit there?"

"Please, yaar. Main already frustrated hoon; at least let me sit on that side so I can talk to my friends," Garv pleaded.

"Alright, let's make a deal. Hum alternate days mein baithenge. Ek din tu baith ja, aur ek din main baithungi," Anshika finally compromised.

"Thank you! Kya main aaj baith sakta hoon?" Garv asked eagerly.

"Okay, but Garv, please don't disturb me."

Garv grinned, "Nahi hoga, Anshika, disturb aapko."

The next day, Garv made sure to sit on his designated side. His friends noticed and couldn't resist teasing him.

"Aaj pehle aa gaya, kya baat hai bhai!" said Mahesh and Nishant, laughing.

"Arey ghanta! Compromise kiya hai ek din ek din ka," Garv muttered.

Anshika shot him a look over his language, hearing his choice of words.

"Bhai, ek baar side mein aana," Garv whispered to his friends. "Tum logon ke saath gaali niklegi toh tumhe mujhe maarna padega!"

The boys laughed, knowing it wouldn't be easy for Garv to hold back.

Days passed, and Garv started noticing small things about Anshika. One rainy day, he noticed her shivering from the cold breeze entering through the windows. Garv, sweating from playing in the corridors earlier, quietly stood up, turned off the fans, and closed the door to keep out the chill.

"Bhai, kya kar raha hai? Fan kyon off kar diya?" a classmate questioned.

"Bhai, fever ja sa lag raha hai," Garv replied, coming back to his desk.

Anshika glanced up and gave him a soft smile. "Thanks, Garv."

Caught off guard, Garv simply smiled back and walked off, feeling a strange warmth in her gratitude.

In their last period, a challenging math class, Garv struggled with a trigonometry problem.

"Kya hua, Garv?" Anshika asked, noticing his frustration.

"Kuch nahi, ek sum samajh nahi aa raha. Kal Mahesh se samajh lunga," he replied.

"Mujhe batao, main samjha deti hoon," she offered, starting to explain.

Halfway through, however, the math teacher interrupted. "Garv, stand up! Tum dusron ko tang karne ke bajaye khud padhoge ya nahi?"

Without a word, Garv stood and walked out of the class, where he found Nishant already waiting, also banished.

"Bhai, tu bhi kya kiya?" Nishant laughed.

"Yaar, ek sum samajh nahi aa raha tha. Socha Anshika samjha de, aur sir ne galat samajh liya," Garv sighed.

As the day went on, Garv noticed Anshika's friends playfully sticking a piece of paper on her back that read "Aunty." Anshika, visibly upset, walked toward the washroom in tears.

Later that afternoon, as they packed up to leave, Garv noticed Anshika eating alone. He approached her quietly.

"Anshika, mere maths ka sum mein help kar dogi?" he asked, trying to lighten her mood.

"Mahesh nahi samjha raha ab aapko?" she replied with a slight smile, realizing he was just looking for an excuse to talk.

They shared a small laugh before Garv walked away, feeling a bit closer to her.

Days turned into weeks, and bit by bit, Garv and Anshika grew more comfortable with each other. Garv noticed how Anshika brought out a softer, more thoughtful side in him, and Anshika started relying on him for small moments of support. The walls between them slowly faded, and both of them began looking forward to the unexpected companionship they were building together.

Chapter 4

Heartstring woven

"Bhai, mil sakta hai kya aaj?" Garv asked over the phone.

"Tu bol, Golu! Sab theek hai na? Tution ke baad mil lete hain terrace par," Ronak replied, sensing something was up.

A few hours later, on the society terrace, Ronak greeted him, "Bhai! Kaisa hai? Mahine ho gaye yaad nahi kiya mujhe tune."

"Yaar, kuch share karna tha, aur school walon ke saath toh nahi kar sakta," Garv admitted, his tone unusually serious.

"Bol na, kya hua?" Ronak prodded.

"Yaar, mujhe lagta hai kisi se pyaar ho raha hai," Garv said, almost in disbelief at his own words.

"Londe, sach mein? Kaisi dikhti hai?" Ronak smirked, amused.

"Bhai, bohot sweet si hai, thodi akdu, lekin dil ki acchi hai," Garv said with a shy smile. "Bas mujhe samajh nahi aa raha mere saath kya ho raha hai."

"Dekho, Golu, jo ho raha hai hone de. Tujhe samajh aa jayega kya karna hai. Waise, khush ho ja - ek acchi ladki dosti kar rahi hai tere se," Ronak teased.

Garv laughed, feeling lighter. After saying goodbye, he went home, but he couldn't get Anshika out of his mind.

Once back, he texted her: _"Can I call you? Garv this side."_

Almost immediately, his phone rang.

"Hello! Hi Anshika," Garv greeted, trying to sound casual.

"Hi, Garv! Kya hua?" she asked.

"Vo maths ka sum samajhaogi kya?" he asked, hoping to extend their conversation.

They spent 35 minutes on the call, with Anshika patiently explaining the sums. Garv, in turn, was enchanted by her voice, barely noticing the time pass.

"Anshikaiiiii! Aajao khaane," came her mother's voice in the background.

"Mumma, five minutes!" Anshika replied before turning back to the call. "Garv, mujhe ab dinner ke liye jana hoga. Kal school mein baaki questions kar lena, okay? Good night!"

As he hung up, Garv felt an unusual peace that night, falling asleep with a smile.

~

The next morning, Garv entered the classroom and greeted her, "Good morning!"

"Good morning! Solve ho gaye sums?" she asked, eyes twinkling with interest.

"Haan, bas ek sum reh gaya. Kal poochh lunga," he replied with a grin.

Two days later, the 25-mark test series began. By the last test, Garv was mentally exhausted, especially since maths was his weak spot.

"Baitha kyon hai? Paper likh na," Anshika whispered, noticing him sit idle.

"Jitna aata tha, likh diya," he whispered back. "Sif 18 marks ka likha, baaki nahi aata."

With only ten minutes left in the test, Anshika subtly slid her paper towards him.

"Jaldi kar! Time ja raha hai!" she whispered, glancing around to ensure no one was watching.

Garv, in complete shock, quickly copied the 5-mark answer she'd revealed. He couldn't believe what had just happened, especially from someone as strict as Anshika.

After the exam, Garv gave her a grateful smile.

"Yeh baat kisi ko pata nahi chalni chahiye," she whispered firmly.

"Thank you, Anshika," he replied softly.

Day by day, they grew closer. Garv noticed himself changing - he'd started cracking jokes to make her smile, going out of his way to make her feel comfortable. And in return, Anshika became more relaxed around him, finding joy in his company and noticing his subtle gestures of care.

Slowly but surely, they were becoming each other's confidants, unaware of how much deeper their bond would soon grow.

The results came out, and Garv was thrilled—85%! But as he looked around, he saw Anshika in a heated discussion with her English teacher over a single lost mark.

"Anshika, kya hua?" he asked, curious.

"Poora right likha tha, fir bhi ek mark kaat diya," she fumed.

"Tum itni serious kyun ho yaar? Theek hai na, ek mark hi toh gaya," he said, trying to lighten her mood. His joke managed to make her smile, and she softened.

Their friendship continued to blossom as Anshika began helping him study, and Garv helped her be more patient and relaxed with friends. Their growing comfort was obvious, and even Garv's mom started noticing his constant need to call Anshika for "homework help."

Raksha Bandhan was approaching, and Anshika decided to tie Garv a rakhi as a way to handle her own budding feelings. Sensing what might be coming, Garv and his friend Karthik slipped out of the classroom just before the celebrations began.

"Kahan jaa rahe ho, Garv?" Anshika called out, noticing him leaving.

"Washroom," he replied with a grin. The two boys spent the entire period in the boys' washroom, waiting for the ceremony to end.

When he returned, Anshika smirked. "Saari rakhiyaan khatam ho gayi hain."

"Good," he teased. "Already have enough sisters, thanks."

They both burst into laughter, neither one entirely sure what they were feeling.

Soon after, exam prep kicked into high gear. Garv called Anshika to check in on her study progress, but her mother picked up.

"Hello! Aunty, namaste," he stammered, caught off guard.

"Anshika toh padh rahi hai, beta," her mother said, her voice firm. "Exams mein disturb mat karo."

Garv gulped. "Oh... theek hai, aunty. Bye."

As exams started, their centers were close, so Anshika often waited on the balcony after her papers, watching the river until Garv's bus arrived. They would chat for a while, exchange "all the best," and part ways until the next day.

But after exams, Garv returned to school only to find out from Mansvi that Anshika had left for a family wedding in Ludhiana. Each day dragged by, and his friend Nishant couldn't help but notice.

"Tu itna chup kyun hai, bhai?" Nishant asked one day.

"Kuch nahi, yaar," Garv replied, forcing a smile. "Bas result ka stress hai."

"Chutiya mat bana, tujhe result ka stress kabse hone laga?" Nishant laughed.

Garv's defenses crumbled. "Yaar, samajh nahi aa raha. Uske bina din katna mushkil ho gaya hai."

Nishant grinned knowingly. "Acchi dost hai na? Aur kuch nahi?"

"Yaar, bas itna hi. Acchi dosti hai," Garv replied, as if reassuring himself.

Finally, Garv's phone buzzed. It was Anshika, asking about homework and their results.

"Hello, Anshika! Kaisi ho?" he said, trying to contain his excitement.

"Badiya. Mera homework bata dena," she replied. "Aur, result kaisa tha?"

Garv sighed. "Sab theek tha, bas math mein 59 aaye."

She chuckled. "Koi baat nahi. Boards ke liye mehnat karna. Kuch samajh nahi aaye toh pooch lena."

"Roj call karke homework poochega toh daant toh padegi hi na. Koi nahi, chalo milte hain parso," Anshika said with a teasing smile.

"Good morning," Garv greeted her, his voice light.

"Good morning," Anshika replied.

"Kaise raha trip? Maza aaya?" Garv asked, eager to hear about her experience.

"Kaafi accha tha, yaar. Bahut jaldi din nikal gaye," Anshika responded, her smile reflecting the enjoyment of the trip.

Garv thought to himself, *Mujhe poochna chahiye tha ki kitna jaldi din nikle hain...*

After their conversation, Garv walked off to join his friends, while Anshika waited outside, feeling a mix of frustration and amusement. She had been coming to school early every day for him, but he never seemed to stay focused in class. It felt like he was always distracted, and she couldn't help but wonder if he even appreciated the effort she was putting in.

One day, Deepika ma'am entered the class and made an unexpected announcement: "Jo jiske saath baatna chahta hai, ab baat kar sakta hai."

Garv's heart sank a little. He had hoped to sit with Anshika, but now the situation seemed more complicated. Anshika, on the other hand, was eager to sit with him, even though she was trying to mask her excitement.

"Nahi yaar, log waise hi baatein banate hain. Agar hum saath baithenge, aur zyada baatein banengi," Garv said, trying to keep things casual.

"Toh kya karna hai? Tum Mansvi ko bolo ki woh tumhare saath baith jaaye, aur main Karthik ke saath baith jaungi," Garv suggested, offering a practical solution.

"Ohk, fine," Anshika agreed, though a part of her was reluctant.

For a few days, they followed this arrangement. But soon enough, their entire row of girls was occupied, and they had no choice but to shift to the last row. It was the only place where they wouldn't be teased by their classmates.

The next day, Garv decided to follow Ronak's advice, even though he was reluctant. He planned to avoid Anshika and see how she would react. As the school day started, he took his seat without looking at her, his heart racing with nervousness.

After the first two periods, Anshika noticed his unusual behavior. She tried to get his attention by nudging his shoe under the desk, but he pulled his foot away. Frustrated, she even turned around during class and tapped on his desk, but he pretended not to notice. Finally, she gave up, deciding to confront him during recess.

As soon as the bell rang, Anshika hurried over to Garv. "Garv, kya hua? Mujhse kya galti hui jo tum mujhse baat bhi nahi kar rahe?" she asked, genuinely hurt and confused.

Seeing her reaction, Garv's resolve melted. He realized he couldn't bear to hurt her, even as part of an experiment. He sighed and confessed, "Sorry, yaar. Mere bestie Ronak ne dare dekar kasam di thi ki ek din ke liye ignore karun... bas isi wajah se."

Anshika looked at him, her expression a mix of anger and relief. "Tumhe lagta hai main itni asani se dosti karti hoon, aur tum itna bara prank karke chale jaoge?" She was fuming but also slightly amused.

Over the next few periods, Garv tried his best to make it up to her, doodling funny sketches on scraps of paper and passing them to her. By the end of the day, she couldn't hold back her laughter.

Finally, he looked at her, eyes sincere. "Anshika, pakka promise, dobara aisa kabhi nahi karunga. Sorry, yaar."

She gave him a stern look but then smiled. "Bas, ab dobara kabhi mat karna. Maine tumhe maaf kiya."

In the last period, Deepika ma'am entered the class with an exciting announcement. "Class, we're going on a trip to Lonavala in five days! Anyone interested should bring 2500 rupees by tomorrow."

The class erupted in cheers, and Garv turned to Anshika, excitement evident in his eyes. But the next morning, she greeted him with a downcast expression.

"Good morning, Garv," she said in a low voice.

"Kya hua? Tum itni udaas kyun lag rahi ho?" he asked, concerned.

"Ghar waale mujhe trip pe aane nahi de rahe," she replied sadly.

"Kya? Tum toh sab kuch itna achhe se karti ho, phir mana kyun kiya?" he asked, trying to understand her parents' perspective.

"They're not comfortable with me going alone for three days," she explained.

Garv thought for a moment. "Ek idea hai... lekin sirf tabhi, agar tum ready ho."

"Kya?" she asked, curious.

"Mam se kehdo woh tumhare ghar par baat karein," he suggested.

Anshika hesitated. "Nahin yaar, woh sahi nahi lagega."

But, as it turned out, Deepika ma'am found out and took it upon herself to convince Anshika's parents. By the end of the day, Anshika had the good news but kept it a surprise from Garv.

The day of the trip arrived, and Garv and Devik were among the last to board. He had no idea Anshika was coming along until their buses made a stop for refreshments. When he saw her, his face lit up with surprise and joy.

The days in Lonavala were filled with adventure and laughter, but it was the quiet moments with Anshika that made the trip unforgettable for Garv. The bond between them grew stronger, with each day spent together deepening their friendship.

Little did they know, this trip would be the beginning of something truly special.

Chapter 5

Where Dream embrace

It was trip day, and as usual, Devik was late. Garv and Devik rushed to school, arriving just in time to catch the bus. By the time they stepped onto the bus, all the other students had already boarded.

Garv quickly made his way into the boys' bus with Devik by his side. What he didn't know was that Anshika was also on the trip, and he didn't realize it until the bus stopped for refreshments.

Garv stepped off the bus of XA and XB, stretching his legs.

"Anshika! Mujhe laga, aaj bhi late ho gayi, aur bus miss kar di tumne," Garv said, surprised to see her.

"Anshika, you're on the trip? Seriously? Mujhe bataya bhi nahi!" Garv continued, trying to process this new information.

"Surprise tha! Your plan worked automatically. Mam ko pata chala ki main nahi aa rahi thi, she talked to my mom and convinced her," Anshika explained with a smile.

"Nice," Garv responded, still processing the excitement of seeing her there.

The bus started again, and they waved at each other. Garv couldn't stop smiling—he was beyond happy.

Once they reached Lonavala, Garv, Karthik, Abhishek, and Mahesh were assigned to the same room. Ruchit, Vishal, Nishant, and Keshav were in the next room.

Later, they set off for the Ekvira Devi Temple. Upon reaching, Garv, along with his friends, decided to race to the top of the temple hill. In his rush to win, he completely forgot about Anshika and didn't even look back to see where she was.

Anshika watched him sprint ahead, feeling a bit disappointed that he didn't even wait for her.

After reaching the top, the group started taking photos. Garv and his friends posed, and then—

"Garv!" called out Mansvi.

"Haan, bol," Garv responded, turning to her.

"Meri Anshika ki photo click kar de," Mansvi asked with a smile.

Garv obliged and started clicking pictures of them, and a few of Anshika alone. Anshika, in her own way, tried to catch Garv's attention with her expressions, but he avoided looking her way. He wasn't one for photos, and he didn't want to make things awkward.

After the photoshoot, they all went together to the temple to pray. For the first time in his life, Garv found himself praying for something other than the usual things.

As they finished their prayers and started descending, Anshika called out, "Garv, neeche chalo."

"Chalo," Garv replied, and they slowly began walking down together. The weather was perfect, with the sunset just around the corner, making it a pleasant evening.

As they descended, they were both silent, walking side by side. Their hands brushed against each other from time to time. They both knew they couldn't hold hands openly, as the rest of the group was slowly catching up, and someone might notice, which could lead to complications.

"Wait, nahi kar sakte the chadhte waqt," Anshika said softly.

"Sorry yaar, miss ho gaya," Garv apologized, his face a little flushed.

"Aram se, Anshika," Garv reassured her, his voice gentle.

At that moment, Garv reached out and held her hand, guiding her as they continued to descend. She missed a step, but Garv was strong enough to support her. His muscles were there to handle the situation.

"Hum dheere dheere chalte hain. It will be good," Garv suggested.

"Anshika, tujhe nahi lagi na?" he asked, concerned.

"Chill, physical pain doesn't affect me. Tum bas aram se utro, koi jaldi nahi hai. Hum waise bhi sabse aage hain," Garv said, his tone reassuring.

Their fingers brushed with each step they took, and in that quiet moment, with the sun setting in the distance, it felt like the perfect moment of the trip. Neither of them said anything, but it was clear: sometimes, waiting for the right moment was worth it.

The night of the DJ party arrived, and Garv was in full swing, but his mind was elsewhere. He was desperately trying to find Anshika, calling her multiple times—at least ten. But each time, she didn't pick up. He searched through the crowd, eyes darting everywhere. Finally, when he spotted her, she was standing with her friends, laughing, completely absorbed in the moment. The misunderstanding hit him hard—why was she avoiding him?

Feeling an unusual mix of frustration and confusion, Garv decided to leave the DJ night. Rajat, noticing his mood, followed him out.

"Golu, kya hua bhai?" Rajat asked, sensing that something was off.

"Golu bsdk, yahan kya kar raha hai? Chal, chutiye, nagin dance nahi karna," Devik teased, always the source of light-hearted banter.

"Kya hua, ladayi kari kya? Anshika ne kuch bola?" Devik continued, noticing Garv's angry vibe.

Garv was pounding away at the leg press, using the physical exertion to release his pent-up frustration. It had been a while since he'd felt this angry. After a few minutes, he jumped onto the treadmill, running aimlessly as his thoughts spun. Meanwhile, Anshika, who had been outside, caught a glimpse of him. She passed him a smile, but Garv, still angry and lost in his emotions, stormed into the room without acknowledging her.

Anshika waited for him, standing in the balcony, hoping he would come to her.

"Garv, yahan uppar," she called out softly.

"Bolo," Garv replied flatly, his tone colder than usual.

"Kya hua aapko?" Anshika asked, genuinely concerned.

"It's late, Anshika. Aram se, kal baat karte hain. Agar koi dekh lega, toh scene create ho jayega," Garv responded, trying to push her away, not wanting to make a scene.

He turned and went back into the room, his mind still racing.

The next day, on the final day of the trip, they headed to Tiger Point. Garv, still carrying the weight of the previous night, was trying to keep his distance from Anshika. He needed time to release his anger, knowing that if he let his emotions loose, it could ruin everything.

"Garv," Anshika called out from behind him.

"Haan, bolo Anshika," he answered, trying to sound calm but failing to hide the tension in his voice.

"Kya hua? Kyun weird behave kar rahe ho?" Anshika asked, sensing something was off.

"Phone check kara apne," Garv snapped.

"Straightforward bolo, hua kya, Garv?" Anshika asked, standing her ground.

"Kal DJ ke time, I called you like 10 times, but kuch nahi yaar. Sahi hain, aapne kuch nahi kiya," Garv said, his voice edged with frustration.

Anshika smiled softly, trying to ease the tension. "Garv, sidha aakar baat kar lete, mera vo wala number ghar par hai, mumma ke paas."

"Shit! Tujhe yeh batana nahi tha! Waise hi ek baar daant khana chuka hoon, ab aur?" Garv muttered, feeling embarrassed.

"I'll take care of it, it's okay. But please, sidha aakar mujhse clear karna hota hai. Kya fayda hua, nahi kar raha tu, enjoy na, mujhe karne diya," Anshika said, her voice soft but firm.

"Sorry," Garv mumbled, his anger slowly starting to fade as he realized his mistake.

They took a walk together toward the bus, talking about the weather and small things to break the tension.

As the trip neared its end, it was time to head back to Surat.

"Good news!! Poori XA ek hi bus mein jaane wali hai. Deepika mam ne permission le li," Ruchit announced, bringing a sense of excitement to the group.

Garv felt a mix of happiness and anxiety. All the emotions that had been bubbling inside him were hard to contain now, and for the first time, it felt almost impossible to hold them in.

On the bus, Garv sat alone in the back, listening to songs on his earphones, trying to escape into the music. He needed some space to clear his head.

"Garv," Anshika called out softly, standing beside him.

"Haan, Anshika, bolo," Garv replied, his voice a little more relaxed.

"Kya hua, yahan akele kyon baat ho, aage chalo. Sab khel rahe hain," Anshika said, trying to engage him.

"Nahi, abhi maan nahi yaar. Aap jao, main aata hoon baad mein," Garv responded, trying to avoid the confrontation, still not ready to face his emotions.

Anshika, sensing his discomfort, sat down beside him, trying to talk to him. Garv's heart was pounding in his chest; he didn't want to speak his feelings out loud, afraid it would make things awkward.

Anshika, noticing his unease, got up after a few moments. "Kuch ho toh share kar lo. Aur aajana, aage sab enjoy kar rahe hain, aap bhi aa jao thodi der mein."

Garv stayed quiet for a while, but eventually, he gathered himself and joined his friends. They started playing a game of "Current Current," and everyone was in high spirits.

Garv stood by Anshika's seat, and they held hands discreetly. Garv, with a mischievous glint in his eye, subtly tickled her palm with his finger, causing her to flinch in surprise, feeling the "current" of the game. They continued like this for almost two hours, hands intertwined, and no one could get them out of the game.

Finally, the bus arrived in Surat. They waved at each other, their eyes meeting with a knowing smile, the kind of smile that said everything without needing words.

The tension between Garv and Anshika grows as their emotional connection deepens, yet moments of misunderstanding continue to challenge their relationship. The story shifts back to the school trip, where Garv is struggling with his emotions after seeing Anshika laugh while on the phone. Believing she might be avoiding him, Garv's frustration builds up, prompting him to leave the DJ night with Rajat and hit the gym to release his anger.

Despite his inner turmoil, Garv's connection with Anshika becomes stronger. When she notices him in the gym, she attempts to get closer, but he remains distant. After their brief conversation in the balcony, where Garv tries to avoid an emotional confrontation, their bond is tested again. The last day of the trip brings a chance for them to talk it out, and Anshika reassures Garv, telling him it's okay to be honest.

Back in Surat, the tension doesn't fade completely. On the bus ride back, Garv and Anshika's communication continues to rely on subtle cues and gestures, something no one else seems to notice. Garv remains guarded, still unsure of how to express his feelings, while Anshika senses his discomfort and gives him space. They find a brief escape from their uncertainty in a playful game, where they hold hands, passing a secret message through gentle touches.

The next day, school projects become the backdrop for more subtle tension. Garv's group project with Anshika faces complications, especially when he is caught in a lie during an English test. Anshika's decision to back him up in front of the teacher cements her role as his emotional anchor, but Garv feels guilty about her involvement. Meanwhile, their peers begin to notice the growing closeness between them, and some like Nishant even start to joke about their relationship. However, Garv remains evasive, still hesitant to confront his feelings directly.

With the projects underway, the dynamic between Garv, Anshika, and their friends shifts. Garv finds himself caught between two groups, one with Kajol and Harsha, and the other with Anshika. The playful banter from his friends continues, but there's an underlying tension—his growing feelings for Anshika are becoming more apparent. Despite the challenges and confusion, Garv can't seem to escape the pull of his emotions, and Anshika remains the one constant in his life. As the group works on their school projects, the lines between friendship and something deeper blur further, leaving Garv at a crossroads.

Each day brings them closer to understanding one another, but the question remains: will Garv have the courage to finally confront his feelings and risk everything for the one he cares about?

Anshika hesitated for a moment, her gaze lowered as she quietly fiddled with the soap mold. Garv, noticing the change in her demeanor, leaned in slightly.

"Hey, what's wrong? You look... different today," Garv asked softly, his concern evident.

Anshika sighed, running a hand through her hair before glancing up at him. "It's nothing really... just some things on my mind," she replied, her voice betraying a hint of sadness.

Garv didn't buy it. He knew her well enough to understand that there was more to it. He took a step closer and placed a hand gently on her shoulder. "You know you can tell me anything, right?"

She paused for a moment, looking down at the soap once more before looking back up at him. "It's just... sometimes I feel like I'm not good enough. Like I'm always trying so hard but never quite making it. And with the preboards coming up, the pressure is getting to me," she confessed, her voice barely above a whisper.

Garv was silent for a moment, letting her words sink in. He could sense the weight she was carrying, the insecurities that she rarely showed to anyone else. It wasn't like Anshika to open up like this, and he knew it meant a lot that she was confiding in him.

"You don't need to worry about being good enough, Anshika," he said, his voice calm but firm. "You're smart, you're capable, and you always give your best. That's all anyone can ask for. And as for the preboards—don't stress too much. We've got this together."

Anshika looked up at him, her eyes softening, and for the first time in a while, a small smile tugged at the corner of her lips. "Thanks, Garv. You always know how to make me feel better."

Garv grinned, his usual mischievous spark returning. "Well, that's what friends are for, right? Besides, you're not getting rid of me that easily."

The two shared a quiet laugh, the tension easing between them. As they stood there in the lab, the familiar comfort of their friendship settled back in, and Anshika felt a little lighter.

"Now, let's finish this soap project before we get caught up in any more deep talks," Garv added with a wink.

Anshika chuckled, feeling her mood lift further. "Yeah, let's get back to work. We can save the emotional talks for later."

With that, the two returned to their project, the bond between them growing stronger with every shared moment, every conversation. And though the pressures of school and life loomed ahead, they knew they could face it together.

"Garv, Anshika called out to him.

'Yes, Anshika, what's up?' Garv replied.

'Where are you going?' Anshika asked.

'Heading to the chemistry lab, just checking out the soap there,' Garv responded.

'Wait, I'll come with you,' Anshika said.

As they walked toward the lab, Garv noticed the sadness on Anshika's face. He didn't say anything at first; they continued chatting as they made their way to the lab.

Once inside, they were alone. They examined the soap together, and then Garv asked, 'What's wrong? Why do you seem so sad?'

'Nothing, really,' Anshika replied, though her tone was heavy. 'It's just that time's moving so quickly. Soon, I'll have to leave Surat and go to Chandigarh.'

'Chandigarh? When? And why?' Garv asked, confusion creeping into his voice.

'My dad is getting transferred there,' Anshika explained. 'After the boards are over, we'll be moving in a few days.'

Garv's heart sank at the thought, but he quickly masked his emotions. He knew he had to cheer her up. 'But that's okay, right? Why be sad? We'll still be in touch,' he said, trying to sound upbeat.

Anshika's voice faltered as she spoke again. 'You know how hard it is for me to make friends. I'll miss Surat... I'll miss this school.'

In her mind, though, she thought, *I'll miss you, Garv. Why can't you see that?*

'But just because you're leaving doesn't mean we won't stay connected, Anshika. We'll talk, we'll text, we'll keep in touch no matter what,' Garv reassured her, his voice soft but firm.

'You'll call me every day, like you do now?' Anshika asked, a hint of hope in her voice.

'I'll even say yes to mom's scolding if I need to,' Garv joked. 'I'll do whatever it takes. I'll be there, just like always.'

Anshika chuckled at his antics.

'Look, no matter where life takes us, we'll always remember each other. True friends don't forget. At least, we'll always remember each other's birthdays, right? And real friends, even if their messages don't always reach, they'll still find a way to talk. So don't be sad,' Garv continued.

Anshika smiled, though she still felt the pang of sadness in her heart. 'You have so many friends, Garv. Why would you even remember me?'

'You have no idea how many hurdles I've crossed to be your friend,' Garv teased, 'I can't forget you, not even if I tried.'

The bell rang, signaling the end of the conversation. They walked to class, but neither could shake the feeling that something had shifted between them. Each glance, each smile, spoke volumes.

It was the last day before the vacations, and something unexpected was about to happen.

During recess, Anshika called over Sakshi.

'Sakshi, can we talk for a minute?' Anshika asked.

'Yeah, what's going on?' Sakshi replied, sensing something serious in Anshika's tone.

'I need to talk to you about Garv,' Anshika confessed.

'What did Golu do now?' Sakshi asked with a knowing grin.

'No, no, he didn't do anything. It's just... I've tried to tell him directly, but I can't seem to do it,' Anshika said, her voice barely above a whisper.

'What do you want to say to him? And by the way, don't tell him I told you his pet name, Golu. He'll kill me for it,' Anshika warned.

'I think I like him, but I can't bring myself to tell him directly,' Anshika admitted. 'And yes, I know his pet name. I've known for a while.'

Sakshi raised an eyebrow. 'So, you want me to go and tell him for you?'

Anshika nodded. 'Please, I can't do it. I'm too scared.'

Sakshi, knowing where to find Garv, rushed off to find him. She was determined to help Anshika, no matter what it took.

When she found Garv, she wasted no time. 'Golu, I need to talk to you,' Sakshi said urgently.

'Yeah, what's up?' Garv asked, sensing the seriousness in her tone.

'Anshika likes you,' Sakshi blurted out, before Garv could say another word.

The words hit Garv like a thunderclap. He stood there, stunned, as his mind raced. Anshika liked him? He hadn't seen that coming.

He stared at Sakshi for a moment, trying to process what she had just told him. 'Anshika... likes me?' he repeated, his voice filled with disbelief."

"Look, stop with all this joking around," Garv said, a hint of seriousness in his voice. "I might just end up hitting you somewhere."

Sakshi shrugged. "Well, he wasn't saying anything, so I thought I'd come and tell you. Now it's up to you to figure out what you want to do with it."

Anshika's heart skipped a beat as she recalled Garv's words, but she quickly brushed it off. "You'll call me every day, just like you always do, right?" she asked, trying to make light of it.

Garv chuckled. "Sure, but I'll tell my mom I'm coming to pick something up from your brother. He'll never know."

Anshika couldn't help but laugh at his casual response.

Garv, with a slight grin, continued, "Look, no matter where we go, we don't forget our friends. At the very least, we'll remember each other's birthdays. And for the best friends, even if their messages don't show up on our phones, we'll still talk when we miss them. So, why be sad about that?"

Anshika rolled her eyes, playfully dismissing him. "Right, you've got so many friends, why would you even remember me?"

"You have no idea how much effort I've put into this friendship with you. I swear, even if I wanted to forget, I couldn't," Garv replied, his tone softening.

They both entered the class, the day passing with stolen glances and smiles exchanged between them, as if the world had faded away, leaving just the two of them.

The next day came—the last day before vacations. And something unexpected happened.

Anshika called Sakshi over during recess. "Sakshi, can we talk?"

Sakshi, ever curious, leaned in. "Of course, Anshika. What's going on?"

"I need to talk to Garv about something," Anshika said, nervously shifting her weight.

Sakshi raised an eyebrow. "What did Garv do now? Did Golu mess up again?"

"No, no," Anshika quickly interjected. "He hasn't done anything wrong. I've tried talking to him directly, but I just can't find the courage."

Sakshi's face softened as she listened. "What do you want to tell him?"

"I think I like him, but I just can't bring myself to say it. And by the way, I know his pet name is Golu," Anshika admitted, looking down.

Sakshi's eyes lit up. "So, you want me to tell him for you?"

Anshika nodded, hopeful. "Yes, please."

Sakshi, knowing where to find him, rushed off to find Garv. A few moments later, she found him.

"Golu, I need to talk to you," Sakshi said, catching his attention.

"Yeah? What's up?" Garv responded, trying to act nonchalant.

"Anshika likes you," Sakshi blurted out, and before Garv could react, she turned and walked away.

Garv stood frozen for a moment, his mind racing. "Don't mess with me, Sakshi. I'll smack you if this is a joke."

Sakshi, without turning back, shouted, "I wasn't joking, Garv. Do what you will."

Afterward, Garv was nowhere to be found. He didn't even show up for his next class. He left school immediately, heading straight to his friend Ronak's place.

"Bro, what's wrong now?" Ronak asked, sensing something was off.

"I don't even know, man. I can't figure out what to do," Garv confessed, his frustration evident.

Ronak, ever the prankster, laughed. "What happened? Did someone mess with you?"

"Anshika told me she likes me," Garv admitted, his face scrunched up in confusion.

Ronak burst out laughing. "What? Anshika?"

"No, Ronak, her dad," Garv shot back sarcastically.

Ronak chuckled again. "Well, if she likes you, what's the problem?"

"I don't know if I should say anything," Garv muttered. "What if she changes her mind? I'm not great with relationships, man."

Ronak, sensing his friend's hesitation, opened Garv's Facebook profile on his phone. He smirked as he scrolled through Anshika's profile. "You really need to say yes, bro."

"Seriously, Ronak?" Garv groaned. "Look, I'm not great with this stuff. I don't know if I can handle all her moods."

Ronak nodded knowingly. "Bro, you need to get over this. If you like her, go for it. Don't overthink. And remember, there's a difference between liking someone and loving them."

Garv paused, processing Ronak's words. "You're right. I've got to stop overthinking."

Ronak smiled and nudged him. "Look, things will work out. Just keep your cool. And don't forget—if she's really into you, it'll be worth it."

Garv finally cracked a smile. "Thanks, man. I needed that."

It was late, so Garv hadn't called that day. However, he had completely forgotten that the second round of the Math Olympiad was the next day. In the rush of his tension, he took the Math Olympiad exam, while Anshika was still waiting, hoping for Garv's call.

"Hello! Anshika," Garv's voice echoed over the phone.

"Anshika, it's okay," she replied, her voice soft.

Before Anshika could say anything more, Garv blurted out, "I like you."

"Are you sure?" Anshika asked, surprised.

"Yeah," Garv answered with a smile in his voice.

"Well, if you're going to back out later, just tell me now," Anshika teased, half-joking but with a hint of seriousness.

"If I wanted to back out, I wouldn't have told you this now. I took my time because I really meant it," Garv replied.

Anshika sighed, "You should've called last night. What would have changed if you'd just called then? We could've talked all night."

"I thought about it, but it got late, so I didn't call," Garv admitted.

"I don't think you remembered, but today was my Math Olympiad exam," Anshika reminded him.

"I'm really sorry. I totally forgot," Garv said, genuinely apologetic.

"It's okay, I think I did well on the exam," Anshika reassured him.

"Let's just stay normal and not make this awkward. And study well, okay?" Anshika said, her voice calm.

From that point on, Garv and Anshika would chat for a little while every day, discussing their lives, their friends, and many other things. Anshika even started giving Garv study tips to make sure he stayed focused on his studies.

Then, one day, during the vacation break, Garv called Anshika.

"Hello! Anshika, can we meet?" Garv asked, his voice filled with excitement.

"I want to meet too, but how is that possible? Your image is so perfect that my mom won't let me meet you," Anshika joked, laughing.

"Why? What did I do?" Garv asked, puzzled.

"Every day you call me after school just to ask about homework, and we talk so much. One day, my mom saw me ignoring you in front of her when we were supposed to meet. Then, she noticed you in the school hallway and saw you talking to some of my friends. Afterward, my math teacher indirectly gave you a lecture at home because of it," Anshika explained, amused by the situation.

"That's a bit too much, Anshika," Garv replied, laughing nervously.

"Yeah, my mom is being super cautious now. She says to stay away from you," Anshika teased.

"Okay, let's wait till exams are over. I guess that's our best bet," Garv said.

"You know what? I have an idea. You come to school, and I'll tell my mom that I need to go there to clear up some doubts. I'll also ask one of my friends to come along," Anshika suggested.

"Perfect! I didn't think of that. You're really smart!" Garv replied with a grin.

"Okay, but we can only meet for a few periods. I don't want my mom to catch us at school, so I'll pretend I'm going there for a quick revision," Anshika said, planning ahead.

"Deal!" Garv agreed.

The next day, Anshika managed to convince her mom, and she took her friend along to school, ensuring that she wasn't caught. Garv arrived at school too, but he hid at first to tease Anshika.

Anshika knew that Garv would arrive early, so she wasn't surprised when he didn't show up immediately. "Typical," she thought, "inviting me to meet and then hiding away." But as soon as Garv entered the classroom, they both couldn't stop smiling at each other.

Anshika convinced Garv to wait while she left her friend in the library. Then, they found themselves alone in the classroom. They sat there, talking, laughing, and occasionally glancing at each other.

"Hey, listen. Can you help me with these math problems?" Garv asked, looking at the papers in front of him.

Anshika smiled playfully, "Sure, why not?"

She began explaining the problems to him, though Garv still felt nervous sitting beside her. He awkwardly sat facing the front, unable to bring himself to sit next to her at the same desk.

Before long, Anshika's friend arrived, and Anshika quickly avoided any awkwardness, giving them both a smile before the three of them headed to lunch. Garv, still feeling a little shy, hesitated to take a sandwich from Anshika's tiffin since her friend was present. But Anshika, noticing his discomfort, said, "Come on, take it! If you don't, my mom will scold me for not feeding you."

After lunch, they waved each other goodbye, and Anshika told her friend she'd join her shortly.

"All the best, Garv! Make sure you study well, and don't spend too much time playing on the ground," Anshika said, smiling at him.

"Oh, okay, Ma'am!" Garv replied sarcastically, grinning back at her.

In the weeks leading up to the board exams, Garv had stopped playing cricket every morning. Initially, he had been spending his mornings on the ground, but now, he had reduced it to once a week. He spent more time studying with Devik, trying to keep up with his revision.

When the board exams finally arrived, both Anshika and Garv were assigned to the same exam center, which meant they would get a chance to meet again.

Every day, they met to revise together, with Anshika guiding Garv through his subjects. As time passed, Anshika began to realize that Garv's feelings for her were more than just friendly. She didn't want to say anything, though, fearing it might ruin the connection they had. But deep down, she knew that Garv cared for her deeply. She had witnessed how he had changed, how he took care of her, and how protective he was.

One day, she spoke to her friend, Muskan, about her feelings. Muskan suggested, "Why not give him a hint? Maybe he'll speak up himself."

Anshika sighed, "I've already given him so many hints—holding hands during the picnic, talking every day, meeting secretly at school... What more can I do?"

Muskan smiled knowingly, "Maybe you should just make him emotional. Who knows? Maybe he'll confess."

Chapter 6

"I Love You" and the Long-Distance Relationship Begins

Did the character remember the date? Hell yes! The roller coaster ride is about to start, and life is about to change for someone—at least for Garv.

7th March 2014

It was 4 PM, and Garv's phone rang. It was Anshika calling.

"Hello!! Garv?" Anshika's voice echoed through the phone.

"Tell me, how did you remember me?" Garv teased.

"Nothing, yaar. I couldn't focus on studying since morning. Garv, can I ask you a question?" Anshika asked.

"Go ahead," Garv replied.

"How long have you liked me?" Anshika asked.

"Just out of the blue, why this question? Is everything alright?" Garv responded, surprised.

"Answer me, no escaping," Anshika insisted.

"Ever since we first sat together, about 5 weeks after that, I started liking you," Garv confessed.

"Like me? Can you define that?" Anshika asked, intrigued.

"I don't know how to define it," Garv stammered.

And that conversation stretched for over two hours, with Anshika trying to talk about their picnic, the moments in class where their hands would accidentally touch, and how they never withdrew their hands. How they would silently communicate through eye contact, without words. But did Garv get it? Maybe, but he wasn't sure what to say.

"Yaar, enough. Garv, I love you. I've fallen for you," Anshika said, her voice trembling with emotion.

"Oh, okay," Garv replied nonchalantly.

"What? Okay? I'm not joking, Garv, I'm serious!" Anshika clarified, feeling a little unsure.

"So, I liked you. What's the big deal?" Garv responded, confused.

"That's like, BFF stuff," Anshika added.

"BFF?" Garv repeated, unsure of what she meant.

"Best friends forever," Anshika explained.

"I love you too, Anshika," Garv finally admitted.

"You know what this means, right? Should I explain?" Anshika asked.

"Yeah, I love you too," Garv confirmed.

"Promise?" Anshika asked, a little hesitant.

"Promise," Garv said, his voice firm.

"I'm going to miss you so much, and I don't want to lose you. If I'm giving you my commitment, I will never let you go," Anshika said with determination.

"Don't worry about it. We'll stay friends even without saying 'I love you,' and we won't let distance come between us," Garv reassured her.

"I love you, dumb. I've been trying to make you understand this for so long, but you made me say it," Anshika said, a little exasperated but smiling.

"Sorry, Anshika. I didn't realize it until now, but I love you too," Garv admitted, feeling emotional.

"Are you crying?" Anshika asked, noticing his tone.

"Let me go to my room. If my mom sees me, she'll get worried," Garv said, trying to hide his tears.

"But why are you crying?" Anshika asked.

"I don't know. It just came out. I love you, Anshika. You're so sweet. Always stay the same, never change," Garv said, his voice full of emotion.

"I love you too. You've made me crazy. I'm taking beautiful memories of this year with me to Surat. Come back soon, let's meet," Anshika said.

"Why are you saying this, yaar?" Garv asked, confused.

"Anshika, I'm leaving for Surat after my last exam. I'm going the day after tomorrow," Anshika explained.

"Don't worry, I'll come to meet you soon," Garv said, trying to comfort her.

"Okay, I'll call you later. I love you so much. Always remember that," Anshika said softly.

"I love you too," Garv replied, his heart full of emotion.

Guess where Garv went after this? Yes, you got it—straight to Ronak's place.

Ronak understood immediately when he saw Garv.

"I understand now—the difference between 'I like you' and 'I love you,'" Ronak said with a grin.

"No, yaar, it's all good. But she's leaving in five days, and there are only four days left till the last exam," Garv explained, looking a little worried.

"Let's buy her a gift, then. Something special," Ronak suggested.

"What should I get her? Everything's fine, yaar. Where will the money come from?" Garv asked, still stressed.

"Don't you save any money?" Ronak asked.

"Saving? For what? I just spend whatever I have. My friends and I go out and grab some food or drinks every day," Garv replied casually.

"You're crazy. Go work, get your books together. Don't waste time. We'll figure out something for the gift," Ronak said, pulling Garv along.

The next day, Garv brought all his books, and Ronak brought his as well.

"Did you bring your books?" Garv asked, seeing Ronak.

"Yeah, I had to bring them. You didn't save enough money for the gift, and we'll have to buy something cheap. Also, who knows when you'll both meet again?" Ronak said with a laugh.

"Alright, let's sell these books," Garv suggested.

Ronak led him to the bookstore, and together they sold their books for 1100 rupees. They felt like the shopkeeper had cheated them by giving such a low price.

Afterward, they went to Archies to find a gift. They spent over an hour looking for the perfect gift, but Garv turned down everything from teddy bears to heart-shaped toys.

"Yaar, I can't give her that. How will she even take it, and what will she say?" Garv said, unsure.

"Get her a crystal Ganpati idol. Those work," Ronak suggested.

"Are you crazy? Those are expensive," Garv said.

"They're 1300 rupees, and the ones with water creatures are beautiful," Ronak insisted.

"These things are only worth 300!" Garv said, rolling his eyes.

Ronak, however, wasn't going to give up. "Listen, this is your first love. Do it right. I'll negotiate with the shopkeeper and get it for 1500."

In the end, Garv reluctantly agreed, and they managed to buy the gift.

"Why did you give 400 extra?" Garv asked, surprised.

"Come on, you're getting a great gift. Don't overthink it. Now, let's go grab a drink. The gift is more important right now," Ronak said.

"Love you, bro," Garv said, grateful for his friend.

"Shut up, idiot! Are you planning to make her cry? Just keep your temper in check, and you're good to go," Ronak said.

Ronak had hidden Garv's gifts at his house and gave them to him on the morning of the exams.

Did Anshika know that Garv was bringing her a gift? No, because Garv himself had no idea he'd ever get a gift for anyone, not until that day.

Anshika and Garv had been revising together before the exams. And finally, as soon as the exams were over...

As Anshika and Garv slowly made their way out, Garv suddenly said, "Anshika, open your pouch."

"What happened?" Anshika asked.

"Just do it," Garv urged.

Anshika opened her pouch, and Garv slipped the gift inside.

"What is this, Garv?" Anshika asked, surprised.

"You don't know yet, but we don't know when we'll meet again. How could I let you go without a gift?" Garv replied.

"When did you get this? How?" Anshika was curious.

"I'll tell you when I get home, but right now, just take care of yourself. And please, stop with that sad face. It looks better when you smile," Garv said, his voice soft but sincere.

"When will we meet again?" Anshika asked.

"Soon, Anshika. Please, don't be sad. If you're sad, I feel worse. But you can't let tears show. If you want to cry, smile and do it in secret. Just be careful, and I'll see you soon," Garv reassured her.

"I love you, Anshika," Garv said, his voice full of emotion.

"I love you too. Take care," Anshika replied, her voice tinged with sadness.

Garv felt terrible that day. Whenever he felt down, there was one thing that made him feel better: speed. He grabbed his cycle and set off, trying to forget the weight on his chest.

His tuition friends always teased him about his "Hyabusa" riding skills, and this time was no different.

Garv called Devik downstairs. They were both a bit out of shape that day, but that didn't stop them from making it through.

A tempo came from one side, and a truck was coming from the other. Garv skillfully weaved between them, with Devik shouting from behind, "Are you trying to kill us, or what?"

But Devik and Garv had a bond that was hard to break.

"What's going on, idiot? Did your paper go that badly?" Devik asked, his tone teasing.

"Anshika's going back to Chandigarh," Garv replied.

"So what?" Devik shrugged.

"We told each other we love each other," Garv said, smiling despite the chaos around him.

"Idiot! Who does that? That's not something you share like a regular conversation. Damn, today felt like we were dancing with death!" Devik laughed.

That day, Devik couldn't resist spreading the news to everyone at tuition. And soon, the "Last Day Party" was being planned — a celebration of Garv's love story, where Devik, Garv, Rishabh, Chaan Chaan (Garv's nickname for him), and others like Sheetal and Jigar were all invited. Even though Jigar was from another batch, he was a good friend of both Garv and Devik, and his presence would play a role in future events.

The Last Day in Surat

"Hello, Garv!" Anshika greeted over the phone.

"Yeah, Anshika, what's up?" Garv replied.

"Thank you for the gift," Anshika said, her voice sincere.

"I already told you, no thanks needed after saying 'I love you,'" Garv joked.

"Can you come meet me? Nishant and Abhishek are coming over, and they want you to join," Anshika asked.

"I'll try, but give me half an hour. I'll figure something out if I can," Garv said, determined.

Half an hour later...

"The only way I can make it is by cycling over," Garv explained.

"Are you crazy? No, don't do that," Anshika replied, worried.

"Yaar, the only friend who can join me right now is out, otherwise, I'd come with him. I can't afford an auto ride, because he charges 400 bucks just to get me there," Garv said with frustration.

"Forget it, Garv. Don't come by cycle," Anshika insisted.

"How did you get the gift in the middle of exams?" Anshika asked, genuinely curious.

Garv then told her the whole story, explaining how he'd managed to bring the gift despite everything going on. Anshika was impressed and told him, "You have such great friends. If I ever got stuck somewhere, I know I wouldn't have to worry. They'd get me out in no time."

"Take care of yourself, Anshika," Garv said, his voice softening.

"Yeah, you too. Don't play around too much, you've got marks all over your hands," Anshika teased.

"Don't worry. My skin heals quickly. Chill," Garv laughed.

"I love you, Kimpu," Garv said, smiling.

"I love you, Golu," Anshika replied with a smile of her own.

Chapter 7

Fortune Double edge

Anshika and Garv were talking about their future. Anshika was clear she would stick to science, but Garv was uncertain. He thought about switching to science too, or at least taking a private admission if nothing else worked out.

Anshika wanted him to choose science, but she never said it outright. The day the grades came in, Anshika scored a perfect 10.00 CGPA, while Garv scored an 8.4.

"What's your score?" Anshika asked.

Garv lied, telling her he had scored 8.8 CGPA.

Anshika and Garv continued their conversation, talking about what they would do next. Garv knew his grades in maths and English had messed things up, but he still wasn't satisfied. He had lied to Anshika, and many of his friends from his dad's office had scored above 9 CGPA. That night, Garv knew he was going to get a speech from his dad.

"Hello, Anshika. Yes, go ahead," Garv answered the call.

"Move aside," Anshika said, waving her hand.

"Mom wants to talk to you," Garv added.

"Congratulations, Anshika!" Garv's mom called out warmly.

"Thank you so much, Aunty," Anshika replied, smiling.

"Here, talk to Garv," Anshika handed him the phone.

"Yeah, Anshika, what's up?" Garv answered.

"I don't even know what to say. Why did you lie to me, Garv?" Anshika's voice quivered with frustration.

"I'm sorry," Garv said, regret evident in his voice.

"You have no idea how bad it felt, Garv. I told my friend about your marks, saying you scored so well, and she was like, 'No, Garv has 8.4 CGPA.' It hurt so much!" Anshika explained.

"I'm really sorry. I was scared, Anshika," Garv admitted.

"Anshika, I love you because you understand me and care for me. I know you're not a scholar, but please, don't lie to me," she said, her voice soft yet firm.

"I promise, I'll never lie again. I'm really sorry, Anshika," Garv pleaded.

"What have you decided? What will you choose?" Anshika asked, her tone softening.

"I'm leaning towards science, but my family insists I should take commerce with math. They say I'm not cut out for science, especially after my poor performance in the boards. They say I should just take commerce with math," Garv explained, sounding uncertain.

"Think about it, maybe they're right. But don't make a decision you'll regret in two years. You have to choose what feels right for you," Anshika advised.

In the end, Garv decided to take Commerce with Math. The reason? His father didn't like IP, and Garv felt that if he didn't take commerce, there'd be no point. Everyone else was doing it, and it took time to succeed in the field.

Classes began, and soon, Garv found himself bonding with Anuj, who became a mentor and a friend to him. "Anuj, what's the deal? Are you seriously telling me to stop joking around or I'll get into trouble?" Garv teased him one day. Anuj was more or less a reflection of Garv's old self. Their friendship grew stronger over time, and soon, their friends started asking, "Are you two brothers or what?"

Chapter 8

She is the Best

You might be wondering how Garv's long-distance relationship was going. Well, it had its ups and downs. Garv was still immature when it came to understanding love, while Anshika was passionate and mature in her feelings.

During the summer vacation of 11th grade, Garv planned a surprise trip to Ajmer with his cousin to visit his grandparents. On the morning of the trip, Garv's dad had accidentally read the 'I love you, good morning' text that Anshika had sent. And guess what? That evening, Garv was supposed to leave for Ajmer, but it was Sunday, so he spent the entire day with his dad. Garv had no idea that his phone had disappeared, and his mom informed him about it. Garv's dad said, "Tell Golu not to get involved in this stuff; he's the topper. But you have to work hard, son."

Garv told his mom, "We're just good friends, mom. If you want me to stop talking to her, I can't do that. I won't let go of my friendship."

His mom gave him a stern look and said, "Your dad has asked you to stop. You're going to focus on your studies now."

And so, Garv reluctantly stopped messaging Anshika. When he spoke to her, he told her everything, and she cried. But he couldn't go against his mom's wishes, so he packed his things and left for Ajmer with his cousin.

When they arrived, Garv wasn't feeling too good, but he wanted to give his grandparents the surprise they deserved. He reached their home, and his grandfather was sitting at his clinic. His grandmother called out to him, ordering his grandfather to bring some Kadhi and Kachori along with Jalebi for breakfast.

Garv had breakfast, met his friends, and then went to the terrace to reflect on the situation. Anshika kept calling, but Garv didn't know what to say. Around 1 AM, Anshika called again, and this time, Garv picked up.

"Anshika, please, can we just talk?" Garv said, sounding exhausted.

"Anshika, I asked you not to message me in the morning. Anyone could have read it. Why don't you understand?" he added.

"I'm sorry, Garv. Please, don't be upset," Anshika said, her voice pleading.

"Do you think I didn't want to talk to you? I'm just as hurt, but you were being careless," Garv replied.

"I was careless? You're the one who—" Anshika began, but Garv interrupted.

"Yeah, I know. I'm the bad one here," he said, admitting his mistake.

"Okay, I'm sorry. Just don't go, please," Anshika begged.

"I'll come back, but only under two conditions," Garv said, his tone lightening.

"Okay, what are they?" Anshika asked.

"First, no more morning messages," Garv stated.

"And the second?" Anshika inquired.

"I want five kisses, over the phone," Garv said, with a playful smile.

"Seriously? Who negotiates like this?" Anshika laughed.

After a moment of hesitation, Anshika agreed, sending Garv five virtual kisses over the call. They spent the next few minutes telling each other, "I love you," before finally settling down.

"I'm sorry, Anshika. I never want to make you cry again," Garv said sincerely.

"I love you, Garv. It's okay, as long as you understand," Anshika replied.

"Will you marry me someday?" Anshika asked, her voice tentative.

"We'll get married?" Garv asked, still processing her words.

"I'm going to beat you up if you don't stop asking me that!" Anshika teased.

"No, I'm serious. We will get married," Garv said confidently.

Anshika realized that Garv still didn't fully understand the depth of love, but that didn't matter anymore.

"Do you love me, Garv?" Anshika asked, unsure.

"Yes, I do," Garv replied firmly.

"Always?" Anshika questioned.

"Always," Garv promised.

"Okay then, I love you. Good night," Anshika whispered.

"I love you, Kimpu," Garv whispered.

Anshika had decided to make him watch the *Ye Hai Ashiqui* serials, where love stories often played out.

t had been two years since they entered the 11th and 12th classes, and someone had changed a lot during that time. How? Well, you'd have to see for yourself to understand.

The friendship between Anuj and Garv? Neither of them even remembers exactly when it began. But whenever they tried to recall, they realized that it was deep, and the bond they shared was beyond understanding. It wasn't about when it started or how, it was about the mutual respect that made them inseparable.

Both Anuj and Garv shared one common passion - watches. Every one or two months, they would buy a new one, a fresh addition to their growing collection. This pattern continued through their entire 11th and 12th classes. Sometimes, they'd even exchange watches. The two of them were so similar in temperament—short-tempered and determined—that no one dared to confront them.

But then, one day, Garv received heartbreaking news—Ronak had met with an accident and was no longer alive. Garv couldn't bring himself to visit Ronak's house for months. He didn't know how to process the grief. Every week, he would go to the place they used to hang out, where he would have long conversations with fruit beer, Devik, and Jigar.

How did Garv feel about it? He never really told anyone. Did he cry? Yes. For five or six days, despite not wanting to, tears would come at night. But he didn't want to appear weak, so he stayed cheerful in front of everyone.

One day, in a playful mood, Devik accidentally broke Garv's favorite watch—a "Tag Heuer" replica. Garv's anger flared up. But just as he moved toward Devik in fury, something stopped him. He thought about it for a moment, calmed down, and let it go.

That day, after school, Garv went to pick up Devik for tuitions, as usual.

"Sorry, Golu bhai," Devik said, genuinely apologetic.

"Don't worry, idiot. It's not a big deal. The watch can be replaced," Garv replied, though his anger wasn't easy to dispel. He knew his anger could destroy things, so he learned to control it.

In the 11th grade, Garv's English teacher complimented him. "Garv, you've really changed. You've become more calm. Your mom told me you're a different person now." His grades also improved. In Maths, he scored 87 out of 100, a huge achievement for him.

Anuj and Garv were almost inseparable—whether it was at school, tuition, or the playground. Anuj had helped Garv become calmer, his anger more manageable. Together, they studied, worked hard, and made it through the year. But even though Garv had grown, he never forgot Ronak. A friend like that could never be forgotten. No matter how far they were, he'd always carry the memory. He'd said it once: "The way you value friendship, if you can stick to that, even a hundredfold, you'll always be content."

11th Grade: Garv and Anshika's Relationship

In the beginning, Garv didn't truly understand the meaning of love. But both of them tried their best. Anshika, who had taken a dummy admission, only needed to attend her tuitions, whereas Garv had to wake up at six in the morning for school and then attend tuitions until 8 p.m.

But despite the exhaustion, the relationship was new, and they found time for each other. The boy who used to sleep for nine hours was now surviving on three. They waited each night for everyone else to fall asleep, so they could talk until 3 or 4 a.m. But once a week, Garv had to face Anshika's anger, because he often dozed off while waiting for 12 a.m. to call her. The following day, he'd apologize, often reaching out to Nishant, who was also Anshika's friend, to convince her to forgive him.

"Why no video calls?" you might wonder. Well, after Garv's 10th grade results, he finally got a touchscreen phone. But during the summer vacation, he was caught watching adult content, and his dad smashed the phone. Before this, they would have video calls once a week, but the internet was expensive, and if only Ambani had come to their rescue, life might have been a bit easier.

Their Journey in the 12th Grade

In the 12th grade, everything seemed to be going well. Anshika and Garv's bond was growing stronger every day. They spent their time supporting each other. Garv would often try to explain to Anshika that competition was fine, but it should be healthy.

One day, on the 7th of March, 2015, Garv, completely exhausted from his busy schedule, forgot that it was their first anniversary. Anshika, understandably upset, was hard to deal with. Garv didn't know what to do. He went to Rajat for help. The two of them sat on the terrace, discussing how to fix things.

Rajat helped Garv by creating a collage of pictures of him and Anshika and sending it with a heartfelt apology letter. When Garv finally called Anshika, he was desperate.

"I'm sorry, Anshika," he pleaded.

"Who forgets something like this?" Anshika replied, still upset.

"Please forgive me. I love you, and I miss you so much. Please, come and hug me," Garv begged.

Though they were far apart, their love sign—a kiss on the fist—was always exchanged when they missed each other. Finally, Anshika accepted his apology, and they both exchanged kisses over the phone. They promised to talk later that night.

Rajat, smirking, teased Garv, "I never thought you'd change this much, bro."

"Shut up, you idiot. I'm only changing for her, not for the rest of the world," Garv replied, his voice firm.

The bond between Anuj and Garv, despite everything, remained untouched. Anuj never cared much for Garv's relationship drama, staying focused on his own world.

April 27, 2015 - A Day Garv Would Never Forget

It was Anshika's birthday, and Garv had remembered, of course. But, as fate would have it, he fell asleep by mistake. It was only when the clock struck 1 AM that he woke up with a shock. 25 missed calls. 50 unread text messages. Panic gripped him as he dialed Anshika's number.

Anshika picked up on the first ring, and Garv immediately knew something was wrong. She had been crying for the last hour, her breath hitched, barely able to catch her sobs. He couldn't stand it. His heart ached as he began to sing her favorite song, *Tum Hi Ho* from *Anshikaqui 2*, hoping it would soothe her. He pampered her with all his love, apologizing over and over, trying to make up for the hours he had lost.

Finally, Anshika calmed down and said softly, "Yaar, aap bahut gande ho. Jab dekho tab sojate ho, samajh hi nahi aata."

"I'm sorry, Aanshu. Please, maan jaao," Garv begged, his voice filled with regret.

"Garv, aapko pata hai na? Aapke alawa aur kisi ka wait nahi karti main. Aap se hi expectations hoti hain. Agli baar se aise tang mat karna, warna main aapki class laga dungi," Anshika warned, a hint of a smile in her tone despite her irritation.

"Yes, Anshika," Garv replied, feeling relieved that she was at least speaking to him again.

"Good night, Garv. And AGD," she said.

"AGD?" Garv asked, confused.

"Anshika Garv Dreams," she teased.

"I love you, and I'm sorry. Please, don't cry anymore. Let's stop crying now, okay? We'll meet soon," Garv's voice trembled as he spoke.

"Haan, love you a lot. Good night," Anshika whispered.

"Good night. And tomorrow, don't forget to eat the chocolates I'll bring for you," Garv teased.

"Haanji," Anshika replied, a small smile on her face.

May 2, 2015 - A Day That Changed Garv's Life Forever

That day would forever remain a scar on Garv's heart. He was in tuition when he received a call from his brother, who worked at his father's office. His voice was urgent. "Golu, jaldi ghar aa. Urgency hai."

Garv's heart sank. "Kya hua? Papa theek hain na?"

"Papa ke saath hum hain. Tu jaldi ghar aa. Ajmer jaana hai. Dada nahi rahe," his brother replied, and the words hit Garv like a ton of bricks.

Garv stood frozen. His mind raced, but nothing made sense. What was happening? He didn't know how to react. He quickly told his tutor that he had to leave, and Anuj, ever supportive, accompanied him.

"Kya hua, Golu?" Anuj asked, noticing the sudden tension in Garv's face.

"Dada nahi rahe," Garv whispered, fighting back tears.

"Chal, tu mere saath ghar chhod leta hoon," Anuj offered, trying to lighten the mood, but Garv's world felt like it was collapsing.

On the drive, Garv texted Anshika, pouring out his confusion and emotional turmoil. "Mujhe samajh nahi aa raha. Kya karoon? Mera mind process nahi kar paa raha."

Anshika, sensing his distress, skipped her class and wrote back. "Agar tujhe zaroorat ho toh, main class mein nahi hoon. Par, Garv, agar kuch serious hai toh, main baat nahi kar paungi. Hum sab jaldi road trip par nikal rahe hain."

Back at home, the house was filled with a heavy atmosphere. Garv's mom and brother were crying. He found his father sitting quietly in his room, tears silently streaming down his face. It was the first time Garv had ever seen his father so vulnerable. Garv walked over, and without a word, hugged him tightly.

"Golu, bola tha main ek mahine pehle, ki operation karwa lete hain. Tumne kaha tha agle mahine, lekin...," his dad whispered, his voice thick with emotion.

Garv had no words. He couldn't speak. He just held his father, trying to offer silent comfort.

His father had been scheduled to go to Jaipur with Dada for an appointment on May 8th, but now the trip had taken a darker turn. The arrangements were already made, and Garv's father was too proud to let anyone know how badly it had hurt him.

"Papa ko bua ko bataya?" Garv asked softly.

"Nahi. Phuphaji ko bata diya. Vo sabko lekar aa rahe hain. Dada ki tabiyat kharaab thi, toh Ajmer jaana padega," his dad replied, his voice strained.

The whole family gathered, and soon, everyone was in the car, heading to Ajmer. As they reached their destination, Garv was surrounded by his father's friends, who were doing their best to manage the situation. His dad's friends, as well as his cousins, tried to reassure Garv, but he could see the sadness in their eyes.

When they reached home, Garv walked straight to the back compound. There, his grandmother ran to him and enveloped him in a tight hug. "Golu, mein hoon na, sab kuch theek ho jayega. Dekho, papa bhi ro rahe hain. Koi sambhalega unhe?"

His aunt joined in, comforting him as well. Everyone was crying, but Garv tried to stay strong. He kept reassuring them, but he couldn't hold back his own tears anymore.

Later, Garv and his cousins, along with his father's friends, walked to the Mokshdham carrying Dada on their shoulders. Dada, a retired government doctor who had started a free clinic in his retirement, had always been loved and respected by the community. His passing left a void that would never be filled, but at least Garv knew his Dada had earned his respect and love throughout his life.

During the next 11 days, Garv did everything he could to help around the house—fetching water, cooking, bringing vegetables, and cleaning. When he got a moment, he would walk to the garden, the place where his Dada used to take him, and he would sit there, remembering him, silently praying to Lord Hanuman to never let go of the people he loved.

"Garv, aap sahi ho," Anshika's text came as a comforting reminder, even as Garv struggled to find his balance.

Garv's voice trembled as he spoke, his emotions raw. *"Haan Anshika, sahi hoon mae ab thoda,"* he sobbed softly.

Anshika, always the comforting presence, responded with warmth and care, *"Baccha, it's okay, you can cry. At least mere samne toh theek hain na?"* Her voice was gentle, offering him the space to express his feelings without judgment.

Garv nodded, his tears slowly subsiding as her words gave him the comfort he needed. *"Haanji,"* he whispered.

Anshika, trying to reassure him even more, continued, *"Love you a lot. Mae hoon na apke paas."* Her love was evident in every word, providing a sense of solace in his troubled moment.

Garv took a deep breath, attempting to regain his composure. *"Haanji, chalo mae karta hoon yaar. Aram se call, abhi bye."* His voice, though shaky, was filled with the promise of better days ahead.

Before ending the call, Anshika made sure to leave him with a reminder of her care. *"Kuch bhi ho, Garv, msg kardena please."*

"Haanji," Garv replied softly, his heart heavy yet comforted by her unwavering support.

Chapter 9

Aggressive Garv was back

As soon as the vacations ended, exam time arrived. Garv found himself in a sad zone due to the stress of his personal life, where he tried to find comfort in his favorite dishes, talking to Anshika, and distracting himself. This, however, began to reflect in his marks. While he did decently in BST and Economics, there was a significant drop in Accounts, almost 20 marks lower than usual. Out of 80, he scored only 52. This was bound to create trouble during the parent-teacher meeting.

In the Parent-Teacher Meeting: Accounts Teacher: "Garv, can you bring your mom here? I need to talk to you both."

Garv: "Yes, ma'am."

Accounts Teacher: "Garv, why such a significant drop in your marks? You were doing fine earlier, but now it's like you're slacking off. Is everything okay? Have you been hanging out too much with Anuj? Or is something else going on?"

Garv's Mom: "No, he's not involved in any business. He's in a service industry."

Accounts Teacher: "Then what's going on? Is he distracted by some girl? Is he hanging out with bad influences? Or just wasting time?"

Garv: "No ma'am, nothing like that."

Accounts Teacher: "Please focus, Garv. This won't help with the boards. Get your act together."

Garv: "Yes, ma'am."

After the Meeting: Garv: "Damn, the accounts teacher really went off on me!"

Anuj: "Why, what happened?"

Garv: "I scored badly in accounts, and she gave me a lecture about wasting time!"

Anuj: "Don't worry, man, this time you didn't even show up for the meeting! You're lucky."

Garv: "Right! Managed to escape."

Later, Garv's landline bill arrived—around 4000 rupees, an amount too high, all thanks to long calls. Garv's uncle helped trace the number, and it turned out to be his cousin Sakshi. Apparently, they had been talking about studies, and Garv's uncle decided to change the plan to avoid future excess charges.

The Landline Incident: Garv was trying to keep the calls hidden, using the landline to stay in touch with Anshika. They had a secret agreement to avoid using mobile phones, since it was too risky and expensive. But even with the precautions, it was clear that something was going on.

Then came Garv's birthday, and of course, it didn't go as planned. Despite a small celebration with friends at midnight, Anshika wasn't happy.

Anshika (on call): *"You still don't understand, do you? This time is mine, you need to respect that!"*

Garv: *"It was just half an hour with friends!"*

Anshika: *"I'm upset. You should apologize."*

Garv: *"Okay, okay! Don't be mad. I love you too. I'll make it up to you."*

Later that evening, Anshika called again, and this time, the conversation took a drastic turn.

Anshika: *"I'm sorry, Garv, but we can't talk anymore."*

Garv (shocked): *"What happened?"*

Anshika: *"Aayush saw our chats and showed them to my mom. My mom told my dad, and now it's all messed up. My dad says either I get married or forget about it all."*

Garv (hurt): *"Thank you for the gift, Anshika."*

Anshika: *"Please, Garv, don't be like this."*

Garv: *"I don't know what to say."* And he ended the call, feeling broken.

The next day, Garv's temper was back. One of his classmates, Tarun, had crossed the line when he used abusive language about Garv's mom. Garv couldn't hold back and ended up beating him, slamming him to the ground.

Garv (yelling): *"Don't mess with me again, or next time, I'll throw you to the ground for real!"*

Soon after, a Kabaddi match was scheduled, and Garv's skills in the sport, honed since his days in RSS, came in handy. He was known for his speed, strength, and experience in the game. His team, supported by his classmate who was the headboy, was ready to take on the competition.

Garv's aggressive side had returned, but he was also determined to make things right with Anshika. The twists in his life seemed endless, but Garv was ready to face whatever came his way.

Garv had always been the dependable one in the group, offering help wherever needed. But when it was his turn to select a team for the upcoming event, things took an unexpected turn. The plan was clear: Garv would pick a few members for his team, but when Saumya suggested adding Hardik and Keshav to the mix, Garv was less than enthusiastic.

Keshav, known for his playful antics, and Hardik, who had a knack for mischief, weren't exactly the type Garv wanted for serious gameplay.

"Bhai, phir tum hi khel lo," Garv said, not wanting to deal with the distractions they would bring.

Saumya, however, insisted on picking at least one of them, and Garv reluctantly agreed to search for another player. With his usual determination, he started organizing the team, tackling the situation head-on. As he went about his search, his junior, Madhav, urged him to give it a try. "Bhaiya, try toh marne do," Madhav said, encouraging Garv to make the best of the situation.

Garv, still annoyed, responded sharply, "Kaam kar, raid marne aa. Agar tu mujhe out kar paaya toh, main match nahi khelunga, baas." His frustration was evident, but Madhav insisted, and soon enough, the match began. When Madhav got too close during the raid, Garv, in a burst of anger and raw power, used his wrestling skills to toss him aside with a belly-to-belly suplex, just like in WWE.

The entire situation escalated when the Headboy yelled at Garv, "Benchod, kyon gussa kar raha hain bhai tu, meri gaand marvaega?" Garv shot back, "Akhand lodu hain, mana kardiya, nahi khel sakta samajh hi nahi raha tha. Ab vapas aaya galti se na toh maa kasam, F5 de dunga us chutiye ko."

As the days passed, Garv's patience wore thin. Three days had gone by, and there was still no message or call from Anshika, which only fueled his anger. He couldn't focus on anything but the growing frustration. The first match of the day was between the Blue House and the Red House, with Garv facing off against Anuj. Garv won the toss, and as the match began, he took the lead, pushing his team forward with almost 13 points within the first 20 minutes.

But trouble struck when Saurabh, Anuj's cousin, tried to tackle Garv, and in the process, ripped Garv's new Adidas t-shirt. Enraged, Garv grabbed Saurabh's shirt and dragged him into his court, showing the power he had in the game. "Golu chutiya hain kya? Jaanwaroin jaisa kyon kar raha hain?" Anuj shouted, angry about the whole situation.

"*Tere bhai ne meri t-shirt kyon phadi?*" Garv shot back, his frustration spilling over. Anuj tried to calm things down, apologizing, but Garv was already fuming. He had no patience for these distractions.

As the match continued, Anuj fought back aggressively, scoring seven points in ten minutes, but Garv regained his composure and extended the lead to 16 points in the last 10 minutes. After the game, both Garv and Anuj, despite the tensions, shared a brief hug, knowing that it was just a game, and their friendship would endure beyond it.

Later, Garv's mind wandered to Prince, who had been trying to tease him from the sidelines, despite not even playing in the match. "*Garv, tayaar rehna, hum harayenge tujhe,*" Prince mocked, but Garv, his determination unwavering, responded, "*Haan, theek hain. Agar Green House hara paya na inko, jo bole jitna bole vo baas.*"

The match began, and Garv proved his mettle by leading his team with powerful raids and impressive tackles, earning points for his house. But in the back of his mind, Anshika's absence gnawed at him, intensifying his frustration. During one particular raid, Vishal tried to dash Garv out, but Garv, using his speed and strength, threw Vishal into his own court.

The game became increasingly intense, and even though Garv's team dominated, he couldn't shake his mounting anger over Anshika's silence. Hindi Sir intervened and stopped Garv from raiding once more, which only further aggravated him. Garv eventually helped his team secure a 28-point lead, proving once again his superiority in the game.

After the match, Garv, now exhausted and emotional, approached Hindi Sir and apologized. "*Tum accha khele baas, yahan tum bhul gaya tum doston ke saath khel rahe ho, na ki professionally ground pe,*" Hindi Sir reminded him, a hint of understanding in his voice.

That evening, after the match, Garv finally received the long-awaited message from Anshika: "*Sorry Garv, ghar par sab sahi honae ka wait kar rahi thi.*"

Garv, still irritated, called her immediately, his voice tinged with frustration. "*Ek message bhi nahi karna hota aapko? Sahi hain.*"

Anshika apologized, explaining that she had been waiting for everything at home to settle down before she could reach out.

The two talked for hours, sharing everything that had happened in the past four days. Anshika, always the voice of reason, reminded Garv, "*Garv, aapko samaj kyon nahi aata ki gussa sahi cheez nahi hain? Kya ho gaya Anuj aur aapki ladayi hoti toh?*"

Garv, ever the protector, responded, "*Mae chahae kuch bhi kar loon, itna pata hain ki vo khada rahega, bhai hain hum dono.*"

Anshika smiled softly, "*Sahi hain, sabko bhai banate phiro.*"

The call ended with mutual declarations of love. "*I love you a lot, Garv,*" Anshika said.

"*Love you, Anshika,*" Garv replied, his heart finally at peace.

As Garv's life started to settle into a rhythm, he focused more on his studies. With only three months left before the 12th board exams, he spent most of his time in the library. He worked hard on a business studies project that involved creating his own virtual watch company, researching specifications and costs. His business studies teacher was impressed, and although the external examiner deducted a couple of marks for his nervousness, Garv's teacher fought for him, ensuring he received full marks.

As the internal exams came to a close, Garv was more determined than ever to make his future the best it could be. But even in the midst of his academic focus, Garv never forgot the lessons of friendship, love, and growth.

When the external examiner arrived for the mock project evaluation, Garv got flustered. He fumbled and lost 2 marks out of 20. But then, his teacher, Mam, stepped in. She fought for him, convincing the examiner to give him the full 20 marks. Afterward, outside the classroom, Mam grabbed Garv by the ear and scolded him.

"Everything was going well, why did you blank out in the middle?" Mam asked sternly.

"I don't know, Mam. Suddenly, I just blanked out on the last question," Garv replied.

"Don't worry. I've made sure you got your 20 marks. Just focus on doing well in the boards now," Mam reassured him.

"Yes, and thank you, Mam," Garv responded, grateful.

The same thing happened in Accounts. Garv knew the answer, but when the examiner asked the last question, he got confused. His Accounts teacher gave him a look that made him realize he had made a mistake. However, Mam still managed to secure 20 marks for him.

"You're crazy, Garv! When you knew the answer, I was giving you hints with my expressions. Why did you change your answer?" Accounts Mam asked, clearly frustrated.

"Sorry, Mam," Garv said, apologetic.

"Don't worry, just focus on the upcoming preboards and prepare well," she advised.

"Yes, Mam," Garv replied.

Preboards began, and Garv did well in all subjects except for Maths. He scored only 52 out of 80. He had put in so much effort, but the marks didn't reflect it. Maths Mam, who was also the vice-principal of the school, called Garv to ask why he wasn't performing well in Maths.

"Maths is really important, Garv. I know you're preparing for the entrance exams. You need to do better," she told him.

Garv was determined. As the board exams approached, he spent almost all his time in the library, with just a few minutes of phone calls with Anshika at night. Despite his exhaustion, he studied relentlessly. Even during his Accounts leave, he spent ten days focusing on Maths because he feared losing marks in the subject. When the results came, he scored 85%, but unfortunately, he lost 12% in both Maths and English. However, he was happy with his 99 in Accounts.

After the board exams, Garv, Anuj, and Devik started attending tuition together. Their daily schedule was from 9:30 AM to 4:00 PM, and afterward, they studied together. Anshika, who was also busy preparing for her JEE and Mains exams, would occasionally argue with Garv. He couldn't always give her the attention she needed because so much was at stake for him. But slowly, Garv began to fall in love with her, realizing how much she meant to him.

Anuj and Garv spent a lot of time together. During study breaks, Anuj would teach Garv how to play poker. Anuj was also a chaiholic, so whenever Garv was home, Anuj would make tea for both of them. Garv's personality started changing as he became more patient, controlled his anger, and softened, especially after spending time with Anuj and Anshika.

Anuj was someone Garv could rely on for anything. Despite Garv's political views and dislike for Shahrukh Khan, Anuj insisted on dragging him to the movie *Fan*. Garv reluctantly agreed and watched the entire film, proving that if you were in Garv's good books, he would do anything for you.

Finally, the entrance exams were over, and Garv was eagerly waiting for the results. First came the IIM Indore result. Garv did well in logical reasoning and English but struggled with Maths, which caused his score to fall short. Disappointed, Garv lost hope for the other results too. However, Garv's father arranged a meeting with a renowned CA, who tried to convince him to pursue CA. Despite his reluctance, Garv started preparing for the CA entrance exam.

But his heart wasn't in it. Garv continued attending tuition and spent time with his friends, not fully invested in his CA preparation. When the results for Symbiosis and NMIMS came in, Garv got into Symbiosis Noida and NMIMS Mumbai. However, he didn't make it into Symbiosis Pune, which led Anuj to switch to NMIMS Mumbai as well.

Garv was torn between his options, overwhelmed by the countless suggestions he had received. After three days of careful thought, he called NMIMS Mumbai, only to find out that the deadline had passed for admissions. He was offered a seat if any remained, but that seemed unlikely. Broken and defeated, Garv accepted his fate. He chose to follow his father's wishes and pursue CA, despite his resentment.

"Son, if you clear the IPCC, I'll send you to the Big 4 in Bombay or wherever you want to go," his father told him, handing over a demand draft for 2.5 lakhs to cover the NMIMS Mumbai fees.

Garv had forgotten that the admission timeline had passed. He called NMIMS Mumbai, hoping for a seat, but by then, the chances were slim. Reluctantly, he accepted his fate and chose CA, feeling trapped by his parents' wishes and cursing his situation.

Chapter 10

Change in the Life of The Fire

Garv agreed to stay in Surat, and while his friends went off to their respective colleges, he found himself all alone. No one was there to share a soda with him, nor to tease him or scold him. It was in this solitude that Garv and Anshika began to grow closer. They celebrated their second anniversary together, and as time passed, people started to believe that Garv had chosen to pursue CA. But deep inside, he wasn't ready for that degree. In fact, he started neglecting his studies, hoping that by failing, he could finally convince his parents to let him do whatever he truly wanted.

During this time, Garv and Anshika began spending more and more time on video calls. Finally, Garv bought a new mobile, and their connection deepened. Anshika, on the other hand, got into Chandigarh University for a BTech in IT. She had also received an admission offer from SVNIT Surat, but due to her parents' knowledge of her relationship with Garv, they didn't allow her to take the admission in Surat.

Garv began to influence Anshika in small ways. She had always been introverted and fiercely competitive, but he wanted her to understand that life wasn't always about being alone and perfect. "You need to change a little, Baccha," he told her. "Life is about letting go, about forgiving, and enjoying the little moments with others." Slowly, Anshika began to listen to his advice and started making a few friends at college.

Life was going smoothly until one fine day in June 2015, Anshika went to a party with her family. She sent Garv some photos of herself in different angles. Garv, sensing a change in his feelings, didn't know how to express his admiration. Anshika, a bit upset at his lack of response, texted him later that evening.

"What happened? Didn't I look good?" Anshika texted.

"Why are you saying that, Baccha?" Garv replied.

"No comment, nothing at all." Anshika's tone was playful but hurt.

"I didn't know what to say... you were looking amazing, Baccha," Garv tried to make amends.

"What didn't you know how to say? Tell me." Anshika pressed.

"I wanted to kiss you so badly, but I just couldn't find the words... You're such a beautiful person, and I'm so lucky to have you with me." Garv's confession was genuine.

"Stop buttering me up, okay?" Anshika teased.

"I really want to come there and kiss you, Cutie Pie." Garv sent the message with a smile.

"Then come over. Why don't you?" Anshika challenged.

"It will take some time, Jaaneman, but once I come, just remember—you'll have to share everything with me: blanket, pillow, all of it." Garv joked.

"Come soon, I miss you so much, Baccha." Anshika's message was filled with longing.

That night, the two lovebirds shared a long and intimate conversation, lost in the world of their fantasies. Their connection deepened further, and love began to fill the air.

As time went on, Garv continued to isolate himself. He made a few friends at his tuition, but since he wasn't passionate about CA, he didn't hang out with them much. Instead, he started focusing on his fitness. After two years of neglecting his health, he decided to join the gym. But after just fifteen days, Garv injured his knee again, reminding him of the injury from his 12th class kabaddi match. He had ignored the injury back then, and it had worsened over time.

Garv went directly to the doctor from the gym, where he was told that his ligament had torn and surgery was required. He called Anshika to update her.

"Are you okay? Don't do anything stupid. Keep the vehicle there, and take an auto home. If you don't, I'll call your mom," Anshika warned, her voice filled with concern.

"Don't worry, Baccha. The doctor said it's a normal surgery. I'll be fine in about 1.5 months," Garv reassured her, though he wasn't fully convinced.

"You're crazy! Why do you take things so lightly? Go home, tell your mom about it, okay?" Anshika insisted.

"Yes, Baccha, I'll message you once I'm home." Garv promised.

After undergoing surgery, Garv was advised to take at least 30 days of bed rest and then go through another 30 days of physiotherapy. However, Garv was worried about how it would affect his exams. He had planned to fail but only in a way that would let him convince his parents. But once the surgery was done, Garv was determined to heal quickly. In just 10 days, he started his physiotherapy, changed his diet to include eggs and non-vegetarian food, and by the end of the 30 days, he was back to tuition, studying hard with his friends, Pritesh, Ghori, Savani, Polkal, and Vasu, who kept him motivated.

On his birthday, Garv decided to give his mock exam a try. He quickly realized how unprepared he was, and told Anshika about it.

"It's okay, Baccha. You still have 10 days. Try to cover as much as you can." Anshika reassured him, always supportive.

On that birthday, Anuj surprised Garv by showing up with two other friends to celebrate. They cut the cake together and went for dinner, lifting Garv's spirits.

10 Days Left for the Exam

Garv dove into his studies. He analyzed the syllabus and tackled the easiest sections first, covering 70% of it in the last 10 days. He skipped Accounts, overconfident that he would do well in that subject. On the exam day, he carefully approached the MCQs, but when he saw the Accounts paper, he realized how different it was from what he had studied for his 12th boards. Nevertheless, he managed to answer the MCQs that could at least get him passing marks.

When the results came out, Garv found that he had passed the exam. He was ecstatic, especially since he had barely managed to scrape through in Accounts with the exact passing marks. His father, knowing Garv's love for watches, gave him a Casio Edifice as a gift. It was the first watch Garv had bought for himself in over a year.

On result day, Garv shared his happiness with Anshika:

"*I made it, Baccha.*" Garv's voice was filled with relief and joy.

"I love you, you worked so hard, I saw it. You used to talk to me all night long, but you stopped," Anshika said.

"Sorry, but if I hadn't, I would've failed. It was about my self-respect, baby. Go to sleep," Garv replied.

"I'm happy you cleared it, I was doubtful. I wondered how you'd do it in just 10 days, but you made it. I love you so much, Garv," Anshika said, her voice filled with pride.

"I love you, baby," Anshika whispered softly.

As the nights went by, Garv and Anshika's bond grew even stronger. They started to explore fantasies of traveling the world together, hand in hand. Garv found himself increasingly captivated by her expressions, so much so that he began to predict how she would react to their conversations. He wasn't always accurate, but he was getting to know her more deeply than ever before.

Garv's love for Anshika grew stronger, and they began to share their fears and experiences more openly.

"You don't have any fears," Anshika said, almost as if she couldn't imagine him feeling scared of anything.

"I fear nothing in this life except for my father. Nothing else scares me, baby," Garv replied.

"Have you ever thought about me leaving? Doesn't that scare you?" Anshika asked, her voice quieter now.

Garv fell silent, the weight of her words settling heavily on him. He didn't want to think about it.

"I'm just joking, Garv. I'm not going anywhere," Anshika reassured him with a gentle smile.

"Yeah, okay. Goodnight," Garv responded, still uneasy.

"Are you angry, Garv? Please tell me," Anshika asked, concerned.

"I can't let you go anywhere. If you do, I wouldn't know what to do. You've added another fear—losing you. How could you even think about it? Let's talk tomorrow. Goodbye for now," Garv said, his voice tinged with sadness.

"Sorry, I was just teasing. I'm awake, and if you want to call, please do," Anshika said, trying to soothe him.

"The day I leave, Anshika, you'll regret it, and even if you want to change my mind, I won't be able to. Just remember that," Garv said, his voice firm but sad.

He ended the call, feeling a little lost, and went for a ride at 2:00 AM. He asked his brother to cover for him, making sure no one knew he was out. Garv couldn't stop thinking about Anshika's words. He drove aimlessly on the highway, letting the music of Arijit Singh heal him as the speed of the ride helped clear his mind. By the time he got home at 4:00 AM, he sent Anshika a message on Hike: *"I love you a lot, and please don't talk about leaving. Come back soon."*

Anshika, who had been awake, called him. "I'm sorry, Garv. I didn't mean to upset you. Please, get some rest," she said softly, making him feel at ease enough to sleep peacefully.

However, Garv was struggling with his studies. For the first four or five months, he wasn't serious about his exams. But with only two months left, he finally realized he had to get serious. He started studying hard with his CA friends, Pankaj and Shreyansh, and his Gujarati friends. He told Anshika that he wouldn't be able to talk much now, as his focus was entirely on his exams. Anshika was upset, but she supported him, understanding the situation.

Finally, the exams began, and Garv realized it wouldn't be easy to pass. With only one day of leave between exams, he pushed himself, giving his all, knowing that his center was his school, where he felt comfortable. After the exams, Garv texted Anshika, "*I think I'll clear one group, but the audit is still a worry.*"

"Don't worry, you've worked hard. Everything will be fine," Anshika reassured him.

"By the way, listen, I'll be starting compulsory ICAI training classes in six days. They'll go from 6 AM to 8 PM, so I won't be free," Garv informed her.

"Hmm," Anshika responded.

"I love you, that's non-negotiable, baby. What can I do? The training will last until December 23, and then the exams will be from December 27," Garv added, sounding apologetic.

"Will you talk to me for at least seven days? I'm missing you so much, baby," Anshika said, her voice filled with longing.

"Yes, Babaji," Garv chuckled, trying to lighten the mood.

The exams finally ended, and Garv received a call from Ghori.

"Maheshwari, you free?" Ghori asked.

"Yeah, I'm free, bro. What's up?" Garv replied.

"Come over to my society, we're going to Pritesh's farmhouse," Ghori said.

"Alright, I'll be there in 15 minutes," Garv said, excited to catch up with his friends.

At the farmhouse, the group gathered around a roundtable conference. It felt like Pritesh had organized everything. Pritesh, the owner of a diamond company, and Ghori, the owner of a textile company, were both down-to-earth, thoughtful people. Their kindness was overwhelming, and they believed in helping others grow together.

"Come, Maheshwari!" Pritesh called out.

"Hey, bro, what's up? The whole crew is here?" Garv asked, surprised.

"We're planning a trip, we need you to organize it," Savani said, grinning.

"Where are we going?" Garv asked eagerly.

"We're thinking of Rajasthan, Maheshwari. It's your responsibility to plan the whole trip and figure out the budget. We'll meet in two days and discuss it," Pritesh said.

"Looks like we're going on a long trip, huh?" Saurabh laughed.

"When's it happening? I still have that compulsory training," Garv replied, hesitant.

"After December 28, bro. Don't worry," Pritesh reassured him.

They spent the afternoon enjoying Gujarati lunch brought from Pritesh's farm, sipping on five liters of buttermilk from his cows, all while watching *Fast & Furious* in Hindi.

Later that night, Garv messaged Anshika, "I'm planning to go out and have fun."

"Where are you going? Come over here and meet me," Anshika replied, hopeful.

Garv thought for a moment. "I could do that, but I have to convince my friends. They're obsessed with Rajasthan, and convincing them might be tough."

"Please, just come over, I miss you so much," Anshika urged.

"I promise, baby. I'll do my best to change their minds," Garv said, reassuring her.

Garv's friends were unaware of his love story. Garv had a strong ability to convince people, so he devised a plan. He organized a trip across Rajasthan, knowing it would likely be rejected. Along with it, he also planned a trip to the northern region and presented it to them.

"Hey, Maheshwari, did you make a plan?" asked Pritesh.

"I've made the plan, but there's something I need to discuss with you all," Garv replied.

"What's up? The plan isn't working?" Ghori asked.

"Look, we leave from here in a car, and you want to go around Rajasthan. During this season, hotels in Rajasthan will be expensive, and it would take at least 20 to 25 days for the whole trip. Our budget will be around 60K. Do you think this budget works for everyone?" Garv explained.

"Man, you're kidding, right?" Polkal exclaimed.

"This is too much, yaar," Vasu added.

"So, what do you think, Pritesh and Ghori?" Garv asked.

"Let's go with whatever everyone prefers. We won't go alone," Ghori and Pritesh agreed.

"Well, I've got another idea. How about we go to North India?" Garv suggested.

"You made a plan for that too?" Ghori asked.

"Yes, I did. We'll first go to Delhi, then leave for Chandigarh the same day. We'll spend two days there, then head to Manali, Shimla, Kasoli, and

Manikaran, and finally return via a flight from Delhi to Surat," Garv explained.

"How much will this cost, Maheshwari?" Pritesh asked.

"Well, I estimate it will cost a maximum of 50K. This includes drinks as well—if you guys drink, otherwise you can cut back and it will be around 10 to 12K. Plus, we'll get to enjoy some snowfall," Garv replied.

"This trip sounds good to me. What do you all think?" Ghori said.

Everyone agreed, but Ghori and Pritesh insisted on removing Delhi from the plan and just visiting Chandigarh.

Garv convinced them by showing the pollution index of Delhi, explaining that it wasn't worth going there. He also highlighted all the special spots in Chandigarh to make them reconsider.

Finally, Garv's plan was set in motion. But there was one hurdle left: convincing his parents. He started with his mom, trying to get her to convince his dad. But surprisingly, his mom wasn't convinced. She thought a 12-day trip was too long and that he shouldn't go alone. So, Garv directly asked his dad for permission, explaining the entire plan and who he was going with. To his surprise, his dad immediately agreed, and even his mom was shocked. It turned out that Garv's younger brother had already spoken to their dad about the trip, and they both thought it would be good for Garv to go and enjoy himself.

Now, the MCS and IT batch had started, and Garv was enjoying the classes. He was a great speaker, always able to make people laugh. Every day, the class would ask him to speak about something in front of everyone. He even had a few confrontations with teachers and students due to his political views, as Garv was a strong right-wing supporter and couldn't stand people who spoke against his beliefs without solid facts. Having seen Gujarat develop since his childhood, he was always ready to defend what he loved.

Finally, December 20th arrived, and Garv decided to play a little game with Anshika.

"Baccha, I've got a surprise for you," Garv said.

"What is it? Tell me the surprise!" Anshika replied eagerly.

"Why should I tell you?" Garv teased.

"Just tell me already!" Anshika said.

"Guess what? I'm coming to see my jaaneman," Garv responded.

"Stop fooling around, Garv. Are you serious? Tell me the truth," Anshika insisted.

"1st January 2019 will be the date of our first date, baccha," Garv announced.

"Are you really coming to meet me, Garv?" Anshika asked, surprised.

"Yes, baccha," Garv confirmed.

Garv sent his tickets to Anshika and told her, "You plan everything; I'll be free after my exams on the 28th of December. I'll only have two days for shopping, so you plan everything and let me know."

Anshika taught Garv how to speak proper Hindi, as Garv's Hindi was a bit rough compared to the more respectful Hindi spoken in the North, where "ji" is often added to sentences.

"Okay, I'll follow your advice, but I'll be meeting you alone, right?" Garv asked.

"No, my friends want to meet you too. So get ready for that," Anshika teased.

"Haanji, Mohtarma," Garv responded, playing along.

On the other side, Anshika was counting the days to meet Garv, planning where to take him, what gifts to buy, and everything else. Meanwhile, Garv and his friends were caught in trouble when someone from their class was found with an exam paper before an IT training exam. They stood together in front of the ICAI president, insisting that they had no idea the paper was the same as the exam. The president told them to come clean or face suspension.

Garv, never one to be intimidated, suggested they seek help from their teacher. Since Ghori and Pritesh had strong connections, their teacher advised them to tell the president they would involve their lawyers. The president, realizing the situation was serious, backed off when they mentioned their lawyer friends. The issue was resolved on December 30th, and the group went shopping together.

Garv was stressed because, although he had booked the trip, he hadn't accounted for other expenses. But on the evening of December 31st, just as he was heading to the station, his dad transferred 50K to him for the trip. Garv thanked his dad with a message: "Thank you."

Chapter 11

The First Date and the Best Date of Garv's Life

Finally, Garv and his buddies boarded the train. You know the best part of being with Gujaratis? They're always prepared! They were carrying 500 theplas and two XL-size bags full of snacks, biscuits, and everything imaginable. Garv and the Savani brothers, the twin brothers, were sitting together, while the other four friends were in the next coach. It was the night of December 31st, and they were planning to party, but they didn't have any drinks with them. But as luck would have it, their friends from L&T, sitting nearby, had brought a 2-liter cold drink bottle filled with whisky. As soon as they opened the bottle, Garv noticed the strong smell. They asked, "Garv bhai, is the smell that strong?" Garv smiled and replied, "Bhaiya, it's pretty strong!" After a while, Garv and the Savani brothers joined them. They partied the night away, ringing in the New Year.

Later that night, Garv messaged his friend Harshana (whom he'd met through MCS). "Behen, free hain kya?" he texted.

"Haaan, bolo, kya hua?" Harshana replied.

"Yaar, ek help chaiye muje," Garv asked.

"Seriously? Tuze help chaiye, Garv?" Harshana responded, a bit surprised.

"Masti nahi, Harshana," Garv clarified. He went on to tell her about Anshika and how he didn't have a gift for her because of all the chaos before the trip. He asked Harshana for ideas on what to do for Anshika.

Harshana, teasing him, replied, "Garv, just be normal with her. Find a nice restaurant and plan a candlelight dinner. But please, don't be awkward. It's been so long since you've met, and you're not the type to open up suddenly, so just be yourself and don't make her feel uncomfortable."

"Ohkz Lambu," Garv responded with a grin.

"Your secret's safe with me, but you owe me a big treat!" Harshana added.

"Sure," Garv agreed.

Just then, Anshika called Garv. Her exams and projects were finally over, and she was feeling emotional about meeting him after such a long time. "Garv, are you excited to see me?" she asked.

Garv, feeling a bit anxious, responded, "Anshika, I'm feeling a little anxious. I don't know why, but I just am."

Anshika, being sweet, comforted him, saying, "I love you, and I'm sending you lots of kisses. Go to sleep now, and we'll meet soon."

The next day, January 2, 2015, Garv woke up early, full of excitement. He got ready and shared his location with Anshika. She messaged him that she was on her way, and Garv couldn't help but feel that every minute was dragging on. As he waited, he thought he saw a girl getting off the bus who resembled Anshika, and he went after her, but then he realized it wasn't her. Just then, Anshika called.

"Garv, wait for 10 minutes please. I took the wrong bus. I'm on my way now," Anshika explained.

"No problem, Baccha. I'm waiting for you," Garv replied, his heart racing.

Finally, Anshika arrived, and when they saw each other, Garv got awkward and forgot to hug her back. Anshika, noticing his discomfort, gently took his hand, and they walked towards the taxi stand together.

"Kidhar ja rahe hain, Anshika?" Garv asked, still a bit flustered.

"Aapko kuch nahi poochna. Aaj jahan mein le kar jaaungi, chup chaap chalna hai," Anshika said with a playful smile.

They got into a taxi, and this time, Garv didn't feel awkward as Anshika held his hand. They both smiled at each other, and Garv squeezed her hand, whispering, "You're looking beautiful and very cute."

Their first stop was Sukhna Lake. The weather was perfect—around 7 degrees in Chandigarh, with a foggy but pleasant atmosphere. They walked side by side for over an hour, and Anshika, feeling carefree, grabbed Garv's hand tightly, not worried about anything.

"Kuch toh bolo," Anshika nudged him.

"Nahi samajh aa raha kya bolun, Baccha. Abhi tak believe nahi ho raha ki aap mere saath ho," Garv admitted, still in awe.

"Main hoon, Baccha. Aapke saath hoon, sab kuch sach hai," Anshika reassured him, her voice soft and sincere.

After their peaceful walk at the lake, Anshika took Garv to the Garden of Silence. It was such a serene place, but in the back of Garv's mind, he was worried about someone from Anshika's family seeing them together.

As they walked through the garden, hand in hand, Garv felt like this was the best date of his life, one he had dreamed of for so long. It wasn't just about the place or the perfect moment—it was about the connection they shared, something that was finally becoming real after all the time spent apart.

Garv and Anshika sat there, their hands intertwined, gazing into each other's eyes. The moment was so peaceful, so intimate, that even the noise around them seemed to fade. Garv, trying to pull his gaze away, was met with Anshika's soft command. "Look at me, only at me," she whispered, her eyes searching his, as they began to talk.

They spoke for hours, reminiscing about the last four years, how their bond had strengthened, how they had grown together through both the good and the challenging times. Anshika, with a playful glint in her eyes, asked, "Garv, how do I look to you?"

He chuckled softly, his voice a little shy, though he meant every word. "You're the kind of person who can make someone change their entire plan for you," he said, his eyes locking with hers. "How could I not love you? I know I'm awkward, but... yeah, I love you."

Anshika, her heart fluttering, pulled his hand from his shoulder. "Stop being awkward," she said gently. "You're making me uncomfortable now. Please, just... be yourself."

They both laughed, the conversation flowing effortlessly as they talked about the future, about how they wanted to move forward together. Time passed unnoticed, until the bustle of the growing crowd reminded them that the evening was slipping away. It was 11:00 PM.

Anshika, eager for a moment of closeness, stood up and gently tugged Garv's hand. She led him towards the Sanctuary near Sukhna Lake. With a mischievous smile, she tried to kiss his cheek, but despite her efforts, she couldn't quite reach. Garv, with a teasing grin, asked, "Why are you jumping, Anshika?"

Ignoring his teasing, she made another attempt and this time, her lips brushed against his cheek. As Garv felt the warmth of her kiss, his cheeks flushed pink. He smiled, his heart racing, as Anshika took his hand and wrapped it around hers, walking beside him in contented silence.

Later, as they sat by the lake, Anshika handed Garv a tiffin filled with sandwiches. "My mom made these for me," she said, a hint of pride in her voice. "But I know you love them, so... please, have some." Garv took a bite, savoring the familiar taste. Anshika noticed how he adjusted his pace to match hers, knowing she liked to eat slowly. Her heart warmed at the sight.

When she finished, Anshika told him, "Baccha, I need to head to college, but I'll be back in an hour."

Garv, reluctant to let her go, pleaded, "Please, don't go. We can do it tomorrow, can't we?"

She smiled, dialing her friend to confirm if she really needed to be at college. Her friend assured her it wasn't urgent. "I'll be back in an hour, I promise," Anshika said, holding his hand with affection.

Garv, after she left, joined his friends at the Rock Garden. As soon as he arrived, they gathered around him, a teasing grin on each of their faces. "What's up, Maheshwari? Why do you look so sad?" Ghori asked, his tone lighthearted.

"It's just... the day's going too fast, yaar," Garv replied, his tone wistful. "I'm going to miss her a lot."

Pritesh clapped him on the back. "Man, you've really done it. You've waited for her, trusted her, and now look at you. Not many can say they've found a love like that."

Garv's eyes softened. "I waited for her, took my time. There's no one like her. We've fought, we've made up, but it's always worth it. Either she's the one, or no one is."

That evening, Anshika called Garv and invited him to their favorite lunch spot. As they sat across from each other, Garv couldn't help but be mesmerized by the sparkle in her eyes. They ordered Malai Kofta and Naan, and Garv, as always, tried to match Anshika's pace with the food. He knew she ate slowly, and he was content to savor the moment, even if it meant stretching out the meal.

Anshika, sensing his care, smiled lovingly at him. Her eyes said everything—*I love you.*

Afterward, they went for dessert. Anshika, who never shared her sweet treats with anyone, surprised Garv by ordering two pastries—Red Velvet and Blueberry. "You choose," she said. Garv, knowing how much she loved Red Velvet, picked the Blueberry, and in a rare moment, Anshika shared her pastry with him. Garv, who usually finished desserts in a few bites, took 45 minutes to savor each one, savoring the sweet taste and the even sweeter company.

Their day continued at Leisure Valley Garden, where Anshika gifted him a bracelet, a wallet, and a perfume. As Garv kissed her palm in thanks, he felt a pang of guilt for not bringing a gift for her. He apologized, explaining that his shopping had been rushed, and that his friends had eaten the chocolates he'd intended to give her.

Anshika smiled, squeezing his hand. "You've already given me the best gift, just by being here with me," she said softly, her eyes filled with affection.

Later, she joked about what to tell her friends. Garv, ever the problem-solver, suggested they go shopping, but Anshika, looking at the time, reminded him that it was already 5:00 PM. "We don't have much time left, Baccha," she said with a smile.

As the evening came to a close, Anshika, surprising Garv again, suggested they go to the movies. Garv was taken aback, knowing she wasn't usually the movie type. But she explained, "It's 4 degrees outside. Let's go to the theater and enjoy the warmth together."

They ended up at an almost empty theater, the film *Tiger Zinda Hai* playing on the screen. Garv held Anshika's hand, his gaze soft as he watched her, her head resting gently on his shoulder. After a while, she caught his attention, her gaze intense and full of affection. Garv, feeling overwhelmed, pulled away briefly, but Anshika, unable to resist, kissed his cheek.

Garv, wanting to kiss her lips, glanced around to make sure no one was watching. As they shared a brief moment, he kissed her forehead, writing "I love you" on her palm. Her smile grew even more radiant, and Garv, sensing her fading smile, kissed her forehead once more, reassuring her, "I'll come back soon. And as long as we're not together, I'll always make the effort to see you."

Anshika, wrapped in his arms, hugged his left arm tightly, her heart full as Garv rested his head on hers.

"Do you even want to watch the movie, Garv?" Anshika teased.

"I've already seen it, Baccha," he replied, a twinkle in his eye.

"Then let's go outside. I need all your attention right now," she said with a playful smile.

"Let's go," Garv agreed, content to follow her lead, as they left the theater together, ready to make the most of their remaining time.

Anshika and Garv stepped outside, and Anshika asked, "Now, what do we do? It's already 7:45 PM, and I need to get back to the hostel by 9:30, or else they won't let me in."

Garv, with a mischievous grin, suggested, "How about we head to Sukhna, where our date began? We can end it there, too."

Anshika smiled and nodded. They took an auto, and along the way, Anshika hugged Garv's arm, knowing that soon they would have to part again. The thought made her feel a little uneasy, so she held on tight. Finally, they reached Sukhna Lake.

The area was dark, and the temperature had dropped to 3°C. They began walking, talking about how much they would miss each other. Then, Garv's phone rang—his mom was calling.

"Kya kar raha hai, Golu?" Garv's mom asked.

"Bas, maja kar raha hoon. Ek dost hai Chandigarh mein, usse milne aaya hoon," Garv replied casually.

"Thik hai, dhyaan rakhna. Zyada party mat karna," his mom cautioned.

"Haan, Mumma. Chalo, abhi bye. Main baad mein baat karta hoon," Garv said, ending the call.

Anshika, walking behind him, teased him, wanting to speak to his mom. Garv, in a playful tone, warned, "Marwa doge aap!" Then, Anshika got a call from her mom but didn't answer immediately. First, she rehearsed what she would say. Afterward, she called back.

Garv laughed, "What's with the rehearsals?"

Anshika shot back, "I'm not a pro at lying like you!"

"Ek baat batao, itni asaani se jhoot bol lete ho. Mujhse toh aise jhoot nahi bolte," Anshika said.

"What do you want to know? I'll tell you all the answers, honestly," Garv responded.

"Chup ho jao! Aur aao idhar. Agar aap sach mein pyaar karte ho, toh mujhse bhi bharosa karna," Anshika said, her tone softening as she hugged him tightly.

Garv returned the hug. "Baccha, please don't be sad. I'll come back soon. If you're sad, I'll be sad too, and then the whole trip will be ruined."

Anshika held his hands and felt how cold his palms were. Without thinking, she started rubbing them to warm them up. They were so lost in the moment that neither noticed it was already 9:10 PM. Garv urged Anshika to hurry, and they rushed to the exit, waiting for their cab.

"Anshika, I'm not sure we'll make it on time," Garv said.

"Are you saying that with happiness, or are you worried? I can't tell," Anshika teased.

"Let's go to the hotel together. We'll have plenty of time to talk," Anshika added.

Garv felt a bit uneasy. Things were moving faster than he was comfortable with, and he also worried about Anshika's relatives seeing them together, since her parents didn't know she was dating. He was also concerned about the respect she might lose in her hometown.

Still, Garv called his friend Savani and told him, "Bhai, make sure the room is clean. If Anshika can't get into the hostel, we'll come to the hotel."

Savani teased him, but Garv stayed firm. "Bro, I'm not going to talk about this with you. We'll stay in that room alone, alright?"

After some banter, Garv and Anshika reached her hostel. Anshika's friends assured her, "Don't worry, we'll get you in. Just give us 5 minutes."

Anshika hugged Garv and said, "Baccha, always stay with me. I'll miss you."

With a final hug, Anshika walked towards the hostel gate, and Garv waited until she disappeared inside. He was sad, but he headed to his hotel afterward.

That first date made both of them realize how much they cared for each other and how hard their future might be, given the distance. They knew they'd have to figure out how to manage it.

Chapter 12

Did Their First Date End?

Garv finally reached the hotel, feeling low. He didn't know when he and Anshika would meet again. Suddenly, he heard voices from upstairs.

"Bhai, up here! Hurry up!" Savani called out. His friends had been waiting for him to start the party.

"Bhai, you made me wait longer than my ex ever did!" Savani joked.

"What do you mean? I didn't make you wait," Garv replied.

"We've been waiting for an hour to start drinking. We can't begin without you!" Savani complained.

"Not tonight, bro. We'll drink after we go to Manali," Garv said.

"You're asking for trouble, I'm telling you. Don't mess with me," Savani teased.

"By the way, how was the date?" Ghori asked.

"It was great, bro," Garv answered.

"Then why the long face? Next year, we'll meet again. If you stay sad, who will make the party fun?" Pritesh added.

Garv finally took off his jacket and put his phone on charge. He joined his friends to enjoy the evening, though he'd already told them he wouldn't drink hard alcohol tonight—only beer. Two hours later, he checked his phone and saw 25 missed calls from Anshika and her friends.

He quickly called her back, but it was her friend Sheru who picked up.

"Haan, Garv, how are you? We've been trying to reach you."

"I'm fine. What's up? Is Anshika okay? Why all the missed calls?" Garv asked, concerned.

"Aapko kya farak padta hai? Humne 30 calls kiye hain. Milke baat kar lo, Anshika ko toh milne ke baad aap bhool gaye," Sheru teased him.

"No, no, it's not like that. As soon as I arrived, I started talking to my friends," Garv explained.

"Nothing. Garv, we have a surprise for you," Sheru said.

"A surprise? What's that?" Garv asked.

"Tomorrow morning, at 5:00 AM, are you coming to meet us?" Anshika asked, her voice cheerful.

"Of course, Anshika! I'll be there, don't worry. I'll come and meet you," Garv replied.

"Don't be late, and please pick up the call when we call you. We'll be waiting for you. We'll book everything for you. Just come and meet us," Sheru reminded him.

"Got it! I'll set my ringtone and get some sleep. See you tomorrow morning," Garv said.

"I love you, baccha," Anshika said softly.

"I love you too," Garv whispered back.

Garv had stopped partying, telling everyone that he was going on a date the next morning. No one forced him to join, because they all understood how important she must be to him. That's the best thing about male friendships—they don't need to say anything, everyone just understands, and they go to any lengths to support their friend's love.

Garv woke up at 4:00 a.m. to the sound of his alarm. He got ready in the next half hour and called Anshika.

"Did you wake up, baby?" Anshika asked.

"I'm ready too, Anshika," Garv replied.

"I haven't woken up yet. I'm getting ready now, and I'll wake up the others too," she said.

"Okay, you get ready. I'll come by cab to pick you up," Garv suggested.

"No, wait, I'll book the cab. You won't know which gate to come to," Anshika replied.

So, Sheru booked a cab for Garv. He was in love with the city—its air, its people, the peaceful life. Garv always loved to smell good, and it showed. Every month, his 100ml perfume bottle would be emptied. As soon as he got into the cab, the driver complimented him. "Paaji, that perfume smells really good," the cab driver said, and their conversation began. They talked about different places Garv and his friends could explore in Manali and Shimla. Garv, curious, asked, "Paaji, will I find any flowers around here?"

The driver responded, "Right now, nothing's open. Things start opening around 9 a.m."

As Garv was about to get out of the cab, the driver wished him good luck with his love life.

Garv smiled and nodded.

Garv then called Anshika.

"Are you here, Garv?" Anshika asked.

"Yes, baby, I'm standing outside the gate," Garv replied.

"Okay, wait a moment. We're just coming out," Anshika said.

Garv's eyes immediately searched for her, his heart skipping a beat as soon as he saw her. Anshika, wearing a red-purplish jacket and a cute winter cap, with her hair cascading over her shoulder and her smile from a hundred meters away, sent a shiver down his spine. "Good morning, baby. Why didn't you wear your jacket?" Garv asked. "Nothing, yesterday when I reached the hotel, my shirt got all sweaty from the back, so I didn't wear the jacket," Anshika explained. "That's fine, you don't even feel the cold, do you?" Garv teased. "I love you, beautiful," he whispered.

The two sweet souls walked together, with Sheru and Chetna trailing behind. They were the only friends Anshika hung out with and played a very important role in their love story—always kind and helpful.

"Hello, how are you both?" Garv greeted them.

"Hello, we're good. How are you?" Sheru and Chetna replied cheerfully.

"We're doing great too," they said, continuing their walk through the cool, soothing morning breeze of beautiful Chandigarh.

"Ahem, Garv, we have a few complaints," Sheru said with a grin.

"Go ahead," Garv replied, puzzled.

"You don't like your phone, so why don't you change it? There are so many good phones in the market now," Sheru teased.

"Sorry about last night, I forgot my phone was on silent mode," Garv admitted.
"You know, last night, Anshika gave us quite a few scoldings for you, right?" Sheru and Chetna said, laughing.

"Yeah, I forgot to bring her gift. I know, I'm sorry," Garv replied, sheepishly.
"She gave us a real class last night! But how could you forget the gift?" Sheru teased.

"I was planning to bring it, but I got caught up at the last moment and forgot. It just slipped my mind," Garv explained.

"No worries, Anshika's fine with us. But you better make it up to her," Sheru said with a wink.

Anshika was a bit ahead of them, walking with Chetna, so Garv and Sheru shared a quick chat.

"Alright, Garv, let's talk about the gift. I need your help," Garv said to Sheru, his voice full of sincerity.

"I don't know what gift to give Anshika, and next time I can't even wait, because I don't know when we'll meet again. I have to give her something," Garv said, looking troubled.

"It's okay, take your time to think. We'll think it over, decide, and then arrange to deliver it to her hostel," Sheru reassured him.

"Done, but you have to let me know soon because I've never bought a gift for anyone, especially not for a girl," Garv admitted.

"It's fine, we'll manage. But hurry back. Anshika really loves you," Sheru said with a smile.

"Yeah, I'll go. But after today, take care of her because I know she's going to cry. I trust you'll take care of her, but don't let her cry," Garv said, his voice filled with concern.

They both smiled at each other, and then Garv and Anshika started walking again.

Garv couldn't help but feel sad. He knew neither of them knew when they'd meet again, and time was slipping away so fast. Garv took her hand, gently rubbing her fingers, and whispered, "I love you," before kissing her forehead and pulling her into a tight hug.

"Please come back soon, and stay longer next time," Anshika said, her voice tinged with sadness.

"If you're this sad, I won't come. It's better I just call you on video and see you smiling rather than upset," Garv teased, trying to lighten the mood. Anshika gave him a gentle smile, and they continued walking back toward the hostel.

"What did you ask from God?" Anshika asked.

"Guess what I asked for," Garv replied with a playful grin.

"I don't know. Please tell me," Anshika said, curious.

"Garv," Anshika called softly.

"I'm right here, Anshika," he replied, his voice full of affection.

Anshika smiled and said, "I'm right here, by your side."

For the first time, Garv felt the fear of losing something precious. He realized that long-distance relationships were no joke—they required commitment and a lot of patience. But as long as they stayed strong together, he wouldn't give up. Garv knew that he would be the one handling all the emotions, but the applause would come from both of them. He silently prayed for her strength, calmness, and happiness.

"Stay with me forever, and we'll be happy together. That's my prayer," Garv said, his voice filled with sincerity.

"I love you a lot," Anshika replied, her voice soft and warm.

"I love you too, baby," Garv whispered.

Anshika, though feeling low, tried to hide it behind a sweet smile, not wanting Garv to feel sad. She wished, deep down, that he would stay with her, that he wouldn't go on the trip. But Anshika knew Garv couldn't stay, so she finally hugged him again, urging him to come back soon.

"Take care of yourself, and don't be sad. I'll always be available. Whenever you want, just call. I'll be on the phone the whole time. I promise, baby," Garv said, his voice soft and reassuring.

"Take care, Garv, and come back soon," Anshika's friends called out to him as he made his way to the cab.

Garv waved at Anshika, giving her a comforting smile, before the cab pulled away. After a few minutes, the distance between them grew, and the reality of long-distance hit hard. They had met in person, and now, the waiting seemed endless. But no matter the distance, love always kept them connected.

Garv reached his hotel, and as he sat there looking at the selfie they had taken that morning, he kissed the photo before calling Anshika.

"Hello, Garv. Anshika has fallen asleep," Sheru answered the phone.

"Alright, good. Whenever she wakes up, tell her to call me. I'll be waiting," Garv said.

"Will do," Sheru replied.

"Take care of her. Stay with her," Garv reminded him.

"Of course," Sheru answered.

"Thanks, and goodbye," Garv said.

"Goodbye," Sheru responded.

The trip officially began, and the group headed toward Manali. Garv sat alone on the last seat of the bus, listening to "Tiger Zinda Hai," his first movie date song. He could feel the lingering touch and scent of Anshika. Garv, ever the observer, could almost smell her fragrance in the air and feel the warmth of her fingers on his. His friends tried to lighten the mood by encouraging him to join in the fun, but Garv couldn't help but feel every second of his date slipping away from him.

Soon, the group started dancing, playing, and having fun on the bus. As they neared Manali, Garv and Anshika were calling each other, talking about their day. But just as Garv was about to reach Manali around 6:00 pm, he got a call.

"Baccha," Anshika said in a horrified voice.

"Anshika, what happened? Are you okay? Where are you?" Garv asked, his voice laced with concern.

"I'm at home, but I think someone saw us together," Anshika said, her voice trembling.

"Why do you think that, baby?" Garv asked, trying to calm her.

She explained that a relative of hers, someone who hadn't visited in a long time, had asked if Anshika was home. Anshika was worried because they lived near the place where Garv and Anshika had been hanging out.

"Don't worry, baby. If they come, just let me know. We'll figure it out," Garv reassured her.

"But if they tell my parents, I won't be able to face them," Anshika said, anxiety rising in her voice.

"I'm here, baby. If anything happens, I'll come to Chandigarh. Just call me. I promise I'll be there," Garv said firmly.

"Promise, Garv? If my dad gets angry, don't leave me alone," Anshika pleaded.

"Just tell them I'm coming. I'll handle whatever comes. Don't worry, I can take care of everything. Just keep me updated, and I'll let my friends know I might have to go back to Chandigarh," Garv assured her.

"I love you, Garv," Anshika said softly.

"I love you too, cutie. Don't worry, everything will be fine. I'll be there if you need me," Garv said, his voice filled with love.

"Keep me posted, okay?" Anshika asked.

"Yeah, I will. Take care," Garv said before ending the call.

Garv had confided in his friends about everything, and they responded with their usual lightheartedness. "Don't worry, Maheshwari, we'll come with you. We'll handle everything and take care of the trip back to Chandigarh," they reassured him.

But Garv, always calm under pressure, replied, "Bro, you're not needed right now. Enjoy yourselves. I'll take care of it."

Pritesh and Ghori, though, were not so easily convinced. "No way, man. We're coming with you. We can't leave you hanging," they insisted.

"Fine," Garv chuckled. "But what if things get out of hand? What will you do?"

"We'll be outside, keeping a lookout. You handle the situation; we'll be ready if anything goes wrong," Ghori replied with a grin.

Garv smirked, shaking his head. "Yeah, I'll be fine, don't worry. I've been through worse."

But then, Ghori, always the realist, warned, "If things escalate, you'll be on your own inside, so if you get hit, don't come crying to us. We'll wait outside."

"I'm telling you, I can't lose my cool with him. I just... I can't be angry, can't curse anyone, and I sure as hell can't fight. I don't know why, but when I face him, I just freeze. Everything calms down, and I don't know what's happening," Garv admitted, his voice quiet, almost lost in the moment.

He paused, thinking back to everything he'd endured. "The physical pain? Sure, I could handle that. But this mental stress... it's something else. I've never known how to deal with it, not without Anshika."

Garv's friends, though worried, understood. They knew that when it came to Anshika, Garv would move heaven and earth for her. Nothing mattered more to him than making sure she never felt alone. Even though his own struggles weighed heavily on him, he had promised that he would never quit on her—no matter what.

The evening had fallen, and at 7:30 p.m., a blanket of snow covered the ground. Garv sat, waiting for Anshika's call. He had braced himself for the worst-case scenario, prepared for anything that might come his way. In that moment, he called his sister and her husband, telling them everything that had happened, just in case he needed them. He knew that whatever Anshika's father might do, he couldn't predict.

Savani, his friend, tried to calm him, offering a drink to ease the tension. But Garv, always serious about handling things himself, declined. "I'm not going to show up drunk. I need to keep my head clear. This isn't the time."

Finally, Anshika called. Her voice, though shaky, was filled with relief. "Baccha, he's gone. He didn't say anything. He just came by and left. Everything's fine now."

Garv's heart skipped a beat as he heard the news. "I knew it," he said softly, more to himself than to her. "I told you everything would be fine. Don't worry about it now. I've got everything handled here."

"I love you so much, Baccha. I'm sorry," Anshika whispered, her words full of emotion.

"Don't apologize, Anshika. Whatever happens, I'm always here for you. Just relax now. I'm going to take a little break and sort things out myself. I'll call you in a couple of hours, okay?" Garv reassured her, his tone calm, yet unwavering.

Anshika smiled through the sadness. "I'll wait. But you better enjoy yourself. I want you to relax too."

With that, Garv turned to his friends and announced, "Alright, I'm going to enjoy tonight. I've been through enough."

He spent the evening partying, enjoying the snowfall and the rum that flowed freely among the small group. Even those who weren't drinking joined in, dancing and celebrating as the stress lifted from Garv's shoulders. The cold air didn't bother him. In fact, it made the moment feel more alive, more real.

Suddenly, his phone rang. It was Anshika.

"Garv," she said, her voice teasing yet concerned. "What are you doing? You're out there in the snow without a shirt on?"

Garv laughed, his joy unmistakable. "I'm just living in the moment, Baccha. Don't worry, it's all good."

Anshika couldn't help but smile, though a touch of worry lingered in her voice. "You're crazy. Please, at least put on your shirt. You're going to get sick!"

But Garv, always the rebel when it came to letting loose, just grinned. "I love you, Anshika. This moment, it's everything. You're the only thing missing."

She sighed, a mix of affection and frustration in her tone. "You really are impossible."

He grinned wider, his heart full of love. "If you hadn't had that incident, I might've just kept quiet, enjoyed my drink, and gone back to the room. But this... this is a moment I won't forget. You might not be here physically, but you're always with me in spirit."

Anshika, though still a little annoyed, couldn't help but feel her heart swell. "You're such a hopeless romantic. Always have been."

"Maybe," Garv said softly. "But this trip has shown me something. It's given me the strength to believe that we'll make it through everything together. I'm madly in love with you, and I promise you—no matter what happens, I will never leave you."

"We'll make it happen," Anshika said with conviction.

Garv's smile widened. "I love you so much, Kimpu."

"I love you too," she replied, her voice full of warmth and affection.

That night was unforgettable for both of them. They began making plans for their next meeting, talking about what they would do when they finally met again. Garv, for the first time during their conversation, felt tears welling up in his eyes. He was missing her touch more than words could express. In that moment, Garv made a promise to himself—no matter what, he would never hurt Anshika, and he would always be there for her.

"Baccha, you are beautiful," Garv said softly.

"Thank you, Garv. I needed to hear that from you. How do I look to you? Your comments mean a lot to me," Anshika replied.

"I love you a lot, Anshika," Garv whispered.

"I love you too, bacchaji. Now, go ahead and rest. We have to go out tomorrow," Anshika responded, her voice warm.

"Haanji, good night, AGD," Garv said.

"AGD?" Anshika asked, confused.

"Anshika Garv Dreams," Garv replied with a smile.

"AGD, baccha," Anshika chuckled.

That night, Garv found it impossible to sleep. He went out to the waterfall near his hotel, his thoughts consumed by Anshika. As he scrolled through her photos, the hours slipped away, and he nearly dozed off by the waterfall. It was Savani who eventually found him and took him back to his room.

The next morning, Garv texted Anshika as soon as he woke up.

"Good morning, Bacchaji," he sent with a smile.

"Good morning, Garv," came her quick reply.

"We can meet again, Bacchaji," Garv typed, his heart racing with excitement.

"When? Where? Are you coming back to Chandigarh?" Anshika responded, eager to know more.

"We can plan it at the end of my trip, but it'll be brief—only 2-3 hours. After that, I have to catch a flight from Delhi," Garv explained.

"Come back, baccha. We'll meet again. I'm excited. And I still need to kiss you, so be ready!" Anshika teased.

"Haanji, baccha. Okay, I'll be ready. I'll just have breakfast and head out soon. We're going to Salong Valley today," Garv replied.

"Okay, but take care. Don't do anything reckless, alright?" Anshika advised.

"I'll take care, jaaneman. Love you, and bye for now," Garv said, feeling his heart swell.

The trip continued, and while Garv's friends were laid-back and uninterested in adventurous activities, Garv and Savani, with their enthusiasm, decided to hike and do paragliding at Salong Valley. Carrying old monk bottles, they trekked until they reached the paragliding base, both feeling dizzy. When the instructor told them to jump, they hesitated, looking down at the steep valley below. But finally, they leapt, and the 15-minute flight was absolutely exhilarating. They also went river rafting, bungee jumping, and visited Shimla, Kasol, and Manikaran. Despite Garv's friends not drinking, they never judged him and still joined in on the fun.

On the way back, Garv shared with Ghori and Pritesh that he was planning to meet Anshika again. They gave him a 3-4 hour window for the meeting, but fate had other plans. Due to a route mix-up, they couldn't meet in Chandigarh. Instead, they arranged to meet in Panchkula. Anshika, undeterred, traveled 50 kilometers alone by cab to meet him. Garv did the same, and when they finally saw each other, they embraced each other tightly, their hearts racing.

Garv showed Anshika a keychain he had carved and painted for her from Manali. They sat in a garden, talking quietly, savoring their time together. But soon, Garv's phone started ringing—it was his friends, getting impatient and urging him to return. He turned off his phone, unwilling to let anything ruin their time together. For the next half hour, they stayed together, cherishing every moment, knowing it would be the hardest goodbye.

"Baccha, please be careful on your way back. Share your cab's location with me, and call me as soon as you get home," Garv said softly, his voice filled with concern.

"Of course, Garv," Anshika replied, her heart heavy with the thought of leaving.

"Thank you so much, Anshika. For coming all this way, for us. It means the world to me," Garv said, holding her tightly once more.

Anshika hugged him again, and they held hands. Garv kissed her forehead, then they waited for Anshika's cab to arrive. As she finally left, Garv went back to his friends, but his heart was still with Anshika.

The trip wasn't memorable just for the beautiful places and comfortable hotels—it was unforgettable because it marked Garv's first date with Anshika, the moment his heart had been longing for.

Chapter 13

Failure's Taste

After his return to Surat, Garv and Anshika's bond grew stronger. They began planning for the future, imagining how they would meet when Anshika would get her internship next year. On the other hand, Garv was discussing gift ideas for Anshika with his friends. After much contemplation, he finally decided on a watch but didn't want to risk it being a surprise. So, he showed her the watch beforehand. In their relationship, surprises were never a thing. They were always open with each other, sharing everything—no secrets. It was through this honesty that their trust deepened, but Garv had become vulnerable to Anshika in a way he hadn't been with anyone before. In love, sometimes, you need to just let yourself fall without questioning the depth.

Anshika loved the watch, and her words echoed her affection.

"Baccha, I love you a lot," she texted.

"Thank you for the gift! It will always be my best watch, and I'll always take care of it, no matter how expensive the next one is. I love you, Garv. Come back to me soon," Anshika added.

"Haanji, Jaaneman, and I love you more," Garv replied.

After receiving the watch, their bond only deepened. They began talking more openly about their plans for the future, their goals, and how they would make things work when the time came.

January 24, 2018, was a pivotal day for Garv—his IPCC exam results were due. Both he and Anshika felt the anxiety in their stomachs as the moment approached. Anshika, who had Garv's roll number, checked the result first.

"Baccha, you failed by 4 marks," she said, unable to mask her concern.

Garv's response was calm. "It's okay, I expected this. I messed up with the subject I love. No worries, I'll take care of it in the next attempt," he reassured her. "I'll call you later, I need to talk to my family first."

Despite his words, Anshika was upset, but she didn't push him to talk immediately.

"Don't worry, Baccha. You'll make it next time," Anshika consoled.

Garv spent some time with his childhood friends that night—people he had kept hidden from everyone in his circle. These friends were from powerful, business-oriented families, and they had a different lifestyle. That night, Garv needed an escape, so he ended up drinking whiskey and playing poker. It was a way to forget the weight of his failure. He had never tasted failure before, and he wasn't sure how to cope with it.

While returning home, he got caught by the police. He messaged Anshika and his mom, telling them he would be staying at his friend's place for the night and would talk to them tomorrow. He called his friends, and they took him to the police station to get him out without leaving any records. The situation was handled discreetly, and Garv went home, exhausted.

The next day, Garv started distancing himself from Anshika and his other friends. He was determined to clear the first group of his exams, no matter what it took. He explained to Anshika that he couldn't fail again and needed time to focus.

"Baccha, I can't handle my studies if I'm emotionally disturbed. If you need me, just double-tap on Hike and I'll be there, but please, don't get angry at me. I need to focus," Garv explained.

Anshika understood, though it wasn't easy for her. Garv had to remind her every 10 days that he was still there for her, just needed time for his studies.

Then came April 27, 2018—Anshika's birthday. Garv had exams starting in just six days, but he couldn't ignore her. Despite his exams, he promised her he would be there for her that night.

At 11:30 PM on April 26th, Anshika called, her voice playful, "Hello, Baccha! What are you doing?"

"Nothing much. The whole night is yours now. I'll be with you until you fall asleep," Garv replied, keeping his promise.

They spent hours on video call, laughing, talking, and simply enjoying each other's company. It wasn't just a call—it was time they cherished, making memories. Garv couldn't get enough of Anshika's expressions. The memories were captured in screenshots, and they talked about everything—from small moments to big dreams. When Anshika finally fell asleep, Garv stayed awake, ensuring her birthday was perfect.

The next day, Garv went to the library to study for his exams, but Anshika was still sleeping. Later, when Anshika called him after reaching college, she reminded him of his promise.

"After your exams, no excuses, Baccha! I want you every night at 11 PM on video call, just like we did last night," she said with affection.

"I promise, after the exams, all my time will be yours," Garv assured her.

Throughout his exams, Garv became a night owl. Despite the pressure, Anshika was always there for him, even though she scolded him for not getting enough sleep. His routine was exhausting—only three hours of sleep for seven to eight days in a row—but Anshika's presence kept him going. They had their little rituals—before every exam, she would call to wish him luck, and after each exam, they would discuss his paper.

Garv wasn't sure if he wanted to become a CA, even though he was pursuing it. His family had many CAs, and he found the work monotonous. But he didn't have a choice—he had to finish what he had started.

Finally, the exams were over. Anshika waited eagerly for the results, texting Garv constantly.

And then the day came. Garv had spent most of the day either talking to Anshika or out with his friends. At 9:00 PM, the results were released. Anshika, in the middle of dinner, couldn't call Garv immediately, but she sent him a screenshot of his result—it said "Pass."

The news was a relief, but there was still more to come. Garv's Articleship would begin soon, and his life was about to change. But for that moment, it was pure joy. He shared the result with his mother, forgetting to hide Anshika's name in the message. His mom was happy that Garv had passed, and she was pleased with his dedication.

Later that night, Garv shared the good news with his friends—Anuj, Pankaj, Devik, Shreyansh, and Rajat. They all celebrated, even though they didn't need a big party to mark the occasion. For Garv, it wasn't about the achievement—it was about the journey. And that night, Anshika showered him with love, her tears a mixture of happiness and relief.

The next day, Garv made sure to get chocolates for Anshika, texting Shreya to help him pick the perfect ones. She congratulated him, and the circle of love continued.

But even as they celebrated, Garv knew that the real battle lay ahead. The future was uncertain, and they still had many obstacles to overcome together.

Chapter 14

'Things Started Changing for Both Betterment, We Guess'

Finally, Garv joined his Articleship with the help of his friend Krunal. As he knew, the work was monotonous, and since he had been placed in the audit department, the arrival of audit season meant that he got busier. The audit job was good in some ways—the clients treated you like royalty. But deep down, Garv wasn't satisfied. When he lay down at night, he often wondered what the purpose of it all was. He felt like a cog in the machine, just going through the motions. Still, he didn't care much for the stipend, which was just Rs. 2,500 a month. He would take a leave every week, not bothered by the small salary, wanting only to escape the drudgery of it all.

Three months in, Garv decided to switch departments, landing in Income Tax and Loans. The change was supposed to be a fresh start, but working in a mediocre firm had its limitations. The loan files weren't all that interesting, and the Income Tax work was worse than he had imagined. Learning all the complex clauses felt like a chore, but it did give him some unexpected skills. Garv became a regular at the Income Tax office, where he learned more than he ever anticipated—especially the ways people used to save taxes, often through fraudulent means.

One day, Garv found himself in the midst of a messy situation. He had pulled a stunt for a client to save on taxes, only to get caught in the crossfire at the office. He had to call his dad, who had connections inside the system, to get him out of trouble. Garv's boss stepped in to handle the issue, but the incident left a lasting impression on him. He realized the value of connections in this world—connections with powerful and wealthy people could get you out of any trouble. That day, he understood something crucial: power, money, and relationships could open doors and get you out of sticky situations.

But this wasn't the life Garv wanted. After three months, he left both departments behind, searching for something more fulfilling.

Meanwhile, Garv had started smoking, though not on a daily basis—about three times a week, usually with his colleagues. He hadn't told Anshika about it yet, keeping it a secret from her. But one day, after months of feeling stuck and confused, he decided to share his feelings with her.

"Baccha, it's been three months since I joined the firm, and I feel like I'm wasting my time," he told her. "I'm not enjoying the work at all. I feel useless."

Anshika, as always, was understanding. "It's okay, Garv. Take your time. Give it a little more time, and you might start enjoying your work. Or, if it's not for you, maybe you should think about changing fields. But don't be hard on yourself," she reassured him. "You'll figure it out."

But Garv, being the person he was, held on to a different belief. "I know I'm here because of connections—family and friends helped me get this position. I have to behave and trust the process, even if it's not what I imagined. I can't just quit easily, Baccha. I need to make it work, not just for me but also to preserve the relationships that got me here."

Anshika didn't fully understand his approach, but she respected it. She trusted him to make his own decisions and encouraged him to figure out what truly made him happy.

Garv's ethics were simple: once you've gone through a certain path with the help of others, you owe it to them to give it your best. He knew that if he jumped ship too quickly, it would affect not just his career, but also the trust people had placed in him.

Relationships

As time passed, Garv and Anshika's bond grew even stronger. There were no filters in their conversations anymore—everything flowed naturally. If Garv got frustrated about something, he didn't hold back. He would curse the situation in front of her, but Anshika would just smile, always understanding. Every time this happened, they would hug each other, expressing their affection by kissing their fists. Anshika, being patient and calm, wasn't trying to force Garv to change. Instead, she gently guided him through her words and actions, teaching him patience, calmness, and a better choice of language.

Garv, being a great listener from the start, would sit in front of her during video calls, his eyes locked on hers as she spoke. Anshika, curious about how closely he was paying attention, would sometimes test him. But soon, she realized that not only was he a good listener, but he was also a keen observer. Garv could predict her expressions even when they weren't on video calls. He knew exactly how her eyebrows, lips, and eyes would react to certain things she said. Anshika, amused and impressed, would joke, "Seriously, Baccha, where did you install CCTV on me?"

Garv, being his cheesy self, always knew how to add spice to the conversation. Whenever Anshika mentioned the 'CCTV' comment, he would throw in a flirtatious remark that made her blush. He loved seeing her cheeks turn pink, her cute dimples making her even more adorable in his eyes. Her eyes were like an ocean—deep, beautiful, and captivating. No matter the time of day, whether it was the morning or night, Garv would look at her and feel like she was perfect. That was what love was—finding beauty in every moment.

Amidst all this, an incident occurred that tested their trust. One of Anshika's friends, whom Garv knew had met Anshika's parents and was part of her friend group, confessed his feelings to her at a college event.

Anshika, in the middle of a video call with Garv that night, told him what had happened. She expected Garv to be angry, but instead, he smiled.

"Why are you smiling, Garv?" Anshika asked, confused and frustrated. "Aren't you angry?"

Garv remained calm and smiled at her. "I've been telling you for a while now, Baccha. You dress up so well when you go to college, with your hair all open—something like this was bound to happen." He saw the confusion on her face and, before she could snap at him, he continued, "Look, I can fight a thousand people who want to love you, but I can never fight the one person you choose. So, there's no point in me being jealous, dear. If he misbehaves with you, then it's my problem, and I'll handle it like I always have. But jealousy isn't going to help us in a long-distance relationship. Ours is built on trust and attachment. You trusted me enough to share this with me, and that's all I need. He just confessed his feelings, so there's no harm in that, right?"

Anshika, although satisfied with his words, felt a little irritated. She had wanted him to be jealous, to show that he cared. She replied, "Garv, seeing things so maturely isn't always necessary. What if I decide to stop talking to him from tomorrow? Would that be okay with you?"

Garv, with his calm demeanor, responded, "See, Baccha, we're already in a long-distance relationship. There's no point in creating insecurities for myself. Your time is important to me, and I trust you. There's no need to stop talking to him, as long as you're open with him about how you feel, or about us. Boys always understand; they don't let their egos get in the way. It's simple—just tell him the truth."

Anshika couldn't help but smile at his maturity, even though a part of her still wished for a little jealousy. She thought about it for a moment before saying, "I love you, Garv."

Garv, with a loving grin, replied, "I love you, Kimpu."

As the days went by, Anshika's jealousy started to creep in when she saw photos of Garv with his two close female friends, Muskan and Harshana. These girls were his CA friends, and although Garv had always been upfront about their friendship, Anshika couldn't help but feel a pang of insecurity. One day, after seeing a photo where Garv was sitting between them, she messaged him, saying, "Aap chala lete ho, mae nahi chalaungi," referring to the photo where he looked forced to sit between Muskan and Harshana.

Garv, noticing Anshika's unease, calmly responded, "Baccha, they're just friends. You know about them. One of them is already in a relationship with my other friend. So, chill. I'm not going anywhere." He continued, "You trusted me with this, so just know that I'm not falling in love with anyone else. You can trust me, Baccha. I promise you that."

Anshika, still feeling a little frustrated but reassured by his words, replied, "I love you a lot, cutu piee."

Garv, with his usual warmth, smiled and responded, "I love you, Jaaneman." His words were a reminder of the depth of their love and how they communicated their feelings despite the insecurities that sometimes surfaced.

Later, Anshika expressed another concern, "Garv, aapke paas itna saare dost kaise hain? Main toh apne doston ko rakh nahi pati." She was frustrated because, despite her efforts, she never seemed to be able to maintain friendships, unlike Garv, who had a wide circle of friends.

Garv, with his characteristic patience, replied, "Baccha, friends banane ka ek tareeqa hai. You need to make the first move. Call them if you think they're important. Don't wait for them to reach out first. I do the same with Anuj, Devik, and the others. When they visit Surat, they call me first, and we always keep in touch." He continued, "When it comes to making friends, if someone is an introvert, you should initiate. Do them a small favor—it could be the smallest gesture, but it shows you care. For extroverts, ask them for a favor, so they feel like they owe you something. Once the connection is made, you'll know how to handle it. Loyalty is key. Even if they move away from you, they will remember your loyalty. And if they ask for a favor, always help if you can. That's how friendships work nowadays, Bacchaji."

Anshika, a little irritated, asked, "Why do we have to do favors and ask for them? Can't we just be normal friends?"

Garv smiled and gently explained, "School time was different, Baccha. That was pure, simple friendship. Now, we have to work for friendships. You have to initiate and smooth things out. Once the bond is built, it's about maintaining it. Don't get jealous if your friends are doing well. You'll be struggling sometimes, but jealousy only ruins things. Competition is fine, but make sure it's a healthy one. That's how friendships last."

Anshika then recalled the time when Garv and Anuj had a kabaddi fight, jokingly asking him about it. Garv laughed and said, "Anuj and I both knew that the fight was just for the game. Once it was over, we hugged it out. We've never played against each other again. Either we play on the same team, or one of us plays for both teams. That's our rule."

Anshika smiled, understanding that Garv was a person who would go to great lengths for his friends. She couldn't help but wonder how far he would go for her, his girlfriend.

With a loving smile, she said, "Baccha, kabhi mat badalna. Aap hamesha aise hi rehna. Mujhe aap poori zindagi bhar chahiye mere saath, samajh?"

Garv, his voice filled with affection, replied, "Haanji, Kimpu. I will always be yours."

Their bond was unshakable, built on trust, love, and understanding. And in those moments, they both knew that no matter what challenges life brought, they would always find a way to work through them together.

The evolving journey between Garv and Anshika continued to unfold, showcasing their deep bond, the trust they had painstakingly built over time, and their unwavering support for one another. Though their relationship wasn't without its challenges—fights, misunderstandings, and frustrations—they always found a way to reconcile. Garv, with his calm and understanding nature, became Anshika's constant pillar of support, offering her reassurance whenever she felt the weight of the world on her shoulders.

A particularly difficult phase in their relationship came when Anshika faced a series of setbacks. An accident had prevented her from attending an important interview, causing her to miss out on top opportunities with companies like Microsoft and Samsung. As her friends celebrated their success, getting into prestigious firms like Goldman Sachs, JP Morgan, and Google, Anshika couldn't help but feel inadequate. She was also grappling with the looming reality that her two best friends were moving to Bangalore, and she would have to navigate this next chapter alone in a new city.

During this time of self-doubt, Garv's presence was more important than ever. His words, always filled with warmth and encouragement, reminded her that setbacks were just temporary. He assured her that distance would never break their friendship, and though she hadn't made it to her dream companies this time, the opportunity would come again. He was certain of it. "You can crack it next year, Anshika," he had said with the conviction only someone who truly believed in her could convey.

Despite her struggles, Anshika finally secured an internship with Amex. Though she wasn't entirely satisfied, Garv, along with her parents, continued to lift her spirits. "You're surrounded by people who believe in you," Garv reminded her. "Your cousins and friends are there. And trust me, when the time is right, your dream company will come knocking."

After everything settled, Anshika smiled through her tears and thanked Garv. In return, he sent her chocolates—via Sheru, of course—a small gesture that meant the world to her.

Chapter 15

Challenges are there, but apologies and compromises work through everything

The time had come for Garv to give his Group 2 exams. However, he had already told Anshika that he didn't expect to pass this time, confessing that he hadn't taken the exam seriously. He was particularly concerned about his last core theory paper, knowing how much he struggled with theory. When the results arrived in mid-January, Anshika checked his score—130. He needed 150 to pass. Despite the setback, Garv reassured her that he would clear the exams in his next attempt, a promise he made with quiet confidence.

Meanwhile, Anshika was preparing for her internship at Amex. As she left for Gurgaon, Garv decided to take a four-day leave from his Articleship to visit her. It wasn't easy to get permission, but Garv had always been good at convincing his family. His mother, who was unaware of the true reason for his trip, believed him when he said he was going to a book fair in Delhi. Garv had always been fond of books—thanks to his friend Anuj—so his mother bought the story without question. His father, however, was more perceptive. He sensed something was off but allowed Garv to go, understanding that a short break could be beneficial for him.

Garv's relationship with his father was delicate. While he had never been afraid of anyone, he couldn't bear to see his father upset. His father's stern demeanor often put Garv on edge, but it was his mother who would always bear the brunt of their arguments. Garv hated seeing his mother cry, especially when she had done nothing wrong. It was this that made him cautious, always avoiding conflicts with his father.

But now, as the days to be with Anshika grew nearer, Garv found himself counting down the moments. Despite the careful lies and the underlying tension, he was ready for the reunion. His mind was set on spending those precious days with Anshika, cherishing the time they would finally have together after months of waiting.

First Kiss

Garv had saved enough from his stipend and pocket money, his habit of investing in the stock market and mutual fund SIPs paying off. Thanks to his economics teacher in 11th and 12th grade, and the support from his family, Garv had learned the value of saving early. The rest, however, he borrowed from his mother. He and Anshika were both eagerly waiting for their next meeting. But, like many moments in their relationship, this one came with its own awkwardness—not because the topic was about intimacy, but because they had been planning this trip for so long that everything felt a bit too big to handle. Yet, one thing was certain: Anshika always knew how to make Garv feel comfortable enough to open up, to speak about things he was too shy or nervous to discuss.

Anshika teased Garv, laughing as she said, "Baccha, I've told you I like you, I've told you I love you, and I've done so many things first—so now, I expect the first kiss from you!"

Garv smiled awkwardly and replied, "I'll try."

Anshika, with a mischievous grin, warned, "Don't come if you're not ready. I swear, I'll end you if you don't meet my expectations!"

Their kiss, planned in the privacy of a closed room, seemed simple enough. After all, they wouldn't be disturbing anyone. But, as always, life had its own way of turning plans upside down.

With just two days left before Garv's trip to Delhi, the hotel and flight were both booked. Flights were cheaper and saved time, so it made sense. Garv called his friends Muskan and Harshana for an urgent meeting, explaining that he was about to meet Anshika again. The teasing started the moment they arrived.

"Kya hogaya, bhai? Why call us so urgently?" asked Harshana and Muskan.

Garv shared his excitement, and they quickly began teasing him. "Well, I'm going to meet Anshika again. But I'm not sure what to get her. You two need to help me pick something out."

They decided to head to VR Mall, where Muskan and Harshana suggested gifts like makeup and handbags, but Garv was at a loss. Shopping on his own wasn't something he was used to. He usually went with his mom, so he turned to them for help.

"I honestly don't know. I've only met her once before," he admitted. "Maybe we should just go for clothes."

They agreed, and off they went to Zara. Garv found himself surrounded by countless outfits, unsure of what would suit Anshika. Muskan, as usual, was the one trying everything on to figure out what would fit Anshika, while Harshana, too thin to try things on, offered her opinion from the sidelines.

After an hour of trial and error, they finally settled on one dress. Garv purchased it and treated his friends to a meal for helping him out. He left the dress at Muskan's house, planning to pick it up before heading to the airport.

Garv was bubbling with excitement as his flight neared. His flight was scheduled for 8:00 PM. Pankaj picked him up from home, and they swung by Muskan's to grab the dress before heading to the airport. After arriving, Garv called Anshika, and they spent the next few hours talking, excitedly counting down the time until they could meet.

It was 11:30 PM by the time Garv reached Delhi. He told his mom he would be picked up from Kashmiri Gate Metro Station around 6:00 AM the next day since the metro closed at 11:00 PM. What he didn't mention was that he and Anshika had decided to meet up that very night. By 4:00 AM, they had agreed to meet, after teasing Garv for the past few days about how he should come and meet her.

Despite his initial hesitation—since Anshika lived in a Girls' PG and it was already late—Garv found himself unable to resist. He told Anshika he would make his way to her PG by 4:00 AM. Anshika went to sleep, setting her alarm for 4:00 AM, while Garv struggled to pass the time at the airport.

He bought a chicken sandwich, sat down, and tried to distract himself by talking to an employee at one of the stores who was playing PUBG. They played together for a while, but when the employee had to leave for work, Garv was once again left with the ticking clock, the anticipation almost unbearable.

He called Anshika, but there was no answer. For 30 minutes, he called her over and over, but it seemed like she had put her phone on silent. Frustrated, Garv finally gave up, thinking Anshika had fallen deeply asleep. He decided to take a bus to Aero Metro Station and get some rest before meeting her in the morning.

But just as the bus ride was nearing its end, Garv's phone buzzed. It was Anshika calling. He urgently told the bus driver to stop, but the driver insisted there was no public transport in the area. Garv didn't care. He needed to get to Anshika, no matter what.

"Why did you call me so many times?" Anshika teased him when he answered the phone.

Garv never tolerated being made to wait or having his calls ignored. His patience was thin, and he was furious when Anshika didn't pick up. He let her know just how angry he was, telling her that he was coming over but wouldn't speak a word to her.

Anshika, ever unbothered by his moods, simply smiled and replied, "No worries, just come over, and then get angry as much as you want."

Garv tried every possible option to get to her quickly—sedans, luxury cars—but all of them had a waiting time of over 25 minutes. His frustration grew, and just as he was about to lose hope, a cab driver drove past. He stopped and asked Garv where he was headed. When Garv mentioned Gurgaon, the driver directed him to walk 500 meters to the other side of the circle. Without hesitation, Garv offered the driver extra money to take him directly to his destination. Surprisingly, the driver agreed for even less than the price of an Uber.

Garv, who preferred sitting in the front, took his place beside the driver. He didn't like traveling alone in silence; the quiet was boring. As they drove, he started talking to the driver about Delhi, asking where he was from and making small talk.

Finally, Anshika called. "How much longer, Baccha?" she asked.

Garv told the driver to speed up, and after what felt like an eternity, he reached the gate of Anshika's PG. He thanked the driver and called Anshika again. From the gate, he could see Anshika's room lights on and two figures standing at the window. Anshika picked up. "Aap aagaye?" she asked.

Garv waved his hand in confirmation. Yet, despite the fact that he was right there, it still took her five more minutes to come down. During those minutes, Garv couldn't stop thinking about how to approach her. He was also aware that her cousin was awake, and he had never met her, which made him even more nervous.

But when Anshika finally emerged from the door, Garv's heart calmed down. His anxiety melted the moment he saw her. She rushed to him, pulling him into a warm hug in the chilly air. They were both bundled up in jackets, but they could still feel each other's heartbeat.

After the hug, Anshika took care of Garv's suitcase, and they smiled at each other, standing on a quiet road surrounded by trees. For the next ten minutes, there was nothing but the silence of the night around them. It felt peaceful, comforting, yet a little awkward. Then Anshika broke the silence.

"Aapko samajh kyon nahi aata? Mujhe bhi sona hota hai, Baccha. Aap jaldi gussa ho jate ho, ab nikal lo gussa," she said teasingly.

Garv just smiled at her and said, "Sorry." He could smell her hair, her clothes—her scent that never seemed to change. He still couldn't believe that they were together again.

They continued walking, hand in hand, and after a while, they stopped in front of her PG. Anshika, who had been silently wishing for a kiss, was growing more impatient. She had been giving him subtle hints, but Garv seemed oblivious, still lost in the moment. She was almost ready to break, but Garv, oblivious as ever, looked around to make sure no one was watching. Anshika, disappointed that he had broken the moment, couldn't help but sigh.

But the next second, Garv pulled her toward him, looked deep into her eyes, and silently asked for permission to kiss her. Anshika blinked deeply, a silent yes. Without another word, Garv kissed her—softly at first, then with growing intensity. It was their first kiss, passionate enough that they had to pull away to catch their breath.

Garv held her tightly, his hands supporting her back, but after a while, he pulled away slightly, cupping her face in his hands. It was the best kiss of their lives.

They embraced again, tightly, before Garv kissed her forehead. Neither of them noticed the time slipping away. When Garv realized it was already 5:15 AM, he knew he had to leave soon. But he couldn't bring himself to part from her just yet. He made the decision to stay a little longer, thinking he would tell his mom that he had slept at the airport.

The two of them walked for another hour. At 6:00 AM, Garv's phone rang—his mom. He told her he would leave in 15 minutes. Anshika comforted him, saying, "Don't be sad, Baccha. We'll meet again tomorrow. We have almost two and a half days together. Just relax and come when you can."

Knowing Garv wasn't familiar with the metro system, Anshika took him to Sikandarpur metro station, making sure he had a token and knew where to go. Garv waved goodbye with a smile, assuring her he would be okay.

Delhi had always held a special place in Garv's heart. It was a city filled with memories of his childhood summers spent at his Mama's house. His Mama had always showered him with love, taking him out for ice cream and buying him toys. That's why, whenever he visited Delhi, he felt at home.

During this trip, his Mama took two days off work, and they went shopping together. Garv was excited, but the only thing on his mind was the next day, when he would be able to see Anshika again.

Though Garv longed to talk to Anshika, she was busy with work. She hadn't eaten because of her meeting, and Garv, worried, texted her to take care of herself. Anshika reassured him, saying she was fine. Later that night, they both fell asleep together.

The next morning, Garv woke up late, as he had stayed up until 4:00 AM. When he saw Anshika's text, he knew he had to plan carefully to meet her later. He told his Mama that he would leave at 3:00 PM, but his Mama, knowing Garv didn't fully understand the metro system, insisted on coming with him to drop him off. Garv couldn't refuse, so he texted Anshika, and they made arrangements for her friend to pick him up at the metro station.

When Garv arrived at Gurgaon metro station, he was early by 15 minutes. He texted Anshika's friend, who informed him that it would take at least 30 more minutes. Garv, a little frustrated, assured his Mama that everything would be fine. Eventually, Anshika's friend arrived, and after chatting for a while, they both waited together until Anshika finally arrived. The moment they exchanged smiles, everything felt right.

As per their plan, Garv and Anshika's friend took photos together so Garv could post them on his status to reassure his family that he was with friends. But the truth was, Garv didn't need those pictures. Being with Anshika was all that mattered.

After the photo session and a bit of chit-chat with Anshika's friend, Garv subtly signaled to Anshika that it was time to leave. She understood and managed to make an exit as they hailed an auto-rickshaw to her PG. Garv, feeling awkward, couldn't bring himself to look directly into her eyes, so instead, he kept glancing at her through the rearview mirror. He held her hand, trying to avoid the discomfort of eye contact.

They arrived at her PG, and Garv decided to remain outside, as it was a girls' PG, and it would have been too awkward for him to go in. As Anshika packed, Garv called his friend Pankaj.

"Yeah, bro, got some time to call," said Pankaj.

"I just met her, and now we're heading out together," Garv replied.

"Bro, no messing around, don't get caught, understand?" warned Pankaj.

"Relax, if something happens, Tushar's in Noida. I've got some cash, too, so we're fine. We'll handle it," Garv reassured him.

It was Garv's first time being in such a situation, hearing about police raids on hotels and the random checks they did, sometimes forcing unmarried couples to call their families. However, Garv had already talked to his brother, a lawyer, and some friends who had contacts in the police. He made sure he could handle any issues that might arise.

Finally, Anshika emerged with her suitcase. Garv flashed a big smile, teasing her, "I'm on a five-day trip, and my bag is smaller than yours, Anshika."

She rolled her eyes at him but then smirked, "You have no idea how much makeup I carry."

Garv was a rookie in the world of makeup. Lipstick was the only item he was familiar with, but over time, he would learn more from Anshika.

They arrived at their hotel on Bougainville Marg and were given a room on the top floor. Both were nervous during the check-in, eager to skip that awkward part. Once they were in their room, they relaxed on the bed, holding each other's hands, a sense of relief washing over them. The romantic journey they had both been waiting for was finally beginning. Though they were both rookies, the thought of learning together made it exciting.

Chapter 16

Love is in the Air

At last, Garv and Anshika locked eyes, and without a word, they got up from the bed and embraced each other tightly. Anshika, emotional, knew they had both longed for this moment, craving each other's touch for so long. Garv held Anshika close, feeling like she was his little darling—small, cute, and his. They hugged for what felt like an eternity, and then kissed each other, over and over.

But then, Anshika pulled away, a mischievous glint in her eyes. She playfully snapped at Garv's shoulder.

"What's wrong?" Garv asked, puzzled.

Anshika smirked and said, "You ate non-veg this morning when we kissed, didn't you?"

Garv immediately apologized and hugged her again, promising to be more careful next time. The atmosphere between them was getting heated in the cold weather of Gurgaon, but they suddenly realized they had forgotten something essential—protection.

Anshika, teasing him, sent Garv on a mission to buy condoms, reminding him that she had told him to bring them from Surat. Garv hesitated but went out anyway, feeling both awkward and nervous about buying them.

First-Time Condom Purchase

It was an excruciating task for Garv to find the right pack. He didn't know which brand to pick, and the thought of asking the chemist in front of so many people was mortifying. After visiting five or six chemist shops and spending nearly 45 minutes, he finally purchased two packs—10 condoms in each. He didn't know how many they would need but wanted to be prepared.

When he returned to the hotel, Anshika was waiting for him, looking absolutely stunning in a one-piece outfit. She noticed that Garv had worked up a sweat and immediately sent him to take a shower, something he hated but couldn't avoid.

Once he returned, they hugged again, danced in the dim light, and kissed passionately. They weren't sure what they were doing, but they were going with the flow, enjoying the warmth of each other's presence. Eventually, things got a little tricky when they struggled to figure out how to use the condom properly. They wasted a couple of them, but eventually managed to get it right.

However, Garv, overwhelmed with emotions and distracted by Anshika's touch, struggled to control his excitement, leading to an awkward moment. Anshika, sensing his discomfort, hugged him tightly and kissed his forehead.

"Baccha, why do you always get awkward over little things? If I'm with you, I trust you completely. This is new for both of us, so we'll figure it out together. Don't feel embarrassed. I'll never judge you," Anshika reassured him.

"I love you, baccha," Garv replied.

They hugged, sweaty but content. After some time, they decided to take a bath together and get ready for their first drinks date.

Anshika, getting ready, caught Garv staring at her. She teased him, "If you want to kiss me, come here, because once I finish my makeup, I won't let you."

Garv grinned, teasing her back. "We'll see about that," he said, watching her carefully as she applied her makeup, which was like a mystery to him.

She made him sit on the bed and helped him apply moisturizer and serum to his hair, handing him a comb. When Garv went to spray his usual strong perfume, Anshika stopped him, explaining that her nose was sensitive to strong scents. Garv, knowing she had trouble with his usual cologne, applied her milder vanilla mist instead, which she appreciated.

Once Anshika was ready, she asked Garv how she looked, and he gave her a romantic smile. Anshika, knowing he couldn't resist, smiled back and said, "Let's go, before my makeup smudges."

Garv, still captivated by her beauty, held her, kissed her forehead, and then picked her up in his arms. At first, Anshika felt a little insecure because she had gained some weight while preparing for interviews. But as Garv held her effortlessly, she relaxed, and they kissed, the moment more intimate than ever before.

Anshika smiled as she recalled the moment when Garv had lifted her up. "When you picked me up like that, I honestly thought we weren't going to the party tonight," she said, teasing him.

Garv chuckled softly, his eyes glinting with amusement. "Why? What made you think that?"

Anshika hesitated for a moment before responding, a playful edge to her voice. "I thought you might drop me or, worse, make me fall. You know, I'm a bit heavy."

Garv smiled, his tone filled with confidence. "You have no idea. I may not be in perfect shape, but my arms and legs are strong enough. I've got you."

Anshika grinned mischievously. "Let's see tonight then. If we don't make it to the table, I'm blaming you!"

The cab ride was a mix of quiet comfort, their hands gently clasped together, eyes occasionally meeting, as they eagerly awaited their destination—Cyber Hub. As they drove through the streets, Garv found himself captivated by the view, a sprawling urban landscape that felt like a different world. It was unlike anything he had seen in India, and for a moment, it felt like something out of a dream.

They arrived at their destination, and Garv was instantly smitten with the vibe of Gurgaon. It was nothing like the busy streets of Mumbai's BKC; this was something entirely different, a world of its own. He knew he was in love with this place at first sight.

Together, they roamed through the Cyber Hub, popping into shops like Miniso and Uniqlo. Anshika, ever the shopper, found her favorite winter clothes store, but Garv wasn't quite as impressed. He couldn't understand the allure of winter wear—boring colors, limited options. He wasn't interested.

Anshika, however, picked out a few things for herself and her mother. They then made their way to a bakery, where Anshika couldn't resist ordering a cheesecake. "I've been here with my manager before," she remarked, and Garv smiled at how comfortable she seemed, no matter the situation.

After the bakery, they headed to Social, a lively place with music and energy that pulled them in immediately. Anshika, ever the spontaneous one, asked Garv to sit next to her. But Garv, preferring to face her so he could look into her eyes, hesitated. Seeing her disappointment, he gave in and sat beside her.

They ordered garlic bread and spaghetti, along with a tower of LIIT. Garv, who had never been much of a drinker, took a sip and was surprised by how much he liked it. Anshika, tipsy and playful, teased him about her drink being served less than his, and Garv quickly made sure to pour her more.

They shared a moment of laughter, holding hands as they relaxed into the cozy atmosphere. The time seemed to fly by, and before they knew it, two hours had passed. Garv noticed that Anshika, now clearly tipsy, was even more adorable than usual. He, however, was completely in control, handling his drinks like a pro.

As the evening wore on, Anshika leaned in close, her words soft and teasing, "I could kiss you right here."

Garv smiled, avoiding her gaze. "Let's go. The room's waiting for us."

Anshika pouted, not ready to leave just yet. "No one here knows us. We could stay a little longer."

Garv chuckled, his voice filled with playful caution. "Baccha, I'd rather not risk it. You know how it would look if anyone saw us together."

Anshika pinched his side, and they both laughed, leaving the place behind.

It was a long walk to the cab stand from Social, and Anshika, now quite drunk, needed support. Garv walked behind her, his hand gently on her shoulder, making sure she didn't trip. She rested her head on his chest, the warmth of her touch comforting him. It was moments like these that made him feel at peace, knowing she felt safe with him.

"Hold me tighter," she murmured, her voice full of vulnerability.

Garv leaned down to whisper in her ear, "Don't worry, I've got you. You won't fall, I won't let you."

Finally, they reached the cab, and Garv helped her inside. As they made their way back to the hotel, Anshika, still drunk, hugged him tightly, telling him she would slap him if he ever tried to leave her. Garv promised, "No matter what, baccha, I'm always here for you."

That night, as they cuddled under the blankets, the two of them, so different in many ways, found a perfect balance. Garv preferred the coolness of the air, while Anshika liked it cozy. But they both agreed to share the blanket, Anshika making sure to warn him not to throw it off.

Garv smiled and settled in beside her, knowing this was a night he would never forget.

The next morning, as the first rays of sunlight filled the room, Anshika woke up early. She couldn't resist watching Garv sleep, his face peaceful and calm. She smiled, enjoying the quiet before she gently woke him up, kissing his lips before pulling him back into her arms.

Garv, still half-asleep, kissed her back, his lips lingering on hers for a moment before he pulled away. "You're too cute," he whispered, settling back into the warmth of her embrace.

Anshika's parents called around 10:30 AM, and Garv, resting his head in her lap, listened to their conversation. He felt a deep sense of contentment, a feeling of being loved and cared for, something he had never experienced before. As they talked, Anshika gently played with his hair, and Garv couldn't help but smile, savoring the simple moments that meant everything to him.

They ordered breakfast and spent the rest of the morning making the bed, laughing, and just being with each other. Garv knew this was what it was all about—small moments of happiness, together.

They kissed each other, and soon their breakfast arrived. Anshika had ordered Dosa for herself and Parathas for Garv. But, of course, Anshika could never end her brunch without something sweet. After finishing their breakfast, they lay down on the bed, cuddling, talking about old times. Their 5th anniversary was coming up in two months, but Garv knew he wouldn't be able to make it. He was about to switch firms and wouldn't be able to take leave. Still, he assured her that after his exams in May, he would visit her again before her internship was over. Anshika became emotional, knowing that tomorrow they would have to part ways again, and she didn't know when they would see each other next. Garv hugged her tightly, comforting her. "We will make it, baccha, no matter how difficult it gets. We'll make it through together," he said. They kissed again and wrapped themselves in the blanket. It turned into one incredibly romantic afternoon. They didn't even realize when they fell asleep, and when they woke up, it was already 5:30 in the evening.

Anshika teased Garv as she wore his shirt, but he wasn't in the mood for jokes. He wanted to go shopping with her since the dress he bought for her was too big. Anshika got upset as she wanted to hug him tightly, but Garv, sensing her disappointment, picked her up in his arms, kissed her lips, and said, "The whole night is ours, but if we don't go shopping, I might feel bad. Let me break the myth that boys don't love shopping."

Anshika got ready, and they went shopping, joined by Anshika's cousin. When they arrived at Ambience Mall, Garv was impressed by what Gurgaon had to offer. The mall was huge. They spent time window-shopping and talking with Anshika's cousin about their day, how they felt, and what they were up to. Then they went to Zara, where the sale season brought a large crowd. Garv's task was to pick dresses for Anshika, while she and her cousin tried on outfits in the changing room. Zara was chaotic during sales, and they finally finished shopping, heading to the food court. Garv avoided holding Anshika's hand because of her cousin, as sometimes it felt awkward. They dropped her cousin at the PG and returned to the hotel. Anshika tried on the peach-colored sweater they had picked for her, and they grabbed Old Monk on their way back. That night, it was party time. Anshika ordered Nachos, and they started dancing to her favorite song, "Tum Hi Ho" from Anshikaqui 2. As they drank, Anshika felt physically drained, so Garv suggested she lie down on the bed, and he gave her a back massage. The night became even more romantic when Anshika handed him her moisturizer, and he continued the massage. His touch relaxed her body in a way she hadn't felt before. She hugged him tightly, and the night flew by. They didn't realize how time passed until it was already 4:00 AM.

Finally, they fell asleep, still holding each other, feeling as if they would never be apart, no matter what life threw at them. When they woke up at 10:00 AM to the sound of the alarm, Garv didn't want to leave the bed. He knew he would be cuddling his pillow again soon, so he hugged Anshika tightly, smiling at the love marks he'd left on her while they slept. Anshika smiled and kissed him. They stayed in bed for a few more hours, but soon it was getting late. Garv had a flight to catch back to Surat. Anshika packed his bag for him, knowing he wasn't great at organizing it. She hugged him tightly, tears rolling down her beautiful cheeks, asking him to promise he would never leave her. Garv kissed her forehead and reassured her. Anshika knew how much he loved her, how he respected her, and how he always asked for her permission before touching her. She was falling deeper in love with him with each passing day, and he knew she trusted him with her heart and self-respect. She cared for him like a mother, and each meeting made their bond stronger.

Anshika took out the chocolates that Garv's mom had made, and they shared them, kissing each other afterward. They left the hotel, and Garv dropped Anshika off at her PG before heading to the airport. As he sat in the cab, tears welled up in his eyes. He called Anshika and told her how badly he would miss her and how he would come back soon to meet her. "I love you so much, Bacchaji," he said.

"Baccha, hum milenge jaldi, vapas. Thank you for coming to meet me," Anshika replied.

Garv finally boarded the flight and fell asleep. When he landed in Surat, he realized how much he missed Anshika, but sometimes flights were just a blur—one minute, he was in her arms, and the next, he was back in Surat. Pankaj was waiting for him at the airport, and they went to a pan shop. Garv lit a cigarette, lost in the memories of their trip together. Pankaj teased him, saying, "Throw that cigarette away, or I'll take a photo and send it to Anshika." Garv threw it down immediately. He had never been afraid of anything, but Anshika's sweet anger was something else entirely.

Meanwhile, Anshika was exhausted and went to sleep. She messaged Garv on hike, sending him AGD and loads of hearts. Garv told Pankaj that he would be joining Kumbhat since he wasn't enjoying the work at his current firm. Both of them knew how difficult it was to get an articleship, but they kept trying.

Garv and Pankaj tried hard to get him into Kumbhat, but they weren't having much luck. Since Garv had only cleared one group, the firm wasn't interested at the time. So, Garv reached out to his brother, who was connected in the builder lobby. His brother spoke to the director of the firm, and after a couple of days, Garv was called for an interview. The director, who didn't really want to hire anyone, asked Garv a few questions. One of them was about Negative Beta. Since Garv had an interest in the stock market, he was able to answer, and the director hired him. As he left the firm, he bumped into an old friend from his CA batch, who was working part-time there. She warned him that he would be getting a tough team, but Garv didn't care. He was just happy to have made it into the firm and was confident he could handle whatever came his way.

On the other hand, Anshika was struggling with office politics, and Garv had already warned her to be careful with her manager. He had always told her that sometimes when girls are nice to everyone, people can take it the wrong way. But Garv chose not to push it further, knowing that if he did, she might feel like he was being controlling. Instead, Garv did his best to help her navigate through the office politics since she was struggling to handle herself. It often irritated her, sometimes more than her period days.

Whenever Anshika felt low, Garv would send her shakes and a cake jar because, he knew, sweets had the power to change her mood in seconds. Meanwhile, Garv's articleship at Kumbhat was moving along, and though he had good colleagues, his boss was a pain.

Then, March 7th, 2019, arrived—their 5th Anniversary. That night was the best night of all. Garv had already ordered a cake for her, with "5th Anniversary" written on it. They celebrated on a video call, tears of happiness rolling down their cheeks. Anshika cut the cake on camera and kissed Garv through the screen. Afterward, she excused herself for about 20 minutes to share the cake with her friend and cousin in the PG. When she returned, she said:

"Baccha, please never go anywhere, I need you, always, understood?"
"I'm not going anywhere, do you think I want to?" Garv replied, a little sarcastically.
"When you get angry sometimes, I get scared that we might fight, but I trust that we will never leave each other."

"We'll work it out," Garv spoke, with a hint of humor.

"Last time, you did something, and I'll never forgive you for that. I trust you now, but if it happens again…"

"I promise, it won't," Garv assured her.

"Sorry, but now, come over here quietly." She added.

A few days earlier, Anshika's period had almost skipped. Garv had started to remember her cycle because he knew exactly when she'd need chocolates and comfort. For the past few months, he'd learned how to manage her moods during those days—calmly and lovingly. When Anshika mentioned that her period was late, Garv immediately told her to get the medical kit ready, although Anshika hesitated. She feared that if something went wrong, her family might find out and cause a scene.

Anshika started crying, telling Garv that she was thinking of ending everything. Garv snapped at her, "Don't say that. I'll call your mom if you keep talking like this. We've celebrated together, and I will be there if anything happens. Don't worry, I'm here for you."

She realized, at that moment, that he was standing by her, no matter what. So, she kissed him good night and said, "AGD."

The next day, Garv messaged her to check if her period had arrived. When Anshika snapped back, asking him to leave her alone, he didn't mind. After a while, she tested with several kits, and all of them came out negative, which relieved her. Soon after, her period started, and she sent Garv a dance emoji with a red lady. Garv, still at the office, didn't quite understand what was happening, so he called her.

"What happened? What's this emoji?" Garv asked.

"We are safe now. Periods arrived." Anshika laughed in relief.

Garv, of course, ordered an almond rose milkshake for her, knowing how tough the first day of her period could be. He reminded her to rest and use a hot pillow for comfort because he knew that would help her feel better. He stayed up that night, peacefully sleeping on video call with her.

Later, during their Anniversary night:

"I'm sorry, baccha. I won't do it again, I promise," she said. "We've been through so much in these five years—so many fights, our first date, our first kiss. You know we're total opposites, but I promise, on every good and bad day, I will always need your time. Just remember, you give me your time, and I'll give you 90% when you're at 10%. But if that 10% ever turns into zero, I will lose, and I don't want to lose you."
"I'll always be here for you, Garv. You know, you're the most important part of my life. I've never been this close with anyone else, and no one else has ever understood me like you do. You know how I'll react, how my smile looks, everything. I love you, and I promise, I'll always be there for you."
"I love you, Jaaneman. I don't know how to prove my love, but if you ever doubt it, just call me, and I'll be there right away. Just remember, we'll never lie to each other, because trust is what keeps us connected. And there are more gifts waiting for you tomorrow."
"Gifts? Seriously? You don't need gifts, you know that."
"I want your time. That's all I ask for. If you want a gift, I'll buy something you like when the time comes."
"I love you so much, Garv. Thank you for making me feel so special every single time. Today, I give you the 'Love You More' title."
"Seriously? You're giving me the title?" Garv pretended to be sad.
"Don't get too happy, it's only for today!" Anshika laughed, and Garv tried to look sad. She laughed at him, sending him tons of flying kisses before they finally went to sleep on video call.

As the days passed, Garv and Anshika grew closer. Garv set a routine to check on Anshika every day—waking her up in the morning, calling her after ten minutes to make sure she was up, and calling again to ensure she had breakfast. Anshika, being lazy about eating, often skipped it, so Garv made sure to remind her. Throughout the day, they checked in with each other to make sure everything was fine, especially with their work pressures. Garv would ask Anshika how her day went and if her mental peace was intact. If something bothered her, Garv would find a way to cheer her up, all while balancing his own exams and work schedule.

Not every day was perfect, though. Garv knew everything about Anshika's office because they were gossip buddies. And while Anshika was struggling with office politics, Garv—who actually enjoyed playing the political game—decided to teach her a few tricks to help her avoid getting caught in the crossfire.

He shared some key tactics with her:

"Fake it till you make it," he told her. "Never let anyone see you struggling unless you trust someone completely. People don't care about your weaknesses, so always act confident—even if you're not feeling it. Don't ever share your problems instantly. Keep your anger and vulnerabilities in check, but don't let anyone see you falter."

Another piece of advice was: "Your work should speak for itself. People need to know what you're doing, even if they don't ask. You're so good at what you do, but you struggle with managing people. So make sure they see your efforts, so they recognize your worth."

He also told her: "Stop getting irritated by every little thing. There will always be someone jealous if you're doing well, but that's okay. Just don't snap at everyone—unless they cross the line, then let them know where they stand."

Garv also taught her how to break the hierarchy when things weren't going her way. "If your boss isn't being helpful, sometimes you have to break the chain and respond in the sweetest way possible. Make him feel a little embarrassed while still making him realize he was wrong."

But Garv had sensed something was off with her Project Manager. Although he was married, he seemed to be getting too close to Anshika over the past three months. Garv understood that being overly nice to everyone could sometimes be misinterpreted, and warned her: "You need to be careful. People might not always have good intentions. It's better to rethink how you're handling your relationships in the office."

However, Anshika brushed it off, thinking Garv was just being jealous. After all, her manager was married, and to her, Garv's concerns seemed like mere imagination.

Now, let's get back to the story:

The morning of March 7th arrived. Garv, knowing the day wouldn't be easy, went to the temple to pray for their strength. He was determined to fight through whatever came their way. Afterward, he called Anshika—it was 8:30 AM, and Garv was her human alarm clock, always calling her to wake up.

"Good morning, Jaaneman," she greeted him cheerfully.

"Good morning, Bacchaji," he replied with a smile in his voice.

"Yaar, come here already. I just want a hug, and then we can sleep the whole day. I don't feel like waking up today," she said, her voice drowsy.

"Bacchaji, get up. Don't be stubborn. I'll come back soon, I promise. As soon as my exams are done, I'll come to you," Garv reassured her.

"I love you. Please, just let me sleep for a little while longer," she pleaded.

"Okay, half an hour, then I'll call you back, alright? And happiest 5th anniversary to us," Garv teased.

"Happiest 5th to us, Garv. I love you so much. Now let me sleep, and you wake me up when it's time," she replied, drifting back to sleep.

Garv got ready for his office, but before leaving, he called her again.

"Baccha, please wake up. Either decide that you're not going to office today, or let me know so I can let you sleep," he said.

"Don't mess with me. I have to go to office. I'm up. I love you, okay?" she said, half awake.

"Okay, Jaaneman. Let's do this. I'll talk to you soon."

Garv and Anshika stayed on video call as Anshika started getting ready. She insisted that Garv stay on the call while she finished getting dressed. Garv, unable to refuse her, messaged his boss about being late due to a vehicle breakdown.

As Anshika got ready, they chatted, smiled at each other, and laughed. She eventually finished getting dressed.

"How do I look today, Baccha?" she asked, twirling.

"Don't ask me that question, alright? You always look good," Garv answered, teasing her.

"Yaar, come on!"

"Baccha, what do you expect? You wake up with messy hair, and then send me pictures of yourself every morning. You look amazing—except when you overdo the makeup."

"You're crazy, I love you, Garv."

"Haanji, Jaaneman. I love you too, Bacchaji. Now go to the office peacefully and come back soon. The gifts will be on their way."

"Please tell me what you're sending me. What is this? I'm your Baccha after all," she said, her voice curious.

"Let it be a surprise. You'll find out soon enough," Garv replied, secretly still unsure of what to gift her.

"Alright, I'll wait for it. Love you."

"Love you too, Bacchaji. Have a great day, and if you remember, call me. I'll pick up."

"Love you, Bacchaji. Bye for now."

That day, as Garv walked into the office, his boss snapped at him. But he didn't let it bother him. He wasn't about to let anything ruin his mood today. Today was special. He had more important things on his mind.

He was struggling with what to get Anshika. His usual go-to colleagues, the guys, were terrible at giving gift advice, so he turned to his office friends for help. But to explain what he needed, he had to share the whole story—who Anshika was, show them her picture—and before he knew it, the three girls were grinning, teasing him.

"Sahi hai bhai, tune bataya hi nahi humko!" one of them laughed. "Essae behen bolta hai!"

Garv couldn't help but blush. He wasn't used to having three girls dissecting his love life, but he had no choice. Finally, after some more laughter and chatter, they settled on the perfect gifts: a bouquet of Ferrero Rocher from Ferns and Petals and a box of donuts, because Anshika loved sweets.

Garv quickly placed the order and made sure to ask the florist to add a personal note. He typed out some romantic and heartfelt lines for her, feeling the excitement building. Now, all he had to do was wait for Anshika to finish work, and then she'd receive her surprise.

At 5:00 PM, Anshika called him, telling him she was on her way home. Garv immediately called the delivery person, ensuring that the gifts would be delivered by 6:00 PM. With that taken care of, he headed to his quiet spot, the place he always went when he needed to clear his mind.

A little later, he called Anshika and asked her to come outside her PG. Anshika, thinking Garv was there to meet her, eagerly agreed. But Garv, ever the smooth talker, explained, "Baccha, abhi office se leave nahi le sakta, varna main abhi aata. Par tera gift aa gaya hai. Be on video call while you get it."

Anshika stepped outside, her heart racing. When the gifts arrived, her face lit up with surprise and happiness. She rushed back to her room, excited to open them. But there was a small mishap—the florist had forgotten to remove the price tag from the bouquet.

"Yeh kitna expensive tha!" she laughed, holding up the tag for him to see. Despite the mix-up, Garv could see the joy in her eyes. She kissed the screen, thanking him. "I love you so much, Garv. This is so thoughtful."

Garv's heart swelled as he smiled. "I love you too, Jaaneman. I thought flowers were a romantic gesture, but I get it. I'll take care next time."

Anshika teased him, "Theek hai, toh phir daant khana, mujhse."

He chuckled. "Koi na, aapka chehra dekhkar daant khane mein koi dikkat nahi hai, Jaaneman."

Anshika's face softened, but she was still a bit irritated. She knew that whenever she scolded him, Garv just stared at her with that smile, making it impossible for her to stay mad. She sighed and hugged herself through the video call, missing him more than words could say. "Come back soon, Garv. I miss you so much when I'm out with other couples. I want this long-distance phase to end."

Garv's heart ached as he saw the longing in her eyes. They both knew it would take time, but they were committed to making it work. Despite their differences—Anshika being more introverted and competitive, while Garv was the laid-back one—they knew they had something special. Their understanding and compromises made everything work between them.

Before hanging up, Anshika gave him one last kiss through the screen. "I love you, Garv. Just come back soon."

Garv smiled. "I'll be there soon, Jaaneman. And then we can finally be together, no more long-distance."

Anshika stepped outside to receive her gifts, her face lighting up with happiness. And when the gifts finally arrived, her joy was unmistakable—she was thrilled. She took them to her room eagerly, but there was a small hiccup—the florist, Ferns and Petals, had forgotten to remove the price tag from the bouquet. Still, Anshika adored the thoughtful gesture, and her happiness shone through as she kissed the screen multiple times.

"I love you so much, Garv," she whispered, her heart full. "These are perfect."

Garv smiled, feeling warmth spread through him. "I'm glad you love it, Jaaneman. We'll talk properly tonight, but I'm heading to work now. We'll catch up later, when I get home."

Anshika sent him one last kiss through the phone, her eyes filled with meaning. "Hurry back, baccha. Today is just for me, you should understand that."

With that, Garv's colleagues caught wind of the five-year anniversary surprise, thanks to none other than Dii, who couldn't resist sharing the news. In celebration, Garv decided to treat them to a party. But all he could think about was getting home quickly. He was eager to talk to Anshika, especially after receiving her text.

"Baccha, I know you love me a lot, but we need to talk about something," Anshika "Haanji, baccha, did you get your gift, Jaaneman?" Garv asked, his voice warm with affection.

"I love you so much, Garv, and thank you. It was really thoughtful," Anshika replied, her voice soft but teasing. "But are you crazy? You didn't have to send such an expensive bouquet. I don't like flowers when they're too pricey—flowers can't even be kept properly, you know. Don't be sad, though. I loved that you wanted to make me feel special. It really made me happy. I'm just saying, don't spend so much on flowers next time. Otherwise, I love you, and thank you for loving me so much, baccha."

"Haanji, Jaaneman, I love you a lot too. I understand. I thought flowers were romantic, but I get your point. But I can't promise I won't do it again," Garv admitted with a sheepish smile.

"Fine, then, you'll have to bear my scolding," Anshika said, her voice playful yet stern.

"No worries. I wouldn't mind taking the scolding if it means I get to look at your face, Jaaneman," Garv responded, his tone lighthearted.

Anshika rolled her eyes, knowing all too well that whenever she scolded Garv, he'd just stare at her with that sweet smile of his, making it impossible to stay mad at him. She sighed, feeling the warmth of their connection. "You're impossible," she muttered, but her heart was soft as she hugged her phone, missing him more than words could express.

"I miss you too, baccha," she whispered into the call. "You need to come back soon so we can party, enjoy, and go shopping. I miss you so much when you're not around, and seeing other couples together just makes me wish this long-distance phase would end soon. But I know it'll take time. And once we're together, we're going to have so much fun."

Garv smiled, his heart full of understanding. Despite their vastly different personalities, they'd managed to make it work—compromise and understanding were the foundation of their relationship, and that was enough to make it last.

had written.

His mind raced as he headed home, his anxiety building. What had he done wrong? Was something off? He wasn't sure, but he hoped the conversation would clear everything up.

Garv reached his room, shut the door behind him, and sat down. His heart was pounding, and he could feel the weight of uncertainty pressing down on him. He picked up his phone and dialed Anshika's number, his nerves tingling as he awaited her voice on the other end.

On the other hand, Garv was struggling in his new office. His boss was unbearable. The issue with Garv was simple: you could make him work long hours without a problem, but if you didn't explain things properly and expected him to figure them out on his own, frustration was inevitable. Garv could work tirelessly, listening to music, as long as he was taught properly once. But he hated being given unnecessary pressure without clear instructions.

It was a tough situation, but he knew that working under someone meant dealing with things like this. So, Garv kept his cool, trying not to let the office stress get to him. However, after their anniversary, things started to get harder at work. On top of that, Anshika was becoming harder to reach, and Garv began to feel the strain of their long-distance relationship.

One thing Garv really hated was when Anshika went to house parties with her colleagues. He wasn't upset because he didn't want her to go, but he had one simple request: that she handle her drinks well and at least message him during the night to check in. The problem was that Garv knew Anshika got easily drunk, and when she went out partying, he made sure she carried pepper spray for her safety. It wasn't about controlling her; it was about caring for her well-being.

Then, just ten days before Anshika's birthday, something happened. Garv had asked her to message him while she was out, and he waited the entire night, but she forgot. That small act set off a chain of frustration in Garv's mind. He couldn't concentrate on his studies, and everything seemed to go wrong. He was upset, and the next morning, when Anshika called him, he avoided her call. It was a Sunday morning, and he had gone to the library. Anshika, hurt and confused, didn't understand why Garv was acting this way. She thought it was just about the message, but for Garv, it was deeper—he could let a lot of small things slide, but repeating the same mistake over and over was what made him snap.

When Garv finally took a break for lunch, he called her back, but his frustration boiled over, and he snapped at Anshika. The words were sharp, and Anshika, equally frustrated, told him not to talk to her anymore. She snapped back, and Garv, in his own frustration, didn't care. He only wanted to make sure she was okay, and if she was, then everything else could wait. He stopped calling her for the rest of the day, and only messaged her to check if she was alright.

The tension hung heavy, but the day finally arrived—Anshika's birthday, 27th April.

Garv called Anshika on her birthday night. She was partying with her PG group, and when she told him she'd be there in half an hour, Garv, still angry, was stubborn. He couldn't wait that long, especially after the way things had been going. "It's okay, you enjoy. I'll be sleeping anyway, need to go to the library, can't wait for long hours," he told her coldly before hanging up and switching off his phone.

Anshika was hurt. It was her birthday, and she wanted to talk to him, to clear the misunderstandings between them. Garv, however, had his own reasons for his behavior. He had been prioritizing her above everything, and he expected the same from her in return. But when that didn't happen, it became too much for him, and he switched off his phone, going to sleep instead.

Anshika, though, couldn't let it go. She tried calling him, but his phone was off. Feeling sad, she typed a long emotional message to him, hoping he'd understand that she loved him too.

The next morning, when Garv didn't call her to wake her up, Anshika felt irritated by his anger. She called him, wanting to talk, but Garv, still upset, replied, "We'll talk tonight, if you have time, okay? For now, go to the office, take it easy."

"I love you, na baccha," Anshika said softly.

"Haaji, love you too," Garv replied, then hung up, feeling conflicted. He knew the fights were becoming toxic, and he didn't want to lose Anshika. But something had to change. He needed to tell her what he needed, or things weren't going to work out.

Chapter 17

Never break Trust

Anshika, on the other hand, had always been fond of her birthdays. As the eldest and only girl in her family, she was used to being pampered. She would always get excited about her special day. After celebrating at the office, she came home around 7:00 PM and immediately texted Garv, asking him to call her urgently.

"Haanji, bolo, kya hua?" Garv replied.

"Please, pehle mood sahi kar lo yaar. Aise gussa rehne ka matlab nahi hai. Main maan loongi, jab exams ke baad aaoge, mere paas," Anshika texted, hoping to resolve things.

"I'm not coming, Anshika, not even after exams. I'm not in the mood. You tell me, what was so urgent?" Garv responded coldly.

"Please, Garv, don't stay angry. On your birthday, toh aur kaise? I'll see what I can do," Anshika pleaded.

"Please baccha, jaldi kar. Main Shreyansh ke ghar aaya hoon padne ke liye. 10 din baad exams hain, agar tumhe bhool gaya ho toh," Garv texted back.

"I'm sorry, Garv," Anshika replied sadly.

"All good, Anshika. Kya ho gaya? Why are you so sad? Tell me," Garv asked, trying to understand her better.

"Yaar, why can't someone just be a good friend? Why do people have to make things complicated?" Anshika texted, feeling frustrated.

"Anshika, please, be straightforward. What happened? Did someone say something to you?" Garv asked, now worried.

"You remember what you told me about the manager? Well, today after the party, he asked me for a drive. I didn't know why. I invited his wife, but he came alone. Why can't people just be friends, Garv? Why does it always have to be something more?" Anshika typed out, hoping he'd understand.

"Did he misbehave, baccha? If yes, do you want me to handle it or tell your dad? Someone needs to deal with it if there's an issue," Garv responded, his protective side kicking in.

"No, baccha, please, don't do anything. I just wanted to let you know," Anshika replied, not wanting Garv to take action.

"What do you want from me then? Tell me," Garv asked.

"I'm sorry for not listening to you," Anshika responded, her tone apologetic.

"Anshika, it's okay. Being friendly with someone is not a crime. But I've told you before, your intentions may be good, but sometimes you can't expect the same from others. When your friend confessed his love to you, did you see me reacting like this? No, right? So, relax. If he tries to do something wrong, I'll take care of it," Garv said, trying to ease her concerns.

"Please don't take any action yet," Anshika pleaded.

"I won't take any step until you tell me to, baccha. But please avoid such situations if you can. I'm protective because I care about you. So, play wisely," Garv advised gently.

"I promise I'll try to avoid these kinds of gatherings," Anshika assured him.

"I'm just saying, play wisely. That doesn't mean you have to cut all these things out. Abhi chill karo, batao kya khayenge?" Garv asked, trying to lift her mood.

"I'm not in the mood," Anshika replied, feeling exhausted.

"Chalo, give me 10-15 minutes. I'll be back, okay?" Garv said.

"Please don't go," Anshika requested, hoping he would stay.

"I'll be back in 10 minutes, baccha," Garv reassured her.

Garv then called Anshika's cousin, who lived in the same PG, and told her to set up a surprise birthday party for Anshika. He arranged Bacardi Apple Rum for them and made sure the party was set in her cousin's room. After everything was ready, Garv called Anshika again.

"Bacchaji, chalo party karne ke liye tayaar ho jao!" Garv called cheerfully.

"Haanji, Harshi (cousin) told me, I love you, Garv," Anshika replied, still a bit overwhelmed by everything.

"I love you 3000," Garv responded with a smile.

"I love you 3000?? What's that?" Anshika asked, puzzled.

"It's from Avengers: Endgame. You'll get it once you see the movie. Now, get ready and enjoy the party," Garv teased.

"Are you not going to talk to me? You always get angry and then don't speak," Anshika asked, feeling a little playful.

"Nahi baccha, enjoy the party. If anything happens, call me. My phone's ringtone is set just for you. I'm going to study with Shreyansh now," Garv replied.

"Okay, I love you, bacchaji," Anshika said, feeling a little lighter now.

"Yes, jaaneman. Happiest birthday, my baccha! Enjoy the party, and if anything happens, call me. Bye!" Garv said, making sure she was okay.

"I love you, and thank you, bacchaji," Anshika replied with a smile, ready to enjoy the rest of her birthday.

The tension in the air was palpable as Garv stood outside, his cigarette burning slowly as the night wore on. His thoughts were a whirlwind, trying to make sense of what had just happened. Anshika's lie had cut deep, and although she was genuinely sorry, Garv knew that trust once broken was hard to rebuild. The way she had acted, hiding the truth about her manager being at the movie, made him question everything. He wasn't angry because of the movie itself but because she had felt the need to lie, to hide something so trivial. It wasn't about the event; it was about her choice to conceal the truth from him, even though he had always trusted her.

As he stood there, Garv's mind wandered back to all the moments they had shared. He had never questioned her intentions before, and this incident gnawed at him. He took a long drag from his cigarette, feeling the bitterness of the smoke fill his lungs, trying to push away the gnawing feeling of betrayal.

His phone buzzed in his pocket, breaking him out of his thoughts. It was Anshika, calling again.

"Hello?" Garv's voice was a little more controlled now, his anger having simmered down slightly.

"Are you home now?" Anshika's voice came through, soft and tentative.

"No," Garv replied, his voice steady but distant. "Still outside."

Anshika hesitated for a moment, then said softly, "Please, don't stay angry. I know I messed up, but please talk to me, don't shut me out."

Garv felt the knot in his stomach tighten, but he knew he had to remain firm. "I'm angry, Anshika, and I don't think that's going to go away just yet. Maybe when I get home, I'll calm down, but for now, you need to understand that what you did hurt me."

Anshika's voice wavered with regret. "I'm sorry, Garv. I didn't mean to hurt you, I swear. It's just... I didn't want you to feel bad. I thought it would be okay..."

"It's not okay, Anshika," Garv interrupted, his voice tinged with frustration but also concern. "If anything were to happen to you, I wouldn't know what to do. I love you too much to just let it slide. You're not some casual friend, and I can't just let things like this go. I want you to be safe, but also, I want honesty between us. You can't hide things from me."

Anshika fell silent for a moment, then replied, her voice small but sincere, "I understand. I'll never hide anything from you again. I promise."

Garv took a deep breath, trying to ease the tightness in his chest. "I need some time, Anshika. I'm not ready to forgive right away, but I will. Just give me a little time, okay?"

"Take all the time you need, Baccha. I'll wait for you," Anshika said softly.

Garv smiled faintly despite himself. "I love you, Anshika. I really do, but I need this time to clear my head."

"I love you 3000," Anshika whispered.

"Goodnight, Anshika," Garv replied, his heart heavy but his resolve firm.

As he walked back home, he felt a strange mix of relief and frustration. He knew it would take time to heal, to rebuild the trust that had been shaken, but he also knew that he couldn't let one mistake define their relationship. It would take patience, understanding, and time—but he was willing to try, for her and for them.

When Garv finally returned to his room, he sat down at his desk, pulling his books in front of him. Exams were just around the corner, but his mind kept drifting back to Anshika. He knew he had to focus, but deep down, he also knew that this was far from over. Trust, once broken, required work—and he wasn't sure if he could fully get past this just yet. But for now, he would take things one step at a time, just like he always did.

Garv's relationship with his younger brother Dhruv is one of unwavering support and love. Dhruv, despite being six years younger, was always there for Garv, willing to help in whatever way he could. Garv had convinced their parents to let Dhruv pursue science with maths instead of commerce because he didn't want his brother to follow the same CA path he had been stuck in. Garv ensured that Dhruv had everything he needed, from his school admission to tuitions. He treated Dhruv as both a brother and a companion, and Dhruv adored him, never questioning any request Garv made.

The bond between the two was deep, and their relationship was built on mutual trust. They fought like any siblings would, but their fights were never serious. Garv, who was focused on his exams, wanted Dhruv by his side to study through the nights. Despite the tough journey to cracking exams like the IIT, Garv was confident he could get into a good private college. He made it a point to study together with Dhruv, often staying awake until 5 am. Dhruv, ever the loyal brother, never once complained, even when Garv needed space or support.

The brothers' relationship was strong enough to endure moments of frustration. Garv would often lash out in stress, but Dhruv would take it all in stride, knowing that Garv would eventually come to him with apologies. Their dynamic was simple yet powerful—an understanding that no matter what, they would always have each other's backs.

Garv's love for his brother extended to even the smallest gestures, like kissing Dhruv's forehead, just as he did for Anshika, the one person Garv loved deeply. The bond between the brothers was so strong that even when Garv faced his exams, his brother supported him through it all, making sure that no matter how stressful things got, he wouldn't be alone.

As Garv approached his last exam, he found himself particularly stressed about a theory paper involving IT, which he had no interest in.

He called Anshika, asking her for help. Though their relationship had been a bit distant that day due to some lingering frustration, Anshika immediately cancelled her plans and patiently walked him through the concepts he was struggling with. The flowchart question, which had once seemed impossible, became clear under her guidance, and Garv found himself laughing at how easy it had actually been.

The conversation between them ended with Anshika offering him comfort and affection, telling him she was waiting to see him once his exams were over. Despite the stress of his final exam, Garv was determined to make plans to meet Anshika. As soon as he left the exam center, he called her and shared his post-exam experiences. He described his paper as borderline but joked that it might just be enough to pass.

Anshika, as always, supported him, teasing him about his overthinking but also scolding him for not realizing how easy the exam had been. They spent the rest of the day together on the phone, with Garv sharing his plans to visit his friends in Mumbai for a weekend getaway.

Despite Garv's parents being okay with him occasionally drinking, they always reminded him to keep things in moderation. They trusted him, knowing he had earned the independence to make his own decisions, but also relied on him not to take it too far. Garv's plans for the weekend were a way to relax after the tension of the exams, and it was clear that he was ready to enjoy some downtime before things got even busier.

Chapter 18

Poker Face Works and Misunderstandings

Garv had devised an elaborate plan for his trip to Gurgaon, one that would keep his parents from suspecting anything. He knew that if he told his mom the real reason for his trip, she'd have questions, especially considering how close she was to Anshika. Garv had a unique relationship with his mom, where he would often share details about his life, and she would show affection towards Anshika as well. This made it difficult for him to be open about meeting Anshika alone, as it would raise suspicions. So, he decided to create a story to avoid any complications.

He told his mom that he was going to spend the entire day with his friends, Pankaj and Shreyansh, who had a good reputation in front of his family. Garv explained that they were going to Dumas, followed by lunch, a round of CS (Counter-Strike), and then a movie. He assured his mom that no food would be needed for him that day, and everything seemed set.

The plan had a few trusted people involved—Pankaj, Shreyansh, and even his brother, Dhruv, who always had his back. If anything went wrong, Garv knew that Dhruv would handle things. The day had been mapped out with perfect precision, and even his office friend, Nishant, was in the loop.

However, as the plans unfolded, Garv faced a few unexpected hurdles. His friend Devik, who was supposed to accompany him to Bombay, had to cancel due to work. In the last minute, Garv reached out to Anuj, a good friend who always came through. Anuj had been one of Garv's earliest friends and had been there for him in the past. They had shared many moments—riding together to Dumas for chai, talking about life, relationships, and anything that came to mind. Garv had even confided in Anuj about his relationship with Anshika and how much he hoped everything would fall into place soon.

Anuj was a bit confused when Garv asked him to come along just for a photo shoot in Bombay. He questioned the need for it, but Garv, in his usual style, reassured him: "Tujae dikkat hain toh bata." Anuj laughed it off and agreed, knowing full well that when Garv called, it was usually for something important.

The morning of the trip didn't go as planned. Garv had set an alarm for 7:30 AM, but of course, he overslept. He woke up at 8:10 AM, with just 30 minutes left before his train was scheduled to leave. He couldn't afford to rush too much; if he acted in a hurry, it would look suspicious to his parents. So, he remained calm, waiting until his father left for work before rushing to get ready. He knew his father left for work around 8:15 AM, and once that happened, he sprinted to the station.

Despite his best efforts to stay calm, Garv had a mini panic attack when his dad called him during his rush. To avoid his dad hearing the train station announcements in the background, Garv quickly stepped outside the station and called him back.

"Tu nikal gaya kya Dumas ke liye?" his dad asked.

"Haan, papa. Bas Bhatar cross kiya hai," Garv replied, carefully choosing his words.

His dad warned him about traffic near the bridge, but Garv quickly recovered from his slight slip-up. He reassured his dad, telling him that he had taken another route due to the reversing vehicles. His dad, satisfied with the explanation, told him to travel safely and ended the call.

Once his dad was off the phone, Garv took a deep breath and rushed to catch his train. In his haste, he accidentally boarded the wrong compartment, sitting in the G section instead of the H section, where his seat was. The guy sitting in his seat immediately got up, and Garv slid into the seat with relief, calling Anuj to update him on his journey. Then, he called Anshika to wake her up, laughing at the mess he had made of the morning.

As Anshika got ready for her day, Garv narrated his struggles, and she teased him, warning him not to get too angry with her. After talking for a while, Garv settled in for a nap on the train. He later realized that his seat wasn't occupied, and it wasn't until the ticket checker came around three hours later that Garv learned he had been in the wrong section. By then, he just wanted to sleep and didn't bother to make the switch.

Eventually, Garv arrived in Bombay, still in one piece, though slightly exhausted from the hectic morning. He had to smile through all the confusion, knowing that his journey was just beginning, and the real challenge of maintaining his poker face was still ahead.

The struggle began when Garv found himself unable to get an auto or a cab to Anuj's place. Frustration built up inside him as the minutes ticked by, and after fifteen minutes of waiting, he finally couldn't take it anymore. In a fit of exasperation, he called Anuj and lashed out, venting his anger. To his surprise, Anuj was laughing on the other end of the line. "You're standing on the wrong side," Anuj said with amusement before guiding Garv through the steps to find an auto. A video call followed, and Garv was finally directed to the right spot, where he found his ride.

By the time Garv reached Anuj's place, it was already 12:45 PM. Anuj's apartment was on the extreme side of Bombay, a cramped one-bedroom flat where mattresses were spread across the kitchen floor, as ten people lived in the small space. It was a typical bachelor pad—barely functional but lively. The center of the living room was vacant, intentionally left open for the hookah circle, which became the focal point of their gatherings. They lit cigarettes and began making plans for where to take Garv for his photoshoot.

Before long, they set off for the local bar, though neither of them had ever drunk together before. They reached the bar, ordered four bottles of Kingfisher Ultra, and soon, the booze hit them hard. Garv, having learned from the Manali trip that hard liquor took longer to get to him, quickly discovered that beer had an immediate effect. But Anuj, the tea enthusiast, was unaffected by the alcohol. "After beer, you're going to have chai?" Garv asked in disbelief. But Anuj, as always, was insistent. "You haven't had chai like this," he said, dragging Garv to a nearby chai shop. Resigned, Garv agreed, and they ordered two clay cups of piping hot chai. Surprisingly, Garv found himself enjoying it.

After the chai, they headed to Juhu Beach. There, in the quiet of the night, Garv lit four cigarettes. Anuj, who had noticed the unusual number, raised an eyebrow. "What's going on, man? This isn't our usual smoke," he remarked. Garv, a bit too tipsy to hide the truth, confessed about the fight with Anshika and the manager incident. Anuj scolded him, saying, "If she told you the truth, stop giving her a hard time. But I know you, you won't let go of it easily." Garv, stubborn as ever, wasn't ready to drop the matter. Anuj, understanding his friend's nature, advised him to not think about it too much and speak to her calmly once he was back. "You're in love with her, bro. Don't make it worse by overreacting," Anuj added.

They spent two hours at the beach, but Garv knew time was running out. He had to catch his train back, so they rushed back to Anuj's apartment. Garv snapped some photos of the city along the way, but Anuj, noticing his friend was more focused on getting pictures than actually enjoying the moment, shot him a look. "You're just here to take photos, huh?" Anuj said with a grin. "Fine, I'll take the pics for you," he teased. They took a selfie together before Garv reluctantly made his way to the station.

At 5:30 PM, Garv boarded the train, only to discover that it was one of the worst train rides of his life. The train, scheduled to arrive in Surat by 10:30 PM, was running behind schedule and barely moving. Garv knew the delay was going to throw off his carefully planned evening. He had already messaged Anshika to let her know he was on the train, but with his phone battery rapidly draining, he knew he'd have to speak with her once he was home. By 10:45 PM, when his phone was down to 5%, Garv realized he had made a huge mistake. He had told his family that he would be home by 11:00 PM after a movie screening. His parents would definitely be concerned if he didn't show up on time.

As the train crawled through the stations, Garv's frustration grew. He had already called Pankaj around 8:30 PM to brief him on what to do in case his phone died and his parents called. He'd told Pankaj exactly how to handle the situation based on the time of the call—if his parents called at 11:10 PM, Pankaj was supposed to say he was still on the way and would be home in 30 minutes. This was the plan they'd devised to cover for his lateness.

When Anshika's call came in, Garv reluctantly answered, his patience thinning. "Baccha, let's talk when I get home, my phone's at 2%," he said, his tone worn out. Anshika, understanding the situation, asked him to drive slowly and take care. "Call me once you get home," she added, before her voice cut off as Garv's phone battery finally died.

Garv felt the weight of his mistakes, knowing he was running out of time. By the time the train was approaching Surat at 11:30 PM, it was barely moving—limping at 5-10 km per hour. Desperate to make it home on time, Garv decided not to wait for the train to reach the station. He jumped off at a slanted structure near the parking lot, his bag in tow, and ran to his vehicle. Within ten minutes, he reached home, but the situation was far from ideal.

At 11:50 PM, as Garv arrived at his society gate, he spotted his father on his bike, searching for him. Garv approached him cautiously, knowing what was coming. "Where were you?" his father demanded, anger evident in his voice. Garv, always quick to read the situation, remained calm. He knew his father's temper all too well. Without a word, he lowered his head and adopted an apologetic tone. "Papa, let's go upstairs and talk," he suggested, trying to defuse the tension.

Once inside, his father let loose, scolding him for being careless and switching off his phone. "If you keep doing this, I won't let you go to

Bombay next weekend," his father warned. Garv, adopting a pitiful expression, explained that his phone had died and he'd left it in his bag. He spun a quick story about forgetting the phone in the theater after dropping Pankaj off and rushing back to grab it. "That's why I was late," he said, hoping his father would buy the excuse.

Garv's brother was smiling from the corner, watching him, when Garv turned to his dad and asked, "Why did you go looking for me?" His dad replied, "I was just saying you probably got stuck somewhere, but your mom wouldn't stop worrying. She thought you might have had an accident since it's unlike you to take so long, and then she started giving me a headache with her worries." Garv shook his head, smiling, and hugged his mom. "You're going to give me a heart attack one day," he said, and his mom tugged on his ear, playfully scolding him. Eventually, his parents went into their room.

After charging his phone, Garv called Anshika and told her everything. She burst into laughter, barely able to catch her breath. When she calmed down, she said, "Baccha, there's a problem." Garv's heart skipped a beat, already feeling exhausted from the day, but he quickly asked, "What happened?" She asked, "Did you book your tickets?" Garv replied, "No, I'll do it tomorrow." Anshika suggested, "Let's plan for next week," but Garv shook his head. "It's not possible. I don't have any leave next week." Anshika then mentioned, "My dad might be coming to Gurgaon because it's my last month here before I go back to Chandigarh. He'll be picking up my things this weekend."

Garv thought for a moment and replied, "We'll figure something out. At least I'll book my one-way ticket for now." Anshika asked, "Why only one-way?" Garv hesitated, then said, "I'm low on budget." He had invested in Yes Bank and didn't want to withdraw from his account. "I'll take the train one way, at least." So, Garv planned to reach Gurgaon by train on Saturday morning and return to Surat on Monday morning by flight. Anshika agreed to handle the plans, and Garv booked his one-way flight tickets.

That night, Anshika jokingly told him, "Please forget the manager thing, okay?" Garv assured her, "I'm coming, Baccha. We'll figure it out when I'm there."

The next day, Garv told his friends Nishant, Nikhar Bhaiya, Jainex, and Jash about his close call and the trip to Gurgaon. They all joked, "Bro, you got lucky!" Then, Garv asked his friend Pankaj, who lived in the same building, to help him book the tickets because Garv didn't have an IRCTC account. They looked for tickets but couldn't find any in the third or second class. Garv wasn't sure about the first class, as it would eat into his budget, so he asked Pankaj to book a Sitting AC ticket from Surat to Delhi. Pankaj mocked him, saying he'd pay for Garv's flight ticket instead since 15 hours of sitting straight wasn't easy, but Garv insisted on booking it. Eventually, Pankaj booked the ticket, knowing Garv wouldn't change his mind, and it cost Garv only 900 bucks.

Friday finally arrived, and Garv and Anshika were busy making plans for how to spend the weekend and what new romantic things to explore. Anshika reminded him to bring protection from Surat so she wouldn't have to buy it herself. Garv teased her, "That's your punishment for lying about that movie. You'll be buying it this time." Anshika shot back, "Fine, don't expect anything." Garv just shrugged, not caring.

On Friday, Garv left home at 6:00 PM because, according to his story, his train to Mumbai was at 7:15 PM, and it would reach Mumbai by 11:30 PM. Garv had planned it this way because his Delhi train was at 8:30 PM, and it would reach a station at 11:30 PM. He called Devik to make sure he would be available for a conference call with his dad to reassure him that Garv had reached Bombay safely. Garv's dad knew Devik from childhood, so there was no risk of anything suspicious. Garv also paid a coolie 300 bucks to get a local train ticket because he didn't want to stand in the crowded train. He hated the smell of people and couldn't stand it. He updated his WhatsApp status, "First time traveling in Local Train."

At 7:15 PM, Garv called his mom to tell her he had boarded the train. Finally, his train to Delhi arrived at 8:30 PM, and he found his compartment, but when he sat down, he realized he had messed up. He had expected decent seats, but they were worse than the seats in his school bus. So, he put his bag on the seat and sat on the train stairs, talking to Anshika. The train was delayed by 30 minutes, so he called Devik again and asked him to stay available until 12:15 AM. Garv saw that his dad's last seen was at 10:30 PM, which meant he must have gone to sleep, and Garv felt relieved.

By 2:00 AM, Anshika went to sleep, and Garv wasn't enjoying the journey. However, a guy, a laborer from Surat, came and sat on the stairs with Garv. Since Garv loved to talk to anyone, he struck up a conversation with the guy, who worked in a textile firm. As they talked, the guy pulled out a country roll cigarette, and Garv cringed. He hated the smell of cigarettes, but he had no choice but to endure it. After some more conversation, they didn't even realize it was already 10:00 AM, and they had reached Mathura station. The laborer got off, and Garv finally went inside to relax, stretching his legs on the seat.

Anshika's voice crackled through the phone, filled with impatience. "Hurry up, Garv! I'm waiting for you," she said, her tone both playful and demanding.

Garv let out a tired sigh, rubbing his eyes. "I'm really exhausted, Anshika. I haven't slept all night. I think I'll just crash," he replied, his words slow with fatigue.

Anshika's response was quick and teasing. "Prove it! Go ahead and sleep, but if you do, I'll be mad at you."

Realizing the smoke from his previous conversations had likely clung to his clothes, Garv stood up, glancing around. "One second," he mumbled to himself. He rushed to the washroom, quickly changed into fresh clothes, spritzed on some cologne, and readied himself for the next part of the journey. He was almost there.

The train pulled into the Delhi station. As the doors opened, Garv rushed out, his heart pounding. His only worry was running into his uncle—his mama—who had no idea Garv was in Delhi. According to the story he'd told at home, he was supposed to be in Mumbai. The fear of being caught made him quicken his pace.

As soon as he stepped outside, Anshika's voice buzzed again, urging him to take the metro. "It'll be faster, Garv!" she insisted, almost pleading.

But Garv, never a fan of public transport, frowned. He wanted comfort, not the hassle of crowded trains. His eyes scanned the area for a cab, and spotting one, he approached the driver. "How much to Gurgaon?" he asked.

"600 bucks to Gurgaon," the driver responded without hesitation.

Garv raised an eyebrow, incredulous. "Are you out of your mind, paaji? I've been traveling to Delhi since I was a kid, and you're telling me 600 bucks for Gurgaon? I came all the way from Surat to Delhi for just 900 bucks. You're charging me that much for a short ride?" he shot back.

The driver hesitated, and then asked, "How much will you pay?"

"350 bucks, not a penny more," Garv replied firmly.

After a brief pause, the driver agreed. Garv climbed into the cab, settling into the back seat. He was so drained that he immediately closed his eyes, hoping to steal a few minutes of rest. His phone buzzed in his pocket–Anshika again.

With a sleepy groan, Garv answered. "Yeah, baby, what's up?"

"Where are you? I'm still waiting here," Anshika's voice came through, sounding a bit frustrated.

"Just twenty more minutes, little one," Garv mumbled.

"I told you to take the metro, didn't I? But you never listen to me," Anshika said, a hint of annoyance in her voice.

"Sorry, jaanu. Don't scold me now, I'm on my way," Garv replied, trying to ease the tension.

"Okay, but don't stop the cab, and come straight to my PG. Don't make any noise, I'm still packing," Anshika instructed him firmly.

"Got it, baby," Garv replied, smiling despite his fatigue.

As the cab neared Anshika's PG, Garv's exhaustion began to fade. The sight of her, waiting for him, was enough to shake off his tiredness and frustration. He walked straight to her room, the world outside fading into the background as he focused on her.

The moment he saw her, all his anger and weariness disappeared. He felt his heart race, and for a brief moment, he was lost in her presence. Garv smiled to himself, stepping closer as if drawn by an invisible force.

Garv lay down on Anshika's bed, exhausted and waiting for her to finish packing. But the silence was too much for him, and he couldn't resist. He stood up, walked over to her, and wrapped her in a tight hug. Anshika playfully slapped his shoulder, a smile tugging at her lips as she whispered, "Wait, baccha," before pulling the curtains down. They stood there for a moment, wrapped in each other's arms, savoring the connection.

Once Anshika finished packing, Garv helped pick out her clothes, though she smiled and teased him, "What does it matter? No matter how nice the clothes, you'll still love me," she said, shrugging. Garv blushed, and with a sheepish grin, he picked up their suitcases, ready to leave. They booked an auto and decided to stay at the same hotel, as Anshika's dad was coming the next day and it would be more convenient.

Arriving at the hotel, they requested the same room they had stayed in before, and luckily, it was available. As soon as they stepped inside, Garv enveloped Anshika in a tight hug, pressing a kiss to her forehead. The warmth of the moment made Anshika's eyes well up, her voice soft with emotion. "I'm sorry about the manager situation," she murmured, her guilt lingering.

Garv simply smiled, brushing it off. The moment he saw her, all his frustrations had vanished. He pulled her closer, burying his face in her hair, just happy to be with her.

"Your perfume," Anshika began, pushing him back slightly, "It's too much. Go freshen up first," she said, shooing him toward the washroom.

But Garv, being his playful self, pulled her in with him. After a quick shower, Garv, feeling the weight of exhaustion, was ready to sleep. They had lunch together, and soon after, Garv fell asleep in her arms like a baby. Anshika smiled as she gently tapped his back, her own eyes drifting closed as she hugged him tightly.

They woke up around 5:30 PM, and Garv kissed Anshika before they both got dressed. It had started raining, and Anshika, who was prone to catching colds, wrapped herself in a warm sweater. They settled on the balcony, hands intertwined, and Garv opened up about the issues he was facing at work. Anshika, however, hated hearing about his office. She had her reasons: when her dad was in Surat, one of the directors at Garv's office had caused him a lot of trouble.

Garv tried to explain his perspective. "When a consultant is hated by bankers, it means they're doing their job right. We have to present things in a way that bankers can't prove wrong, even if it's flawed in its original form," he said, his voice calm but firm.

But Anshika, being an ethical person, didn't understand the cutthroat world of the Surat market. And Garv's admiration for the very person her dad hated? That didn't sit well with her. She didn't understand how Garv could respect someone like that, but he couldn't help it—he admired the man's aura, his personality, and his sales skills.

Their discussion turned into a heated argument, and soon, they both retreated to their phones in silence. But Anshika's curiosity got the better of her. She noticed Garv smiling at his screen, chatting with someone. She asked for his phone, and Garv, always confident, handed it over without hesitation.

Anshika scrolled through it, finding an entire gallery filled with screenshots of their funny video calls and candid moments. Garv sat back, enjoying the playful jealousy it sparked in her. He teased her, knowing how it would make her react.

When Anshika scrolled through his WhatsApp chats, Garv warned her, "Please, avoid the group chat. Trust me, no one would like the way we talk to each other."

Anshika laughed at the messages, making Garv chuckle too. He pulled her into a tight hug and whispered, "My phone's password is your number, my card's pin is yours, and the combination for my dates is yours too. I have no problem with you checking my phone. I'm good with having only one don in my life."

Anshika smiled, kissing him before pulling him close for a dance. Their laughter filled the room, but just as things settled, Anshika's phone buzzed with a message from her manager. Garv's mood shifted instantly, and Anshika noticed. "We need to get ready," she said. "We're going shopping. Let's go to the mall."

Garv, however, had other plans. "We need to be back by tonight, the India-Pakistan match is on," he reminded her. But Anshika, sensing his mood, tightened her grip on his hand and led him to the mall.

As always, Anshika made her way to Miniso first, playing with the stuffed toys there. She insisted that they pick out candles, but Garv, not in the mood for shopping, was reluctant. Frustrated, Anshika left the store, with Garv following behind. He tried to make it up by taking her to other shops, but she remained distant.

Anshika's mom called during their shopping, asking her to buy something for her and her brother. Anshika, realizing she could trust Garv's judgment, began asking him for his opinion on the items she should buy. Garv was surprised at how many options there were for women's clothes, and as he began learning about different dress styles and sizes, he found himself enjoying the shopping experience—though he knew he had ruined her mood earlier.

To lift the mood, he discreetly ordered some Old Monk from his contact. After finishing their shopping, they headed back to the hotel. As soon as they entered the room, Garv hugged Anshika tightly, but she resisted, reminding him of the tension still lingering between them.

He apologized, promising to be back in a few minutes. Anshika, not wanting him to go out and smoke, stopped him. "Go buy candles instead," she told him, knowing he loved to watch the India-Pakistan match. Garv, sensing her reluctance, kissed her deeply.

As he went out in search of scented candles, he called her to let her know he couldn't find what she wanted. "Just come back," she urged him, her voice filled with longing. It had started raining, and Garv quickly returned to the hotel. When he entered the room, he found Anshika wearing his favorite top, and she had already ordered pizza. The Old Monk was already there, and they snuggled into the blankets, sipping drinks as they watched the India-Pakistan match—though, for the first time, Garv wasn't fully focused on the game.

They were four drinks deep when Anshika, with a mischievous smile, turned off the match and dimmed the lights. She pulled Garv into her arms and whispered, "Listen carefully."

She gently kissed Garv's forehead and whispered an apology. "I'm sorry for what happened," she said softly. "Let it go, Garv. Holding onto it will only ruin what we have." Offering him her phone to check, she waited for his response, but Garv pushed it aside. Instead, he cupped her face in his hands and kissed her lips. "I'm really sorry, Baccha," he murmured. "I promise it won't happen again. Just please, never lie to me."

They embraced each other tightly, the weight of their words hanging between them. Garv swept her into his arms, and they danced together, their lips meeting in a kiss that was both tender and passionate. Anshika playfully asked to see Garv's muscles, and with a grin, he flexed his arms and legs, his muscles firm and solid beneath her touch. She laughed, telling him, "You should slim down a little. You'd look even better."

Their kisses grew more intense, the kind of kisses that came with a deeper understanding, and though they were still learning, it felt natural between them. Their intimacy was different now—more confident, though still filled with some awkwardness. They shared a lighter moment as they joked about the videos they had watched, laughing at their attempts to figure out the popular positions. The night was filled with intensity, but also with love, and it felt like they were closer than ever before.

As the night ended, Anshika set an alarm, knowing her father would be arriving in the morning. They fell asleep, their bodies intertwined, the warmth of their closeness soothing any lingering tensions between them. Though they might fight or feel hurt at times, every moment like this brought them closer, solidifying their understanding and love.

At 6:30 AM, Garv was jolted awake by Anshika's cries. He immediately saw her, her face contorted in pain, her hand trapped awkwardly beneath his back from the night before. Garv rushed to her side, his heart racing. "Calm down, Anshika," he urged gently. He rubbed her arms, trying to ease the tension in her muscles, and made sure she wore some warm clothes to help prevent any further cramps. But nothing seemed to ease the pain.

Anshika, in a panic, cried out, convinced her hand was fractured. Garv, however, knew it was just a cramp, but the sight of her distress made his chest tighten with anxiety. He quickly shut all the doors and switched off the fan, the heat of the room growing as he focused all his energy on massaging her hand. He applied pressure with his strong hands, trying to stretch her muscles and ease the pain.

For an hour and a half, he worked tirelessly, his own body drenched in sweat from the effort. Finally, after what seemed like an eternity, Anshika began to relax. She threw herself into his arms, apologizing for freaking out. She could see the sweat on his brow, the strain of his concern.

"Sorry, I got so worked up," she said, pressing a kiss to his lips. Garv smirked, teasing her gently, "You're lucky you didn't kill me with that freak-out, Jaan. I swear, you almost took the life out of me with that."

Anshika giggled, the tension finally breaking. They both knew they were stronger together, their bond deeper than ever.

A soft kiss landed on Garv's forehead, followed by a gentle apology. "I'm so sorry about what happened," Anshika whispered, her voice filled with remorse. "Please, don't let it ruin our relationship." She offered him her phone, a silent plea for understanding.

Garv, however, dismissed her gesture with a tender kiss. "Don't worry, Baccha. I promise it won't happen again. Just please, never lie to me." Their embrace was a silent vow, a promise of unwavering trust.

Later, as they danced and kissed, Anshika's gaze fell upon Garv's muscular physique. She admired the strength in his arms and legs, a solid foundation for their love. A playful smile tugged at her lips as she suggested he tone down a bit for aesthetic purposes. Their shared laughter was a testament to their growing intimacy, their passion burning bright despite their inexperience.

As the night deepened, they explored the depths of their love, their bodies entwined in a passionate embrace. They laughed together, their shared vulnerability strengthening their bond. The night was filled with love, laughter, and a touch of playful exploration.

The next morning, Anshika's peaceful slumber was shattered by a sharp pain in her hand. She cried out in agony, her hand cramping painfully. Garv, startled awake, rushed to her side, his heart filled with concern.

He soothed her with gentle words and tender caresses, but the pain persisted. As her father's arrival loomed, Anshika's anxiety grew. Garv, determined to alleviate her suffering, employed a more vigorous massage technique. His strong hands worked tirelessly, pushing through the pain.

Finally, after what felt like an eternity, the pain began to subside. Anshika, overwhelmed with relief, hugged Garv tightly, her tears of gratitude mingling with his sweat. Garv, exhausted but victorious, chuckled, "You nearly scared the life out of me. Now, go meet your father. I'll explain everything later."

Anshika kissed Garv's forehead and told him that she was sorry for what had happened. She urged him to let it go from his mind because it would ruin their relationship. Anshika offered her phone to Garv to check, but he set it aside and kissed her on the lips. He told her that he was really sorry, and promised that it wouldn't happen again, but asked her to never lie to him. They hugged each other tightly, and then Garv picked Anshika up in his arms. They danced and kissed, and Anshika wanted to see Garv's muscles, so he flexed his arms and legs, and she could feel that they were very strong. She told him that he should get a little slimmer so he would look better.

Then their lips met, and they were passionate, though they were still learning. They didn't feel awkward, and they had used fewer condoms compared to before. That night was intense and romantic, but they weren't able to figure out some positions that are popular among Indian people. They laughed together watching videos about it, and then kissed each other. Anshika set an alarm because her father was coming to Gurgaon the next day. In the morning, Garv heard Anshika's screams and saw that she was crying because she had a cramp in her hand from sleeping with her hand under Garv's back. Garv tried to calm her down, rub her arms, and have her wear warmer clothes, but nothing was working. Anshika was freaking out because her father was coming in 2 hours. Garv started giving her a massage, but he was hesitant to do the kind of massage that boys do for cramps, since he didn't have much time. Anshika believed her hand might be fractured, but Garv knew it was just a cramp. Seeing her cry made Garv anxious, so he closed all the doors and turned off the fan, and gave her a strong, forceful massage with his hands to warm up her muscles.

After 1.5 hours, she finally felt better. Anshika jumped and hugged Garv tightly, apologizing for freaking out, since she could see he was sweating from turning off the ventilation. Garv gave her a sly smile and said he would tell her father what happened, and that he was being completely honest with her.

Garv gave her a playful smirk, his eyes glinting with mischief. "You almost drained the life out of me, Baccha," he teased. "Come on, let's go meet your dad, and I'll show you just how much energy you've drained from me today."

Anshika, still feeling a bit guilty for her earlier panic, told him to rest. "I'll be back in two to three hours, once Dad leaves the PG," she said. But Garv, ever the protector, insisted on going with her. They walked together to her PG, Garv smiling at the sight of her, and Anshika, seeing the slight anxiety on his face, returned the smile. He held her hand tightly, as if reluctant to let go, but finally, he dropped her off at her PG and walked back to his room.

Exhausted from their late night and the emotional rollercoaster of the morning, Garv collapsed onto his bed. They had barely slept, only catching a few hours after 4 AM. He grabbed a small drink of Old Monk to relax and, feeling the weight of the night, drifted into a deep sleep.

An hour and a half later, Anshika returned and rang the doorbell. Garv, deep in sleep, was oblivious to the persistent ringing. She tried calling him multiple times, but he didn't answer. It wasn't until another 15 minutes had passed, and Garv's alarm blared, that he groggily woke up. The panic set in as he saw Anshika's name flashing on his phone, her calls coming through non-stop for the past 20 minutes.

Thinking the worst—maybe her dad had found out about them—his heart raced. He quickly answered the call, his voice filled with concern. "Anshika, what happened? Is everything okay?"

Anshika's voice came through, calm but urgent. "I'm outside, Garv. Can you open the door?"

Anshika gently told Garv to rest, reassuring him that she would be back in two to three hours once her dad left the PG. However, Garv insisted on accompanying her, and together they walked to her PG. Garv couldn't help but smile as he looked at Anshika, and she returned the smile, noticing the concern in his eyes. He gripped her hand tightly, feeling protective as ever. Finally, after walking her to her PG, Garv headed back to his room, exhaustion setting in. They had barely slept, having stayed up until 4 AM, and after giving Anshika a soothing massage, Garv drank some Old Monk to ease his tiredness and fell into a deep sleep.

An hour and a half later, Anshika returned and rang the bell. Garv was deep in sleep, unaware of the persistent ringing. Anshika called him several times, but he didn't stir. Fifteen minutes later, his alarm went off, and when he saw all the missed calls from Anshika, panic gripped him. He feared that her dad might have found out about them. Frantically, he called her back. "Anshika, what happened? Is everything okay?"

Anshika's voice was calm yet urgent. "I'm standing outside, Garv. Can you open the door?"

Garv hurriedly opened the door, and as soon as Anshika stepped inside, she threw her arms around him, scolding him for making her wait outside. Without a word, Garv scooped her up into his arms and gently placed her on the bed. As he lay beside her, he whispered, "I just want to sleep, please don't disturb me." And with that, he nestled into her warmth, drifting off to sleep like a baby. Anshika, holding him tightly, followed him into slumber.

Hours later, Garv woke up, the soft afternoon light filtering into the room. He looked over to see Anshika sleeping peacefully, curled up like a cute baby. He kissed her forehead, and she instinctively hugged him tighter in her sleep. Garv smiled and ordered lunch, gently waking her after a while. "It's already 3:00 PM," he said, his voice soft.

They exchanged a smile, both feeling a quiet joy in each other's company. Garv had learned so much in his time with Anshika—he had figured out what made her tick, what sensitive points to touch, and what made her feel loved. They spent the rest of the day together in the room, enjoying each other's company in the most simple, intimate way.

As the night wore on, Garv knew it was time to leave. His flight was at 5:00 AM, and goodbyes were always hard. As he held her in his arms, the familiar scent of Anshika's perfume lingered on his shirt. He smiled, knowing he wouldn't wash it for days. Anshika kissed him, her lips pressing against his as she tried to make them swell with love. Garv returned the kiss with all the passion he felt. The goodbye was coming, but their love had grown deeper, their longing for each other palpable.

Garv drove Anshika back to her PG and, even though it was time to leave, he couldn't help but step out of the car to hug her tightly once more. He kissed her forehead and stood by, watching as she walked to her room. He waved at her until she disappeared inside, and then, with a heavy heart, he left for the airport.

Arriving at the airport, Garv finally called his mom to let her know he had boarded the flight. He assured her not to call before 9:00 AM since he would be asleep. He had told her he'd reach Surat at 9:30 AM, but the truth was, Garv's flight was delayed, and he would actually arrive at 7:30 AM.

As he waited at the quiet airport, Garv became drowsy. The silence was only interrupted by the hurried footsteps of passengers racing toward the gate. Realizing the final call was being made, Garv scrambled to make it to his gate in time. He boarded the flight just in time, his heart pounding. The flight finally took off, and he reached Surat, where Pankaj was waiting to pick him up.

The drive home was long, and as they sat together, Pankaj chatting away, Garv couldn't help but think about Anshika. He realized that, despite the distance, the connection they shared had only grown stronger. When he got home, his mom noticed his lips were bruised and slightly irregular in shape, but she said nothing.

Exhausted, Garv took a sick leave, the strain of the past few days catching up to him. As for Anshika and Garv, their bond continued to deepen, both emotionally and physically. But one thing was clear: love is a beautiful thing, and when you give it your all, you must promise yourself to always give without fear, for if you fear losing it, you might lose yourself in the process.

Chapter 19

Office Fights and Buddy in Trouble

After returning to work, Garv's life fell into a routine, but the friction with his boss only grew. His boss's constant bad language and rude behavior pushed Garv to his limits. The office dynamics were tough for him, but he found solace in his colleagues, particularly Nikhar bhaiya, Jainex bhaiya, and Nishant. Nikhar, a mentor figure, always had his back, providing guidance and support. Despite his own struggles, Nikhar saw potential in Garv and made sure to teach him valuable lessons, taking him along to meet bankers and clients so he could learn firsthand. On the other hand, Jainex was a complex character—difficult to handle yet fiercely loyal to his friends. Jainex, though he'd left his CA course at its final stage, often advised Garv and others to focus on their studies and not give up on their degrees, a piece of wisdom that stuck with Garv.

Despite his growing frustration with his boss, Garv tried to keep his cool, knowing that his colleagues were his lifeline. He continued to study the stock market with his friend Jash, who shared his passion for mutual funds. Together, they spent hours researching the best investments, which became one of Garv's greatest escapes. But as his work environment became more suffocating, the tension inside Garv built up.

Meanwhile, life outside the office had its own rewards. Garv finally passed his Group 2 exams, with a perfect score of 150. The excitement was shared with his friends and colleagues, and Garv immediately called Anshika to share the good news. She was overjoyed, sending him kisses even though she was at work. It was one of the rare moments of happiness in Garv's life, but that brief celebration was soon overshadowed by the chaos at work.

To cope with the mounting stress, Garv started avoiding clubs. After a wild night out in Bombay where he and his friends were hit with a massive bill of 75,000 rupees, Garv vowed never to set foot in one again. It was a hard lesson, but it taught him that there were better ways to enjoy life without spending ridiculous amounts of money.

Back in the office, Garv's relationship with his boss continued to deteriorate. His boss's attitude was unbearable, but Garv never let it show. Instead, he found a way to get Anshika the help she needed from her difficult reporting manager in the US. He suggested Anshika send a well-crafted email asking for help from a colleague named Imran, who had a connection with the manager. Surprisingly, it worked, and Anshika found some relief.

Despite Garv's frustrations, Anshika's encouragement kept him going. However, his patience had a breaking point. On his birthday, he told his boss he would be taking the day off, and his boss, taking it as an affront to his ego, reported him to the director. The situation escalated, and Garv found himself face-to-face with the director the next day. He was ready to snap, but the director, sensing his frustration, handled the situation calmly, advising him to keep his cool.

But as the pressure at work mounted, Garv's frustration reached a tipping point. He had been dedicating endless hours to the office, working even during his Articleship time, but there was little to show for it. His hard work seemed to go unnoticed, and the unnecessary pressure continued to rise. It all came to a head in December when Garv decided he'd had enough. The stress and constant cigarette breaks to manage his anxiety were taking a toll, and he finally decided to quit.

That day, when he told his boss he was leaving for his tuitions, his boss tried to pressure him to stay. But Garv wasn't having it anymore. In front of the office staff, he lashed out, confronting his boss about his behavior and the constant mistreatment. Garv threatened that if his resignation wasn't accepted and he wasn't given his relieving letter, he would have to involve his uncle, who worked in income tax. This move took the boss by surprise. The director, who had been informed of the situation, intervened and called Garv's boss to sort things out.

Garv's patience finally paid off when his resignation was processed, but not before the director chewed out his boss for two hours. Garv left the firm after serving his one-month notice period, feeling a mix of relief and bitterness.

However, the real trouble was just beginning. While Garv had managed to escape the toxic work environment, a more personal storm was about to hit him hard.

Anuj was more than just a best friend to Garv—he was his brother. They didn't spend much time together, but they always knew that when the time came, one phone call would be enough for them to stand by each other. It was on a quiet Sunday morning in January 2020 that Garv received a call from one of their school friends, and what he heard shook him to his core.

"Bhai, have you spoken to Anuj lately?" the voice on the other end asked.

"No, yaar, it's been about a week. Why, what happened?" Garv replied, a growing sense of unease creeping into his voice.

"You won't believe it, Bhai. He sent a weird message to his brother this morning, and now he's not picking up his phone. He's just gone... no one knows where."

Garv's mind raced. Anuj was a strong guy, always the life of the group, the one who could always be counted on. To hear this about him was hard to process. He immediately informed his parents, telling them he would be out for a few hours. He texted Anshika to let her know not to call him until he reached out to her again.

Determined to find his brother, Garv started searching through all the places where he and Anuj had spent time, hoping to find him. Hours passed, and frustration mounted as he came up empty-handed. Finally, a call came from Anuj's brother, who revealed that Anuj had left Surat. Garv quickly teamed up with him, and together, they went to the station, hoping to find some clue about Anuj's whereabouts. After much searching, they finally located his vehicle.

After a long and tense wait, Anuj spoke to his mother, and finally decided to come back home. But, despite the relief of knowing he was safe, the situation was never discussed among friends or family. Anuj was always a joyful, carefree guy—his sudden disappearance didn't seem to make sense. Garv and Anshika later discussed it, and they both agreed that it was best not to confront Anuj about what happened. They knew him too well—he was strong, but something had hit him hard. With time, they hoped, he would open up when he was ready.

Chapter 20

A Boon Amidst a Crisis

As the world grappled with the spread of COVID-19, Garv found himself in an unexpected position of comfort. When the lockdown hit India on March 25, 2020, Garv had just left his job at the firm, and with his six-month stipend already in hand and a fixed deposit of two lacs maturing, he was in a much better financial situation than most. On top of that, he and Anshika had just celebrated their 6th anniversary together with a virtual dinner date, and while the world around them faced uncertainty, they were focused on each other.

The lockdown wasn't a blessing for Anshika, though. As a placement year student, she found herself navigating a tough economy, with opportunities shrinking as companies postponed hiring. But Anshika was determined. She threw herself into her work, focusing on competitions and staying ahead in her studies. Garv, meanwhile, was diving deep into the stock market. His daily routine started with watching the SGX Nifty and catching up on market news via CNBC. He became fixated on the idea of investing in blue-chip stocks, convinced that the market's downturn would eventually turn around, but not everything went as planned.

Garv's first big mistake came with the SBI credit card IPO. He also invested in ITC and a few other mid-cap stocks, which he believed were at discounted prices and would recover quickly. But the market kept free-falling, and Garv's investments didn't look as promising. Undeterred, he turned to options trading and spent hours learning the ins and outs of the market. He practiced risk management and built patience—something the stock market, he learned, demanded in spades.

In the meantime, he and Anshika spent hours watching vlogs from Flying Beast and his group of friends. They admired how he pampered his daughter, and it gave them ideas for how they would raise their own children one day. Garv would often tease Anshika about how he would love their daughter more than her, joking that he would take her on solo trips and shopping sprees. Anshika, in return, would scold him, but it was all in good fun.

Their relationship reached a new level during the lockdown. Garv even began to show an interest in Anshika's world of makeup and fashion. He joined her makeup and fashion group on Instagram, and though it was a new world for him, he threw himself into learning about the latest trends. From lipsticks to foundation shades, Garv became an expert, much to Anshika's amusement. His Instagram feed was filled with makeup brands and products. But more than just the shopping, he enjoyed talking to Anshika about it, discussing everything from makeup to clothes.

In return, Anshika loved hearing Garv talk about his passion for watches. He'd stopped buying them, but he always believed a good watch could make a person stand out, adding to their personality. And while the stock market consumed much of his time, Garv also had a few things he indulged in—like perfume. He never compromised on his scent, believing that smelling good added to his confidence.

To wind down, Garv would often play PUBG with his friends—Anuj, Rathi, and others. It was their way of staying connected in the midst of a global crisis.

Over the two months that followed, Garv started to regain control over his emotions. He had learned the hard way that greed had no place in the stock market, especially when trading options. After wiping out a chunk of his capital, he took a break, revisited his strategies, and practiced on a demo account. He also began learning more about hedging and volatility, which helped him grow more patient in his trading. Meanwhile, Anshika made a bet with him—she claimed he didn't know every stock in the market, but Garv surprised her by naming prices of shares off the top of his head. Their bets were always playful, a reminder of their special bond.

To find balance, Garv took up his old hobby of cooking. He'd always loved preparing meals, but had let it slip as his life got busier. Now, with extra time on his hands, he started cooking meals for his family, experimenting with dishes like Biryani, Malai Kofta, Pasta, Paneer Gravy, and even Galouti Kebabs. He knew how to chop vegetables perfectly and which spices worked best. Anshika would tease him, joking that he should become a "house husband" and cook for her every day. Garv would laugh it off, but in his heart, he knew one thing for sure—he'd do anything to make Anshika happy, even if it meant spending the rest of his life cooking her favorite meals.

As the lockdown continued, Garv felt a sense of contentment. He was growing emotionally, professionally, and personally. And most importantly, he was happy—because he knew, in Anshika, he had found his soulmate, his anchor, and the love of his life.

Garv knew one thing for certain: Anshika was highly career-oriented. He could sense that she was facing a crisis at this stage of her life—not that she wasn't doing well, but she wasn't satisfied. And deep down, Garv understood that Anshika would never be truly content until she reached the pinnacle of success. He had learned over time that in a relationship, as in life, there can't always be two swords in one sheath. He was ready to make any compromise necessary because, in the end, all he wanted was peace—peace that came from lying beside her at night, holding her close.

He was prepared for anything, even to take on the role of a house husband if it meant that Anshika could chase her dreams without distraction. But there was one thing he made clear to her: he wouldn't sit idly at home. He'd find a way to start his own business, something he could manage from home so that he could still take care of their life together without feeling bored.

Anshika, curious as always, asked him, "What will your family say about that?"

With a gentle smile, Garv replied, "They won't interfere, as long as I'm happy. And my happiness comes from seeing you happy."

As time passed, their love for each other deepened. On the other hand, Garv was trying to rebuild his losses in the stock market. He had started trading again, cautiously minimizing his risks by hedging his positions and using stop-loss strategies. It was a slow process, but Garv knew he couldn't afford another significant loss. He had to tread carefully, playing the long game.

Then, Anshika's birthday arrived on April 27th, 2020. With the lockdown in place, Garv decided to surprise her with a gift unlike any other. He reached out to his friends and Anshika's friend, Sheru, to gather video clips wishing her a happy birthday. Sheru even managed to get videos from Anshika's family, and together, they compiled the footage into a heartwarming video. At the end, Garv included his own personal message: a poem, a few heartfelt lines, and a promise to always love her.

When Anshika saw the video, tears welled up in her eyes, and Garv could see the joy on her face. In that moment, he promised himself that no matter what, he would always strive to make her happy, for his love for her only grew stronger with each passing day. Anshika, too, realized that Garv's love was unconditional, and that no matter what happened, he would always be there for her.

But there was a side to Garv that Anshika didn't know. He had been struggling silently, hiding his frustrations over the financial losses he'd incurred. He didn't want to worry her, knowing she would scold him for the decisions he'd made. So, he kept it to himself.

Despite this, he remained determined. He resumed his trading, focusing on controlling his emotions and minimizing his losses. His patience grew thin as the process was slow, but Garv knew he had no other choice. Meanwhile, Anshika decided to join him and his friend Devik in trading, though Garv soon realized that options trading wasn't for everyone. He preferred to give them stock picks but trade alone in silence, as constant questions and interruptions disrupted his focus.

Around this time, Garv's MCS (Master of Computer Science) course began, consuming twelve hours of his day. He found solace in it, particularly when it came to discussions about business models. Garv had always been passionate about speaking and debating, and he relished the opportunity to express his thoughts.

In one class, his professor assigned a project to create a business model, and Garv proposed the idea of a creche service. He knew that, in today's world, with both parents working full-time, affordable childcare was a pressing need. He convinced his group to pursue the idea, and within a few hours, he had crafted an entire unit economics and revenue model. When it came time for the presentation, Garv's speaking skills shone. He didn't bother with complex slides, believing in the power of a strong introduction and a well-timed Q&A session. Though their group finished second, Garv received accolades for his ability to answer questions and speak confidently.

However, his focus on the stock market never wavered. After a two-day hiatus, Garv dove back into trading, but things took a turn when a classmate criticized the BJP government during a debate. Garv, a firm supporter of the right-wing, could no longer stay silent. As the conversation shifted to complaints about rising prices and unemployment, Garv, calm but determined, stood up.

"How has this government affected you personally?" he asked the student, who rattled off a list of grievances. With quiet confidence, Garv began listing the achievements of the current government, from Gujarat's success stories to national-level changes. He made his point clear without directly attacking the student, choosing instead to gently dismantle his argument, all while maintaining a composed demeanor. His friend Nishant, who sat nearby, texted him to calm down, but Garv knew he had made his point.

And so, life continued—Garv trading, learning, debating, and loving Anshika with every ounce of his being. Their relationship deepened, each day bringing them closer to a future where they could face anything together. No matter the struggles, Garv was determined to make Anshika happy, and in turn, she continued to be his anchor in the chaotic storm of life.

Finally, Garv had finished his batches, and it was Anshika's placement month. However, due to a lack of companies hiring, she chose to go with the one she had done her internship at—American Express, where she had already received a PPO (Pre-Placement Offer). Her family was happy, and so was Garv. But that night, during their video call, Anshika seemed really disappointed.

"Baccha, kya hua? Kyon sad ho?" Garv asked, concerned.

"Yaar, mehnat toh kari thi, na. Manaye nahi mila jo chahiye tha. Mujhe pata hai, na aapko, raat raat bhar baithkar coding ke competitions aur sab mein success nahi mila," Anshika replied, her voice tinged with frustration.

"Baccha, jitna package mila hai, please samajh. Already COVID chal raha hai. Varna dusri company mein ho jata. Aur last baar tha ki aap baad mein bhi desakte ho na," Garv reassured her, trying to calm her down.

"Haan, baad mein bhi desakte hoon, but mere doston ka toh ho gaya na, main reh gayi," Anshika's voice cracked with emotion.

"Baccha, suno. Apne aap ko judge karna ho toh wait till at least age of 30-32. Aur tab bhi agar nahi kar paaye, toh regret karna. Kyunki tab tak show-off wali life chalti hai, aur koi stable nahi hota. Once you cross that age and you're living peacefully, enjoying the life you wanted, then you've made it. Competition karo doosron se, it gives motivation, but satisfaction bhi rakho taaki life peacefully jee pao," Garv said, trying to soothe her.

"Aapko pata hai, na, mehnat ki thi maine," Anshika replied, her voice heavy with the weight of her disappointment.

"Main ne kabhi mana kiya? Mujhe pata hai tum kya deserve karti ho, aur 5-6 saal mein tum sabko beat kar dogi, kyunki tumhare paas dedication hai, jo tumhe karna hai usme. So, theek hai na bacchaji, you will make it work," Garv spoke with conviction.

Anshika slowly started crying.

"Bolo Anshika, strong ho, nahi haar manegi aur nahi royegi," Garv encouraged her, his tone soft but firm.

"Haan, main strong hoon. Is baar nahi hua toh kya, I will crack what I want," Anshika said, wiping away her tears.

"Haan, baccha, chalo ab happy ho jao. Aur meri party kahan hai? Ye batao," Garv lightened the mood.

"Aap aaoge toh tab dungi, abhi nahi milegi. But mujhe kya gift milega, ye batao," Anshika teased.

"Soch rahe hain, mil jayega tumhe apna giftie, baccha," Garv joked.

"I love you a lot, baccha. And thank you for always supporting me," Anshika said, her voice full of gratitude.

"Aajao, chalo hug kar lo aur sojao," Garv responded, wrapping up the call with warmth.

Garv called Shreya to arrange a special gift for Anshika. Since Shreya was at home, they decided to send her some sweets. Shreya contacted a friend who baked macarons, and Garv requested her to decorate them with hearts and a Maldives theme. He told her that the order should come from Sheru because Anshika's family didn't know about Garv yet.

The next day, Anshika received the macarons, and she immediately recognized that they were from Garv because of the Maldives-themed macaron. She called him, her voice full of joy, and gave him many kisses.

"Guess what, my family loved the macarons! And I'm so happy after eating the sweets. You really made my day," Anshika said, her happiness evident.

Did Garv and Anshika fight? Yes, there were some fights. During the COVID lockdown, while it was risky to go outside, some of Garv's friends, who were living outside the city, had their families contract COVID. Garv delivered fruits and medicine on their behalf because his friends knew he would never say no to helping them. But Anshika, concerned for Garv's safety, scolded him, saying it was their responsibility, not his. She was worried that Garv might catch COVID.

Garv, however, believed that once you make friends, you help them in their time of need, no matter the cost. Anshika understood this when one of her relatives needed oxygen gas later that year in Delhi. She told Garv about it, and he immediately contacted a friend in Noida, who confirmed that he could arrange it. Garv then asked Anshika if he should send it, but Anshika hesitated because she didn't know how to explain it to her father.

After a few hours, her father arranged the oxygen, and the situation was sorted. That night, Anshika asked him,

"Baccha, ek baat batao. Aapne us dost se kab last baat ki thi?"

"Hoga 6-7 months, kyun? Kya hua?" Garv replied.

"Toh aapko help chahiye, aapne usse call laga liya?" Anshika asked, still unsure about the whole thing.

"See, saare type ke friends hain mere paas, aur mujhe pata hai kaun kis level tak ja sakta hai. Woh jo banda baitha hai Delhi mein, hum baat nahi karte zyada, but hamari dosti acchi hai. Jab bhi woh zaroorat padti hai, hum milte hain aur baat karte hain," Garv explained.

"Aapne usse mere baare mein bataya ki mujhe requirement hai?" Anshika asked, still processing everything.

"Nahi, maine usse bola ki bhai meri family mein urgent requirement hai, kya jugad ho sakta hai?" Garv clarified.

"Love you a lot, baccha," Anshika said, her heart softening.

"Love you, jaaneman," Garv responded, his voice full of affection.

On the other hand, Garv had successfully covered his losses and begun averaging down, gradually rebuilding his position. As his exams drew near, anxiety started to settle in. Along with the pressure of his CFA exams, Garv realized he had gained some weight over the past months. So, he decided to take action—not only to prepare for his exams but also to get back in shape. He started cycling daily, riding between 11 to 15 kilometers in an hour. Although he loved food, which had gotten out of control after COVID, he was determined to maintain his physical strength.

Then, Diwali arrived. Anshika had an unusual request—she wanted to learn poker from Garv. At that time, Garv was staying at his neighbor's house, taking care of it while they were away for a month. Pankaj's exams had already started, and Garv knew that it was time to focus on his own studies as well. So, he stopped trading in options and joined Pankaj, Shreyansh, and Muskan in their study sessions. Every day, Garv studied, and in the evenings, after long hours of revision, he and Anshika would play poker together.

The nights were chilly, and they were drawn to each other. They started playing strip poker, with Garv being the competitive player he was, always trying to win. But in front of Anshika, he didn't mind losing; he'd go all-in, knowing it was never a bad thing to lose the game when it was in front of the one you loved. Those nights were a blend of relaxation and fun, after long hours of work and study. After playing, they would talk and sleep on the phone, comforting each other and drifting off peacefully.

But as December came, Garv's schedule changed. He fully immersed himself in CA studies, putting aside all other distractions, including his investments. His new routine involved studying late into the night after speaking to Anshika, making sure she was asleep before diving into hours of study. He would then sleep in the afternoons, guiding Anshika on political matters when she needed advice. She had grown into a capable student and was now moving smoothly through her professional life. Garv's guidance helped her develop new tactics, and she felt more at ease in her career.

But life, as it often does, didn't always follow the plans they made. Sometimes, despite all the effort, results weren't favorable. No matter how much time one spent trying, if the outcome wasn't what people expected, it seemed to invalidate everything. People failed to understand that just because someone was going through hard times didn't mean they were enjoying it. If a person didn't give up, it was a sign of their resilience, not their failure. It only took a moment to turn things around, yet not everyone had the patience to wait for that moment. Most loved the honeymoon period, but not the struggle that came before success.

Readers, remember this: always trust your heart and mind. If you rely on others, bad luck can easily turn into a bad life over time.

Chapter 21

Playing the Role of Catalyst and Keeping Patience

Finally, January came to a close, and Shreyansh and Garv found themselves studying with renewed focus. But there was good news to celebrate—Pankaj, their friend who had taken his exams in November, had passed his CA exams. The boys couldn't have been happier for him. It was a moment of victory for their entire friendship, and the joy was infectious. Boys, they believed, never envied each other's success. They uplifted each other, always rooting for the growth of their friends. And that was what made their bond unbreakable, stronger than even love at times. The depth of their friendship was like gold, precious and rare.

Pankaj had been through tough times in his personal life, and this success meant the world to him. Garv and Shreyansh knew the road ahead would still be hard for him, filled with challenges, but they stood by him, always. No matter what.

As their studies progressed smoothly, Garv had started smoking again. He knew the harmful effects, but the stress of his exams led him back to the habit. Anshika, of course, was unhappy with it. Garv, however, was open with her, admitting that he didn't like what he was doing. He had never wanted to end up in the core CA field, and the uncertainty of his future made him feel restless. He promised Anshika that once he was done with his CA, once he had more clarity about his path, he would quit.

To those who don't smoke, I hope you will never touch it. You might be tempted to try other things—weed or alcohol, for instance—but cigarette addiction is real, and it sticks with you like no other. It might not be more powerful than love, but for many, it becomes a crutch they rely on.

Then, in March 2021, the pandemic hit again. COVID-19 was back, and just like last year, Garv and Shreyansh were hopeful that their exams might get postponed. They slowed their pace, thinking the exams would follow the same pattern as before. But then, in April, ICAI made its announcement—exams would proceed in May. Panic set in.

They had to get back to studying, pushing themselves harder. On top of that, both Garv and Shreyansh had family members who were affected by the virus. Nishant, one of Garv's close friends, was also preparing for the exams but had tragically lost his mother in the second wave of COVID. Garv, along with his friend Arpan, went to offer their condolences and suggested that Nishant take the exams in November.

As if the stress wasn't enough, Garv himself caught a viral infection. His carefully planned study schedule got thrown off. Frustrated, he kept pushing through, taking medication and injections to keep his energy up during the exams. But despite all that effort, Garv was devastated. His results were a blow to him. He had failed three out of eight papers. The one that hit hardest was Audit, where he scored a measly 39. He had hoped for a better result, at least a pass in the first group, but the damage had been done. He now had to face eight papers again in three months.

Through all of this, Garv knew one thing: he had to stay calm. If he let his frustration get the best of him, it would only make things worse. Meanwhile, he was getting increasingly strict with his younger brother. He wanted to make sure his brother didn't make the same mistakes he had made. Garv pushed him to work hard for his entrance exams, especially the private college ones. His family had invested so much into his education, and Garv couldn't let his brother fail.

Despite the pressure, Garv's focus never wavered. He continued studying and managing his time as best as he could, while also making sure his brother stayed on track. They studied together whenever possible, making their way through the chaos as a team.

After the exams, Garv finally told his mother he was going to Gurgaon to meet his friend and take a break. He had planned to relax after everything that had happened, but the best part was that he was finally going to meet Anshika. It had been nearly two years since they'd seen each other, and now that Anshika had started her job, they decided it was time to reunite.

Garv booked a train to Gurgaon and a flight back. By then, he had stopped taking pocket money from home. He had enough savings from his small investments to cover his daily expenses. The moment he arrived in Gurgaon, they checked into a hotel, but things didn't go as smoothly as they had hoped. They got into a big argument on the very first day.

The fight was unexpected. They had been apart for so long, and even though they were both eager to be together, old tensions resurfaced. After a long day, though, they finally settled down. Garv, tired and drained from his stressful weeks, lay next to Anshika. In a long-distance relationship, it's not just the physical intimacy that you miss. It's the feeling of being close, of falling asleep next to the one person who makes you feel safe, relaxed, and loved. Anshika could tell that Garv was stressed and tired, so she wrapped him in her arms and held him like a child. She helped him drift off to sleep, soothing him after all the chaos in his life.

When they woke up the next morning, Garv opened up to Anshika about his exams. He wasn't sure he'd be able to manage both groups in November. It felt too risky, and he wasn't sure if he could handle the pressure. But Anshika, ever supportive, encouraged him to try. She wanted him to succeed, and she didn't want him to give up. She also didn't want to face another long stretch of time without him. They began to talk about their future plans—how they could eventually live together.

But a new fight arose when Anshika brought up Garv's dad and his decisions regarding their future.

Garv's father had made a lot of tough choices, especially when it came to Garv's career. He had pushed him into CA, though Garv didn't have the passion for it. But he'd also supported him financially to go to college. Now, when Garv expressed his desire to pursue CFA, his father didn't object. There was a guilt in his father's eyes, a realization that Garv wasn't happy in the field he was in. But Garv had made peace with it, knowing his father had only wanted the best for him.

The conversation was difficult. Anshika, not fully understanding the dynamics of Garv's family, questioned why his father had chosen CA for him. Garv, feeling defensive, lashed out. He explained how, despite the struggles, his father had been there for him when it mattered. He wasn't just a strict figure; he had given Garv the freedom to choose his own path. After a tense silence, Garv managed to convince Anshika that there was more to the situation than she realized. He had promised to support his brother's future, making sure his younger sibling was set up for success as well.

At the end of their conversation, Garv turned to Anshika, his voice steady but firm. "Whatever amount you're going to invest in the house, I'll match it. That was the plan, right?" he said, his gaze unwavering. But his tone softened slightly as he continued, "You can say anything to me, Anshika, but please, watch your words. You know how strict my dad is. I can handle a lot, but there's a line." He paused, his frustration still palpable, but it was clear that he wasn't going to let it escalate any further.

Anshika's words about his parents had struck a nerve. Garv wasn't sure if it was because they were harsh or because they had come from her. He had always held back from criticizing her family, even when she was scolded by her mother. He would always tell her it was okay, but he never spoke ill of her mom. But this time, it had gone too far.

The fight had taken a wrong turn, and Garv, his patience wearing thin, spoke again. "If we don't stop this now, I'm leaving the hotel." His tone was serious, but he didn't want to fight; he just wanted peace.

Anshika, realizing the intensity of the moment, quickly apologized. But Garv, needing time to cool off, didn't respond immediately. He simply sat in silence, his mind racing. He hated fighting with her, but the things she said about his parents, it was something he couldn't easily let go. If it had been anyone else, the relationship might have ended in that instant. But with Anshika, he knew better; they would work through it.

Fifteen minutes passed before Garv finally calmed down. He took a deep breath, drank some water, and turned to see Anshika lying on the bed. She was crying. The sight of her tears made his heart ache.

"Aap kyon ro rahe ho, Anshika?" Garv asked softly, his voice full of concern.

"Nothing, yaar. I don't want to talk to you right now," she mumbled, her voice choked with emotion.

Garv sighed, a mix of sadness and understanding filling him. "It's okay, just think about who started it. If you think what you said was okay, then it's fine." He tried to be rational, but inside, his emotions were a whirlwind.

Anshika had hoped he would console her, but instead, he turned away and lay down beside her, facing the other way. The distance between them made her feel even worse. She started crying again, overwhelmed by guilt.

Garv noticed her sobbing and couldn't bear it. He reached out, but Anshika didn't let him hug her. He gently made her sit up, his voice firm but tender. "Was I rude, Anshika?"

"Yes, I'm sorry," Anshika whispered, her voice barely audible. "But do you think it was right for you to say you would leave me alone in the room? If you had really gone, I don't think I could've ever spoken to you again."

Garv shook his head. "I wouldn't leave you alone here, Anshika. But you can say whatever you want to me, just not about my parents." His voice softened as he spoke, but there was an underlying strength in his words.

Anshika's breathing had become shallow, tears still flowing freely. She was upset, but Garv couldn't stand seeing her cry. He hugged her tightly, rubbing her back gently, trying to soothe her. But Anshika couldn't stop herself from feeling guilty. She couldn't help but cry even more.

Garv hated seeing tears, even his mother's. It irritated him to no end. But for Anshika, he couldn't stay angry for long. He began to tickle her sides, knowing exactly where her most ticklish spots were. Anshika burst into laughter, her sobs subsiding, replaced by joy.

She wrapped her arms around him, burying her face in his chest, her tears now mixed with giggles. Garv hugged her back tightly, his heart lightening with every passing moment.

Later that evening, Anshika went to meet some friends. She invited Garv to join her, but he declined. Instead, Garv spent the time cleaning the room and heading to the market. He picked up some alcohol, including a bottle of Jameson, a can of beer, and a bottle of Sula red wine, before returning to the room.

When Anshika returned, she was surprised to find Garv had not only cleaned the room but also bought alcohol. She hugged him tightly, kissed him, and they danced, their earlier fight forgotten. They promised each other they would face any problem together, no matter what.

Anshika, still frustrated by her work situation, confided in Garv about not getting the promotion she felt she deserved. Garv, always the supportive partner, listened patiently. To lighten the mood, Anshika asked for a massage, but Garv couldn't quite focus, distracted by the fact that his girlfriend was, well, *too* attractive.

Eventually, they both decided to get Garv drunk just to see how he would react. It was risky, but Anshika was curious. After starting with beer, Garv quickly moved on to the wine, but it didn't satisfy him. He mixed himself a couple of strong pegs of Jameson, each one larger than the last.

As the night wore on, Garv became more and more playful, his inhibitions melting away. They laughed, teased each other, and danced until Garv, now tipsy, began acting like a child. His usual composure was gone, replaced by an innocence Anshika had never seen before.

He started to complain about feeling hot, so he removed his clothes and lay down on the bed. Anshika laughed, trying to keep him cool and calm, but Garv, now acting almost childishly, insisted on going outside for fresh air.

"No, you're not going outside like this," Anshika laughed, stopping him from leaving the room. She took him to the balcony instead, where they shared a quiet moment, just the two of them. Eventually, Garv's exhaustion kicked in, and he begged her to take him to bed.

Anshika helped him to the bed, and they spent the rest of the evening chatting, with Anshika recording their funny conversation. She smiled as she realized that after a night of drinking, Garv had become like a child—playful, innocent, and completely lovable.

By morning, Garv kissed her awake, and Anshika, though exhausted from taking care of him the night before, couldn't help but smile at his affection. They spent the rest of the afternoon together, tangled in love and laughter.

As they scrolled through Google, looking at apartments in Gurgaon, Anshika's love for the city grew, and Garv promised to make their dream of living together a reality. Later, they went out for some shopping and fun, before Garv had to leave for Surat. Their goodbye at the hotel was bittersweet, filled with promises of a future where they would always be together.

Anshika packed his bags—because, as usual, Garv was terrible at it—and as he left for the airport, they exchanged one last kiss and hug, both longing for the day when they could be together, every night.

That flight was the worst for Garv. He couldn't figure out how he was going to handle the pressure of both CA and CFA. His plan was to clear at least one group to make things easier, but deep down, he knew he had messed up. When he landed, Pankaj was there to pick him up. Garv asked Pankaj to take him to a pan shop, though Pankaj was always the clean guy and had never touched a betel nut. Garv, however, smoked, and as they walked, he asked Pankaj to help him come up with a plan to clear both the CA and CFA exams. Garv didn't want to fail the CFA, as it was costly, and if he failed, it would be a waste of his father's money.

To cope with the stress, Garv smoked a pack of cigarettes. The weight of expectations from his parents, friends, and most of all, his better half, was bearing down on him. The pressure was immense. To relax, he started playing CS with Pankaj and Shreyansh on Sundays, and during the weekdays, every 2-3 hours of studying, he'd step out for a smoke, analyzing the remaining course and how he'd finish it. Around this time, he started meeting Rathiji, who had just returned from Kolkata. Rathiji was also stressed, dealing with the decline of his family's business due to COVID. Whenever Garv took breaks, Rathiji would hang out with him, sitting together, listening to music, and smoking cigarettes. Within a few weeks, Rathiji had also started smoking with him.

Meanwhile, Anuj was setting up his new business in textiles and was doing well—Anuj was a workaholic, always focused on his goals. Since Garv couldn't meet them individually, he asked them to meet together. Anuj and Rathiji, who had known each other from tuition back in 2015 but lost contact over the years, rekindled their friendship. Now, the three of them were inseparable.

Boys' friendships are the best thing—no matter how tough life gets, a simple phone call, and the group is there. They didn't offer solutions or advice; they just sat together, had tea, and smoked, providing comfort in silence. For Garv, they were his stress-relievers.

On the academic front, Garv studied with Nishant, Shreyansh, and Arpan, preparing for the November exams. He didn't celebrate any festivals—no Ganesh Chaturthi, no Janmashtami, nothing. Finally, the exams began. Garv's first exam was his favorite subject, but it turned out to be ridiculously lengthy—more complex than the Bhagavad Gita. Though he was confident he could handle it, as soon as he opened the paper, he knew it was going to be a challenge. The entire class was turning pages frantically, even after the reading time had ended. It was a tough 45-

50 mark paper, and Garv did his best, but he wasn't sure of his performance.

He knew that clearing this paper wasn't enough; he had to perform well in the others too to maintain the average required to pass. After the exam, frustrated, he called Pankaj to come over and stay the night, so Garv could focus on the next paper. The second paper was about the stock market, and Garv was confident that he had done well. But then came the dreaded audit and law paper. He managed average performance in both.

For Group 2, Garv asked Nishant how he was studying, and the two of them studied late into the night. Nishant, Arpan, and Shreyansh were all studying together over the phone after the first group exams, as they were all feeling exhausted. In Group 2, Garv struggled with Direct Tax since he had never worked in that field—he loved to present himself and play to his speaking strengths. The Direct Tax paper was above average, and Garv tried his best, knowing that he was on the verge of passing.

When the final exam was over, Garv was unsure about two subjects: FR (Financial Reporting) and Direct Tax, but he put them out of his mind and focused on his CFA exams. The CA final exams were done, and now he had to manage the eight subjects of CFA. Garv studied late into the night, revising what he could. On the night before his CFA exam, anxiety hit. After such long, competitive exams, he hadn't taken a proper MCQ test in a while. But Anshika calmed him down, and Garv went on to give the exam, completing it 20 minutes before time. He was confident about most of it, but the FR section still left him uncertain.

Meanwhile, Anshika, who had shifted back with her parents for work-from-home, planned to visit Gurgaon. Garv discreetly told his mom that he was going to meet Anshika and would attend an interview at a Big 4 CA firm. He met Anshika at New Delhi Station after waiting for an hour. She gave him a look—he had gained some weight, but they didn't care. They took a cab to the hotel, and Anshika had packed sandwiches made by her mother, knowing that Garv loved them. Hand in hand, they entered the hotel, but the room they had been promised was not what they received.

Anshika, furious, stormed the reception while Garv, awkward in front of the lady, suggested they book another property. But Anshika wasn't having it. She bargained hard and managed to get a suite with a balcony and a peaceful view. Relieved, they hugged each other tightly, and Garv kissed her to help her relax. They took a bath together, then went to Cyber Hub. They shopped, had dessert to celebrate her promotion, and ended the night at Social with drinks. Anshika's beauty had grown over the years, thanks to her skincare routine, and as they sat there, sipping beers and Chinese food—Anshika's favorite, though Garv wasn't a big fan of food with drinks—it was the perfect end to a stressful few weeks.

The warmth between Garv and Anshika always felt like a sanctuary from the chaos of life. In moments like this, their bond deepened, for in each other's presence, it felt as though nothing could tear them apart.

Sitting in the cozy rooftop café, with the night alive around them, Garv sensed Anshika's unease. Her smile was there, but her eyes carried the weight of unspoken thoughts. In these silent exchanges, they understood each other better than words ever could.

Anshika broke the silence, her voice carrying the vulnerability that had been hidden beneath her calm demeanor. "You know how much I love you, Baccha," she said softly, her gaze lingering on him, as if searching for something.

"I know," Garv replied, his voice steady, without a hint of doubt. "I never doubted your love for me." He took her hands in his, feeling the warmth and reassurance in their touch. "And no matter what happens, I'll always be here for you."

She let out a sigh, her fears finally spilling out. Her heart, torn between the love she felt for him and the pressures from her family, weighed heavily on her. Yet, despite the turmoil within her, she found solace in Garv's unwavering presence.

"I'm scared, Garv," she admitted, the words a mix of frustration and worry. "I love you, but there's this whole other world I can't escape. My family, their expectations... I don't know how to handle it."

Garv listened intently, understanding the depth of her conflict. His gaze softened, and though his own challenges loomed large, he knew this moment was not about him. "Anshika," he began, his voice calm, "when you need me, I will always be here. Whatever you face, we'll face it together. I'm not going anywhere."

She met his gaze, the vulnerability in her eyes slowly replaced with trust. She knew, deep down, that no matter how much the world tried to pull them apart, they had something that no one could take away: each other.

"I don't care what the world says," Garv continued, squeezing her hands gently. "What matters is us. You and me. And I'll always be here, no matter what."

Anshika felt the weight of her worries lift slightly as she held onto Garv's words, knowing they were true. They didn't need to fight the world—they just needed to keep fighting for each other.

The rest of the evening passed in laughter, teasing, and shared glances that spoke volumes. When they returned to their hotel room, the weight of the world seemed a little lighter. In that moment, with all their challenges, they had each other. And that, Garv knew, was everything.

Anshika knew Garv loved her unconditionally, yet a sense of restlessness had taken over her. She asked him, her voice laced with a mix of concern and curiosity, "Garv, what if one day I get into an accident and forget everything—forget even you?"

Garv didn't hesitate, his gaze unwavering. "If that happens, I'll have your two best friends speak to your parents, and I'll be there for you. To take care of you, at least."

"But what about love, Baccha?" Anshika's voice faltered, her eyes searching his. "Will you be able to love me the same way? Will you still want me?"

Garv's expression softened, his love for her clear in his words. "Have I ever compared my love to yours? No. I love you in my own way, Anshika. And in return, all I want is your love. I don't need an exact measure of it, just you—mine, until my last breath."

Her voice trembled as she spoke again, "But if I can't fight for us... if I'm too scared to go against my family, will you look after yourself? Will you be okay?"

Garv's heart ached at the thought, but he kept his composure. He ordered more drinks, needing something to steady his mind. As the drinks arrived, he excused himself to grab ice cream for both of them, his hand gently holding hers as he returned. "Anshika, promise me something," he said, his voice raw with emotion. "Promise me you will fight for us. It won't be easy. It might take months... but don't lose hope. If you do, don't ever look back, because once you do, I won't know how to handle it. I can't lose you." He paused, his eyes moistening as he spoke the words that had been weighing on him. "You are the reason I'm still standing. You give me purpose, a reason to fight through my failures."

Anshika, deeply moved, squeezed his hands tighter. They had been through so much, and yet, they were still here—together. "I'll never betray your trust, Garv. I promise," she whispered, her voice steady, but her heart was full of doubts.

Garv's eyes searched hers, trying to understand the depth of her fears, but his love for her outweighed any uncertainty. "I trust you," he said, more to himself than to her. "No matter what, we'll get through this. This is just a hard time... and it will pass."

They held hands, silent but resolute, as they left the café. Back at the hotel, the tension between them was palpable. Garv hugged her tightly, kissing her forehead, before asking her to change. He needed space to clear his head, to sort through the emotions swirling within him. He sat in the balcony, lit another cigarette, and tried to breathe through the unease.

Anshika, knowing how much Garv hated his habit, approached him silently. She kissed him, and as she pulled back, he instinctively withdrew, the taste of smoke lingering on his lips. "I know it's bad for you," she said softly, her fingers brushing the cigarette from his hand. "But don't let it come between us."

He smiled faintly, tossing the cigarette away and turning to her. She sat on his lap, wrapping her arms around him. In that moment, the world outside disappeared. It was just the two of them—promises made and hearts intertwined.

The night that followed was unlike any other. Their passion was fierce, raw, and beautiful, a silent understanding passing between them. No words were needed; their bodies spoke everything they felt for one another. Wrapped in each other's warmth, they slept soundly despite the cold winter night.

Morning came too soon. Garv kissed Anshika awake, the soft press of his lips sending a wave of warmth through her. They bathed, got dressed, and prepared to leave. Anshika packed his bag, and they left for the train station. Garv held her hand tightly, not wanting to let go.

In the cab, the driver tried to make small talk, trolling politics, but Garv, ever calm, remained quiet. Anshika flashed him a reassuring smile, sensing his mood. When they arrived at the station, Garv carried their bags, walking her to the platform where her train was waiting.

"Come with me to Chandigarh?" Anshika asked, her voice hopeful yet resigned.

Garv hesitated but nodded. "Of course, Baccha. I'd love to." But he knew that after dropping her off, he couldn't go with her. Her father would be there to pick her up, and he couldn't intrude.

"Never mind," she said gently, her voice soft with understanding. "There's no need."

They shared a quiet moment, standing together in the cold, waiting for her train to depart. Garv held her close, and they whispered their goodbyes just as the train began to pull away. He watched until she was out of sight, feeling the sting of separation.

Once she was gone, they called each other, the distance between them never feeling as far as it was. "I love you," Garv said, his voice thick with emotion.

"I love you too," Anshika replied, her words like a promise.

After the call, Garv made his way to meet his old friend, Tushar. The two had been friends since their CA tuition days, and it had been a year since they had caught up. Tushar, who was living in Noida and setting up his business, greeted Garv with enthusiasm. They went to a local bar, cracked open beers, and talked about life, love, and everything in between.

"Boys never really have the answers when it comes to emotions," Garv joked, trying to lighten the mood. "But we're always there for each other, even if we don't know what to say."

Tushar laughed, agreeing wholeheartedly. "We may not have solutions, but we can make each other laugh, at least."

Garv dropped Tushar off after a night of casual conversation and headed to the airport. Meanwhile, Anshika had reached home, and they spent their flight talking about their time together. Their words were sweet, almost cheesy, but it felt right—like a reaffirmation of their bond.

As Garv boarded his flight, he couldn't shake the feeling that something was about to change, but what, exactly, he didn't know yet. The trip to Gurgaon was over, but the journey of their relationship was only beginning.

Anshika's voice broke through the silence, a soothing yet worried tone creeping in as she spoke to Garv. "I know things have been tough for you lately, and I can sense the frustration in your voice, but you don't have to carry this alone, Garv."

Garv, sitting in the same quiet room, leaned back into his chair, hands gripping the edge, feeling the weight of his emotions pressing down harder with each passing second. He had always been the one to take charge, to figure things out himself, but now he felt lost—caught in a cycle of self-doubt and failure.

"I just want to be someone who doesn't need to be fixed, Anshika," he murmured, his voice barely audible over the distance that had grown between them. "I've tried so many things… but it just feels like nothing ever works out. I'm stuck."

Anshika's soft but firm response came through the phone, "You're not stuck, Garv. It's okay to feel this way. It doesn't make you any less strong or capable. Everyone faces their own battles. We all have our moments of doubt. You don't have to have everything figured out right now. Just take it step by step. I'm here for you."

Garv's chest tightened, the vulnerability he had buried so deep inside finally bubbling up to the surface. Anshika's words were a balm, but they weren't enough to stop the flood of emotions rushing through him. He had been fighting so hard, trying to keep it all together, trying to be the person she believed in. But deep down, Garv knew he was breaking, and he couldn't keep hiding it any longer.

"I… I don't want to disappoint you," he confessed, his voice shaking ever so slightly. "I've failed so many times. And now I don't even know if I can keep going."

Anshika was quiet for a moment, as if gathering the right words, then spoke with a calm, unwavering certainty. "Garv, your failures don't define you. The fact that you keep trying, that you don't give up—that's what matters. And I'm not here to judge you for your mistakes or to ask you to be perfect. I'm here to stand beside you. Always."

For a brief moment, Garv let himself believe it. He let himself feel the weight of her words, letting them settle into the parts of him that felt most broken. She had always been his strength, the one person who knew how to reach through his walls and pull him out of the darkest moments. But now, there was still something gnawing at him—something he couldn't ignore any longer.

"I don't know if I can keep doing this, Anshika. I'm exhausted, and I'm scared," he admitted, his voice breaking. "What if I can't make things work? What if I lose you in the process?"

Anshika's voice softened, but there was a firmness behind it that reminded Garv of her unwavering love. "You're not going to lose me, Garv. But you have to take care of yourself first. Don't lose yourself in trying to fix everything. Take a step back. Breathe. And remember that no matter what happens, you're not alone."

Garv sat there for a long while after their conversation ended, the weight of her words lingering in the air. The storm of emotions didn't pass immediately, but for the first time in what felt like forever, he allowed himself to believe that there might be a way out of the darkness. Maybe things didn't have to be perfect. Maybe he could just be, for once, without the pressure of being everything to everyone.

He didn't have all the answers, and he didn't know what the future held, but for the first time in a long while, Garv let himself trust that he didn't have to go through it all alone.

Garv's heart raced as he heard Anshika's voice, her sobs echoing through the phone. He felt the weight of her words crushing him—he knew something was wrong, but to hear her say it aloud, to hear her say it could be cancer, shattered his world.

He did his best to comfort her, trying to keep his own emotions in check, though inside, he was a storm of helplessness. He promised her that everything would be fine, that it was nothing serious. But as the conversation ended, he couldn't shake the feeling that everything was hanging by a thread. His world was teetering, and the person who meant everything to him was facing something so terrifying, something he couldn't control.

Days passed, and Garv found himself in a state of constant emotional turmoil. His frustration with Anshika's dedication to her interview had turned into anger, but deep down, he knew it was his own insecurities and fears manifesting. She had to focus on her future, just as he had to focus on his own struggles. But the reality of his own failure—his broken confidence, his inability to balance his dreams and his love for her—gnawed at him.

The phone call with Anshika about her health was the breaking point. Garv, unable to bear the thought of losing her, sought solace in a temple far from home. Sitting in silence, he prayed fervently, desperately wishing for the strength to deal with whatever news came. His tears were unstoppable, as he clung to memories of Anshika, her childhood photos he kept close. In that moment, the pain of his failures seemed to fade, replaced by the overwhelming fear of losing the person he loved more than anything.

Returning home, he confided in his mother, sharing his fears and promises. He had no idea what the future would hold, but he knew one thing: if Anshika needed him, he would be there, no matter the cost.

Later that night, when Anshika called him again, asking him to promise that he would move on with his life, no matter what happened to her, Garv's heart broke even more. He could feel the weight of her words. He knew she was trying to protect him, to ensure he wouldn't fall apart if the worst happened. But Garv couldn't make that promise—not without her.

And so, he promised himself that he would stand by her, whatever the outcome. He wouldn't let her face this alone. His love for her was unshakable, and as he whispered words of comfort into the phone, he vowed to be by her side, no matter how hard it would get.

"Baccha, I promise you one thing," Garv said, his voice trembling with emotion, "If the reports come back with bad news, till your last breath and last fight, I will be with you. And I won't just be on a call. I'll come to Chandigarh, to your home, and live with you. If I have to beg in front of your parents, I'm ready to do that. But I'll be there with you, bringing all my books and stuff. I'll study there and work in Chandigarh itself."

"Why do you love me so much, Garv? Tell me," Anshika's voice quivered.

"Baccha," he said softly, "I got two things from my father—anger and the ability to maintain relationships. In that, I learned love too. I know both of them, just at the extreme level."

"Aap pakka mere paas rahenge phir, what about the business plan you made, the one you argued with me about?" she asked.

"Remember one thing, Baccha, careers can change and mold, but the one person you want to spend your entire life with—you can't change that. It's not just about loyalty," Garv answered firmly.

"You know I'll never compromise on my career, Garv."

"Have I ever told you that you have to? I'm ready to be your house husband if that's what you want. And when you told me we might have to shift to the US, my stand was simple—give me some time, and I'll be there. Wherever you go, I'll walk with you. But never let your ego get in the way, because if that happens, I'll lose myself," Garv said, his voice steady.

"Pray the reports come back negative. But honestly, if something goes wrong, I'll die happy because I'll know you'll be there with me. And I know how much you love me," Anshika said, her voice barely a whisper.

Garv's eyes welled up with tears, but he cut the call quickly, unable to show his vulnerability. He rang her back normally, trying to sound composed. "In cancer, not everyone dies, okay? If the reports are bad, we'll fight it together. I won't let you give up," he reassured her.

As the emotional chaos surrounded him, Garv returned to his exams in May 2022, his third attempt. He pushed himself through it all, but once again, he failed. The results were a blow to his already fragile patience. When the scores came out, Garv didn't want to face his family, especially his father. He told his mom he would be back in a few hours and asked her not to call him. In despair, he went to Dumas Beach, smoked a pack of cigarettes, and gathered the courage to tell his dad that he would no longer pursue a degree that was draining him.

While he was struggling with his own failures, three positive things happened: Anshika got into Amazon, she received her "Coding Diwa" award, and his brother secured a seat at VIT Vellore. He felt a momentary relief and joy for them, particularly Anshika. He had always known the effort she put into her coding competitions, and when she finally succeeded, he felt an immense sense of pride. Though his exams had been a mess, seeing her grow was a source of happiness for him.

When she complained that he didn't seem happy for her achievement, Garv, not one to easily express emotions, sent her a box of macarons and pizza. He may not have known how to show his happiness, but he was deeply proud of her. The success of her hard work was the sweetest music to his heart.

Garv also felt a sense of pride in his brother's admission to VIT Vellore. He knew that his work in getting his brother into a good college was finally done. His father had been disappointed with Garv's own IIT-JEE scores, but Garv had taken a stand, reminding him that not everyone can get into that college. He wanted his brother to be content, not burdened by expectations. Garv didn't want him to feel the same pressure he had, and seeing his brother happy made Garv forget his own pain, at least for a while.

Then came a grand wedding at home. His cousin was getting married in Udaipur, and the entire family gathered to celebrate. For the first time, Garv had a drink with his father, his uncle, and his brother-in-law. By this point, Garv had gained weight, his physical activities having taken a backseat due to the stress of his degree. The pressures of his life—his failing exams, his family's expectations—had driven him to stress eating and smoking.

At the wedding's Sangeet night, when Garv saw the expensive whiskey at the bar, something inside him broke free. It felt like a once-in-a-lifetime opportunity, and he drank around 18 Patiala pegs with his favorite cousin and other relatives. For the first time in years, Garv danced his heart out on the dance floor for over two hours, something he hadn't done in a long time.

As his cousins complimented his moves, one of them teased him about his weight, warning that he wouldn't find a beautiful girl to marry if he didn't lose some pounds. Laughing it off, Garv told them about Anshika and their future plans. He was just waiting for the right time to make it happen. Everyone raised their glasses, toasting to the future.

The next day, Garv sat down with his cousin, Garima Di, to discuss his options. He knew she had been through the same journey, having dropped her CA path at one point. Garima, understanding his confusion, suggested several courses that could be completed in one to two years, tailored to Garv's interests. He took her advice seriously, feeling a glimmer of hope for the first time in a while. Together, they enjoyed the remainder of the wedding, but Garv's mind was already consumed with the uncertainty of his future.

When he returned home, he found out that his buddy, Rathiji, had gone through a breakup. Rathiji had been struggling with it for days, and Garv, despite his own burdens, stayed by his side. No matter the time—whether it was late at night or early in the morning—Garv answered his calls. It took Rathiji about 15 to 20 days to start feeling somewhat better, but he still wasn't fully back to normal. Eventually, he confessed that his ex had cheated on him. Garv was furious, not because of the betrayal, but because he knew how loyal Rathiji had been to her. Rathiji had supported her through some of the toughest times in her life, including the struggles her business had faced during COVID. But when things got tough for him, when he couldn't keep up with material gifts or offer the support she wanted, she turned her back on him. Garv, though angry, refrained from any revenge—after all, the woman was his old school friend. Instead, he blocked her, reinforcing his belief that loyalty and friendship were above all else.

Garv had already witnessed the heartbreak of two of his friends in the past, both of whom had been betrayed by women they loved. It was one of the hardest things to experience, and Garv couldn't quite understand what drove them to make such decisions. It made him question how difficult it was to read people's true intentions. But life went on.

After dealing with the emotional mess from the breakup, Garv brought his CA exam results to his mom. He admitted to her that he didn't have much energy left, not just physically but mentally. His brother, who had witnessed Garv's sleepless nights and stress, stood by him, offering quiet support. He knew the toll the exams had taken on Garv, who had been burning the candle at both ends, smoking to cope with the pressure.

When his father came home, Garv's mom sat him down to discuss Garv's situation. Garv's father called him out into the hall, and for the first time, Garv lashed out. He had kept his frustrations bottled up for so long, but now, the anger poured out. "I told you from the beginning that I'm not interested in CA! You pushed me into this, but I've seen my cousins fail at it. It's not that I didn't try, but sometimes enough is enough. You just want me to follow your path because all your contacts are CAs, but that doesn't mean I should be one too!" Garv's words hit hard, and he pressed the wrong button when he mentioned taking out a loan and using his savings from investments and his small business to balance things out. The words were harsh, and though his father had never reacted emotionally before, this time, he simply took a deep breath and walked away, locking himself in his room. Garv could hear his father's tears through the walls. No father wants to hear that their child feels like they've ruined their own future.

Garv's mother, upset with his outburst, told him to leave the house. His grandmother tried to intervene, but Garv was already at the door, emotionally exhausted. He called Anshika, hoping to find solace in her words. What he wanted to hear from her was that she would wait for him. He needed her support more than ever, as his life seemed to be falling apart. Anshika, despite being busy with her successful career, understood. "I'll wait for you, Garv," she said. "But I'm moving to Bangalore next year, and I won't be able to live alone there. It's not going to be easy, but I'll try to make it work."

That night, Garv lay awake in torment. He had made many emotional decisions in the past that had only led to pain. He knew he needed to take a step back, think things through, and talk to his father again. The next day, when his father returned from work, Garv decided to give his last attempt at the CA exams. His father, ever the pragmatist, told him that if he could dedicate himself fully, he would get one last chance to prove himself. "Give us a gift for our 25th Anniversary on February 1st, 2023," his father said, and Garv agreed. Though the road ahead was still difficult, Garv had made a decision.

Alongside his CA preparations, Garv also enrolled for the CPA exams, a course that could be completed within two years. It was a costly venture, but he needed a backup plan. Just as Garv was beginning to focus on his future, a new crisis struck—his father's brother, Garv's uncle, suffered a brain stroke and was left in a critical condition. The family's stress levels skyrocketed, with Garv's father rushing to Ahmedabad to care for his brother. Meanwhile, Garv took on the responsibility of managing things at home.

In August, when his brother joined college, Garv decided to accompany him, as his father was still occupied with hospital duties. Garv had always been close to his brother and wanted to be there for him. But Anshika wasn't happy with Garv's decision. She felt frustrated that Garv was always getting pulled into family matters, and it was taking a toll on his studies. She didn't understand why he couldn't focus on his future. It reminded Garv of the time when her own family had been in turmoil—when her Nana had fallen ill, and her mother had been the only one looking after him, while Anshika argued that it was her Mama's responsibility to help. Garv had always supported her, but now, he needed her to understand that his family needed him too

Garv's journey was filled with immense emotional turmoil, personal challenges, and moments of growth, despite the intense struggles he faced. The turmoil from his CA exams, the stress from family pressures, his friends' relationships, and his own aspirations created a complex landscape that was difficult to navigate.

When Garv failed his CA exams again, his breaking point arrived. He felt defeated, exhausted from the constant battles with his own self-confidence and the relentless expectations placed on him. But as he took some time to reflect on his future, he realized that staying on a path he didn't believe in would only keep him stuck. This led him to make the bold decision to pursue something different—something that aligned more with his passions and strengths.

Despite all the setbacks, Garv found solace in the success of those around him. Anshika's hard work and eventual recognition at Amazon inspired him. His brother's success in getting into VIT Vellore also gave him a sense of pride, knowing that he'd played a significant role in guiding him. These small victories were a reminder that success isn't always defined by traditional paths.

The wedding in Udaipur marked a turning point in Garv's life. It allowed him to temporarily escape the pressure, let loose, and enjoy the simple pleasures of life. His dance moves, his laughter with family, and the heartfelt conversations with his cousin Garima helped him realize that life isn't all about achieving a specific goal—sometimes, it's about finding moments of joy and connection.

When his friend Rathiji faced a heartbreak, Garv's loyalty and sense of duty to his friends came to the forefront. His understanding and patience during Rathiji's tough time demonstrated his deep capacity for empathy and support. Despite the heartache, Garv knew that loyalty was a value that could not be compromised, even when it came to his friends' relationships.

At the end of the day, Garv decided to take the advice of his cousin and explore options outside of CA. His resolve to look into foreign courses showed that he was not afraid to change direction. He was ready to carve out his own path, even if it meant taking risks and stepping away from a future planned by others.

Garv had witnessed two of his friends go through heartbreaking breakups in the past, and each time, it had left him shaken. It was painful to see how these girls, whom he knew well, had made decisions that were beyond his understanding. In both cases, he couldn't quite grasp what had driven them to break his friends' hearts. But now, after all the chaos surrounding his exam results, Garv sat down with all the quotations for his courses and took them to his mother. With his usual calm demeanor, he told her that he didn't have the strength to continue sacrificing his self-confidence any longer. His brother, who had witnessed Garv's sleepless nights of studying and knew just how much stress he had been under, supported him quietly.

When Garv's dad finally returned home, his mother had already discussed his plans with him. His father called him into the living room and, despite the frustration that had built up between them, told Garv that failures were a part of life. He reminded him that he had never taught him to give up. But Garv, his patience worn thin, couldn't hold it in anymore. He snapped. "From the beginning, I've told you I'm not interested in this course. I've seen our cousins suffer, and it's not that I haven't tried. Sometimes enough is enough," Garv shouted. "You wanted me to do CA because all your contacts are CA. But that doesn't mean I should follow that path."

His words were harsh, but in that moment, Garv couldn't hold back. "I will take the loan, or I'll use the savings I've made from investments and some of my business earnings," he said, his voice cold. It was rude, he knew that. But his father, who had always remained calm and detached in these moments, didn't react emotionally. Instead, he simply nodded and walked away, locking himself in his room. Garv broke down, tears flooding his eyes. No father wants to hear that his son has failed to meet expectations. It hurt Garv more than he was willing to admit.

His mother, witnessing the breakdown, told him to leave. His grandmother tried to stop him, but Garv, in a moment of overwhelming emotion, walked out anyway. He needed to talk to someone, and so, he called Anshika. He told her everything—the failure, his decision to go abroad for further studies, and his plan to move on from the CA. He needed to hear her say she would wait for him, but Anshika, who had her own demanding career, couldn't make such promises easily. Still, she said, "I'll try to wait for you, Garv. But I'm moving to Bangalore next year, and I can't live alone there." Garv's heart felt like it was breaking again, but he didn't say anything. "Just sleep on it," he told her. "I need to think too."

That night, Garv wrestled with his thoughts. He knew he had made mistakes in the past—emotional decisions that had led him here. The next day, he decided he would talk to his father again. When his dad came home from work, they had a long discussion. Garv's father finally relented, telling him that he could take one last attempt at CA and promised to support him if he gave it his all. "Give us a gift on our 25th Anniversary, Garv. Make us proud," his dad said.

It was a relief, but Garv's path forward wasn't without challenges. His dad's brother had suffered a brain stroke and had been left in a critical condition. The family was on edge, and Garv's father had to travel to Ahmedabad to be with him, leaving Garv to manage everything back home in Surat. It was stressful, especially with his brother starting college in August, but Garv, despite his exhaustion, chose to take care of things.

But Anshika wasn't happy about it. She was frustrated that Garv was so involved with his family matters when he needed to focus on his studies. She couldn't understand why Garv kept putting his family's needs above his own, just as she had done with her own family when her Nana was sick. Garv, though, had a different perspective. He told her, "If you found yourself in the same situation, and your brother was out, would we not take care of your family?" Anshika, always stubborn, avoided a fight with her mother but couldn't reconcile with the way Garv was handling things. She didn't treat her Nana as well as she should have, and Garv remained silent, unable to react to the ongoing drama in his life.

Life was a constant struggle for Garv. His personal battles, family pressures, and the emotional weight of his decisions made it difficult for him to see any clear way out. But in the middle of it all, Garv knew one thing for sure: he had to keep going, even if everything around him seemed to be falling apart.

Through all the chaos, Garv learned the importance of taking ownership of his life. He realized that it was okay to fail, to change his mind, and to take risks. His journey was not about perfection but about learning and evolving, always with the support of those who cared for him.

Garv's story is a testament to the strength of resilience, friendship, and the courage to forge your own path despite the odds.

In October, Anshika asked Garv to come to Bangalore to meet her. She was visiting the city to look for a place to stay, as she was planning to move there in a few months. Garv, however, told her he couldn't make it. His exams were approaching, and his family was dealing with a lot of chaos. But Anshika, with a hint of frustration, reminded him that he had found time to drop his brother off at college and attend to other family matters. She got upset and told him, "Tell your mom that you need a break, and you'll go meet me in Bangalore. It will help you focus better on your studies."

Garv felt hurt by her words. She didn't seem to understand the pressure he was under, the emotional turmoil he was experiencing. But she kept pushing, and her friends told him it would be fine to go for just two days. In an impulsive decision, Garv fabricated a story. He created a fake email saying that he had been invited for an interview with one of the Big Four firms in Bangalore, a position he had already applied for, but the interview had been online. Without giving it a second thought, he booked a flight from Vadodara to Bangalore.

He told his mom not to mention anything to his dad, as his father was going to be away for a few days. Garv was low on money, having invested most of it, but he knew who to turn to. He called Rathiji and explained his situation, promising to repay him as soon as he could withdraw money from the market.

The next morning, Garv flew to Vadodara, where he learned that the airport would open only at 5 AM, and his flight was at 5:45 AM. To kill time, he wandered the night bazaar and grabbed a packet of cigarettes. He called Anshika to talk, but their conversation was far from pleasant. Garv let it slide because, after all, they were both intoxicated.

"Hey Anshika, talk to me now. I'm sitting here all alone," Garv said.

"You're meeting friends, aren't you? You're gonna meet them after such a long time. Let me party with them first, please," Anshika replied.

"Seriously, I'm not stopping you from partying, but can't we talk for a bit? I'm sitting alone on the road right now. Who else can I call? Tell me," Garv said.

Anshika's friend, Chetna, chimed in, "Garv, you're coming tomorrow, right? Let Anshika enjoy tonight with us. We'll talk later."

Garv responded, "I'm going back to Surat, Chetna. But I'm just asking to chat for a while."

"Yeah, go back to Surat. But you won't get what Anshika can give you here," Chetna teased.

They both laughed.

"If you wanted what you're talking about, I wouldn't have gone through all this trouble to fool my family just to meet you. I could've just used my contacts in Surat, booked a hotel, and it would've been cheaper. Trust me," Garv said, half joking.

He then ended the call and switched off his phone. Garv ordered some Maggi and tea to pass the time. He ended up talking to the vendor, who turned out to be a friendly Gujarati man. Garv didn't realize how quickly time passed, and before he knew it, it was 3:30 AM. He switched his phone back on and saw a message from Anshika: "Sorry, good night."

Garv felt a pang of sadness. Why was it that no matter how hard he tried to give, he always seemed to be the one to make more effort? Why did it feel like girls assumed that boys just wanted physical intimacy?

From his own experience, Garv knew that most boys, deep down, simply yearn for the simplicity of a comforting embrace. They just wanted to rest their heads on the laps of their loved ones, seeking solace in the quiet warmth of a hug, a momentary escape from the whirlwind of their lives. It's strange, he thought, how as boys grow older, they no longer seek the comfort of their mother's lap or the same affection they once did as children. It's as if something shifts, and they begin to carry their burdens alone. Perhaps it's a rite of passage, or maybe it's just how things happen. But Garv was sure of one thing—if a boy doesn't have that unconditional love, the kind his mother gives, then nothing else compares. There was no love like that.

When it came to relationships, Garv had always believed that physical intimacy was secondary. Sure, it could be arranged, but it was the emotional connection that truly mattered. Physical closeness, in his experience, just made you more committed. And he couldn't help but laugh at the unpredictability of relationships. Especially when it came to understanding a girl's emotions. That was something no one could really predict. He had joked with his friends, saying that on his worst days, he'd trust playing poker more than getting involved with a girl. After all, losing money was bearable—but losing emotions? That was a different kind of pain, one that lingered far longer.

Finally, Garv arrived in Bangalore. The city welcomed him with its perfect weather and bustling energy. It was the kind of place that made you feel alive. Nishant, his friend from the firm, had moved to Bangalore after clearing CA and had promised to show him around. Nishant led him to Sheru's house, where they met Anshika once again, along with Sheru, Chetna, and her cousin from Gurgaon. After the Chandigarh trip, it felt good to reconnect with everyone. They sat down for breakfast, shared a little chit-chat, and caught up on life.

Anshika, though, could tell something was off. She knew Garv was still affected by the incident from the night before. There was an unspoken rule between them—no fights in front of others. So, Garv kept his calm, masking his emotions, though the weight on his heart didn't vanish. They decided to head to the hotel nearby, the one they had reserved for their stay.

Once they were in the room, Anshika wrapped her arms around Garv, pulling him close. "Just relax," she whispered, sensing the turmoil inside him. Garv had a lot on his plate, and the incident from last night was just another layer to his stress. But when he looked at Anshika, something inside him softened. With her in his arms, he could momentarily let go of everything else. He hugged her tighter, as if her touch was the only thing that could ground him. They shared a kiss, slow and tender, and for a brief moment, Garv forgot about the world outside.

A little while later, Garv stepped out to get something for Anshika. He returned with beers and Bacardi Cranberry, hoping to lighten the mood. He'd already given her a gift earlier, a little something to mark her first time in Bangalore. He'd also asked his friend Akhil, a friend of Devik's who he had met online, to bring over some drinks for Anshika and her friends, as they had reason to celebrate. Anshika had recently landed a job at Amazon, and Garv was beyond proud of her.

However, Garv hadn't quite realized that his choice of whisky might not be to their liking. Anshika and her friends teased him for picking the wrong kind of drink, and Garv, though slightly embarrassed, took it all in stride, laughing along with them. It wasn't the kind of thing to ruin the mood—especially not when they were together, enjoying each other's company.

Anshika and Garv spent the evening partying, but Anshika could sense that something was off. Garv was quieter than usual, his mind clearly preoccupied. He had always been the steady one, but tonight, he was feeling something he had never experienced before: insecurity. It was strange, he thought, how he had always been the one to encourage Anshika to step out of her shell and embrace the world. And now, as she blossomed into the extroverted person she was becoming, he couldn't help but feel a twinge of jealousy. For the first time, he felt like he was losing control of the situation. The tension of his own life—the pressure from the interviews he had given, his uncertain future—was beginning to weigh heavily on him.

Anshika noticed the change in him immediately. Without a word, she pulled him into a tight embrace, holding him as if to say, "I'm here, don't worry." And just like that, the world seemed to quiet down for Garv. They spent the next two days in the hotel, wrapped in each other's arms. It was the kind of emotional comfort that only love could bring. They talked, they laughed, and yes, they even got lost in thoughts of past fights, but it was in these moments of vulnerability that Garv realized how much he treasured this connection.

For Garv, it was more than just love—it was a sense of security he never thought he would find. He had never imagined that someone could love him the way Anshika did. She treated him like her baby, with such tenderness and care, and Garv knew deep down that this was the kind of love he had always longed for. The kind that made him want to fight for it, no matter the odds. He had always promised himself he would never give up on love, and now, more than ever, he was willing to give it his all.

As the days passed, they shared their hopes and worries. Garv opened up about the interviews he had given, his uncertain career path, and the challenges he was facing. They found solace in each other's presence, and for a while, the world outside the hotel room didn't matter. It was just them—lost in their little bubble, finding peace in each other's arms.

By Sunday morning, it was time to check out. They left the hotel and headed to Sheru's house. Sheru had already arranged for the maid to cook lunch for them, and Garv, feeling both grateful and content, sat down to enjoy the meal. However, there was something that still weighed on Garv's mind. He needed to meet Akhil, the friend who had helped deliver the gift to Anshika earlier. He didn't want to take his friendship for granted, so he told Anshika he would be back in two hours.

Anshika, though, was a little upset. She didn't like the idea of Garv leaving, but Garv was firm. "I'll be back in two hours," he reassured her. Sheru, sensing the tension, quietly told Anshika, "He's just meeting a friend, it's no big deal."

For Garv, friendship meant everything. It was something he had always valued deeply. When he arrived at Sheru's house, he was met with teasing remarks. "This is the friend who came all the way to Bangalore Airport just to drop you off? Seriously?" they joked. But Garv just smiled. Boys' friendships, he knew, were different from others. It didn't matter how much time passed or how little they spoke. There were no expectations, no standards to meet—just the unspoken understanding that they would always have each other's backs.

After his time with Akhil, enjoying beers and thanking him for the gift delivery, Garv returned to Sheru's house. As soon as he stepped inside, Anshika wrapped her arms around him, her hold tight and warm. "You need to finish your CA quickly and come live with me," she said softly, her voice filled with concern. She was finding it hard to manage everything on her own, and she wanted him by her side.

Garv, always striving to give his best, nodded. "I'm trying, Anshika. I promise, I'm doing my best."

As the day drew to a close, their emotions took over. The connection between them deepened, and what followed was an intimate moment. They kissed with a passion that had been building for days. Without a word, they locked the door to Sheru's room, craving the privacy that allowed them to truly be themselves. The world outside didn't matter. In that room, it was just them, holding on to each other, needing each other more than ever.

Later that night, Garv's flight to Pune loomed. The direct flights to Gujarat were too expensive, so he had booked a flight to Pune, planning to take a train to Bombay and then to Surat. As he prepared to leave, he knew that this trip was just another chapter in their long-distance love story—one that, despite the challenges, would continue to grow stronger.

Here's the passage rewritten in a more polished novel style:

The travel had been exhausting, but Garv knew that his trip, though draining, was worth it. As soon as he reached the station, his friend Rathiji was there to pick him up. They shared a smoke together, catching up on life and love. Rathiji had just come out of a difficult breakup, while Garv was doing everything in his power to save his own relationship. They spoke about their struggles, offering each other support in silence, both understanding how hard it was to face the weight of expectations.

Once home, Garv gathered his books and headed over to his bua's place. He was determined to make the most of the next few weeks, but the pressure of his CA exams was beginning to take its toll. Garv had already decided to cut his sleep down to four hours a night, pushing through the fatigue and exhaustion. As the exams approached, he barely slept at all, reducing his rest to just two hours a night. His body was running on empty, fueled only by cigarettes and Red Bull, and by the time the final exam arrived, he was completely drained.

The last exam day, in particular, was the hardest. Garv felt like he could barely keep his eyes open, and the exhaustion hit him so hard that he collapsed on the road while walking back from a smoke break with Rathiji and his buddy Sonu. At first, they laughed, but when Garv didn't stir, panic set in. They rushed over to him, pouring water on him and slapping him lightly to wake him up. He had even peed himself, which made the situation worse in their eyes. But after several minutes, Garv stirred, groggy but awake. His first thought wasn't of his health, but of the syllabus he still had to cover before the next exam. Despite everything, he was determined to push forward.

He sat down at a nearby shop, ordered tea and another cigarette, trying to calm his nerves while Sonu sat beside him. Garv had always been someone who refused to show weakness, even when it seemed like he was falling apart. He never let anyone drive him, even in the toughest times, not even after surgeries. He drove himself because he didn't want anyone to see him as fragile.

By the time they returned to his bua's home, Garv's family had heard about what happened and was understandably worried. But Garv was too focused on what lay ahead to think much of it. He took a quick bath, tried to relax, and then called Anshika, explaining everything. "Don't worry," he told her, "I'm going to sleep now, and I'll text you when I wake up." His mother insisted on staying near him, and he finally settled down to sleep at 9:00 PM. After a short rest, he woke up at 12:30 AM, texted Anshika, and they shared a video call. Anshika kissed him through the screen, and Garv, exhausted but relieved, told her to go to sleep while he continued his revision. He knew that his best shot at doing well on the exam was to stay focused, even if it meant sacrificing his well-being.

That night, he ordered more Red Bulls, pushing himself into a second wind. The exhaustion was overwhelming, but he managed to push through. Garv knew he needed rest for the important scoring subjects, and he was determined not to let his anxiety over the Direct Tax paper ruin his chances. When the exams finally concluded, he felt drained but satisfied, certain that he had given his best.

A few days later, his Garv bhaiya from the firm arranged an interview for him at a bank, which had a direct connection to the national head. When Garv met the man, he was stunned by his presence—towering at nearly seven feet with broad shoulders and a solid physique. The national head, a retired army officer, asked only a few questions about sales and showed little interest in technicalities. "This guy isn't going to last long in a desk job," he joked, referring to Garv. And it was true—Garv wasn't someone who thrived in an office setting; he longed for independence.

Despite that, Garv took the opportunity to negotiate, using his potential sales skills to get a better package. With the help of his boss, he managed to secure a Deputy Manager grade, skipping two levels that most others would have started from. It was a small victory, but one that gave him a moment of satisfaction.

Later that night, Garv, Nikhar bhaiya, and Arpan celebrated, toasting to new beginnings. Arpan had been a source of emotional support for Garv, especially with his plans to eventually move to Bangalore. Arpan had connected with Nikhar bhaiya through Garv, showing how important relationships and networks were for the future. Garv had kept in touch with everyone from the firm, knowing that these connections would prove valuable later on.

When Garv finally returned home, he sat down with his father to discuss the offer. He was ready to accept the package, confident that sales was the right path for him. He was beginning to feel like things were finally falling into place. As Garv moved forward, his business was also starting to show promising results, further solidifying his decision to take the leap.

Not every moment in life is the same. They say time heals, but the truth is, time doesn't heal—it only forces you to live with your wounds.

Sometimes, it even throws more pain your way, either to strengthen you or break you completely.

For Garv, it felt like time was doing nothing but testing his endurance, pushing him to the edge. He had made the decision to accept the job offer, moving forward with what seemed like the right choice. Yet, deep inside, he couldn't shake the uncertainty. Despite the opportunity he had in the wholesale finance sector, dealing with builders and their funding, Garv was still unsure of his path. He didn't feel the sense of fulfillment he had hoped for.

Anshika, ever the support he needed, couldn't quite grasp the depth of his frustration. She understood his sacrifices, the relentless effort he had put into everything. But she couldn't fully understand the weight of his internal battles, the way he saw his future. To her, this job was a win, a step forward. To him, it felt like settling.

And then, the day he had been dreading arrived—the day of the results.

Garv would never forget that day. It was the day all his efforts seemed to shatter in an instant. He had passed everything, except for that one subject—the one that had destroyed his average score. He had been so close, but in the end, that one failure overshadowed everything. It crushed him. All the hopes of his family, his friends, and especially Anshika—they all hung on him. But now, they all seemed to be slipping through his fingers.

The devastation was suffocating. His father's expectations for the 25th Anniversary gift, Anshika's belief in him as her soulmate, the dreams his friends had for him—all of it came crashing down. Garv didn't know what to do with himself. He felt hollow. He wanted to cry, but his mind wouldn't let him. The internal struggle—keeping a smile on his face while silently breaking down inside—was something only those who truly knew him could comprehend. But Garv never shared that pain with anyone. His silence was the only thing keeping him from falling apart.

In an attempt to escape, he went to the beach, sitting there for hours, smoking to numb the pain. It was the worst feeling he had ever known—the desire to break down, but no tears would come. His mind refused to let him cry, even though his heart screamed for release. Garv hated himself for feeling so weak.

As he sat there, lost in his own despair, his phone rang. It was his father. The call was like a cruel reminder of everything he had been avoiding. But this time, it wasn't anger in his father's voice—it was understanding, love, and concern. His father told him that if he wanted to pursue higher studies abroad, it was okay. His happiness mattered more than anything else.

Garv didn't know how to respond. His father was offering him a way out, a chance to start fresh. But he couldn't make that decision in a moment of such turmoil. He wasn't sure of anything anymore. So he told his father he needed a few days to think it over.

For Garv, everything seemed tied to Anshika. His future, his career, his life—everything depended on her. He had spent so much of his life trying to make her happy, keeping promises, and putting her needs first. But now, he wasn't sure if that was enough. He wasn't sure if he had it in him to keep giving, especially when he wasn't sure if she understood the depth of what he was going through.

He knew love was supposed to be a two-way street. But when it came to his own feelings, he had always been blind. Love had consumed him completely. And he had seen it happen to others—the way they changed after falling in love. They adapted, they took on responsibilities, they became something else. It was true—when love hits you for the first time, it changes you. But after that, life moves into the realm of duty and responsibility.

Garv wasn't sure he was ready for that change.

That night, Anshika found herself on the verge of giving up on their relationship. It had been a rough road, and she wasn't sure if she could continue. Garv, however, had other thoughts. Calmly, he told her, "I just need 1.5 years. When the new financial year begins, I'll come to Bangalore and sort everything out." He had a plan, a way forward. They both agreed that this would be the path they would take. Garv knew that when a girl begins to give up, the journey ahead gets incredibly difficult, but he also believed that if they weathered the storm together, they could make it.

After some contemplation, Garv decided to accept the bank offer. Was it the right decision? Maybe, but only if the road ahead didn't remain so unclear. Only time would tell.

January 16, 2023—an important day for Garv and his friends. The group was buzzing with excitement because everyone knew that this breakthrough moment was crucial for his life. Before Garv's new job began in Bilimora, they decided to throw a party at Jigar's flat. Anuj, Garv, and Rathiji went there, and it turned out to be one of the best nights they'd ever had. The music was loud, the drinks were flowing, and Rathiji, the sweet guy, had a little too much to drink. As usual, the boys took care of him, but not without teasing him mercilessly first.

Later that night, after everyone was drunk, they made their way to the terrace, lying on the floor and gazing up at the starry sky. After a few minutes, Rathiji started feeling unwell, so Jigar took him downstairs. Anuj and Garv were left alone. As they lay there, Garv opened up to Anuj, telling him how he was feeling—how he'd lost all his self-confidence and how uncertain he was about his future. It was a raw conversation, and Anuj, as always, offered him a listening ear.

"Golu, you know, a few years ago I left home," Anuj confessed, breaking the silence.

"Bhai, how could I forget? You left and left me in the lurch," Garv replied with a grin.

"I was lost, Golu," Anuj continued. "Everything seemed wrong. I didn't know what I was doing. College life was chaos, and then an opportunity came up. I took it, thinking I'd figure things out later."

Garv listened intently. "You could've told me, bro. I didn't know what was happening with you. If you had, I would've understood. But I never asked, because you were my brother."

Anuj gave him a reassuring smile. "Look, you know that bad times don't last forever. We're all here with you. Don't give up now, okay? Don't lose hope."

"I've come too far, bhai. I won't give up now," Garv said, his voice firm.

That night, for the first time, Anuj spoke to Anshika. And during their conversation, Anshika shared something important with him—she asked him to tell Garv to quit smoking. Anuj, who knew Garv better than anyone, replied, "Don't worry, Anshika. Once Garv moves in with you, he'll quit on his own. But right now, no one can make him stop if he doesn't want to."

They spent the next hour lying on the terrace, watching the sky. Garv couldn't stop thinking about his future—how he would manage his job, his studies, and the life he wanted to build with Anshika. He knew that once he was with her, his problems would fade. She was his healer, the one person who could make everything better.

Anuj, seeing the weight of Garv's thoughts, told him, "Listen, I know you, Golu. Working for someone isn't your thing, but stay calm. Just get through this phase. You'll figure it out."

That night was memorable, and Garv felt a sense of relief. He was ready to face his new journey.

On January 16, Garv officially joined the bank. His luck was on his side, as he already knew his boss, Nikhar Bhaiya, and colleague Monika di, from his previous firm. This connection eased his transition into the job. His boss, who worked in Ahmedabad, came to Vadodara that week, explained the work culture, and introduced Garv to some of his business connections. Garv was advised to reach out without hesitation if he ever needed help. His boss, understanding that Garv was new, reassured him that it was okay to ask for support. He also gave him a heads-up about certain people Garv should be cautious of—people who could cause trouble, people like "snakes."

Garv, determined not to fall into office politics, focused instead on his studies and managing everything else in his life. Wearing his blazer, he started cold calling various sites, building connections as part of his retail job.

But as with all new beginnings, there were bumps along the way. The first was his training in Ahmedabad. Waking up early hadn't been easy, especially since he'd been up late studying. He forgot to ask his mom to wake him up, and when he checked the time, it was already 7:30 AM. Panicked, he called his mom, told her he was heading to Ahmedabad by vehicle because he had missed the train at 6:30.

In his rush, he took the expressway, which was only for four-wheelers, and only realized his mistake when he reached the toll gate. He had to exit at Anand and talk his way out of a fine with the police. Garv was good at talking his way out of tight situations, and the officer let him go. Despite the hiccups, he managed to reach Ahmedabad in time for his training, a two-day program.

Garv shared a hotel room with another guy from Surat. Over dinner, he began forming a connection with him. He knew he could use this friendship to expand his business connections in the future. Garv understood that the key to getting favors was offering favors first. So, he treated his new friend to dinner, and when the training ended, Garv received a bag for acing the training competitions. He gave the bag to his new roommate as a gesture of goodwill. The guy was thrilled, and Garv was content knowing that small acts of kindness went a long way in building relationships.

It was the last day of his training, and Garv, eager not to miss his friend Nishant's wedding in Surat, sought permission from HR to leave early. The excitement of the occasion pulled him away, but there was one problem: none of the trains were available at the time he needed. Undeterred, Garv made a snap decision—he would drive the 260-270 kilometers from Ahmedabad to Surat himself. The distance didn't seem daunting; he was determined to be there for his friend.

The road stretched before him, and he drove tirelessly, covering the distance in a mere four hours. But there was something else bothering him. He didn't want to tell his family that he had driven all the way from Ahmedabad to Surat. His dad would undoubtedly snap at him, possibly even make him quit his job. So, when Garv reached Surat, he stopped by Pankaj's place to change his vehicle, hoping to avoid raising any suspicions at home.

Once he changed, he rushed to his family home, quickly freshened up, and headed to the wedding venue. He had barely made it in time—the last seven vows were being exchanged when he arrived. As soon as Nishant saw Garv, a bright smile lit up his face, the joy of seeing his best friend at such a pivotal moment filling the room. Garv couldn't help but feel a warm sense of happiness as he watched Nishant, the groom, marry the love of his life.

The evening carried on with shots of whisky in a private room, surrounded by friends and family, and Garv knew that he had been a part of something special. He had arranged the bottles of whisky himself for his own wedding one day, but tonight, it felt like the perfect way to celebrate Nishant's big day. Exhausted but content, Garv knew he needed to leave early the next morning for Vadodara for work.

Before heading back to his hotel, he clicked a few pictures, waved goodbye to Nishant and Yashoda, and then headed to his home. The exhaustion of the day settled in as he finally talked to Anshika. She scolded him immediately, her concern clear in her voice. "What were you thinking, driving all that way on the highway?" she fretted. "You're crazy. Either start wearing a helmet, or I'm telling your mom about all your wild stunts!" Garv smiled, trying to calm her down. He soothed her, and soon enough, she was asleep like a baby. He closed his eyes, imagining the day when he would marry the love of his life, a day he knew would be the best of his life.

The following morning, he had to head back to Vadodara. The routine was still fresh and challenging, but Garv was slowly getting used to it. His mornings started with a call from his mom, waking him up as she always did. He would get ready, wear his blazer, and text Anshika to let her know he was leaving for the office. The rest of his day would be spent meeting builders and consultants, followed by a quick stop at the local pan shop for some gossip with the shopkeeper. Then, he'd return home, study for a few hours, and talk to Anshika before either heading to bed or studying more, depending on his energy.

February 1st, 2023, arrived. It was his mom and dad's 25th anniversary, and though his mom had told him not to plan anything—because his uncle wasn't in good health—Garv had other plans. He had quietly arranged for all the building members to gather at his flat at midnight, along with his bua, phuphaji, and cousins. A cake was ordered, and gifts were ready for his parents. Garv, despite his mother's request to keep things low-key, surprised them by showing up in Surat with all the celebrations prepared.

His parents were stunned, and their joy was palpable. Garv had learned a lot from his father, not just about business but about love, romance, and how to care deeply for someone. His dad was a true romantic, always making time to care for his mom, and Garv had taken those lessons to heart. He knew how to surprise her, how to make her feel loved, just as his dad had done for years. That night was a testament to the 25 years of love and care that had shaped their family.

After the celebration, the family members slowly trickled out, leaving Garv to rest. He couldn't wait to share everything with Anshika, telling her about the surprise and how happy his parents were. As he lay down to sleep, he felt a deep sense of peace. But the very next day, life threw him a curveball.

He had planned to return to Vadodara the same day, but he hadn't informed his office that he would be working from Surat. On top of that, he had a business meeting scheduled for February 2nd. He booked his train tickets in advance, planning a quiet dinner with his parents before heading back. However, as Garv quickly learned, life rarely unfolds as planned, and soon enough, a new challenge awaited him—one he hadn't anticipated.

February 2nd was shaping up to be one of the worst days of Garv's life. He had finished his work smoothly at the office and was just about to leave around 1:30 in the afternoon, eager to head home. That's when his phone rang, and the caller ID showed Ritik's name—someone Garv hadn't expected to hear from. Ritik was a junior of Garv's and a school friend of Sonu, Garv's cousin.

"Haan londe, kaisa hai? Yaad kiya aaj mujhe, bhai?" Garv answered, his voice cheerful.

But Ritik's response wasn't the usual casual banter. Instead, it was laced with a seriousness that immediately made Garv's stomach tighten.

"Golu bhai, tu kahan hai?" Ritik's voice cracked, heavy with emotion.

"Bhayi, main Vadodara hoon. Kya hua? Bol na, bhai kuch kaand kiya tune?" Garv replied, trying to lighten the mood, but the shift in Ritik's tone had him on edge.

"Golu... tere phuphaji ka accident ho gaya hai..." Ritik said, his voice trembling.

Garv froze. "Bhai, kya bol raha hai? Sahi hai vo? Main aa raha hoon Surat, tu rakh dhyaan unka aur Sonu ka," he stammered, struggling to process the words.

Ritik's next words shattered him. "Golu... he died on the spot. The truck... the truck hit him."

The world around Garv seemed to collapse in that moment. His heart pounded in his chest as the news sank in. His mind couldn't register the reality of it—just yesterday, he had been with his phuphaji, making arrangements for the dinner that was supposed to happen tonight. Now, everything felt like a cruel, twisted joke. Garv could hardly breathe.

He barely processed the words as he rushed out of his office, his legs moving on autopilot. "Ritik, bhai, Sonu ka dhyaan rakhna, uske saath rahiyo. Main jaldi pahuchta hoon," Garv said, voice shaky but determined. He had to be there. He couldn't believe this was happening.

Frantically, Garv searched for trains, but everything seemed to be against him. No trains were available at that time. His mind raced as he dialed his father's friend at the office, praying for a way out, a way to get to Surat, to his family.

Garv's heart was heavy with disbelief as he spoke into the phone.

"Bhaiya, papa ke saath kisi ko bhejna, mere phuphaji nahi rahe..." Garv's voice broke as he said the words he never thought he'd have to say.

"Golu, hum sab tere papa ke saath hain. Tu chinta mat kar. Tu aram se Surat aa jaa," Dad's friend reassured him, his voice steady but laced with sadness.

"Ek baar papa se baat karna," Garv requested, his throat tight with emotion.

"Haan Golu, bol," came his father's voice, distant and sorrowful.

"Papa, kuch bhi nahi ho sakta? Matlab kuch toh ho payega?" Garv's voice was a mixture of hope and desperation.

"Nahi Golu, maine baat ki hai. He died on the spot," Dad said, his words a cruel confirmation of the tragedy.

Garv felt as if the ground beneath him was slipping away. "Chalo, aap dhyaan rakho. Main Surat aa raha hoon, 6:00 baje tak," Garv said, trying to regain some composure.

"Aaja tu jaldi," Dad urged him.

Garv immediately texted Anshika, explaining what had happened. He knew she would be in meetings, so he didn't want to disturb her, but he needed her support. He typed out the message quickly: *What happened, please call whenever you get free.*

Anshika saw his message and quickly replied, *I'll call you in half an hour. Till then, take care.*

Garv headed home, his mind numb, still trying to process the loss of his best phuphaji. He couldn't comprehend it—just yesterday, he had been with him, planning everything. Today, he was gone, and Garv couldn't handle it. He felt a well of emotion rising in him, but he wasn't used to crying, not like this.

When he reached home, he opened his almirah and pulled out the bottle of whisky he had bought for a night with friends. But today was different—he had nothing but a few hours to himself, and Anshika wouldn't be available for a while.

Garv poured himself a drink, the liquid burning as it went down, but he didn't care. He poured another, and then another. Three pegs later, the tears started to fall. They came silently at first, but then, they couldn't be stopped. He began to remember every moment spent with his phuphaji, every summer vacation, every Holi they had celebrated together. Phuphaji had been the one to teach him how to ride a cycle, and later, a car. Holi was his favorite festival, one he celebrated every year with his phuphaji, who always joined in the festivities like a child.

Phuphaji had been the most selfless person he knew. He had never turned anyone away—whether it was family or the community, he was always ready to help. Garv's tears came faster now, the memories flooding him. He loved his phuphaji so much, and now he was gone.

In his haze, he put his phone on airplane mode, downed the last of the whisky, and curled up in the corner, scrolling through pictures of his phuphaji. The grief overwhelmed him, but it wasn't enough to stop the process of remembering, of reliving all the moments they had shared.

After a while, Garv realized that Anshika's meeting might be over. He switched his phone back on, and sure enough, her message had come through. He immediately called her, his voice shaky as he tried to find comfort in her words.

"Baccha, aap kaise ho? Aap nikal rahe ho Surat?" Anshika asked, concern evident in her voice.

"I don't know how I'm doing right now... I have an hour until my train," Garv replied, his words filled with pain and confusion.

"It will be okay, Garv. I'm here for you, remember that. Don't be sad, you have to support everyone when you get there," Anshika reassured him, her words a small balm to his shattered heart.

"Yeah, I'm going to take a shower... I'll feel a bit better," Garv muttered.

"Why are you showering now?" Anshika asked, confused.

"I had a drink... I was alone, and I didn't know what else to do. But I'll feel a bit better after showering... and then maybe I can rest a little on the train," Garv explained.

"Garv, you promised me. No drinking, no matter what happens. Why did you do this?" Anshika asked, a touch of worry in her voice.

"I know, baccha. I promise, I won't drink alone again. I just... I didn't know how to handle this. It's just... it's just that my phuphaji was the only one who really understood me. My heart is breaking, and I don't know what to do," Garv confessed, his voice cracking as he spoke.

"Aap ro rahe ho, baccha?" Anshika asked softly, her concern deepening.

"No... I'm okay. I'll be fine. The train is leaving soon, I need to go. I'll call you when I get there," Garv replied, trying to steady himself.

"Please, take care. Get there safely and call me as soon as you reach," Anshika urged him, her voice full of love and support.

"Haan, I will," Garv promised, trying to find strength in her words as he prepared to leave.

The tension and sadness Garv felt were palpable, yet he wore a mask of composure. Despite the overwhelming grief inside him, he chose to stay strong, hiding his emotions from everyone around him. His mind replayed every moment spent with his Phuphaji, the man who had been his rock, guiding him through both good and bad times. Now, with his loss, Garv had to face the reality that his confidant, his mentor, was gone.

The journey to Surat station was long, and although Garv tried to distract himself with his thoughts, he couldn't stop the flood of emotions. Anshika's texts, meant to soothe him, were left unread. Garv needed to be alone, to process everything by himself. He couldn't let his family see him break down, especially not in front of his Bua, who still had no idea what had happened.

Upon arriving at Surat, the first thing Garv did was head to the familiar "pool" spot with his friends, a place where they would meet to unwind. It was a place that symbolized comfort, but that evening, it felt like nothing more than a ritual. Anuj, who noticed the subtle signs of distress, asked Garv if he was okay, but Garv brushed it off, putting on a façade of normalcy. He didn't want to be treated differently.

As Garv went about his day, trying to handle the logistics of his Phuphaji's passing, the heaviness of the situation weighed on him. He comforted his Bua with words of reassurance, pretending that everything would be fine, even though deep down he knew that things would never be the same. The reality of his Phuphaji's death still hadn't fully hit him. He was stuck in a state of disbelief, caught between holding back tears and having to be the strong pillar for his family.

Finally, as the night wore on and Garv's family began arriving to confront the devastating news, he braced himself for the inevitable. He knew that once the truth was revealed, it would be a turning point for everyone involved. But Garv stayed focused on his role as the protector of his family, hoping that the pain would eventually pass, but also dreading the moment when it would all become real.

Through it all, Anshika's messages of support remained a comforting presence, though Garv couldn't bring himself to read them yet. He would call her when the time was right, when he was ready to accept the weight of what had happened and share it with the one person who had always been there for him. But for now, he had to focus on the moment, on his family, and on the process of moving forward, even when every part of him wanted to break.

The weight of the moment hung heavily in the air as Garv sat quietly with his Bua and the women of the family who had always cared for him—his mother, Dadi, Building Aunty, and his cousin sister. He watched their pain, their tears, as they too processed the loss of Phuphaji. His heart ached, but he held it together, his resolve strong, at least for now.

Garv's father called, informing him that he and Sonu had finished the necessary procedures at the hospital and were on their way to the house. They would finally tell Bua the truth about what had happened. Garv knew that this moment was only going to make things harder. Tomorrow, Bua's other children would arrive, and the truth would spread further. Garv's mind raced with a prayer—he hoped time would pass quickly so he could manage everything that was coming.

When Sonu and his father finally arrived, the truth was told, and the emotional weight of it all seemed to hit everyone at once. Garv's father held his sister tightly, his grief evident in his embrace. Garv's own emotions surged as he saw Sonu, his younger brother, holding it together with impressive strength. Sonu didn't cry, but Garv couldn't help but hug him tightly, offering what little comfort he could. Their bond was unspoken but deeply understood. Garv turned his attention to the women of the family—his mother, Dadi, and Bua. He could hardly bear seeing the three most important women in his life in such pain. He reassured them with his usual strength, trying to stay grounded for them, even though his heart was breaking too.

The family gathered for dinner at Sonu's neighbor's house, though Garv had no appetite. He knew that if he didn't eat, Sonu wouldn't either, so he sat beside him, offering support. As they ate, Sonu's tears began to fall, and Garv couldn't hold back anymore. He hugged his brother and promised that he would always stand by him, no matter what. It was in this moment that Garv realized how much he had been holding in.

Needing a release, Garv called his friends to meet up at their usual spot—the "pool." They all gathered there, as always, waiting for him. Garv lit a cigarette, lowered his head, and began talking about his Phuphaji, the memories they had shared, the love and guidance he had received. It was then that he finally broke down. The tears came without warning, flowing freely as he cried like he never had before in front of anyone. His friends, who had always seen him as strong and almost invincible, now understood the depth of his pain. They embraced him, rubbing his back, silently offering their support. Garv sobbed for ten minutes, a release he hadn't allowed himself in days.

Once his tears subsided, anger took over. Garv was furious, and his friends knew better than to try and calm him down. He called a friend to tell him he was going to make the truck driver pay for what he had done. He promised that once the ceremony was over, he would make sure that driver would face the consequences of his actions. His anger was a fire that no one could extinguish, and his friends, though concerned, understood that Garv needed to vent.

Later that night, Garv stayed with his Bua, taking care of her as best as he could. He couldn't bring himself to sleep, not with the weight of the situation pressing down on him. As the house quieted, he finally decided to call Anshika around 1 AM. He had ignored her messages earlier, unable to find the strength to respond.

"Aapko samajh kyun nahi aata? Ek baar bata sakte ho na? At least msg karke ki kaisa ho yahan tension nahi hoti muje," Anshika's voice was filled with concern.

"I'm sorry, Baccha. But you need to understand the situation. Please try to think about it. And, just come here and rest, okay?" Garv replied, his voice soft but tired.

"Did you tell Bua, Baccha?" Anshika asked, her worry evident.

"She's asleep now. I told her, but she's not doing well. Tomorrow is going to be a busy day, so I might not be able to talk much. Please, don't be angry with me," Garv explained, trying to reassure her.

"Please, just take care of yourself. I'm always thinking of you," Anshika said, her voice warm with love and care. "I love you a lot, Garv. Please take care, and if anything happens, just call me. At least text me."

"I will, Baccha. Don't worry about me. I'll be fine. Now go sleep, okay? Tomorrow is going to be a long day," Garv said, trying to comfort her, though the weight of the day still hung heavy on him.

"Good night, Garv. AGD," Anshika responded before hanging up, her affection clear in her words.

Good night, AGD baccha' Garv

Garv sighed deeply, staring into the quiet night. Tomorrow was going to be a tough day, but he knew he had to face it head-on, just as he always had. But for tonight, he would try to rest, for his family, for Anshika, and for himself.

As Garv sat at the Pan shop, the air felt heavy with tension. His thoughts were consumed by the recent events—the loss of his phuphaji, the devastation his family was enduring, and the burning anger that churned inside him. Sonu's suffering only fueled the fire. Garv couldn't stand to see his friend in pain, especially when it was caused by something so senseless. His mind constantly drifted back to the driver, the one responsible for the crash, who had somehow vanished. Garv had promised Sonu that he would get to the truth, no matter what. No matter the cost, he would make sure that driver paid for what he had done.

But as he sat with Sonu's friends—lawyers, all of them—at the Pan shop, each one offering their own advice, Garv felt a growing conflict within. They told him to think carefully about the consequences of his actions. If he went after the driver physically, the case would be destroyed, and justice would slip away.

Garv listened, though his anger still burned. He felt the tension in his body, the frustration pulsing beneath the surface, but deep down, he knew they were right. He wasn't the type to sit idly by, but this time, his instinct for vengeance had to be tempered with reason. His phuphaji wouldn't want his legacy to be tainted by rash decisions. He couldn't dishonor him like that.

His friends, who had known him for years, spoke from experience, urging him to hold off and trust in the law. Garv, though still seething inside, finally nodded. They were right. He had always acted on impulse, but now he had to think about the bigger picture. The truth would come out, but it had to be done the right way. His phuphaji's memory deserved nothing less.

When the meeting ended, Garv felt the weight of the world on his shoulders. He wasn't in the mood to celebrate or talk. His mind was focused on finding the person who had been riding the bike and knew what had truly happened. It wasn't going to be easy, but Garv was determined. His resolve was unshakeable.

Later, when he sat with Sonu, the two of them talked in quiet voices. Sonu's eyes were hollow with grief, but Garv saw a glimmer of hope in them when he promised that he would find the truth. They spoke long into the night, and Garv made it clear—he would do whatever it took to find the truth, no matter how long it took or how difficult it might be.

Just then, Sonu's friend—a junior to Garv—arrived to meet him. He had heard about the situation and wanted to show his support. Garv appreciated the gesture, but he wasn't in the mood for sympathy. He simply nodded, acknowledging him, but his thoughts were already elsewhere, focused on the task ahead.

As the group began to disperse and the night wore on, Garv found himself alone with his thoughts once again. The day had been long, exhausting, and emotionally draining, with no sign of relief. But Garv had always been a man of action. He had his mission now, and nothing—not anger, not pain—was going to stop him from seeing it through.

"Bhai, sahi hain tu," Shharshank said with a wry smile.

Garv had known Shharshank since childhood. They had been classmates, and Shharshank was not only Sonu's busmate but also Devik's cousin. The two lit their cigarettes as they stood together, the air thick with the tension of their conversation.

"Baas, benchod, yeh chutiyap khatam hi nahi hota," Garv muttered, his frustration clear.

Garv's phone rang, interrupting the silence. He had already asked a few of his friends to dig into the whereabouts of the guy who had been driving the bike. As he spoke into the phone, Shharshank overheard the conversation. Garv's anger was reaching its peak as they still hadn't been able to find the driver.

"Make sure to find where that motherfucker is," Garv said, his voice low but filled with fury. "I'll make him walk straight to the court."

Shharshank, who knew Garv's temper well, felt a knot form in his stomach. He had seen Garv angry before, but this was different. Garv was a force when enraged, and no one dared to cross him. But what Shharshank knew, and what made him fear the situation, was that the driver was his relative.

Finally, Shharshank gathered the courage to speak up.

"Bhai, Golu, ek baat karni hain tujhse," Shharshank said, his voice hesitant.

"Haan, bol, kya hua?" Garv replied, his patience thinning.

"Bhai, vo jo uncle hain, jo bike chala rahe the, vo mere relative hain," Shharshank confessed, his words carrying an uncomfortable weight.

Garv's face remained calm, but he tried to control the storm inside. He had always tried not to let his anger affect his loved ones and friends.

"Bhai, dekh, tu jaanta hain mujhe kaise hoon," Garv said, his tone steady. "Aur yahan baat mere apne paar aayi hain. Main tujhe 10 din deta hoon unhe samjhane ke liye. Varna, phir main apne haath mein le lunga yeh matter, aur phir nahi sununga teri bhi."

"Bhai, main baat karta hoon. It's just that vo dar gaye hain, yaar. Toh vo heart patient hain, isliye he's avoiding," Shharshank explained quickly.

"Dekh, Shharshank, tu bhai hain isliye main kuch nahi karunga 10 din tak," Garv said, his tone now softer but resolute. "But tell him, case nahi ho raha hain, benchod. But without his statement, the case won't stand in court. Agar vo khud aate hain, toh badiya hain. Varna main apne tareeke apnaunga. Main sirf sudhra hoon, lekin agar mera koi royega na, toh kisi ka apna khoyega. Samjha de unhe aram se, aur make sure he talks."

"Maine bola na, bhai, main handle kar lunga. Pakka, tujhe nahi padna padega," Shharshank reassured him.

"Theek hain, bhai. Chal, Sonu se milne chalte hain," Garv said, his voice slightly more relaxed.

Shharshank knew that Garv would give him time due to their long-standing friendship. He believed that he could convince his relative to talk, and he did. The driver and his wife were at his Bua's house to meet her, express their apologies, and settle the issue. Shharshank was confident that his relative would make it work.

Ten days later, Garv found himself standing amidst hundreds of people on the last day of mourning for his phuphaji. In Hindu culture, this day is when the soul of the departed is believed to leave the world. There were political leaders, MLAs, community heads, NGO members, police officers, and more, all there to bid farewell to a well-known figure in the community.

Garv hadn't been able to book tickets in time, so he had driven through the night from Vadodara to be there. A fight with Anshika had delayed him, though, as she didn't understand his need to attend. She felt he should rest and focus on his new job, especially with their anniversary coming up and his sister's wedding ahead. But Garv wouldn't listen.

It was the last day, and Garv hugged his Bua, feeling a mixture of sorrow and comfort. His phuphaji, a man who had always loved him, had known about Garv's arrival, and his Bua was happy that he could be there. Together, they bade him the final farewell, offering prayers for his happiness.

While this was happening, Garv had received a job offer from Kotak Bank in Surat. He discussed it with his dad, weighing the pros and cons. Ultimately, they both concluded that it wouldn't be right to dishonor the commitment he had made with his current employer. Nikhar bhaiya's words carried weight in the office; he was a top performer, and because he had referred Garv, there was no doubt the national head would agree to the interview.

Garv decided to stay where he was and rejected the other offer. Opportunities would come again, but relationships were rarer. He understood that making such a decision early in his career could impact how people in the industry viewed him, and that was something he couldn't afford.

As he settled into his work and took care of the remaining legal matters for his phuphaji's insurance claims and court arrangements, Garv found a small sense of relief. His friends at the bank had been handling the processes with Sonu, who had recently become a lawyer. His senior had taken the case pro bono, ensuring a good settlement.

Now, Garv had the chance to focus on his work. But the emotional turmoil from the loss of his phuphaji lingered. He saw how his father struggled, feeling helpless and alone. Garv had never seen his dad like this, and he understood that the responsibilities on his father had increased.

Despite their complicated relationship, Garv knew that his father needed him now more than ever. So, he began calling him every day. Their conversations had never been frequent, and while it wasn't that they didn't love each other, the father-son bond was one of the most complex forms of love—something that no one could truly understand.

On the other hand, Garv had sheathed his swords. He had put aside his anger and ego because he knew that in the workplace, maintaining calm was crucial. He had decided to avoid office politics, not in the mood for any confrontation, especially with his exams looming. He longed for peace, but things, as always, didn't work out the way he hoped.

Garv and his colleague, Monika Di, had just joined the bank. Together, they were facing an identity crisis, trying to make a mark in a world already ruled by sharks. Sometimes, the enemies you face aren't the competitors in the market, but the ones who dwell under the same roof. And in their case, the real challenge was someone within the very organisation where they worked. Nikhar Bhaiya had warned Garv about this person, but Garv, ever determined, decided to play the game of clean politics, believing that in the end, the best one would always win.

Slowly but surely, Garv began to make his way—reaching out to every consultant, every builder he could connect with using his contacts. He knew that maintaining his composure was the key. He didn't want to get triggered, for if he did, things would turn bad fast.

Finally, the day arrived—the day of Garv's first salary. It was the 26th of February, and the happiest person that day was none other than Anshika. She told him she had never been as happy when her own first salary arrived, nor when she got promoted. She understood Garv's reluctance toward working under someone, but even she could see how much this moment meant to him. They had already been planning their first trip for their tenth year of togetherness and the upcoming ninth anniversary. But there was a dilemma—Garv's sister's wedding was also around the corner, on March 3rd. He tried to talk to his boss, but since he had already taken leave, it wasn't possible to get more time off.

Garv decided to talk to his sister. He explained that he would send her a gift instead of attending, as celebrating with Anshika was more important to him. She was in Bangalore, feeling alone, and this trip was something they had both been looking forward to. The planning for the trip began in earnest. Garv had already shed some weight, dropping from 125 kg to 111 kg. While he wasn't fully in shape yet, he knew it wouldn't take more than two to three months to get there. But his main priority remained clearing the CA exams, as that was the biggest obstacle in his life. The exams kept him from fully focusing on his job and business.

He began shopping for himself and Anshika, buying a tiger-print beach dress for her for the Maldives trip they had always dreamed of.

Though they weren't married yet, to Garv, this trip felt like their first honeymoon. Anshika, in her playful yet mischievous way, had tasked him with buying lingerie to go with the dress. Garv, who knew every detail about her—from sizes to preferences—still found it an awkward task to buy a bra for her. Going to Decathlon, he nervously asked the saleslady for advice on colors. After the awkwardness, he managed to get the right one, and once he called Anshika to tell her about the experience, they both burst into laughter. He also picked up a massager for her, knowing she loved massages. They were ready—flights booked, hotels sorted, everything in place.

His friends were happy for him. They knew this trip would give him the boost he needed to get back on track. But, as always, life has its ups and downs, and Garv was still recovering from the loss of his Phuphaji. In memory of his uncle, he started contributing 5% of his salary to support cows and other needy people. From his first paycheck, he bought gifts for the important women in his life—his mother, grandmother, aunt, and even the building aunty who had helped raise him. Anshika, though a little jealous, understood. Garv reassured her that she was his priority, despite missing his sister's wedding for the trip. He had planned the entire thing with her in mind, and he wanted her to enjoy every moment.

Garv knew Anshika had led a more reserved life, while he, on the other hand, was mischievous and full of energy. It was the perfect combination for a memorable trip. As Anshika said, she would rely on him for the whole trip. She would just enjoy whatever he planned.

Chapter 23

The Best Trip of Their Lives Begins

Garv packed his bags, his excitement growing as he prepared for the most awaited trip of his life. The day had finally arrived—his anniversary with Anshika, and the two of them were about to embark on their first vacation together. The anticipation was palpable, a mix of love and excitement that made his heart race.

He arrived in Ahmedabad, where his close friend Arpan was waiting to pick him up. Arpan, like any true friend, didn't need to ask why Garv didn't just take a cab. In the unspoken language of male friendship, they valued those few extra minutes together—no rush, no agenda. They shared cigarettes, exchanged life stories, and in those moments, their bond deepened without needing to say much. Boys' friendships weren't about grand gestures or constant check-ins. They weren't even about remembering birthdays. It was about being there when it mattered—when life hit hard. That's what made their friendship pure and real. Love may be a diamond, but a friendship like theirs? It was gold.

After spending some time with Arpan, Garv was off to Bangalore, where Anshika was waiting for him. The night had a festive vibe; it was Holi at Sheru's house, a celebration filled with laughter, colors, and old college friends. Most of them were girls, and though Garv wasn't usually one for big crowds, Anshika and Sheru's presence made it comfortable. He was an extrovert, but unknown faces often made him awkward.

Finally, he and Anshika were alone in Sheru's room. As soon as they were together, the world outside faded. They hugged each other tightly, both feeling the relief and joy of finally being together. After catching up with everyone else, the night turned into a celebration. Garv went to a nearby store, picking up beer for the group, but he had something special planned for himself. The bus to Pondicherry was scheduled for 11:00 PM that night, and he had a plan to make the evening even more memorable.

After grabbing a bottle of Black Dog whisky, he tucked it away in his pocket. Back at Sheru's house, he and Anshika settled into the balcony, enjoying the beer. Garv, however, knew that beer alone wouldn't be enough to set the mood he was hoping for. He discreetly mixed the whisky with tap water, and soon enough, the vibes shifted. The Holi festivities were in full swing, and they smeared each other with color, laughing and teasing.

Anshika, with a mischievous glint in her eyes, took Garv into Sheru's room. They locked the door behind them, and in the intimacy of the space, they shared a deep kiss. Then, Anshika took some of the red Holi powder and handed it to Garv. At first, he didn't understand, but when she asked him to apply it to her hairline, he realized the significance. In Hindu tradition, the groom places sindoor on the bride's hair during the wedding—a ritual called "maang bharna." Garv carefully filled her hairline with the red powder, and they hugged again, their connection deepening.

The night was theirs, and they couldn't wait for their trip to begin. After a light dinner, they set off for the bus to Pondicherry.

When the bus finally arrived, Anshika had booked a sleeper compartment, hoping to have a little privacy. However, much to their disappointment, there were only curtains separating the sleepers. But for two lovebirds, that wasn't a problem. They quickly figured out how to secure the curtains, making their own space amidst the bus's lively atmosphere of couples. Garv and Anshika, lost in their own world, shared intimate moments, kissing and holding each other close. Garv's hands roamed, exploring the curves of Anshika's body, and the chemistry between them was undeniable.

After a while, Garv realized his jeans had slipped to the floor, and Anshika teasingly picked them up. Laughing, they cuddled together, the warmth of each other's presence making the long journey feel shorter. They finally drifted off to sleep, wrapped in each other's arms, eager to wake up in Pondicherry.

As the bus neared their destination, the morning greeted them with a soft glow. Garv and Anshika shared a quiet kiss, their faces beaming with happiness. It was their first unofficial honeymoon, a secret getaway, for neither of their families knew the truth. Garv's parents thought he was in Ahmedabad for work, while Anshika's were under the impression she was enjoying the weekend with Sheru and other friends.

They stepped off the bus, their hands intertwined, and hailed an auto to their hotel—**Le Royal Park**. Their adventure was only just beginning.

The check-in time was still three to four hours away. Anshika, with a sly smirk, glanced at Garv and teased, "I told you to plan ahead. So, what's the plan now? Should we sit at the reception, or do you have something else in mind?"

Garv placed a reassuring hand on her shoulder and led her out of the hotel after they submitted their bags. "Don't worry," he said, "I've got it covered." They rented a yellow Vespa, and as he looked at Anshika, his face lit up with excitement. "Are you ready for this joyful trip?" he asked.

Anshika settled behind him and hugged him tightly. In that moment, Garv felt like his dream had finally come true. He had imagined this countless times—Anshika sitting behind him, hugging him, and him comforting her with one hand on her lap. He smiled and said, "Open the map. Let's explore the entire city."

For the next three hours, Garv took Anshika on a whirlwind tour of Pondicherry, showing her the famous beaches and scenic spots. Finally, they found themselves back at Rock Beach, where they stopped at a café overlooking the water. They sat there, enjoying the breeze, as they ordered breakfast, dessert, and a beer.

Anshika looked at him, impressed. "You've shown me all of Pondicherry in just three hours! Now what?" she asked.

Garv chuckled. "Now that we know the best places in town, the next two days are already planned out. You can relax and leave all the planning to me," he said, winking at her.

Anshika reached out and hugged his hand, sensing that something was weighing on his mind. "Are you okay? I know there's been a lot going on with you lately."

Garv kissed her forehead and reassured her, "I'm with you, baccha. There's some stuff on my mind, but this trip will help me clear my head. We'll be fine."

Anshika smiled, comforted by his words. "We're going to enjoy every moment of this trip, I promise."

They ordered a Salted Caramel Cheesecake, and it blew their minds with its deliciousness. Afterward, they walked along the beach, taking photos and creating memories, before heading back to their hotel.

The moment they entered their room, they felt both excited and awkward. It was their first trip together, and everything felt new. They locked the door behind them, embraced each other tightly, and shared a passionate kiss. The intensity of the moment was electrifying.

Garv then handed her a surprise gift: a khakra, some lingerie, and a massager, all with a playful, naughty look in his eyes. Anshika hugged him tightly, and for a moment, the world outside seemed to fade away. They had been through so much in the past few months, but they promised to make it work, to keep fighting for their love. The following year, they both agreed, they would get married—no matter what.

After a soothing bath, they curled up under the sheets and spent the afternoon cuddling. As the day went on, Garv, despite his reluctance to bathe, agreed to take another one with Anshika when she playfully insisted, "If you don't bathe, I won't go anywhere with you!"

Once they were ready, Anshika looked stunning in a red dress that reached just above her knees, paired with delicate bellies and her hair flowing freely. She applied red lipstick, blusher on her soft cheeks, and a matching eyeshadow palette that accentuated her beauty. Garv couldn't help but be mesmerized by her. She playfully kissed his cheek, leaving lipstick marks, before touching up her makeup.

They locked the room, and Anshika, feeling carefree, handed her phone and bags to Garv, letting him handle everything as she reveled in the excitement of the day. She was enjoying being free, trusting Garv to guide their adventure.

In the lobby, Garv caught her admiring herself in the mirror. With a smile, he snapped a picture and showed it to her. She embraced him tightly, grateful for the love they shared, and then they left to explore more of Pondicherry.

Their destination was Paradise Beach, known for its lively parties. Garv had long dreamed of riding with Anshika sitting behind him, hugging him tightly, and today, that dream finally came true. As they made their way to the beach, they stopped along the way to take photos and capture memories.

Once at Paradise Beach, they found a beach bar. Anshika, curious to try something new, tasted Baileys liquor for the first time, drinking six glasses of it, while Garv enjoyed his beer. They spent some quiet moments on the beach, relishing the cool breeze, before sharing a tender kiss.

As the night approached, the security guard blew his whistle to signal closing time. They made their way back to their Vespa, agreeing to return tomorrow for the Saturday night party.

Back at the Rock Beach café, they continued their celebration with cocktails and another slice of cheesecake. Afterward, they bought more Baileys and beer from a wine shop and headed back to their hotel room. The night sped by in a blur of laughter, music, and dancing. They fell asleep in each other's arms, savoring their first morning together on holiday.

The next day, Anshika wore a beautiful green dress, and they headed to Coromandel Café for breakfast. The wait was long, so they decided to shop around. Garv was thrilled to be shopping with her, picking out things she loved and enjoying every moment with her.

Their trip was filled with joy, laughter, and unforgettable memories, each moment bringing them closer than ever before.

They took some bracelets, earrings, and souvenirs with them before heading to a café where they ordered French-style pizza and croissants. The café's vibe was great, but Garv didn't quite enjoy the taste of the food. However, Anshika, who wasn't fond of the flavors either, saved the day, and they decided to head back to Rock Beach. After spending some time there, they went to a café facing the beach. Garv enjoyed a beer while Anshika savored her Chinese food alongside him. Later, they headed to their favorite café for cheesecake and coffee. The café owner, noticing their frequent visits, smiled and said, "You're in Pondicherry, and yet, you always come here." Garv and Anshika couldn't help but smile back at the warmth in his words. After their dessert, they returned to their hotel, with the afternoons proving to be far more romantic than the nights.

However, sometimes, things can get awkward between couples when they try something new after watching videos online. Garv and Anshika, despite the awkwardness, turned it into funny moments, laughing and hugging each other. Anshika then changed into the bikini dress she had bought for the trip, pairing it with a shrug and denim shorts. They made their way to Eden Beach, known as the Blue Beach of India. Anshika had visited many beaches across the world but had never really immersed herself in the waters. She preferred to enjoy the view from the shore. Garv, on the other hand, couldn't understand how someone could not enjoy the waves—it was, after all, the best part of the beach.

They booked a private pass for one hour at Eden Beach, but after half an hour, Anshika asked Garv to extend it for two more hours. They enjoyed the waves together, with Garv holding her tightly as they sat on the beach, sharing a peaceful and romantic evening. Afterward, they took a shower by the beach, and then went back to change for the party at Paradise Beach.

Back at the hotel, they changed into party clothes and took shots of Baileys before kissing each other. They then realized, much too late, that they had forgotten to arrange for transport to the party. But they managed to get to Paradise Beach and enjoyed the party. Garv drank a lot of beer, and Anshika and Garv danced together. Later, they sat on the beach, gazing at the stars. Anshika, wanting to make the moment more fun, asked another couple sitting nearby if they could join them. The other couple welcomed them, and in just five minutes, everyone had bonded. Anshika and the girl went to get some beer, while Garv and the guy chatted and got to know each other.

As the night went on, Garv drank a little too much. He was feeling a good buzz, but he knew he wouldn't be able to drive back. So, he asked the guy for help, and the couple offered to take them back to their hotel. After the party, they went to Rock Beach for dinner. To their surprise, they returned to the same café they had visited earlier. Garv and the guy enjoyed their dinner, and Garv had a couple more beers. When Anshika saw him drinking again, she gestured to the shopkeeper to not serve him any more alcohol, telling him that they were out of stock on Budweiser Magnum. Garv, ever the charmer, talked his way into getting another beer.

By the end of the night, Garv was visibly drunk. Anshika, a bit upset, made sure to handle him carefully, even as he insisted on paying the bill. As a gesture of appreciation for their loyalty, the café owner handed Anshika two cheesecakes. They walked along the beach after dinner, but after a few minutes, Garv got nauseous and vomited on the sand. Anshika, always caring, handled the situation with patience.

The other couple offered to drop them back to their hotel, but Anshika, slightly angry and deeply concerned, couldn't help but feel disappointed in Garv. She felt his behavior wasn't mature. Garv, usually confident and carefree, had always driven himself after drinking. But tonight, with Anshika by his side, he didn't want to take any chances. Despite his usual reckless speed—he never drove below 80 km/hr when alone or with a friend—he had kept it under 50 km/hr throughout the trip, respecting Anshika's presence.

Once back at the hotel, Anshika led him toward their room, still upset. Garv, feeling the effects of the alcohol, tried to avoid the bed, knowing he was going to be sick. As he sat in the bathroom, Anshika grew increasingly worried. "Please, just come to bed and lie down," she pleaded, but Garv ignored her. He didn't want to ruin the room, knowing the mess he was about to make. In his haze, Garv accidentally hit his head on a nearby tap. Anshika, frightened, immediately called his friends—Anuj, Rathiji, Devik—for advice. They reassured her, telling her not to worry too much, that Garv would be fine in a few hours. Despite their calm words, Anshika couldn't help but feel uneasy. They had never seen Garv this drunk before; his usual alcohol tolerance was strong, but tonight he'd mixed too many drinks—wine, whiskey, liquor, and beer.

Garv finally began to feel normal around 4:00 AM. He got back into bed, but the space between him and Anshika was noticeable. He knew he had messed up, and what had started as a smooth trip was now marred by the tension. In the early morning, around 7:00 AM, Anshika woke up, leaned in, and kissed Garv on his forehead, but her anger lingered in the air. She was judging him, and Garv could feel the weight of it. By 8:00 AM, Garv woke up to find Anshika still upset, and he didn't like it. He had come on this trip to enjoy it, but now it felt like it was all falling apart.

Instead of confronting her, he chose silence. He was angry too, but he kept it to himself. He wasn't about to add fuel to the fire. "I'll be back after I drop the vehicle off," he said quietly, trying to keep things calm. Anshika, though, had already begun packing. She wasn't saying much, but she was clearly upset.

When Garv returned after dropping the car off, Anshika was done packing. Together, they left for the bus stop and boarded the bus. They settled into their sleeper compartment, but after about half an hour, Garv realized Anshika was still angry. He could feel the distance between them, so he pulled her into a hug, hoping to ease the tension. He whispered, "I'm sorry," but Anshika's anger was not so easily soothed.

Garv rubbed her feet gently, massaging her as he spoke. "I'm sorry. Please forgive me. I didn't mean to upset you." But Anshika remained distant.

Just then, Garv's phone rang, breaking the silence. It was Anuj.

"Did you leave yet?" Anuj asked.

"Yeah, just about an hour ago," Garv replied, trying to keep things casual.

"Anshika okay?" Anuj probed.

"Yeah, she's fine," Garv answered, though he wasn't sure.

"Golu, come here, we need to talk," Anuj said, his voice serious.

"Sure, man," Garv replied.

"Take care, okay?" Anuj added.

"Yeah, see you soon," Garv said before ending the call.

He kissed his fist and turned to Anshika, saying again, "I'm sorry." She looked at him, her frustration clear.

"Garv, do you even realize how wrong you were this morning?" Anshika asked, her voice tight with emotion. "You went to drop the vehicle off alone, and didn't even ask if I wanted to come. We could have gone to see the sunrise together, but you left in anger. That wasn't right, Garv."

Garv gently took her hands in his. "I'm sorry," he said again, before pulling her into a tight embrace. He knew he had messed up, and he would do anything to make it right.

Sometimes, Garv thought, people don't understand that actions aren't always intentional. The previous night, he had mixed his drinks, and although he could usually handle alcohol, he knew he had overdone it this time. He had avoided driving after drinking, especially because Anshika was with him. Usually, he would drive home alone after a party, without a second thought, but with Anshika beside him, he hadn't wanted to take any risks.

That night, Garv had kept the speed under 50 km/h. On a regular day, he would have driven around 80 km/h, even in the city. But this time, he cared more about her safety than anything. When they reached the hotel, he didn't want to risk throwing up in the room, so he went straight to the bathroom and passed out there.

When he woke up, he could tell Anshika was still upset. He didn't want to disturb her, so he lay beside her, quietly staring at her while she slept. It was all about respect, he knew. And he respected Anshika more than anyone.

Back in the present, Anshika pulled him into a tight hug. "It's going to take time to forget this, Garv. But why? Why do people always focus on the small black dot on a whiteboard, instead of seeing the whole white space? Why can't they understand that?"

Garv kissed her gently, his eyes filled with regret.

He moved toward her feet and began rubbing them softly, his gaze full of apology. Anshika, feeling the sincerity in his touch, hugged him tightly. They shared a soft kiss, and in that moment, the tension between them finally started to ease.

But then, they both realized something: they had left their condoms back at the hotel. They both laughed, a small moment of relief breaking the tension. They hugged each other tightly and fell asleep, the weight of the trip's ups and downs settling in.

Later, back in Bangalore, they took a cab to Sheru's home. On the way, Anshika grew quiet again, lost in thought. They sat down with Sheru, and Garv apologized once more. Sheru, seeing the genuine remorse in Garv, reassured Anshika, "It wasn't intentional. He zoned out, lost in the moment. It's okay."

Sheru served them dinner, but Garv's mood had shifted. He felt like he had broken their unspoken rule: to handle their issues between the two of them, without anyone else getting involved. But now, sitting silently, he felt the weight of what had happened. He had always kept his promises to Anshika, but tonight, it felt like something had changed.

Anshika noticed Garv's silence and knew something was wrong. Then, out of nowhere, she passed out while eating. Garv immediately rushed to her, holding her so she wouldn't fall. Panic spread through him as he kissed her forehead, trying to wake her. "Please wake up," he whispered, his voice desperate.

Garv didn't know what to do—his heart was heavy with worry and confusion. He gently picked her up in his arms, trying to shake her awake. Finally, she stirred, her eyes fluttering open. Garv, tears streaming down his face, placed her back on the bed and kissed her forehead.

Anshika, still groggy, looked at him in confusion. "What happened? Why are you crying?" she asked, pulling him into a tight hug.

Garv gently explained to Anshika, "I passed out out of nowhere," his voice full of concern. She pulled him into a tight hug, as if to reassure herself that everything would be okay. The warmth of her embrace filled the room, and for a moment, all the tension of the past days seemed to melt away.

Then, as if to lighten the mood, Anshika brought out the cheesecake that the café owner had gifted them for being loyal customers. She smiled and said, "Loyalty is what matters in the end. It might be hard sometimes, but when the fruits of loyalty ripen, they are the sweetest. Trust me."

Garv smiled back, feeling a sense of relief. Anshika took a spoon and, with a soft laugh, started feeding him the cheesecake. The taste was sweet, but it was her presence that made everything feel right again. As she fed him, she pulled him into another hug, her voice softer now, but filled with sincerity. "What happened last night... it's okay. Just promise me one thing," she said, looking into his eyes, "Promise me this will never happen again. That you'll never get drunk and pass out like that again."

Garv nodded, his heart aching with the need to reassure her. "I promise, Anshika," he said, holding her hand tightly. "Last night will never happen again." They shared a gentle kiss, the bond between them stronger than ever before.

The time for Garv's flight was drawing near. He knew he had to leave soon, but the thought of parting from Anshika made his chest tighten. They hugged each other tightly for a few more minutes, savoring the last moments together before he packed his things. As he finished, he waved to Anshika's friends and followed her and Sheru to the cab.

Garv gave Anshika a smile, a bittersweet expression on his face, before stepping into the cab. Anshika stood there with Sheru, waving him off, as he disappeared into the vehicle.

Back at the airport, Garv moved quickly through check-in. He needed to get through it fast; the moment he had cleared security, he would call Anshika. He couldn't bear to be away from her for too long. He felt insecure, unsure of how to handle the distance, because to him, she was everything. In his heart, Anshika was the one thing that mattered more than anything else.

Garv called her as soon as he could, his voice full of apology and love. "I'm sorry, baccha," he said softly, his words full of sincerity. "I love you a lot, and I promise, this mistake of mine will never happen again." They spoke for a while, the sound of her voice soothing his nerves, before he boarded his flight back to Vadodara.

Back to his regular routine—back to the chaos of office politics and the insecurities of dealing with colleagues, like the guy in Surat who was always trying to prove something. Despite Garv's growing success, this man was a constant source of tension in his life. But Garv had learned to ignore the drama and focus on the positive: his good colleagues, like Nikhar bhaiya, Monika di, and Vaibhav bhai.

Vaibhav bhai, who was from another NBFC, had always been a mentor to Garv. He knew how to navigate the tough world of sales, especially with the Surat guy making life harder for everyone. Vaibhav had been in the same bank and knew the ins and outs of dealing with difficult colleagues. He took Garv under his wing, showing him how to engage with builders, how to talk to them, and how to handle the pressure of sales.

As Garv spent more time with Vaibhav bhai, he started to understand the nuances of his job. But he made the mistake of neglecting his studies, thinking he could catch up later during his 20-day leave. His sales targets, though, were not as easy to hit as he had hoped. For three months, he was stuck at zero, and when he finally got a few leads, they got rejected. Then, he was handed a file for a Cat A builder by the Surat guy.

Monika di had warned him. "This builder's file is tricky, Garv. It's hard to get out of our system. You sure you want to try this?"

But Garv, eager to prove himself, ignored her advice and pressed on. He spent all his time trying to get the file through the system before his leave, but he wasn't able to. The rejection hit him hard, and the insecurity crept in. Sales were his strength, and he felt like he was failing.

As the exams neared, Garv found himself torn. His bank's Annual Meet was in Udaipur, but Anshika was upset. She didn't understand why he would go; she was comparing his salary with hers, forgetting that everyone started somewhere. Garv, unsure of what to do, asked Nikhar bhaiya for advice. "It's an opportunity, Garv. All the national heads, CCOs, and RSMs will be there. It's a great chance to make connections."

So Garv went. But when he arrived in Udaipur, he found out his boss was on notice period. Garv had been planning to ask for leave in person, but with the situation changing, he hesitated. His boss had always been supportive, though, telling Garv to take time and that business development takes time.

When Garv finally spoke to his boss, it was awkward. "Garv, it hurts me not professionally but personally when I am supporting you and guiding you," his boss said. "You know I'm here for you. But you need to take this seriously."

Garv, feeling guilty, apologized. "I didn't mean to put you in this position, sir. I was just hesitant because I haven't performed well. I thought I'd take care of things after meeting you. I'm sorry."

Garv, still recovering from the events of the previous night, turned to Anshika, his voice tinged with guilt. "I passed out... out of nowhere," he muttered, the weight of the incident pressing down on him.

Anshika didn't respond immediately. Instead, she wrapped her arms around him tightly, seeking comfort, her face burying itself into his chest. The silence between them spoke volumes. Then, pulling away just slightly, she brought out a cheesecake from the café, a gift for their loyalty as regular customers. She smiled faintly, as if trying to lighten the mood.

"Loyalty is what matters at the end," she said softly, cutting the cheesecake. "It may be difficult, but when the fruit of loyalty ripens, it's the sweetest. Trust me."

She took a spoonful and fed him, the moment somehow tender despite the heaviness of their conversation. Afterward, she pulled him back into a tight embrace. "What happened last night... it's okay, but promise me, Garv. Promise it won't happen again. Promise that you'll never get drunk and pass out like that. Not again."

Garv held her close, his voice firm with the weight of his promise. "I swear, Anshika. Last night will never repeat itself. I'll never let you go through that again." He gently cupped her face in his hands, their foreheads touching, before pressing a soft kiss to her lips.

The warmth of the moment lingered for a while, but reality soon crept in. Garv could feel the time slipping away, his flight drawing closer. With a final hug, they both silently acknowledged the impending separation.

As Garv packed his things, he waved goodbye to Anshika's friends. She, along with Sheru, accompanied him to the cab, her face a mixture of sadness and affection. He offered her one last smile before getting into the cab, his heart heavy as it always was when leaving her.

The drive to the airport felt too short. Garv checked in quickly, eager to talk to Anshika, always feeling a sense of insecurity when they were apart. She was his anchor, the one thing that mattered more than anything else in his life. Garv had never cared for his pride, especially when it came to Anshika. Whether or not he was at fault in their arguments, he was always the first to apologize, always ready to put aside his ego to keep the peace. He would do anything for her, even be a house husband, just to spend his life by her side.

He called her once he had some quiet moments, and once again, he said what he always needed to say. "I'm sorry, Baccha," he whispered, a sincere kiss pressed to the phone's receiver. "I love you so much. I promise, this mistake won't happen again."

They spoke for a while, exchanging words of reassurance and love, before Garv boarded his flight back to Vadodara, feeling the weight of the distance between them.

Back at work, things had returned to the usual grind. Garv found himself tangled in the web of office politics, especially with a colleague from Surat, who was as insecure as he was ambitious. But amidst the chaos, Garv found some solace in his colleagues—Nikhar Bhaiya, Monika Di, and Vaibhav Bhai. Vaibhav, a former employee at the same bank, took Garv under his wing, teaching him the ropes of sales. He was more than a mentor; he understood the pressure Garv was under and wanted to ensure he wouldn't suffer the same fate he had.

Garv spent countless hours with Vaibhav, learning how to pitch to builders, how to navigate the complex world of sales. He dedicated himself to the task, thinking that if he could master it, it would be a way out of his growing insecurities. But despite his efforts, he found himself stuck, unable to move forward with his sales targets. And then, he received a difficult file—a tricky one. Monika Di had warned him about it, but Garv, determined to make something of it, pushed forward.

But in the end, things didn't go as planned. With exams looming and his work piling up, Garv was forced to juggle both responsibilities, trying to manage his studies while keeping his sales job afloat. The pressure weighed on him, but he kept his focus.

However, this led to a significant fight with Anshika. She couldn't understand his decision to attend the annual meet in Udaipur when his exams were approaching. To her, it seemed like Garv was prioritizing work over their future. "I don't care about your job, Garv," she snapped, frustration clouding her judgment.

But Garv, seeking advice from Nikhar Bhaiya, chose to go to the meet, convinced it was an important career opportunity. When he got to Udaipur, he learned that his boss wasn't there, as he was on notice. This revelation hit him hard, but he found some comfort in knowing that his boss had always been supportive. They had shared a mutual respect, and Garv knew that despite his fears, he had the backing of someone who believed in him.

His boss's words stung. "Garv, it hurts me—not professionally, but personally—when I'm supporting you, and you're hesitating to take leave. Everyone else knows you're on leave; you're the only one who doesn't."

Garv, feeling the weight of his failure, apologized. "Sorry, Sir. I didn't mean to, it's just… I haven't performed well. And with everything going on at home, I was hesitant to ask for leave. I didn't want to burden anyone."

But his boss was understanding, urging him to prioritize both his work and his exams. "Go ahead, take your leave, but remember, once exams are over, focus on your sales. Monika is counting on you to follow through."

Back in Surat, Garv reconnected with people from different regions—Bangalore, Bombay, and Punjab—thanks to Vaibhav Bhaiya, who introduced him to Karthik from Bangalore. Garv knew that moving there the following year was a possibility, especially with everything that had happened with Anshika.

As the days passed, Garv tried to balance his work, his personal life, and his studies. But there was always something pulling him in different directions. His weight loss journey, his ongoing struggles at work, and the tension with Anshika over money all created a storm in his mind. The argument over finances, sparked by their Pondicherry trip, left a bitter taste between them. Anshika questioned his priorities, and Garv, hurt by her words, couldn't let it go.

In the end, both of them had their own battles. Garv struggled with his job and exams, while Anshika fought her own insecurities, fueled by things said in passing by friends. Despite everything, Garv knew that no matter what, he would always be there for her. But what he didn't realize was that sometimes, when both people are struggling, the smallest things—like an offhand comment or a misunderstanding—could tear at the fabric of a relationship.

And yet, even in the midst of their difficulties, Garv was determined. He would find a way to make things right, no matter how hard it seemed.

Chapter 24

Even Rocks Get Cracks

Garv was finally starting to get on track in sales. He had begun sourcing in the market, fully aware that his performance would determine whether or not he could move to Bangalore. So, he focused on his work, searching for ways to pull the necessary files from the system.

On the other hand, his personal life was anything but smooth. For the first time, Garv saw his dad in a broken state, a sight he never thought he would witness. His father, after his brother's accident, was alone in Surat, taking care of his sister's family while also caring for his brother, who was bedridden due to a brain stroke. After work, his father would visit his sister's house and then go to his brother's, handling everything single-handedly. Garv knew his dad was strong and would manage, but still, this situation brought them closer. If his dad needed someone to talk to, he would call Garv, and Garv always answered. From his childhood, Garv had seen his dad always pick up the phone for him, no matter where he was, and so he did the same.

As for Anshika, things were becoming a bit tense. But Garv held on to a belief: *"No situation is ever so bad that it can't be fixed."* However, he had forgotten one crucial thing—every relationship needs effort from both sides to improve. Lately, Anshika had started complaining, comparing their relationship with others. Most of her complaints were materialistic, but there was one significant concern: all her friends' boyfriends were with them in Bangalore, and she also wanted to live with Garv. Garv tried to stay calm, but deep down, he knew things weren't going the way he hoped.

After the end of June, Garv decided to visit Bangalore. His parents had no idea that he was going; he simply told them he was staying in Vadodara, getting some rest and doing his chores. When he arrived in Bangalore, they spent some quality time together, shopping at the mall, and Garv finally gave Anshika her long-overdue birthday gift. They went clubbing, laughed, danced, and forgot about the world for a few days. When Garv visited Anshika, all her complaints seemed to disappear, and his own frustrations melted away. They cuddled, partied, and shared intimate moments, but after two days, Garv had to return to Vadodara, and reality hit again.

Back at work, Garv continued focusing on his sales performance, boosting his efforts both professionally and personally. Then, in mid-July, the Gujarat team had a farewell party for their boss and a colleague. They headed to a farmhouse in Ahmedabad. Garv was in a good mood, discussing strategies with his boss and colleague, Nikhar bhaiya, when his phone buzzed. It was Anshika calling.

The issue with Garv was that he didn't always understand that answering every call wasn't always the best choice, especially when it could disrupt important conversations with others. He picked up the call, and things weren't looking good. In the past few days, they hadn't been on the same page. Anshika had started partying late into the night, while Garv just wanted some time to talk to her, even if just for a few minutes. Their relationship had become strained, and this call was no exception.

"**Garv, can we talk?**" Anshika's voice trembled.

"**Yeah, sure.**" Garv responded, stepping into a room and locking the door behind him.

"**Garv, I think it's not working between us.**" Anshika's words hit him hard.

"What happened? Tell me." Garv asked, his voice thick with concern.

"We are different, and there's pressure from home as well." Anshika started to cry.

"Anshika, what happened? Please tell me. Something's wrong, I can tell."

"I can't take it anymore, Garv. I'm alone in Bangalore. You don't understand."

"What do you mean? What don't I understand? You say you're busy, but when you want to talk, I'm always here. Yeah, it's a struggle, but I'm trying my best. You know how much I care about you." Garv's voice was strained.

Anshika paused, gathering herself, as they continued on their video call.

"Garv, there's something I need to tell you." Anshika's voice was quiet.

"Go ahead." Garv answered, his heart pounding.

"I met someone, Garv."

"Someone from home or someone else?" Garv asked, trying to keep his composure.

"Someone from home. But I said yes to meeting them."

"And?" Garv's voice was calm, but his mind raced.

"Garv, don't you understand? Something's wrong."

At that moment, Garv felt the flood of emotions rushing through him. His thoughts scrambled like a bullet train, and he fought to hold back his tears.

"Baby, just keep it between us. Do you love me?" Garv asked, trying to keep his emotions in check.

"Yes, I do." Anshika's voice was soft but sincere.

"I told you, baby, after this financial year, I'll mostly be in Bangalore." Garv reassured her.

"Garv, you're not getting it. I'm saying something else." Anshika's voice cracked.

"I know, baby, I know. All I need to know is you love me, that's all." Garv's voice was steady, but the pain was evident in his eyes.

"Why, Garv?"

Garv couldn't hold it anymore. The tears flowed freely, unable to be controlled, as he realized the weight of everything that had been left unsaid.

Kya bolna chahte ho? Main boldeta hoon," Garv said, his voice tinged with frustration. "Clearly, you must have had a good time, spent the night. What else is there to say, Anshika?"

"Aapko farak nahi padta," Anshika replied, her voice cool but hurt.

"You do love me, right? Your mistakes are forgiven. I don't want to know what happened," Garv continued, his voice softening as he tried to reach her.

Anshika, who knew Garv well, understood that he never cried easily. Seeing him cry now broke her heart. "Garv, nothing happened. Please, stop crying. Someone will see you."

The truth was, Garv's boss and colleagues had been calling him nonstop. They knew Garv as the life of the party, and as they enjoyed themselves by the pool, his sister Monika had sensed something was wrong. She knocked on his door, asking him to open up.

"Garv, everyone's waiting for you downstairs," Monika said, concerned.

"Yeah, I'm coming in 15 minutes," Garv replied, trying to gather himself.

Monika, seeing his red eyes, asked gently, "Is everything okay?"

"I'll be down in 15-20 minutes, just some trouble at home... got a bit emotional," Garv explained.

"We're waiting. Let me know if you need anything," Monika said before leaving.

Once she was gone, Garv called Anshika again.

"Baccha, please listen. You know I love you. If you went out and had a drink, and something happened with someone else by mistake, I'd understand. I'll let it go, I promise. It matters to me, but I won't hold it against you," Garv said, his voice shaking with sincerity.

"Aap yeh karke apni self-respect ko girayenge, Garv. Aap samajh rahe ho?" Anshika replied, her tone a mix of concern and confusion.

"Anshika, there's already so much going on in my life. I'm telling you the truth. I love you. I always have, and I always will. You know how much I've changed for you. From the start till the end, it's always going to be you. Ego and self-respect mean nothing when it comes to you. They don't matter in front of you. You're everything to me. I'm sorry," Garv continued, his emotions raw and vulnerable.

"Please don't say sorry, baccha. I'm sorry. Just stop crying," Anshika whispered, her voice softening as she tried to comfort him.

"Anshika, please don't feel guilty. I'm telling you the truth—I won't mind anything. It's just a rough time, and we'll get through it together," Garv said, trying to reassure her.

"Baccha, you go and enjoy yourself now, or everyone will misunderstand. We'll talk later, okay?" Anshika said, her voice full of care.

"You just say the word, I'll listen. I'll always be there. I promise, no matter what. I'm sorry if I've been loud. Have you ever heard me fight, except for with you? I love you. I love you so much, Aanshu. Please don't do this," Garv pleaded.

"Baccha, no worries. You go enjoy, we'll sort this out later. Just relax," Anshika reassured him.

With that, Garv left his room and joined his colleagues by the pool. His boss immediately pulled him in, handing him a beer. Garv dipped his head under the water a few times, his anger cooling in the pool's embrace. He lit a cigarette, taking a long drag, and then his boss pulled him aside.

"Garv bhai, like a big brother, I'm telling you—love isn't one-sided. You have to give it your all, on both ends. You're working hard, but you'll also have to fight for her," his boss said.

"Yes, Sir," Garv replied, listening intently.

"Bro, if she gives up, it won't matter how hard you fight. You're fighting for her, but don't turn it into a competition. Everything will be okay. Chill out," his boss continued, offering advice.

"Thank you, Sir," Garv said, appreciating the wisdom.

The pool party eventually ended, and Garv, Monika, and Nikhar Bhaiya sat together. Nikhar tried to calm him down, sensing Garv's turmoil.

"Garv, what's going on? Don't take so much tension. Nothing will happen," Nikhar said, trying to ease his friend's mind.

"I don't know, bhai. I just... something doesn't feel right. Seriously, I don't understand," Garv confessed.

"Garv, no matter how much you stress, nothing will change. It'll all work out," Monika said gently, offering reassurance.

"Monika, you don't understand. She's the most important thing in my life. She always will be. I can and will fight for her," Garv said with determination.

"You sound like you're ready to die for her, Garv," Nikhar remarked with a chuckle.

"You never know, bhai," Garv replied, his voice serious.

"Bhai, you're a little drunk. Rest now, and then we'll party again later tonight. Take it easy," Nikhar said, trying to lighten the mood.

"Yeah, you're right," Garv responded, though his mind still raced with thoughts of Anshika.

Later, Garv, feeling drained, called Anshika again. Despite knowing something was off between them, he continued talking to her, determined to fix whatever was wrong.

After two days of partying and trying to clear his head, Garv finally returned to Vadodara. He had been waiting to go to Bangalore for five days, and now, as he made his way to the city, he hoped things would get back to normal.

He arrived in Bangalore, smoked a cigarette to calm his nerves, and then took a cab straight to Anshika's house. As soon as he entered her room, Anshika hugged him tightly, kissing him deeply. They held each other, silently enjoying the comfort of being together. It was Thursday night, around 11:00 PM, and they sat hand in hand, quietly sharing the peace they had longed for.

Anshika brought out Rajma Chawal for him, his favorite dish. She had cooked it for him, knowing how much he loved it. They ate together, savoring the simple, comforting meal. Afterward, they cuddled, enjoying each other's company in silence.

"I told you, we're not discussing what happened the other day. Let's just let it go," Garv said softly, wrapping his arms around her.

Anshika hugged him tightly in return, her arms around his neck, her face buried in his chest. They shared a peaceful, romantic night together.

The next morning, they woke up to the soft aroma of coffee. Anshika made coffee for both of them, and they enjoyed it together, sitting close, their hands intertwined.

"Baccha, can I ask you something?" Anshika asked, looking into his eyes.

"Yes, tell me," Garv replied.

"Why do you love me so much?" she asked, her voice soft and filled with curiosity.

"Have I ever asked for anything in return?" Garv replied, his eyes never leaving hers.

"That's not an answer, Garv," Anshika said, a hint of playfulness in her tone.

She cupped his face gently, her eyes searching his for the truth. "Tell me, why do you love me so unconditionally?"

"I don't believe in options or backups. What I have with you, that's my life. I love you for who you are. Nothing else matters. I know things have been messy, but it's okay. This will pass. At the end of it all, I just want to spend my last breath in your lap. That's it, baccha," Garv said, his voice filled with sincerity.

Anshika kissed him deeply, passionately, then pulled away, smiling mischievously. "So, are you partying with my neighbors today?"

"Of course, no problem," Garv answered, his smile returning.

"It means, those five girls are there, that's why," Anshika said.

"Invite your office colleague, Suraj, too. If you get another company, it would be good, kid," Garv teased.

Garv smiled.

"I'm here, your kid," Anshika said sweetly.

"Chill, I'll ask. But if he doesn't show up, we'll still party. Should I say yes?" Anshika continued.

"Yes, I'm in," Garv replied.

Then, Anshika told her friends that they would be there for the party. After that, she and Garv just cuddled with each other, not saying much because their eyes spoke everything. They simply gazed into each other's eyes, letting their lips stay busy with kisses. After a romantic morning, they finished some office work, and then went shopping at the mall. They spent about three to four hours there. Garv enjoyed shopping with Anshika because he loved spending time with her. And yes, when a guy is in love, everything becomes enjoyable, especially if it makes his other half happy—no matter what it is. Trust me, when Garv was a kid, his mom used to tell him to go shopping with her. He never liked shopping for himself and would tell her, "Mom, you know my size, so you pick it out."

Now, Garv had changed a lot. Why wouldn't he? They had almost been together for ten years, and the only thing left was marriage. Garv found relief in only two things: Anshika's smile and Anshika's hug. Well, as evening approached, they headed back home to get ready. Anshika opened Garv's suitcase and picked out his clothes. Once they were both ready, Anshika looked absolutely stunning, but Garv wasn't sure how to compliment her in a meaningful way.

Anshika, looking at him with questioning eyes, asked, "How do I look?" Garv stood up from the bed and walked towards her. Anshika smiled, trying to move away and jokingly said, "Kid, you'll mess up my lipstick."

But Garv was in no mood to listen. He grabbed her hand, pulled her towards him, kissed her lips, and hugged her tightly. "You look amazing. For me, no matter what time it is, you always look beautiful," he said.

Though Anshika's lipstick ended up on Garv's lips, she wiped it off, and then Garv hugged her from behind. They both looked into the mirror, and he kissed her on the cheek. Anshika, with a playful shove, told him, "Let me get ready; we'll be late." After they were both dressed, they went over to Anshika's neighbor's house. For Garv, it was the most sophisticated party he had ever been to because boys never prepare so much for a party. Anshika's friends had cooked bread rolls, sandwiches, and were setting up a cocktail bar. Garv felt awkward and kept asking Anshika not to leave him alone in the kitchen.

He was especially tense because only vodka was available at the party, and Garv didn't really like vodka—unless he was drunk. Knowing he had to drink responsibly since he wasn't with his friends, he still felt a bit uneasy about the vodka. While Anshika and her friends were busy in the kitchen, Garv called Anuj.

"Hey bro, how's it going?" Anuj asked.

"Nothing much, bro. Just the party, but I'm feeling awkward," Garv confessed.

"Why?" Anuj asked.

"Bro, have you ever partied alone with six girls?" Garv asked.

Anuj laughed and told him to chill.

After a few drinks, everyone realized they might run out of booze, so Garv volunteered to go buy more. He went downstairs and grabbed a bottle of Absolute Vodka and a flask of Black Dog whiskey for himself, knowing that after four shots of vodka, he'd need something else. When he came back, they started dancing to the music again. Garv got his cigarette out, and Anshika allowed him to smoke.

At one point, Garv went to the washroom and mixed some whisky with tap water to feel better. He returned, and they began playing a wild game of Truth or Dare. Anshika was eager for Garv to choose a dare. Finally, Garv chose dare, and they were tasked with dancing together. As the music played, they danced closely, with Garv holding Anshika by the waist. During the dance, Anshika kissed him, and they shared a passionate kiss, hugging tightly. The room erupted in claps as they continued, and the shots kept coming. Garv didn't lose his senses, but something felt off. He wasn't enjoying the company, and although he wanted to say something, he didn't want to upset Anshika, who had worked hard to make new friends.

After the party ended, Garv and Anshika said their goodbyes and headed home. Once inside their room, Anshika hugged him tightly and kissed him, and the night turned romantic. Garv, who sweated a lot, didn't mind, and they both cuddled and slept in each other's arms. The next morning, Garv kissed Anshika on the forehead and hugged her even tighter. But something was wrong. Anshika's mood was off, and Garv could sense it. He tried to avoid bringing it up, just cuddling and giving her a massage, but he never could finish it because Anshika was too hot to handle. After a light lunch and watching a movie, they went out again. They went to the mall and then to Vapour, but luck wasn't on their side, as the brewery was closed. Garv wasn't in the mood for canned beer, so he ordered an Old Monk peg for himself.

As they sat in silence, Garv asked Anshika, "Can we go to your friend's house and party instead?"

Anshika, in a rare moment of resistance, said, "Not today, it's our time."

They went to Ironhill instead, but Garv could still sense something was off. He was trying to avoid conflict and held her hand, asking her, "Baby, what's on your mind?"

Anshika smiled and said, "Nothing, I'm fine." But Garv knew that smile was fake. He could read her every expression, having spent so much time on video calls with her. He had screenshots of their photos and dreams of putting them on their bedroom wall.

Knowing her better than anyone, Garv asked again, "Baby, let's go home. We need to talk."

Anshika held his hand, and they paid the bill. On the cab ride back, Garv held her hand tightly, sensing that something wasn't right. They arrived home, and after sitting on the bed, Garv hugged her, asking again, "Baby, what happened?"

Anshika started crying, and Garv knew things were about to get bad. He braced himself, though he knew there were lines no one should cross—lines that shouldn't be ignored or let go.

With a heavy voice, Garv asked, "Baccha, please tell me what happened. It's not going to get sorted like this, and we'll ruin our relationship if we keep going down this path. Please, open up."

Anshika's tears only increased, and her face was streaked with distress. She couldn't bring herself to face him with the truth, but Garv was losing patience fast. She finally spoke, though her voice was barely a whisper. "I kissed someone... mistakenly."

The words hung in the air, and Garv felt his heart drop. He held back his anger for a moment and calmly asked, "When? Where?"

Anshika, trembling, hesitated for a second before replying, "You'll find everything on WhatsApp." She explained everything in a shaky message—how it had been pouring rain, how they had gone to a party with some office colleagues, and how the guy had offered to drop her home when Suraj, the usual ride, had already left.

"He took me to his place first to get a helmet for me," she wrote. "We were sitting on the couch, and I kissed him on the cheek, and then... he kissed me back. After that, I just left."

Garv couldn't believe it at first. His mind raced, trying to piece together what he was reading. Something didn't add up. It wasn't the full story, he could tell. As he finished reading, his anger surged to new heights. Without thinking, he threw his phone at the front wall with all his force, the screen shattering on impact.

Trying to maintain control, he gritted his teeth. But his patience was slipping.

"Anshika, who was he? Tell me his name," Garv's voice was barely restrained.

Anshika shook her head. "Please, I can't tell you. It was my mistake, not his. I don't want to fight."

"Do you hear me? I just want to know who he is. Does he know about us?" Garv demanded.

Anshika stayed silent, her breath shallow, knowing Garv's anger was only growing. He repeated himself, louder now, "I want to know, Anshika!"

Garv's tone turned more menacing, and she flinched. He opened his bag, grabbed his pack of cigarettes, and headed for the door.

"Where are you going?" Anshika pleaded, her voice trembling with panic.

"I need to clear my head. I'm leaving," he muttered.

Anshika tried to stop him, grabbing his arm. She didn't want him to go, not like this, not in this mindset. "Please, smoke in the washroom or the balcony. Don't leave like this, Garv."

Garv didn't respond. He walked toward the washroom, his steps heavy. He slammed the door shut behind him but didn't lock it. Inside, he lit up two cigarettes, inhaling deeply as the smoke swirled around him. But the anger was building again, sharp and violent. He kept staring at his shattered phone screen, reading the message over and over.

His mind was spiraling, and there was only one way Garv knew to release his frustration—through pain. But he didn't want to hurt anyone else; he wanted to hurt himself, to release the anger in the only way that made sense in the chaos of his mind. His fists began pounding the walls, each punch more powerful than the last. The sound of his blows echoed through the small room.

Anshika rushed toward the washroom, hearing the destructive sounds. She flung open the door, her eyes wide with fear at the sight of Garv, his knuckles bruised and swollen from his punches. She grabbed him, holding him tightly, begging him to stop.

"Stop! Please, slap me instead, Garv. Don't hurt yourself," she cried, tears streaming down her face.

Garv looked at her, his face twisted in a mix of anger and helplessness. "No, Anshika. You don't understand. I can't hurt you. You've never seen my bad side. I've kept it buried for ten years, since I fell in love with you. But right now... right now, I can't keep it in. Let me do this... I need to hurt myself so the pain in my heart can be released."

Anshika sobbed as she tried to hold him, but Garv gently pushed her away. His pain, his self-loathing, was too much.

His knuckles were swollen, but he didn't care. He sat down on the bed, cradling his bleeding hand, trying to keep the blood from dripping onto the floor. Anshika rushed to him with cotton, silently offering to help him dress the wound.

"Please, let me clean this up," she whispered, her voice thick with emotion.

But Garv didn't respond. His mind was consumed with the storm of emotions inside him. He knew what he had to do next, but he didn't know if it would make things better or worse.

"I'm leaving," he muttered. "I'm going to the airport."

Anshika refused to let him go. She quickly called Sheru and made Garv talk to him, but he cut the call, his resolve hardening.

He stood, heading for the door. As he reached for the handle, Anshika screamed his name. She stood in front of him, holding a razor, its sharp edge gleaming in her hand. "If you leave, Garv, I'll slit my wrists. Don't you dare leave me."

The words hit Garv like a slap, but they weren't enough to stop him. His mind was reeling. He knew Anshika's limits, knew she wasn't bluffing. His heart thudded painfully in his chest, and before she could react, he snatched the razor from her hand.

Without saying another word, he made a clean cut across his left hand, the blood spilling out, a testament to the overwhelming pain he couldn't escape.

"I told you, Anshika... you don't want to see my bad side," Garv muttered through gritted teeth, his voice barely audible.

Anshika dropped to her knees, sobbing uncontrollably, reaching for his injured hand. "Garv, please don't do this... don't hurt yourself."

But Garv simply looked at her, his eyes filled with anguish. "Don't touch me. I need to be left alone."

As the blood soaked through the fabric of his shirt, Anshika sat beside him in silence. The room was filled with the weight of unspoken words, the suffocating tension between them only growing.

Garv gently placed his hands in Anshika's lap as she began to apply medicine and cotton to his wounds. The soothing motions of her touch contrasted with the storm inside him. He winced as she finished, the coolness of the cotton not enough to ease the ache gnawing at him. Anshika, sensing the tension, moved closer, reaching for him to offer a comforting hug. But Garv, caught in his turmoil, instinctively pulled back.

"I've already booked a cab," Garv muttered, his voice distant. "We're going to Sheru's home. Please inform her."

Anshika looked at him, concerned. "Garv, it's 1:00 AM. It's so late—"

He cut her off, his gaze piercing hers. "You have two options. Either we go to Sheru's place, or I go to the airport alone." His words were blunt, unyielding, as if giving her no space to argue.

Silence stretched between them as they waited for the cab. Garv, still avoiding Anshika's gaze, finally spoke again, his voice quiet but firm. "Who is the guy?"

Anshika hesitated for a moment, then gave in, her voice soft as she spoke the name. "His surname is Gupta."

Garv nodded, the name reverberating in his mind like an echo of something broken.

As they waited, Garv tried to push away the thoughts of Anshika with someone else, his mind struggling to come to terms with the picture she had painted. No matter how hard he tried, the images wouldn't form. It was like trying to catch smoke with bare hands.

Tears began to sting his eyes, unbidden and relentless. Anshika, reaching out to him, tried to hold his hand, but Garv quickly withdrew. She placed her hand gently on his lap, her touch tentative and cautious, as if afraid of further shattering the fragile connection between them.

He couldn't focus. His phone buzzed in his pocket, and without a second thought, he pulled it out, tapping out a message to his contacts. His fingers moved with practiced speed, asking for a favor to erase the name Anshika had just given him—obliterate any trace of it, make it disappear. He messaged three or four of his trusted people, the ones who had the means to handle these things.

Garv's mind was clouded with a mixture of pain and frustration. *Mental pain is the hardest,* he thought bitterly, *because there's no medicine for it. Nothing to numb it.*

The cab finally arrived, and they made their way to Sheru's home. The walk from the gate to the building was a short distance—just two hundred meters—but for Garv, it felt like an eternity. Every step seemed to echo with the weight of his thoughts. As they walked, Garv deleted the messages he had sent. He knew the power of the people he was reaching out to. They were well-connected, dangerous even, in ways that could ruin lives. He couldn't risk them finding out too much. Not now.

If they knew what was going on, the consequences would be severe—not just for the man who had kissed Anshika, but for her as well. Garv's respect for Anshika ran deep, and he could never let her world be destroyed by the choices of others.

His friends—his close circle—were businessmen, political figures, and people with ties to the police. They didn't hesitate to act if someone hurt someone they loved. Garv knew they could find anyone and tear apart their life in a month or less. They would have no mercy. But he also knew the risks. If Anshika's career was tarnished, he wouldn't be able to forgive himself.

By the time they reached the building, Garv's thoughts were still heavy with the weight of everything he couldn't control. His body felt rigid, and the silence between him and Anshika was suffocating. The last fifty meters of their walk were a blur. As they neared the entrance, Garv finally, reluctantly, reached for Anshika's fist, his fingers wrapping around hers, though his eyes remained fixed on the ground, avoiding hers.

He had made up his mind. He needed answers—answers that would guide his next steps. Would he stay and try to fix things, or would he leave? The decision was still hanging in the air, unanswered.

Sheru greeted them at her door and led them inside. The conversation that followed was short and to the point. Sheru, always the curious one, asked Garv what had happened.

Garv, still trying to shield his pain, didn't let his hands be visible. His palms were burnt from his reckless actions earlier. He wore a shirt to cover his wounds, concealing the fresh cuts on his hands, while also hiding the evidence of the burn marks he had inflicted on himself in an attempt to numb his emotions.

"Sarcastic as always, Garv?" Sheru said with a smile, trying to break the tension, but Garv only shook his head.

"Ask your friend, Sheru," Garv said, his voice strained. He needed a break from talking about it.

He turned away and stepped onto the balcony, needing the space to breathe.

Anshika had poured her heart out to Sheru, and Sheru, still processing the weight of the confession, couldn't believe her ears. She stared at Anshika, her voice filled with disbelief as she asked, "Anshika, are you doing this to break up, or has this really happened?"

"No, it happened, Sheru. I made that mistake," Anshika replied, her voice breaking.

Sheru's frustration grew, her anger visible. Just then, Garv entered the room, sitting on the bed with an air of quiet contemplation.

"Garv, how are you? What do you think about everything she just told me?" Sheru asked, turning to him.

"I don't know, Sheru. Honestly, I don't know how to react," Garv admitted, his voice heavy with confusion.

Sheru wasn't satisfied. "No, Garv, this can't go on like this. A decision has to be made. She's done this once; if you forgive her, what's the guarantee she won't do it again? If you get married, will she do this after? Anyone who can cheat once is capable of doing it again."

Anshika's eyes welled with tears, and she looked helplessly at Garv, her sorrow written all over her face.

"I don't want to end this, Sheru. I know it shouldn't have happened, but I'm still waiting for an explanation from Anshika," Garv said, trying to keep his composure.

Anshika's voice was barely audible as she cried. "I feel so alone in Bangalore, Garv. I told you to come, to be with me. I didn't want to be alone here. This doesn't make any sense, and there's no justification for it. I accept that it was my fault."

Garv's eyes were wet with tears, but he fought them back, torn between anger and sorrow. He was trying to keep his calm, especially with Sheru in the room. His tears, though, were reserved only for Anshika and his mother. No one had seen him cry in years—not even his mother, who had always known him as the tough, unshakeable person in their family. But those who truly knew him understood that if Garv stood by their side, they had nothing to fear.

"Anshika, I love you. I can't undo that. Will you ever do this again?" Garv asked softly.

"I feel so alone here, Garv. I struggle too. It's not just you—I'm struggling, and I fight through it. I didn't want to make this mistake, but I did. I am so sorry. I just need you, Garv," Anshika said between sobs, reaching out for him.

Garv paused, his voice filled with emotion. "I'm fighting, Anshika. I'm struggling, but I'm not giving up. I know that if we get through this, we'll be together forever. And that's all I need. My career? It can change, but being with you, growing old with you—that's all that matters to me."

Sheru, still not convinced, asked, "Garv, can you forgive her?"

"There's no option, Sheru. I love her too much. And maybe, just maybe, if it happens again, I'll be angry, but I won't hurt her. I can never leave her. That's not even a choice for me," Garv replied, his voice firm, despite the pain.

Anshika's sobs grew louder as Garv silently pleaded with Sheru to leave them alone, communicating his request through a silent look. Sheru, sensing the need for privacy, stepped out, closing the door behind her. Garv switched off the lights, giving himself the space to cry in solitude. He sat on the bed, staring at Anshika.

"Why do you love me so much, Garv? I don't deserve your love. Please, don't love me like this. I feel so guilty," Anshika whispered through her tears.

Garv took her hands gently in his, his voice steady despite the storm of emotions inside him. "I took time to fall in love with you, Anshika. Once I did, there was no going back. I don't need logic for this. If you need me, I'll always be there. If I'm needed, I'll do whatever it takes to be by your side."

"Will you forgive me?" Anshika asked, her voice barely a whisper.

"It will take time, but don't worry, I won't let you feel it. I'll heal myself, but yes, I'll be possessive for a while. Maybe for a few days, maybe months. Please handle that, okay? I just need to know you're okay, that you're with me," Garv said.

Anshika nodded, her heart heavy with emotion. "Anything, Garv. Just don't leave me."

Garv hesitated, then asked, "Can I ask something from you?"

Anshika looked at him, wiping her tears. "What do you want, Garv?"

"I might sound selfish right now, but yes, I'm taking advantage of the situation. I'm being selfish. But will you remove the CA condition, and then I can promise that I'll be in Bangalore in the next six months?" Garv's voice carried a quiet urgency.

Anshika considered it for a moment before asking, "But Garv, would you marry me if everything falls into place?"

Garv looked at her, his tone steady but filled with resolve. "Anshika, I don't want to run away and get married. You know that. I want both our families there. I can convince my family, but if yours doesn't accept it, then we can't move forward with it."

Anshika's expression faltered. "What if they don't accept us?"

Garv's voice grew more intense. "For you, Anshika, I'd lower my self-respect, my ego, everything. I'll fight for us, even against your family. I'll stand by you, no matter what. If it means fighting for you, then I will."

"Then what about the CA, Garv?" Anshika asked, her voice filled with concern.

Garv looked at her with determination. "Let me focus on my business for the next 6 to 8 months, and I'll make the switch to a decent package in Bangalore. At the same time, I'll apply for a Distance MBA from a good college too."

Anshika nodded thoughtfully, her eyes softening as she replied, "Alright, but promise me one thing—you will clear CA. I mean, I'm willing to take away the condition of CA for our marriage, but you have to clear it, no matter how much time it takes."

"Yes, I promise," Garv said firmly.

Anshika's eyes filled with tears as she gazed at him. "I'm sorry, Baccha. Please forgive me. I love you so much. I may never be able to love you as you deserve, but I love you with all my heart."

"If I hadn't forgiven you, I wouldn't have brought you to Sheru's house, and I certainly wouldn't have taken your hand in mine," Garv said softly, his voice breaking. "In my life, nothing matters more than you."

And then, finally, Garv broke down. His tears flowed freely, and Anshika, heartbroken at the sight of him, gently took his face in her hands. She guided his head to rest in her lap, and she laid her face over his, soothing him with her touch. Garv buried his face in her lap and began to cry, his emotions overwhelming him. Anshika turned him around and kissed his forehead softly, her own tears falling onto his face. They kissed each other, their embrace tight, as if neither wanted to let go.

"I love you so much," Garv whispered through his tears. "I'm sorry you feel lonely because of me. I promise I'll be in Bangalore soon."

Anshika shook her head gently, holding him closer. "Please, Garv, not tonight. Don't say sorry tonight. Just stay with me."

She wrapped her arms around him, pulling him closer, burying his face in her arms as they shared the warmth of each other's embrace. But then, something shifted within Garv. He pulled back slightly, his expression serious.

"What's wrong, Garv?" Anshika asked, her voice soft but confused. "Come here, don't pull away."

"We don't have protection, Anshika," he said, his voice low.

Anshika gave him a playful look. "It's your fault, you know. It's your job to bring the condom."

Garv gave her a look in return, but then he pulled her back into his arms. Anshika whispered in his ear, her breath hot against his skin. "Tonight, let it go. We've been through enough. We don't need it."

And so, they let their passions take over, losing themselves in each other. They were tangled in a wild, sweaty romance, completely lost in the moment. Afterwards, they held each other tightly, their hearts still racing. They went to the bathroom to wash up, then returned to the bed, where they curled up together, their bodies entwined under the blanket. It was already 6:30 in the morning, so they decided to cuddle for a while longer before heading home.

Once back, Anshika took Garv's hand in hers and gently applied medicine to the marks and injuries on his palm. As she did, a wave of anger and concern washed over her.

"Please," she said, her voice trembling. "Never hurt yourself again. If you do, I swear I'll never talk to you again." She pulled him into a tight embrace, her love and worry pouring into the gesture.

They spent the day together, relaxing and enjoying each other's company. They went on a double date with Garv's friend Nishant and his wife. Later, Garv stepped outside with Nishant for a smoke, still processing everything that had happened. He knew he wasn't going to judge Anshika, but the moment still haunted him. Nishant, sensing his struggle, spoke candidly.

"It'll take time, Garv," he said, his voice steady. "But if you've decided to forgive her, then you need to let go. Don't hold on to it. If you keep picturing it, it will hurt your relationship. You've got to let it go, fast, or it'll linger."

The evening went on, filled with laughter, music, and good times, but Garv still couldn't shake the feeling. Later, at home, he and Anshika danced together, their bodies moving as one, lost in the rhythm of the night. They kissed, their passion reigniting, as the night grew deeper.

Finally, the time for Garv's flight arrived. Anshika held his hand tightly, tears in her eyes. "I'm sorry again," she whispered, kissing his forehead.

Garv kissed her lips gently, his hands cupping her face. "Let it go," he whispered. "Give me time to let go of it too. We'll get through this."

He kissed her one last time, leaving his love marks on her lips. Then, he hugged her tightly, as if afraid to let her go. Before leaving, he asked for one of her tops, wanting something of hers to hold onto. She gave it to him, and he took it with him as a reminder of her, something to hold onto while he was apart from her.

Finally, Garv was back in Vadodara, fully immersed in his work. He had set his sights on his core business, knowing that to make the move to Bangalore, he needed to handle countless files and set up his consultant base. His days were filled with intense focus, tipping consultants with his own money and incentives to gain more leads. Despite the growing success in his career, something was missing—Anshika.

Around ten days into his return, Anshika had started distancing herself. It wasn't intentional, but Garv couldn't ignore the fact that she was slipping away from him. It wasn't work that was keeping her busy; it was the after-office parties, the clubbing, and house parties. Garv had no issues with that lifestyle, but what hurt him deeply was her lack of communication. She stopped replying to his messages, and that silence was unbearable.

Garv was staying with Vaibhav Bhai, who had been supporting him through his business efforts and helping him handle the files that he'd taken on during his exams. Vaibhav noticed Garv's condition, especially how he was smoking excessively, and suggested that Garv consider a job with Bajaj in Vadodara, offering a decent 30% hike in salary. But Garv was steadfast. He refused to switch careers now. He had one goal in mind: to be with Anshika, and he couldn't afford to let that slip away.

As the days passed, Garv's frustration grew. He threw himself into his work, focusing on sourcing and handling business, but the silence from Anshika was eating at him. Finally, on the 16th of July, they had a huge fight. Garv couldn't take it anymore—he needed her, but she was too absorbed in her social life to notice.

"Anshika, this isn't about you finding time for me," Garv said, his voice thick with emotion. "It's about you talking to me. Just a simple conversation. That's all I need."

Anshika's response was cold, dismissive. "Okay, decide what you want. Tell me how much time you need, Garv."

Garv's voice cracked as he replied, "I don't need much. Just 15 minutes. In the morning when you're free, at lunch, or at night when you get home. Just 15 minutes when you're free, no matter the time. I'll always wait for your call, and I promise, I'll never skip your calls, no matter where I am."

Anshika responded dryly, "Okay, fine. 15 minutes today, and I'll follow this routine. But now, I'm off to a party. Bye."

The casualness in her tone stung Garv, but he tried to push it aside. What troubled him more, though, was that Anshika wasn't spending time with her college friends, Sheru and Chetna. He was growing more anxious. He didn't know what was happening, and the uncertainty was driving him mad.

In an attempt to avoid overthinking, Garv began staying late at the office, leaving around 3 or 4 AM. His panic attacks had become more frequent, though they were still mild. He refused to show weakness, even to himself. The work kept him distracted, and the file that had been stuck for so long was finally about to be approved. Garv had also planned his trip to Bangalore for the 30th of July, with the intention to take a short break and focus on his future.

But on the 27th of July, just days before his trip, things took a turn for the worse. Anshika had agreed that they would start talking normally again from that night. Garv had waited eagerly for this moment, hoping for some normalcy in their relationship. It was past midnight, and he saw that Anshika was online on Instagram. Yet, she wasn't answering his calls. She wasn't responding to his messages either. Instead, she had just sent a short text saying she was going to a party.

The frustration built up in Garv's chest. He waited until 1 AM, trying to hold it together. He tried calling her again and again, but there was no response—she kept cutting his calls. It was as if she had shut him out entirely. By now, Garv's panic attacks had escalated, and he found himself speeding down the streets in his car, hoping the rush of the road would keep his mind from spiraling. He tried to distract himself, telling himself to be patient, but the emptiness inside him was unbearable.

Finally, around 1:30 AM, he saw that Sheru was online. He quickly texted her, asking if she could help him. She replied almost immediately, and within moments, Sheru was on the phone with him.

Garv's breakdown was the culmination of months of emotional turmoil, frustration, and pain. He had given everything to Anshika, but her actions had left him broken and lost. His tears didn't just express heartbreak; they were a release of the pent-up anger, confusion, and betrayal he had been carrying. Garv had always been patient, always trying to hold things together, even when the relationship seemed to be slipping through his fingers.

Anuj, understanding the gravity of the situation, was one of the few people Garv could rely on for emotional clarity. When he saw Garv's state, he immediately tried to comfort him, even though he knew how deep Garv's pain went. Anuj was right - sometimes, letting go was the hardest thing to do, but it was often necessary for healing.

"Listen to me, Golu," Anuj said, his voice steady but firm. "You've done your best. You can't keep chasing someone who isn't willing to meet you halfway. Anshika's actions speak louder than words. Don't let her hurt you more than this."

Garv was silent for a while, overwhelmed by the situation. He knew what Anuj was saying made sense, but his emotional attachment to Anshika, the love he still felt for her, made it hard to let go. After a long pause, Garv spoke, his voice trembling, "I just... I just don't understand, Anuj. After everything we've been through, why is she doing this? I don't deserve this."

Anuj sighed, his heart aching for his friend. "You deserve someone who will give you the same love, trust, and respect you've given. Right now, it's about healing, Golu. You need to take care of yourself. Let her go, and maybe one day, you'll see that this was the right choice."

The silence stretched between them for a moment, the weight of Garv's pain heavy in the air. He stayed quiet, letting his thoughts swirl in his head. The battle inside him raged on. But eventually, he let out a defeated sigh. "I know you're right, Anuj. I just can't seem to let go."

"You will," Anuj replied softly. "It's going to hurt for a while, but you'll heal. You just have to give yourself time."

The minutes stretched into hours as Garv continued to cry, his emotions raw. The weight of everything seemed too much to carry alone. Eventually, he collapsed onto his couch, exhausted. Anuj stayed on the phone, silent for most of it, just there, offering unspoken support.

It wasn't easy, and it wouldn't be over quickly, but Garv knew deep down that the time to move on had come. The love he had so fiercely held on to was now causing him more harm than good, and as painful as it was, he needed to let it go.

The next morning, after a restless night, Garv stood in front of the mirror. His reflection looked weary, but there was a flicker of resolve in his eyes. It was time to rebuild. Time to focus on himself, on his work, on his future. No longer would he allow himself to be torn apart by someone who couldn't see his worth.

He looked at his phone, saw the missed calls from Anshika, his parents, his friends. For a moment, he felt the temptation to call her back, to hear her voice, to hope that she would apologize and everything would go back to the way it was. But he knew that was only wishful thinking. He had to stay strong. It was time to take control of his own life.

Garv put his phone on silent, locked it away in a drawer, and stepped out into the day. The journey ahead would be difficult, but it was one he would have to take alone, for now. He had a lot to figure out, but he knew one thing for sure: he would never again lose himself for someone who wasn't willing to fight for him.

"Bhai, you know how I am. I went all in for her, Anuj. She made me lose myself," Garv said, his voice cracking with frustration.

"Stop it, Garv. I'm always here with you, you know that. Why are you overthinking it? Everyone's under a lot of stress right now," Anuj replied, trying to calm him down.

"No, Bhai. I'm going to show her how bad it feels to lose someone," Garv said, his voice filled with anger.

He ended the call abruptly and sat on the balcony railing, his legs hanging outside as he stared into the void. Just then, Anshika's video call came through. Garv picked it up, and Anshika immediately noticed the dangerous position he was in.

"Baccha, please get off there! I'm serious, something could happen!" Anshika pleaded, panic rising in her voice.

"If you want a breakup, I'll show you how it's done. I'll be in Bangalore today," Garv retorted, his voice hard.

"Fine, come. We'll talk, but get down from there, please," Anshika urged, her tone softening slightly.

"No more talking today, Anshika. I'm going to give you the best breakup you've ever had," Garv said, his words laced with finality.

Garv quickly booked his flight to Bangalore. Anshika informed her friends and family about his plans, while Arpan, Garv's close friend, became concerned. Arpan had been on his way to Vadodara, but he turned around halfway to join Garv in Bangalore. On the other side, Rathiji and Anuj were also heading to Vadodara, reassuring Garv's parents that they would take care of him.

At the airport, Garv received a call from his dad. He had been trying to reach him, clearly worried.

"Son, please understand how much you mean to everyone. Your family and friends are all so concerned. You don't want to hurt yourself over this," his dad said gently, his voice filled with concern. "I've been through the same. I lost my first love too, and you need to understand that people around you are just trying to help."

Garv listened silently, his emotions swirling inside. He could feel the weight of his father's words, but his anger and pain made it hard to take in. He responded quietly, "I'll be back in a few days, Dad."

Garv then called Pankaj, who also tried to reassure him. "Come to Surat, Garv. I'll go with you to Bangalore," Pankaj offered, knowing full well Garv wasn't likely to listen.

Anuj, however, wasn't too worried. He knew Garv was strong, even if he was acting recklessly now. His main concern was that Garv wouldn't lose control and hurt Anshika, especially considering the deep anger he was holding inside.

As Garv boarded the flight, he received another call from Anshika.

"Did you board the flight?" Anshika asked, her voice sounding more tentative than usual.

"Just pray this flight never lands, Anshika," Garv replied bitterly before abruptly hanging up.

Meanwhile, Sheru had a conversation with Anshika, offering her support but warning her that if things went badly, it would be on her. As Garv's flight landed in Bangalore, he immediately called a cab to head straight to Anshika's house. On the way, he called his mom, trying to maintain some normalcy despite the storm raging inside him.

Garv finally reached Anshika's home, his heart racing with anger and hurt as he walked straight to her flat. He knocked, but when no one answered, he called her. Anshika told him she was waiting downstairs, but in the dark, she didn't recognize him at first. When they finally met, she led him upstairs and into her room.

Garv, still in a storm of emotions, quickly removed his black Batman t-shirt — the one Anshika had gifted him on their anniversary. It held sentimental value for him, not just because of the gift, but because it marked his progress in losing weight. From XXXL to XL, he had worked hard to get there. He started removing other gifts she had given him, placing his mobile and wallet on her bed, then changed into a new t-shirt. In a sudden burst of anger, he stormed out of her room.

Anshika tried to stop him, but Garv shot her a look that made her stop in her tracks. "I don't care. Hit me, but you're not leaving," she said, her voice shaky with both concern and desperation. She quickly called Sheru, asking him to speak with Garv, hoping he could calm him down.

Sheru, understanding Garv's turmoil, tried to convince him, telling him there was no point in running away from the situation. "Sit down and talk with her, Garv. You've come all the way to Bangalore. Don't make it worse," he urged.

Reluctantly, Garv sat on the bed, his head bowed in silence. Meanwhile, Anshika called her mom and Anuj to inform them that Garv had arrived. Her other friends messaged her, asking if she was okay, though Anuj, who knew Garv inside and out, wasn't worried about Anshika's safety. He knew Garv would never hurt her.

Anshika, desperate to talk things through, tried to speak to Garv, but he remained quiet, staring at the floor. After a long pause, Garv suddenly sat up, his anger erupting in the form of tears. "What do you want, Anshika? Why can't you understand how bad you're making me feel?" he asked, his voice trembling. "I asked for your help to get through this mess, but you... you created it in the first place."

Anshika's heart shattered as she saw Garv break down. She realized it wasn't just her fault — her toxic neighbors and friends had influenced her behavior as well. Guilt washed over her, and she rushed to him, wrapping her arms around him as they both cried. "I'm sorry," she whispered, her voice thick with emotion. "I'm not going anywhere. I'm here, always."

But Garv wasn't so sure. His trust had been shattered, and despite her words, he couldn't erase the hurt he felt. They decided to update their friends and family, reassuring them that everything was under control.

Anshika, understanding Garv's emotional state, gently lifted his face into her lap, holding him as he sobbed. "Shhh," she whispered, comforting him as he cried. In that moment, everything seemed to quiet, and she kissed his forehead before pulling him into a tight hug, making him feel safe and loved.

Later, they sat down for dinner. Anshika asked, "Didn't you notice me standing downstairs waiting for you?" Garv replied softly, "You didn't notice me either when I came upstairs. I've been trying so hard to get everything right, to fit into the life I want, and now... if you keep pushing me away, I'm done."

Anshika, a small smile tugging at her lips, asked, "So you came all the way to Bangalore to stop me from breaking up with you?"

Garv's voice was firm but tinged with sorrow. "No. Today, I promised myself that no matter what happens, I'll give you all the things you've given me, and then I'll go to Kodai, eat magic mushrooms, and jump from there."

Anshika's heart stopped, and she cried, holding him tightly. "I'm so sorry," she whispered, her voice breaking.

They ate dinner in silence, their emotions heavy. Then, Sheru called them, telling them to get their act together and focus on making things work. He had already spoken to Anshika and advised her to write down the things they needed from each other. Anshika suggested they do it the next day, and she held Garv close, lulling him to sleep like a child in her arms.

The next morning, Garv knew he had to be in Ahmedabad for a commitment with a builder. He started working early, and Anshika, waiting for him to take a break, hoped they could finally have the conversation they needed. When Garv took a break, they sat down together with pen and paper. Anshika asked him to write down what he wanted from her.

Garv, his eyes still heavy with emotion, wrote just three things: "She will give me time. She will always understand me. The couch in our home will be of my choice."

The weight of the moment hung between them as they sat in silence, understanding that they both had a lot of work to do – together.

Garv, still feeling the weight of everything that had happened, lay down beside Anshika, his mind racing with the events of the past few hours. He stared up at the ceiling, trying to gather his thoughts before he spoke. Anshika, sensing his hesitation, gently placed her hand on his chest, her fingers tracing the contours of his shirt as she waited patiently for him to answer.

Finally, after a long pause, Garv turned his head to look at her. The anger from earlier had faded, but the frustration was still visible in his eyes. "I don't know, Anshika," he started, his voice soft but heavy with emotion. "It feels like I'm constantly trying to fix things, but nothing is ever really right. I'm trying to balance everything – the builder, the family, this house, my career… and then there's you, and I don't know where I stand with you sometimes. It's like no matter how hard I try, something keeps slipping away."

Anshika's heart softened as she listened to him. She understood his frustration, but she also knew that Garv had a tendency to take everything on himself, to carry the burden without asking for help. "I get it," she whispered. "I know I've been difficult, but I promise, I'm not trying to push you away. I just want us to figure this out together. I don't want you to feel like you're carrying it all alone."

Garv sighed, his hand reaching out to hold hers. "I don't want to feel like I'm carrying it alone either. I want to share this life with you, Anshika. But sometimes it feels like we're not on the same page, and it scares me. I'm afraid that if we don't start trusting each other fully, everything will just crumble."

Anshika kissed his forehead gently, her voice steady as she spoke. "We'll figure it out, Garv. We always do. We've been through a lot, and we've made it through. You don't have to carry everything by yourself, not with me. I'm here. I'll always be here."

Garv, though still unsure of everything, felt the weight in his chest begin to lift just a little. He looked at her, seeing the sincerity in her eyes. For the first time in a while, he allowed himself to believe in the promise she was making.

He nodded, the tension in his body easing. "Okay. Let's do this... together."

Anshika smiled softly, her thumb brushing against his hand. "Together." She leaned in and kissed him gently, sealing the promise that they would face whatever came next as one.

And as they lay there, the music softly playing in the background, both of them knew that while the road ahead might not be easy, they were ready to face it, side by side.

Garv, with a calm yet determined expression, agreed to Anshika's condition regarding the home. Anshika, her face lighting up with a smile, responded playfully, "You can do anything for me." Without wasting another second, she pulled him close, kissing him deeply. The night unfolded in the warmth of their embrace, growing more romantic as time passed. They had been so caught up in the argument that they had forgotten about the condom, but since they had been intimate once before, they felt comfortable continuing their connection.

As darkness settled in, they found solace in each other's arms, eventually drifting off to sleep, entangled in a peaceful cuddle. The following morning, Garv kissed her awake, his touch teasing and affectionate. They spent a romantic morning together before having lunch, after which they napped again. By evening, they got ready and decided to visit the mall. Afterwards, they headed to Ironhill, calling Sheru to join them.

On the other end, Sheru's voice rang out, full of concern and exasperation. "Have you two sorted out your mess?" she asked. "Because if you start fighting again, I swear I'll beat both of you with my sandals." Despite the playful reprimand, the tension between Garv and Anshika seemed to ease, and they enjoyed their time partying before heading back home.

They were both exhausted by the end of the night. Back at the apartment, they changed into comfortable clothes and collapsed into each other's arms, finally resting peacefully. The last day in Bangalore arrived, and Garv and Anshika spent the morning cleaning up the apartment. Anshika would be heading back to the office on Monday, so they made the most of the time they had left. With Anshika's roommate out of the house, the couple found themselves free to explore desires they had kept in check before.

As the room grew quiet, they let go of their inhibitions, trying something new that they had been curious about. Their passion intensified, and afterward, they held each other close, savoring the tender moments. Garv promised he would return after a few hours; he had plans to meet his old friend, Arpan, who had come to Bangalore to visit his sister and brother-in-law.

Anshika, understanding and supportive, gave her permission, and Garv headed out to party with Arpan. Upon arriving, Arpan was visibly frustrated with Garv's recent actions. The two friends spent time together, discussing how things had progressed between Garv and Anshika. By the time Garv returned to Anshika, he was an hour late, but the warmth of her embrace upon his return made everything right. They cherished their final hours together before Garv's flight back to Vadodara.

Once back in Vadodara, Garv threw himself into his work. His days were filled with managing his files, and soon, late nights at the office became routine. Despite the chaos, he managed to keep in touch with Anshika, thanks to his multitasking skills. But when the results of his exams came out, everything seemed to shift again. Garv had missed the cutoff by just two marks, and the disappointment weighed heavily on him.

Anshika, upset and distant, started to ghost him. Days went by without any messages, and by mid-afternoon, Garv still hadn't heard from her. Frustrated and confused, he called, but she didn't answer. Hurt, he blocked her, but when Anshika tried reaching out, she found herself blocked as well. Enraged, she stormed over to Sheru's place, venting her anger.

Garv, after some time to cool off, finally gathered the courage to text her. When Anshika called him, the tension between them erupted. She yelled, furious at the mess he had caused. Garv, trying to stay calm, explained, "It takes just a few seconds to send a simple text. Do you have any idea what kind of thoughts go through my mind? It's not about that other guy—it's about your safety. Your 'last seen' kept changing, but nothing else was. At least you could have answered the call or sent a quick message saying you'd call back."

But Anshika, hurt and resolute, felt the weight of their ongoing struggles. She needed space to figure things out, and Garv, frustrated by the distance between them, reluctantly gave her the space she demanded.

Anshika had made up her mind. She felt that Garv wasn't trying to understand her, and their constant fights were driving a wedge between them. It was becoming too much to handle, and in her frustration, she decided to give him the space he wanted. Garv, on the other hand, was grappling with his own demons. The silence from Anshika was killing him. Sometimes, she wouldn't even call for days. The lack of communication was driving him mad, and he could feel himself unraveling.

His brother, seeing the toll it was taking on him, was furious. Garv had come home for a few days to escape the chaos, but his life seemed to be spiraling out of control. The file he had been working on, one that was crucial for his career, was supposed to be approved by the Credit Head with the help of Monika di. But just when he thought he had everything lined up, the builder backed out, saying that he no longer needed the funds. It felt like a gut punch, another failure on top of everything else.

His panic attacks, which had been growing more intense, were only making things worse. He was short-tempered and frustrated, not just with his work but with the situation he and Anshika were in. His brother's anger only seemed to fuel his own, and one night, Garv snapped.

He called Anshika, his voice colder than it had ever been. "What is it with girls?" he said bitterly. "They just do a little bit of makeup, set their eyebrows, put on some lipstick, and suddenly, they think they've got a whole new world waiting for them. But they never think about the guy—the one who has to keep crossing all those hurdles to even get a chance to be with them."

Unbeknownst to him, Anshika was on a trip with her office colleagues at the time, trying to escape from the storm that had been brewing between them. But when she returned, she couldn't hold it in anymore. That night, she called him, her voice shaking with emotion as she cried, telling him what his brother had said to her. The words hit her like a slap, and it was the final straw.

Garv, hearing the pain in her voice, felt a surge of anger. Without thinking, he stormed over to his brother, his hand connecting with his cheek in a sharp, stinging slap. "How dare you talk about her like that?" Garv yelled, his rage uncontainable. "She's not just some girl. She's someone I care about!"

His brother was taken aback, but Garv wasn't done. He grabbed his jacket and stormed out of the house, his heart pounding in his chest. He needed to get away. He couldn't stay under the same roof as someone who would say such hurtful things about Anshika.

Once outside, he immediately dialed Anshika's number again, desperate to make things right.

Garv's voice was soft yet filled with regret as he spoke to Anshika, "Anshika, I had my brother slapped... I'm really sorry. I shouldn't have let myself get caught in the middle like that."

Anshika's voice trembled, and she let out a small sob. "Garv, it hurt me... what he said," she whispered.

Garv gently tried to calm her down. "I promise, Anshika. It will never happen again. I'll make sure of it."

Her sobs quieted, but the tension between them was still palpable. After a moment, Anshika hesitated before speaking again. "Garv... there's something I need to tell you," she said, her voice strained. "I haven't kissed any guy. It was just a story I made up—an excuse for the breakup. We had some vibe, yes, but before anything could happen, I left."

Garv's heart dropped, but he held his composure. "I promise you, Anshika, give me six months. I'll clear my CA. And if I don't, I'll leave... I'll walk away. But you have to trust me."

They agreed—Anshika needed space. They would limit their conversations to just ten minutes a day. Garv reluctantly accepted the condition, hoping this would give them the clarity they needed.

The next morning, Garv woke up to a message from Anshika. It read: "Nothing happened, Garv. No moments, no other guy. I made up the story, and it went too far. Please understand." But Garv wasn't sure if this would put his mind at ease. He wasn't relieved—not really. His mind raced with confusion. Why was she lying again? What else was she hiding? He didn't know anymore.

Still, he let his guard down, focusing on his studies and the work that had piled up. He stopped worrying about the new leads and logins and concentrated only on the cases that were already in progress. In his free time, he studied the subjects that stirred his passion—his CA exam was his next goal. At night, he counted down the minutes until their ten-minute conversation. He would prepare romantic lines, sweet shayaris, and play songs for her, hoping to win her heart back.

Anshika, on the other hand, was still in love. But she was trying her best to be stronger, colder—hoping Garv would eventually give up on her and let her go. For the next twenty days, Garv lived with the weight of his panic attacks. To clear his mind, he would occasionally escape on his two-wheeler, taking trips to Ahmedabad and Udaipur—places where he could outrun his thoughts, focusing only on the road ahead.

No one knew about these trips—not even Anshika. The only time his panic attacks didn't consume him was when he was on the road, calculating the next gap or turn. Riding fast was the only thing that gave him peace.

But Garv's patience was wearing thin. One day, he bought a maroon-colored cord set for Anshika. He had also asked a friend who was coming from Canada to bring back some Sephora lipstick, a brand that was out of stock in India. Anshika had shared the shades she wanted, and his friend brought three of them.

Garv decided it was time to visit her. But he couldn't tell her the truth—he couldn't risk another fight. Instead, he told her that he would courier the gifts to her through a friend in Bangalore. "Just give me your address, and I'll send it over," he told her.

But Anshika, skeptical, insisted, "Why not just deliver it to me directly?"

Garv came up with another excuse, spinning a story to make her believe it was impossible. Reluctantly, Anshika agreed. And so, Garv booked his flight from Bombay to Bangalore, but before leaving for the city, he took a short two-day trip to Surat for office work.

In Surat, Garv went shopping and even treated himself to a facial. He'd lost a lot of weight, now fitting into an L-size instead of his previous XL. It was a small victory in the midst of everything else. He bought her favorite khakharas and chocolates and printed a collage of her photos on glossy paper. He told his friend, Devik, to buy a gift bag and colorful markers, because Garv was determined to win her back—he had a plan.

Once in Bombay, Garv told his family he was heading back to Vadodara for work. But the truth was, he was headed to Devik's place. There, they drank Old Monk and shared memories, sinking into a melancholic mood. As the slow music played, Devik and his roommate, Atharva, listened quietly. It was a reminder of how much had changed since Garv's relationship with Anshika had become strained.

That night, Anshika texted Garv: "I'm going out with some colleagues for a party. I might not be able to talk to you tonight." Garv read her message and simply replied with an indifferent "Okay."

Garv printed out some photos of himself and his girlfriend, Anshika. He wrote some poems (called "shayaris") that he had written for her, and drew some smiley faces on them using colorful markers. He then asked his friend Devik to give the gift bag to Anshika. But Devik brought a small gift bag, which Garv felt was too small. So Garv took his own favorite yellow bag that he had kept for years and told Devik that their friendship was more important than the bag size. Devik sadly gave Garv the bag.

Meanwhile, only Rathiji knew that Garv had gone to Bangalore again, and Anuj didn't know because Garv knew Anuj would get angry at how Anshika was treating him. Garv packed the gifts and photos in Devik's yellow bag and went to the airport. He didn't want Anshika to know he was coming, so he didn't text her. He landed in Bangalore and went to the area near her house around 10:30 am, as he had told her his friend would be delivering the gift then. Garv waited for hours, trying not to smoke so Anshika wouldn't get upset.

Finally, around 11 am, Anshika called him, saying she had slept late and would be out for the gym later. Garv told her he would be there by

11:30 am, and she agreed to meet him on the main road to get the gift. Garv hid near the gym and waited for Anshika. When she came to get the gift, he tapped her shoulder, surprising her. Anshika was shocked to see Garv there. Garv gave her the gift, but he started having a panic attack, with his hands and legs shaking. Anshika asked if they could go to a café or her home, and they went to her home. Anshika was acting very cold and distant. Garv quietly sat on the bed, and Anshika asked him to talk. When Garv asked her to open the gift, she saw the photos and poems he had made for her. This made her emotions soften, and she smiled as she looked at the photos and opened the other gifts inside, like snacks and a dress.

As Garv sat on the couch, trying to hold himself together, Anshika's words echoed in his mind. He was trying so hard to make things work, but with every step forward, it felt like they were pulled back by misunderstandings and unanswered questions. When she asked him, "*Kyon kiya aapne yeh?*" his heart sank. He had to explain everything, to tell her why he was doing this.

He looked at her, eyes filled with honesty, and replied, "*Aap hi ne kaha tha na ki aapke dad apni beti ko aise gift lene nahi bhejte, toh main sidha hand deliver karne aaya hoon. Baccha, aur sort karne aaya hoon ki kya karna chahiye hum dono ko, kyunki yeh mere liye asaan nahi ho raha hai.*"

He couldn't stop himself from adding, "*Aur by the way, main XL se L mein fit ho gaya hoon,*" hoping it would bring a smile to her face, but instead, Anshika just rolled her eyes. He knew she was trying not to let the moment get too serious, but he needed to lighten the mood.

"*Rehne do,*" she said, trying to brush off his comment, but Garv, determined, told her, "*Check karna, pichhe meri T-shirt pe likha hai L.*" He could see the confusion in her eyes, and then her face softened.

Anshika, still looking unsure, asked him, "*Kab jaaoge vaapas?*"

Garv, keeping his cool despite the storm inside, stood up, took his bag, and started walking towards the door. He wasn't leaving yet, but he wasn't sure what more he could say.

"Not like this, Garv," she said, her voice softer now.

The tension was still thick between them, but they were both trying to work through it. Garv sighed, sitting back down, and asked for some water. Anshika went outside to get it, and Garv was left to his thoughts. Her flatmate, sensing the tension in the air, spoke to Anshika while she was in the kitchen. "*He's trying to make you happy, Anshika. He's giving his best effort. Don't leave him.*"

When Anshika returned with the water, she sat next to Garv. She looked at him with a mixture of tenderness and concern, and then asked him something that made his chest tighten.

"*How can you love me so much, despite everything that has happened?*" she asked, her voice shaking slightly.

Garv took a deep breath, his heart aching as he thought about everything they'd been through. He didn't have all the answers, but he knew one thing for sure—he loved her more than he had ever loved anyone before.

"*It's just how I know how to love you,*" he said quietly, his words soft but filled with meaning.

Anshika's eyes searched his face, looking for something—maybe reassurance, maybe understanding. But she still couldn't comprehend why he was holding on despite all their difficulties.

"*Agar main nahi maanti toh?*" she asked, her voice trembling slightly.

"*Main already Devik ko bolkar aaya tha ki shayad aaj hi wapas aa jaunga agar tum nahi maani,*" Garv replied, trying to keep his tone light, but his heart was heavy.

Anshika was quiet for a moment, and then, without warning, she wrapped her arms around him in a tight hug. Garv felt the warmth of her embrace and, for a brief moment, he let himself surrender to it. He rested his head in her lap, feeling the overwhelming rush of emotions he had been holding inside for so long.

As he let go of the facade he had been keeping up, Garv broke down, his body shaking with sobs. He hadn't realized how much the panic attacks and sleepless nights had been taking a toll on him until this very moment. *"I've been suffering from panic attacks all this time... and the only way I've been surviving is by taking sleeping pills..."* he confessed, his voice cracking.

Anshika, her own heart breaking at his words, held him even tighter. *"I'm so sorry, Garv,"* she whispered, her voice filled with regret. She had never realized how much he had been suffering.

As they held each other, Garv felt a mixture of relief and sadness. He didn't feel happy yet, though, because their relationship was so fragile. The last two times they had tried to fix things, it had ended in a fight. So, even in this moment of closeness, a part of him was still uncertain.

Anshika, sensing his doubts, squeezed him tighter and whispered, *"We'll work through it, Garv. I won't let you go."*

After a long, heavy silence, Garv, his voice hoarse, asked, *"Can I ask you something?"*

Anshika nodded, still holding him close. *"Yes, baccha."*

"Has anything happened between you and that guy? Please, just tell me the truth. You've told me three different stories, and I don't understand what's going on," Garv asked, his voice trembling now, his vulnerability laid bare.

Anshika paused, her heart aching at the question. She saw how much this was eating at him, and the last thing she wanted was for him to doubt her. She looked into his eyes, holding his face gently in her hands, and spoke with deep sincerity.

"Garv, nothing happened with anyone. I promise you. You have my word."

Garv felt a weight lift off his chest, but he still couldn't fully relax. He needed to hear it from her, needed to believe it with all his heart. But seeing the certainty in her eyes, hearing the conviction in her voice, something inside him clicked.

He let out a long, shaky breath, feeling the burden of doubt begin to fade, and for the first time in a long while, Garv felt like maybe—just maybe—things could be okay between them.

As Garv hugged Anshika tightly, the weight of the past few days seemed to lift off him, if only for a moment. The embrace was a silent exchange of comfort, understanding, and reassurance. He stayed in her arms, allowing himself to feel something he rarely let others see: vulnerability. Anshika held him just as tightly, feeling the tension in his body, knowing this was more than just a physical act—it was him finally letting go, even if just for a while.

Anshika's voice broke the stillness, her words tinged with the raw honesty she had been holding back for so long. "*Garv, mae aapse darni lag gayi thi us raat ladayi kar baad,*" she confessed softly, her heart aching as she recalled the moment when their argument had escalated. "*Because yes, you got frustrated and your voice got raised... it was the first time I saw you lose control like that.*"

Garv could feel the pain in her words, and it only made him hold her tighter, regretting how things had spiraled that night. Anshika continued, "*You're not someone who breaks down easily, Garv. You're always in control. You're strong, you handle everything, but that night... I saw a different side of you, and it scared me.*"

Her words cut through him, but it wasn't her fault. He had never been one to show his emotions easily. He had always been the rock, the one who stood tall no matter what. But with Anshika, the walls had come down, and he wasn't sure how to handle it. His mind began to drift to another memory, one that revealed just how deep his control ran, even in life-threatening situations.

Last year, Garv, Rathiji, and Devik had been sitting at their regular meeting point, Tea Master, when things took a dangerous turn. Anuj wasn't around that day, and the group was just hanging out when Rathiji got a call from his younger brother. His father had been caught in a perilous situation: he had stumbled upon a butcher shop near a bridge where cows were being slaughtered, and the area was known for being volatile. His father had been alone, and it had quickly escalated.

Rathiji turned to Garv, his face serious. "*Chal, matter ho gaya hain. Garv, let's go,*" he said, his voice tense. Garv, always the protector, didn't hesitate. He immediately told Rathiji to let Devik go home, sensing that Devik wasn't suited for this kind of danger. Garv wasn't one to sugarcoat things, and he knew that this area wasn't safe at night. He had always avoided it himself.

As they made their way toward the location, Garv's mind raced, trying to piece together the information. "*Kya hua hain, bata toh sahi,*" he had asked Rathiji on the way, growing more anxious with each passing minute.

When they arrived, the scene was far worse than Garv had imagined. Hundreds of men stood in the streets, an intimidating presence that filled the air with tension. There were only five of them: Garv, Rathiji, and a few others. Garv's instincts kicked in, and he immediately took control of the situation.

He turned to Rathiji. "*Tell your father to stay silent. We can't afford any mistakes here. Anything can happen.*" The weight of the moment hit Garv hard—he knew that if things went south, they would be outnumbered, and it could quickly turn violent. He knew how quickly things could escalate in that part of town, and Garv wasn't someone who took risks lightly.

Garv's calm exterior masked the storm inside him, but he was aware of how dire the situation had become. He quickly dialed the MLA, his friend's son, and requested immediate assistance. He didn't stop there—he called in support from RSS and Bajrangdal, knowing that they needed backup. Garv's friends quickly responded, and three police vans arrived soon after. But the first 15 minutes of that night had been hell for him. He kept his composure, refusing to let any fear show on his face.

Even though he could have easily started a fight, he knew that would have been a death sentence. He understood that the situation was too dangerous, and with the odds stacked against them, violence wasn't an option. He maintained his cool, never once showing the panic rising inside him. It wasn't until his friends arrived that the pressure began to ease, but even then, Garv stayed vigilant, knowing that his calmness had kept the situation from escalating further.

That was the kind of man Garv was—a man who could handle life-or-death situations with a cool head, never letting his emotions cloud his judgment. But when it came to Anshika, everything changed. She was the one person who could see through the calm exterior. She was the one person who could make him feel everything. And that night, when she saw him break down, it was the first time she had truly witnessed his vulnerability.

As Garv held Anshika in his arms, he realized something important: He could fight the world with his control and strength, but with her, he didn't need to keep up the façade. In front of Anshika, he could be real. And for the first time in a long while, he let himself be that man. The man who needed her, not just the one who always needed to protect everyone else.

Anshika, sensing the depth of his struggle, hugged him tighter, her heart full of understanding. She had seen the man he was, the strength he carried, but she also saw the pain he tried to hide. And she promised herself, right then and there, that she would never let him carry it alone again.

Garv's voice trembled with emotion as he spoke to Anshika, his words coming from the deepest corners of his heart. He pulled her closer, his arms tightening around her, as if to convey everything he couldn't say through just words.

"I don't know how to cry when I'm alone," he confessed softly, his voice barely above a whisper. "And my anger, it turns into frustration. Trust me, I can hurt myself, but I'll never hurt you. Not for a single second. I love you so deeply, you can't even imagine, Bacchaji." His voice cracked slightly as he continued, "I'm sorry if you ever feel that way. But I can't even raise my eyes in *front of you. For the whole world, I can be a devil if they mess with me, but in front of you, I'm always your baby. And I'll remain that way, forever."*

Anshika felt a lump form in her throat. She pulled him closer, her lips pressing softly against his forehead. She kissed him gently, the warmth of their connection radiating through her. She could feel the weight of his words, the honesty, and the depth of his love. She whispered, *"I know, Garv. I know."*

With tears threatening to spill, Anshika pulled away just enough to smile at him, before she stood and walked towards the kitchen to prepare lunch. As she was finishing up, her phone rang, and it was Suraj, her colleague from work. The conversation was lighthearted, but it meant something deeper to Anshika. As she hung up, she turned to Garv and said, *"You need to thank Suraj and Sheru. They've been the ones motivating me, telling me to treat you right, to remember how much you love me. They were right."*

Garv's face softened, and he smiled, embracing her tightly. *"I'm lucky to have you, Bacchaji,"* he whispered, feeling a wave of relief wash over him. They sat down and shared their lunch, but their attention wasn't on the food—it was on each other. Their eyes locked, speaking the silent language of love they had built over time.

As they sat there, Anshika, with a shy smile, said, *"Never give up on me, Garv. I'm sorry too. I know I made you feel unwanted, and that wasn't right."* The words hung heavy in the air, but there was no tension between them. Instead, there was understanding, a quiet bond that was becoming even stronger.

Garv wrapped his arms around her once more, squeezing her gently. *"I'll never give up on you. And don't ever feel like I would. You're everything to me, Bacchaji. Always."*

After a long moment, they stood up and went about getting ready. Garv told her that he needed to leave for Vadodara the next afternoon for some business, but Anshika wasn't too upset. She kissed him, a lingering kiss that told him all the things her words couldn't.

Later, they found themselves at Vapour in Sarjapur, enjoying the lively atmosphere of the club. They sat close, with Garv wrapping his arm around Anshika, their connection palpable. After a few drinks, Garv called Sheru on video, giving her the surprise of their rekindled love and happiness. Sheru beamed at them through the screen, telling them, "*Stay happy, stay together.*"

Garv smiled as he picked up his phone again, dialing Anuj's number. When Anuj answered, the playful exchange between them felt like a small, familiar comfort in the middle of this night filled with new beginnings.

"*Haan, Golu, bolo,*" Anuj greeted him casually.

"*Bhai, tujae ek baat batani thi,*" Garv said, a touch of seriousness in his voice.

"*Bol, kya hua?*" Anuj replied.

"*Bhaii, mae Bangalore aaya tha, tujae nahi bataya. Sorry Bhai, sort hogaya mera aur Anshika ka.*"

Anuj, with his typical teasing tone, laughed. "*Lodu, Rathi ne pehle hi bola tha ki vo keh raha tha ki call karke gaand maar manae usko. Wahi keh raha tha ki tu khud samna se call karke bataega sabse pehle muje.*"

Garv couldn't help but chuckle. "*Bhai, hogaya yaar. Sort le, Anshika se baat kar.*"

After their brief call, Anshika and Garv shared more laughter, enjoying the night. Garv ordered hookah for Anshika, and they continued hugging each other, feeling more connected than ever. When it was time to leave, they called it a night, heading home at around 12:30 AM.

On the cab ride back, Anshika playfully said, "*Mae aapko haath nahi lagane dungi.*"

Garv, in his usual teasing way, replied, "*It's okay, Baccha. Just hug me from behind, that's all I want.*"

When they reached home, the world outside seemed to disappear. They hugged again, kissing each other, and Garv, holding her close, made a promise.

"*Please, Baccha, never think of leaving me. You're the only one who can handle me in this world. Even my mom tells you to keep me in check. But I promise, no matter how tough it gets, I'll be there for you. You focus on your career, and I'll handle everything else. I've got your back, always.*"

Anshika nodded, holding him tighter. She knew, without a doubt, that Garv was the one person who would always stand by her, and she was ready to do the same for him. Together, they were unstoppable.

Anshika kissed him softly, then pulled him into a tight embrace. The warmth between them, the closeness, felt like everything they had ever wanted. That night, they held each other like it was the last time. Anshika buried her face against his chest, her arms wrapping around him as if she never wanted to let go. They cried together, hearts breaking and healing in the same moment. In the silence of their tears, they made a promise to one another—no matter the obstacles, they would fight for their love and eventually be together, bound by the promise of marriage.

As the night wore on, their cries subsided, and they drifted into peaceful sleep, their bodies tangled in the comfort of each other's presence.

Morning came softly. Anshika rose quietly, a smile playing on her lips as she went to the kitchen and ordered Garv's favorite breakfast. Meanwhile, Garv remained sound asleep. Anshika stood there for a moment, simply watching him. She leaned down and kissed his forehead, then wrapped her arms around him once more. She lay beside him, hugging him tightly, savoring the moments before they had to face reality.

An hour passed, and Anshika gently woke him. "Baccha," Garv groaned sleepily, "Please, let me cancel the fight and finish it tomorrow. I don't want to leave you."

Anshika smiled softly, stroking his hair. "Come here, cuddle with me, and stop whining," she teased. "You know work in Vadodara is important too."

Garv gave in with a sigh, letting her pull him close. They kissed again, their lips meeting in a silent exchange of love, and for the next half hour, they just stared at each other, their hearts full of affection.

After a while, Anshika stood up, stretching as she moved to get dressed. She went to the kitchen to bring breakfast for both of them, feeding Garv with her hands as they shared quiet moments together.

With only four hours left before Garv's flight, they spent the time savoring their last moments together. They hugged once more, unwilling to let go, knowing it would be a while before they would see each other again.

Finally, the moment came. Garv had to leave for Vadodara. He kissed Anshika's forehead one last time and waved to her flatmate before heading out to catch his flight. They stayed on the phone the whole time, talking like they hadn't in days. Anshika reminded him to take care of himself and promised that if he felt the weight of anxiety or panic, he should call her, no matter the time. Their old connection, their love, had returned, stronger than ever.

Back in Vadodara, Garv threw himself into his studies, but life had other plans. His worst enemy, the one person he could never stand, was made his boss. The news hit hard, but Garv wasn't one to back down. One day, they clashed, and Garv made it clear that if his boss ever crossed him again, it wouldn't be easy for him. Garv was ruthless with those who got on his bad side, and this was no exception.

Things were moving forward, but Garv's mind was still consumed with his business, which he had handed over to someone else when his mind wasn't in the right place. He focused on his studies, but there was always the nagging thought about what could have been with his business.

Then, Anshika dropped another bombshell—she would be going to the U.S. for fifteen days in October. Garv, determined to see her off, promised that he would be there. "I'll be there, even if it's just for one day," Anshika said, agreeing. But Garv, never one to stick to a simple plan, didn't tell her that he was planning to stay for two days.

As October rolled in, Garv found himself in Bangalore. Anshika video called him, and through the screen, she realized that Garv was already in the city. She was excited, as he never ignored her calls. She knew right then that this moment, him being there, meant everything.

When Garv finally arrived at her building, Anshika rushed to meet him, throwing herself into his arms. She kissed him, her heart full of gratitude for him making the effort to be there. "Thank you for coming, Garv," she whispered against his lips.

Anshika was in a panic. She hadn't packed yet, and there was still shopping to do. With only two days left, she felt overwhelmed. But Garv, ever the calming presence, assured her that everything would be fine. He sat with her as they made a list of what needed to be done, ensuring that all the loose ends would be tied up.

They hugged each other tightly, switching off the lights, and let sleep take over. The world outside didn't matter anymore. All that mattered was the warmth of their embrace, the quiet moments, and the love they shared.

The next morning, Garv had already applied for leave, so he didn't need to work. While Anshika was busy with her tasks, Garv headed to the medical store to pick up the medicines they had listed for her. The store was a kilometer away, and the afternoon heat made the walk exhausting. When he finally returned home, sweat soaked his clothes.

Anshika, seeing him in that state, immediately ordered him to wash up. She had a glass of water ready for him and planted a sweet kiss on his lips. After that, she wrapped her arms around him in a tight hug. Once he had cleaned up, they headed out to the mall to finish shopping for the things they needed. They managed to complete the list, then decided to pick up some alcohol to enjoy later while packing Anshika's things.

Back at home, they started folding clothes, the music playing softly in the background as they shared drinks. But Garv, feeling off for the past few days, noticed that the heat of the afternoon had made him feel lightheaded. He didn't want to worry Anshika, so he kept it to himself, slipping into the living room to lie down.

Anshika, excited about their party plans for the night, grew irritated when she found him asleep. She had hoped to spend more time with him, but he was unwell. Early the next morning, around 6 AM, Garv woke up to a cold chill, realizing that he had caught a fever. He avoided contact with Anshika, not wanting her to catch it. Meanwhile, Anshika had been feeling off the night before and suspected she might catch a fever too.

Garv, ever the protector, made her drink a mixture of 60 ml Old Monk in 200 ml hot water before she went back to sleep. By the time she woke up, she felt better, but her concern for Garv grew when she noticed how warm his hands were. When she kissed his forehead, she realized he wasn't well. She finished the packing on her own, her thoughts on Garv's condition.

At 9 AM, she gently woke him, wanting to spend more time together before she left. She insisted that he take medicine, but Garv, not wanting to risk any bitterness, opted for more Old Monk in hot water, doubling the dose. After about an hour, he started to feel better. They double-checked her luggage to make sure everything was packed, then had breakfast together.

Anshika kissed him, and for a few moments, they shared a quiet, romantic exchange. But as 11 AM approached, it was time to get ready. Anshika's nerves were evident, and Garv, seeing her stress, pulled her into his arms. "Everything will be fine," he reassured her softly. "You're a strong woman."

With that, they made their way to the airport. Anshika's terminal was in a different part of the airport, so Garv took her there first. They clicked a few photos, and he kissed her forehead before wishing her luck. "Don't forget to bring me a gift," he teased, his smile reassuring her. Anshika waved at him with a playful flying kiss before disappearing into the crowd.

Garv, once she was out of sight, took the bus to his terminal. He checked in quickly and called her to pass the time. Anshika, finding herself bored at her terminal with nothing to do, was glad for the distraction. Garv kept her entertained until it was time for his flight. He kissed her over the phone and told her to have a safe journey.

After Garv returned to Vadodara, a few days passed, and he took some time off for his CA final studies. Meanwhile, Anshika was in the U.S. During office hours, and whenever he was at the library, Garv made sure to take breaks to talk to her. Their old routine returned, with Anshika often falling asleep while talking to him. The connection they shared, so deeply rooted in love and trust, was as strong as ever.

Dear readers, I urge you to understand this simple truth—if you love someone with all your heart, no obstacle, no problem, will ever seem too big to overcome. In the end, the person you love is the only one who can truly bring peace to your soul and happiness to your life.

Chapter 25

Good Old Times Are Back

Things had started to feel like the good old times again. Anshika, as she had in the early days of their relationship, began to support Garv more and more. She made time for him, avoiding the distractions of parties and messaging him throughout the day. Garv, in turn, had become less possessive, especially after Anshika decided to distance herself from the toxic group of people he had once been worried about.

Garv spent most of his time in the library, from 10 in the morning until 8 in the evening, diving deep into his studies. After that, he would sleep briefly before starting up again at 2 AM. It was a grueling routine, but Garv knew the importance of focusing on his CA exams. He still felt unsure about his audit paper, but he was determined that with the right approach in the final days, he could turn things around.

He had moved into his Bua's house to avoid distractions, staying completely focused on his studies. When the exam results came in, Garv was relieved—he had cleared Group 2, and as long as he nailed the audit paper, he was on track to becoming a Chartered Accountant. The weight of that achievement filled him with pride, but there was something else on his mind—his birthday.

Anshika had just returned from the US, but she had forgotten to bring him a gift. To make up for it, she drank his favorite whisky, Jamison, but when it came to celebrating his birthday, they had a disagreement. Garv wanted to spend his birthday with her, but Anshika had already planned to visit her home. She asked him to come over after December 6th, and they could celebrate then.

But Garv had already made plans with his friends. His friend Rathiji's birthday was on the 25th of November, and Garv's was on the 27th. They decided to throw a combined celebration at Bhuvnesh's place. Who was Bhuvnesh? He was the new addition to their friend group, someone who had become such a close companion in just four months that he'd even cleaned up Garv's vomit after one too many drinks. Though Bhuvnesh could sometimes be a bit irritating, he was truly a gem of a person, and their friendship had blossomed quickly.

On the 26th of November, the six boys gathered in Bhuvnesh's room to party. It started at 11 PM and went on until 7 AM the next morning. There was dancing, laughter, and a whole lot of alcohol. Garv had already told Anshika about the party, reassuring her that if anything urgent came up, she could always call him.

Around midnight, hunger struck, so Garv and Bhuvnesh headed out to the station to grab some food. In the middle of the street, Garv, feeling the call of nature, took a quick pee in front of a CCTV camera mounted outside a shop. Bhuvnesh, never one to shy away from a bit of mischief, joined him. The two of them laughed like idiots before picking up a parcel of food for their friends. The party continued until the early morning hours, and by the time the rain started pouring down, Garv was ready to head home.

Exhausted, he went back to his place and finally collapsed into bed for a peaceful sleep. It had been one of the best parties of their lives—wild, carefree, and filled with memories they'd laugh about for years to come.

The next month rolled in, and Garv found himself back in Vadodara, ready for the final stretch of the year. After a long time, he visited a temple, offering prayers for his and Anshika's continued togetherness. It was a moment of reflection, a time to be grateful for the love and support they had shared. Soon after, Garv returned to his work, his mind focused on the future, knowing that the good times with Anshika would only continue.

As the year drew to a close, Garv found himself on a high note. His exams had gone well, the party with his friends had been unforgettable, and, most importantly, he and Anshika had managed to sort out their differences. They were stronger than ever, and it felt like everything was falling into place.

However, not everything was perfect in Garv's world. His friend Bhuvi was going through a tough breakup. One evening, when Garv visited Surat around the 2nd of December, he stepped into Bhuvi's flat and immediately noticed the smell of alcohol and cigarettes in the air. Bhuvi was struggling with the aftermath of his breakup, and it was clear he was in a dark place.

Garv stayed with Bhuvi for two days, offering support and trying to help him process his emotions. During this time, Garv thought it might be helpful to call Dinesh, a friend who was known for his love of weed, in an attempt to lift Bhuvi's spirits. However, when they called Dinesh, they were shocked to hear the depth of his own struggles. Dinesh wasn't just in a tough spot; he was genuinely unhappy with his life and had reached a breaking point. He freaked out on the phone, expressing how much he needed someone to talk to.

Garv, without hesitation, reached out to Dinesh's sister to let her know what was going on. Together, they decided that enough was enough. Dinesh's sister took the responsibility to talk to the family, making sure they understood Dinesh's situation and would support him in getting out of the toxic cycle he was in. Garv felt a sense of relief. For him, friends were always family, and he believed in helping them grow, not holding them back.

With that, Garv knew his friends were in better hands, and he could focus on what mattered to him most—Anshika. Soon after, Garv visited Anshika in Bangalore. He had been looking forward to spending time with her, but when she arrived, he was a bit disappointed. While she had brought him bottles of his favorite whisky, Jamison, and Jagger, Garv felt a small sting that she hadn't brought him something that felt more personal, something he could keep for life.

It wasn't about the gift; it was about the thought behind it. He didn't want anything material, but something that symbolized their bond. He told Anshika, "I just expect something from you, baccha." Hearing this, Anshika hugged him tightly, and Garv knew she understood what he meant.

To make it up to her, Garv had bought Anshika something special—cute, expensive iPhone covers for her new phone. He knew she would love them. The thought of seeing her smile when she opened the gift made the whole experience worth it.

They spent the rest of their time together, shopping and enjoying each other's company. Anshika gifted Garv three stylish t-shirts for his birthday and made him try them all on. They laughed and joked, making memories that would last. That night, they had a small party at Anshika's place, with the alcohol she had brought from the US, and they spent romantic days and nights together, talking, laughing, and just being in each other's presence.

As the year came to a close, Anshika asked Garv if he could come to Bangalore for New Year's. Garv, however, wasn't sure. It was quarter-end for him at work, and he had files to manage. He told her he would try but couldn't promise anything. He reassured her, though, that if he couldn't make it, he would come to Bangalore on the 1st of January, so they could start the new year together, in each other's arms.

It was a promise, and Garv couldn't wait to see what the new year would bring for both of them.

After spending those unforgettable days with Anshika, Garv was back at the grind. The office politics, the never-ending work, and the pressure had all returned, but this time with a much heavier burden. The month-end chaos had arrived, and, as usual, Garv was buried in files and paperwork. He managed to survive through it all and reached the final day of the year, December 31st, with the disbursement hanging over him. It was a race against time, but Garv, ever the hard worker, managed to finish the disbursement by 9:30 PM.

With that out of the way, he quickly checked the flight availability and booked one to Bangalore. It was a last-minute decision, and the flight was expensive, but nothing was going to stop him from being with Anshika for the new year. He called her from the cab, telling her he would be there in two hours. Anshika was surprised. "Kab program banaya?" she asked, clearly not expecting him so soon. But when he sent her the flight details, she was taken aback. "17k for tickets, Garv?" she replied. Despite the price, she couldn't hide her excitement and told him to come, saying, "Aap aajao, baccha. Aram se, main wait kar rahi hoon."

The flight was quick, and soon enough, Garv landed in Bangalore. He went straight to Anshika's place, and as luck would have it, there were just fifteen minutes left until the new year. Anshika had planned to celebrate at her friend Suraj's house, who had just moved into her society. But as the night unfolded, the plan changed, and they ended up going to another friend's house. The party was lively at first, but Garv wasn't really feeling it. Something happened during the party that made everything fizzle out, and before long, the party ended.

Garv and Anshika returned to her place, where they set up candles in their room, lit some whisky and Jägermeister, and changed into something more comfortable. They created their own little celebration, away from the chaos, just the two of them. They watched a movie, drank, and danced their way into the new year. When the clock struck midnight, they hugged each other tightly, marking the beginning of a new chapter together.

The night was filled with laughter, love, and a sense of calm that only being in each other's arms could bring. They drifted off to sleep in a peaceful embrace, the kind of night that felt like a dream. As the sun rose on January 1st, Garv woke up to find Anshika still by his side. They spent the day together, shopping, going to clubs, and making plans for the future. It was a day full of hope and dreams, but underneath it all, Garv couldn't shake the tension in his chest. His result was just days away, and he was trying to stay calm for Anshika's sake.

Despite his best efforts to hide it, the anxiety gnawed at him. The future seemed uncertain, and he didn't want Anshika to worry. But deep down, Garv was fighting a battle within himself, knowing that the result could either make or break his dreams.

As the day came to a close, Garv reluctantly boarded the flight back to Vadodara. His heart felt heavy, but he tried to push away the thoughts of failure that crept in. It wasn't the right time to be consumed by the results just yet. He still had to keep up the facade of normalcy.

Finally, the long-anticipated result day arrived. Anshika, as always, was more excited than Garv himself. When the clock hit 10:30 AM, the result was released, and Garv stepped out of the office to check it. His heart raced as he clicked on the link. He had passed the second group, but once again, the first group had slipped through his fingers.

Tears welled up in his eyes. He had fought so hard, and yet, here he was, still falling short. He felt a wave of disappointment and hopelessness wash over him. He immediately called Anshika, his voice cracking as he delivered the news. She was in her office, and hearing her voice in that moment only made the pain harder to bear. Garv, knowing the impact it would have on her, reminded her of his promise. "I will go from your life if this happens," he told her, his voice barely above a whisper. He didn't want her to carry the weight of his failures. He couldn't bear the thought of disappointing her, and so he made that heartbreaking decision.

Anshika was quiet for a moment, not fully grasping what Garv meant. But before she could respond, he assured her that if she needed him, he would be there on the phone, always. The weight of his failure seemed unbearable, and all he wanted was to find solace in his own grief.

Garv then called his parents, bracing himself for their reaction. They weren't upset. In fact, they seemed relieved that he had passed one group, and with only three papers left, it was a step closer. But for Garv, it didn't feel like progress. It felt like another broken dream, another shattered hope. All the plans he had made with Anshika, all the dreams they had shared, now felt impossible.

Anshika called him later, concerned about how he was holding up. She asked him if he was okay, and Garv, despite the tears in his eyes, lied through his teeth. "I'm fine," he said, not wanting to burden her further. She told him they would talk later, but Garv wasn't sure he could talk. Not about this. Not about the failure that now seemed to define him.

The year had begun with so much hope, but now, as the first days unfolded, Garv wasn't sure what the future would hold. All he knew was that, for now, he had to keep his distance from Anshika, despite the love they shared. He had made a promise, and he intended to keep it, even if it meant breaking his own heart.

Garv sat by the beach, his mind a whirlwind of thoughts and emotions. The waves crashed against the shore, mirroring the turbulence inside him. He had been lighting one cigarette after another, each puff trying to numb the ache that he couldn't escape. The world around him felt distant, irrelevant even. It wasn't that Garv didn't know that life doesn't end with one setback, but for him, it was different. Life had always been about Anshika. His plans, his future, his dreams—everything revolved around her. Without her, he couldn't imagine where he'd be, or what he'd even be doing.

Garv never thought about being apart from Anshika. Even after all the fights, the misunderstandings, and the times when it felt like the world was against them, he had always known one thing: He would always be there for her, no matter what. His love for her was the foundation of his world. He couldn't fathom life without her by his side.

But as much as he loved her, he had to admit something to himself: he had put all his hopes, all his happiness, into this one relationship. And now, standing at the precipice of uncertainty, he realized how dangerous that was. It was never wise to place all your happiness in the hands of one person, no matter how much you loved them. As much as he knew Anshika was his world, Garv realized he had neglected the other pieces of his life—his friends, his family, his own well-being. The truth was harsh: he had kept all his eggs in one basket.

"Never keep all your eggs in one basket," he thought. You can make one person your world, but never let your happiness depend entirely on them. If something went wrong, if things fell apart, it would hurt so much that you might not even be able to pick yourself up.

He took a deep breath as the sun began to set, the golden light mixing with the blue of the waves. It was a moment of clarity amidst the chaos. Garv had to find his own way forward, no matter the outcome of his relationship with Anshika. But tonight wasn't the time for all that. Tonight, he needed to go home, face his reality, and deal with the consequences.

With a heavy heart, he turned on his phone, his screen flashing with a call from Anshika. His stomach churned. He wasn't ready for this conversation. He didn't know what to say, how to explain himself. But he knew it had to happen.

He picked up the phone, bracing himself.

"Aapko kuch bolna hai?" Anshika's voice crackled on the other end.

"I am sorry," Garv whispered, feeling the weight of the words he could never take back.

Anshika's tone was sharp, a mix of hurt and frustration. "Garv, bohot jyada gussa aa raha hai mujhe. Sachhi bata rahi hoon," she said, her voice quivering with emotion.

Garv felt a lump in his throat. "Haanji," he replied, unsure of how to respond.

"Sach mein, maan kar raha hai. Chale jaaun main baccha?" Anshika asked, her voice a soft whisper now, filled with a quiet sadness.

"Haanji, baccha," Garv responded, the words coming out more automatically than he intended, a clear sign of the emotional numbness he was starting to feel.

But Anshika wasn't done. "Kya? Haanji? Mazak hai kya? Itna asaan sochte ho aap mere liye? Main pagal ho gayi hoon Garv, kyonki itna pyaar kiya hai aap se," she said, her words like a punch to his chest.

"Sorry, Anshika," Garv whispered again, his voice low, filled with regret.

"Mujae kuch answers chahiye," Anshika replied, the words like a final blow. "Then I will decide what to do. I'll need a few days to think about this, so don't keep your hopes high, Garv."

Garv could hear the finality in her voice. He didn't know what to say anymore, so he simply muttered, "Haanji."

Then came her next question, one that had been weighing on her mind, and undoubtedly on his as well. "Kya socha hai aapne CA ko lekar? Ab batao, aap muje. Kya surity hai ki is attempt mein ho jayega?"

The question hung in the air. Garv knew this was the moment that had been building for months. His CA exams, his promises, his dreams—all of it was wrapped up in Anshika's words. But how could he answer? How could he give her any assurance when everything in his life felt so uncertain?

He closed his eyes, trying to gather his thoughts. He wasn't just fighting for his own future now—he was fighting for the future he had imagined with her. But no matter how hard he tried, he couldn't shake the feeling that he was falling short of everything he had promised.

"Anshika... I don't know," he said finally, his voice a mix of vulnerability and despair. "I just... I don't know."

The silence on the other end felt deafening, as though the weight of their entire relationship was resting on the outcome of this one moment.

Garv rode to the beach, one cigarette after another, as he drowned in his thoughts. He couldn't make sense of what was happening or what he was supposed to do next. Yes, many of you may wonder why he was so fixated, thinking life doesn't end like this. But for him, life had no direction without Anshika. Everything he had planned was with her, and everything he had envisioned for the future always revolved around her. If he didn't get to be with Anshika, he honestly didn't know what to do or why he would do it. That's why he had never thought about being apart from her. No matter how many fights they had, Garv knew one thing for sure—he had given his all. No matter the situation, no matter who started the argument, he always knew that no matter how badly life would mess with them, he wanted to be with her, for her, and never leave her until his last breath.

But trust me, dear readers, never put all your eggs in one basket. You can make one person your entire world, but never sacrifice your happiness for that one person. Never take away the joy you get from your friends or family. If something goes wrong, you'll find yourself so lost, trying to pick up the pieces, not knowing how long it'll take to get back on your feet. Trust me, going all in like that can either make you the most ruthless person or leave you as nothing.

Back to our story, the evening sun dipped below the horizon, its orange glow reflecting on the waves that were growing bigger. It was then that Garv switched on his phone and called his mom. "I'll be home in half an hour," he said, his voice barely above a whisper. After a quick wash-up, he freshened up before heading home, where dinner awaited. Anshika had texted, saying she would call in about half an hour after she had settled in and freshened up.

Just then, Garv's screen lit up with an incoming call from Anshika. His heart sank. This was the worst part for him. He didn't know what to say. His mind made up that they were finally over. He picked up the call.

"I need to say something," Anshika said.

"I'm sorry," Garv muttered.

"A lot of anger is building up inside me, Garv. I'm being honest," Anshika continued.

"Yes?" Garv's voice was almost a whisper.

"Honestly, I've had enough. Do you want me to leave?" Anshika asked.

"Go ahead," Garv replied, his voice almost defeated.

"Why are you so casual about this? Do you think it's that easy to just let go, Garv? Why did you love me so much?" Anshika asked, her voice trembling with emotion.

"I'm sorry, Anshika," Garv whispered again.

"I need answers. Then I'll decide what to do, and I'll take a few days to think. So don't keep your hopes up," Anshika said.

"Okay," Garv replied, his tone soft.

"What do you think about your CA exams? Do you even have a guarantee that you'll pass this time?" Anshika's voice was firm.

"I can't guarantee the CA results, Anshika. I'll give my best. I'm positive—99 percent confident that I'll make it. But the rest is up to fate and external factors. The day the results come out, within one month, I'll be in Bangalore, I promise. And about setting up the house—well, that depends on when our families are okay with it. As for my love for you, I don't think I need to answer that. You already know. I'll always love you, Anshika. And about the cigarettes—I won't make a false promise. I'll quit them for you, but I can't promise that I'll never have one. I just promise that I'll be with you always, and the cigarettes will fade away in time," Garv explained, his voice steady despite the turmoil inside.

"I'll tell you one thing, Anshika," Garv said, his voice sincere.

"Yes, tell me," Anshika replied.

"The decision is yours. But always remember, make it from your heart, not just because you feel you have to. I love you, Anshika, and I will always fight for you. Once I'm there with you, I'll never leave your side, I promise," Garv said, his words full of resolve.

"I love you too, Garv. Now, go to sleep. I'm exhausted, and I'll think things through in the next few days. I'll let you know then. But take care of yourself," Anshika replied, her voice soft but firm.

"Okay. Goodnight. I'm not tired. If you can't sleep, call me. I'll be awake," Garv said.

"Goodnight, Garv," Anshika whispered.

The next day, Anshika told Garv to be free in the evening. She promised to support him but laid down some strict conditions: no going out, no attending weddings, just focusing on work and studies.

Garv nodded in agreement on their video call, his expression serious. She had included the wedding clause because in just fifteen days, their mutual friend, Shreyansh, was getting married. The next day, Garv called Pankaj to tell him he wouldn't be able to attend Shreyansh's wedding due to month-end pressure at work. He specifically asked Pankaj not to tell Shreyansh, as their trio had always been inseparable, and Garv knew Shreyansh would be devastated if he found out.

Everything seemed to be going well until, a few days later, Anshika informed Garv that her roommate wouldn't be home for a few days. Those dates coincided with Shreyansh's wedding. Garv, not wanting anyone to know, secretly planned a trip to Bangalore. He didn't tell anyone. But somehow, Pankaj found out, and the next day, Garv received a call from Shreyansh.

"Don't even talk to me if you're not coming to my wedding," Shreyansh said. "Don't use the month-end excuse, man. You're going to see that girl, and you don't have time for your brother's wedding? Don't even call me after this."

Tushar, a mutual friend from Delhi, also called Garv, urging him to come. Garv felt cornered, knowing Anshika would want him to go. But he also had to figure out how to manage his leave. With only five days left before month-end, he texted his boss to request urgent leave for the following Monday.

Garv scrambled to book last-minute flights, heading from Bangalore to Jaipur, then from Jaipur to Vadodara for his return. His plan to attend Shreyansh's wedding was costing him much more than he expected— flights were expensive, and he didn't even have wedding clothes.

So, Garv and Anshika went shopping, buying new clothes and shoes for the wedding. Anshika even bought him a pair of white sneakers, a gift that Garv appreciated deeply. The two of them spent the night in each other's company, talking about their uncertain future, but making the most of the time they had together.

The next morning, Garv kissed Anshika, holding her close. He felt a surge of emotion after all the struggles they had faced. Every time he saw a wedding, he couldn't help but dream about the day he would marry Anshika, the woman he loved more than anything. He took her in his arms, spinning her around, kissing her once more before waving her goodbye, and left for Jaipur.

Garv was the life of the party, the one who could never be left out. As soon as he landed, Shreyansh had already sent a driver to pick him up. The moment Garv stepped into the car, he got a call from Shreyansh. "You tell me where to stop, bro," Shreyansh said, knowing full well that Garv would never show up to a wedding without booze in hand. This was Jain's wedding after all, and Garv, along with his friends, didn't care about tradition or rules. They were there for the party.

Garv settled into the cab and immediately called Tushar. "What do you want to drink, man?" he asked, already planning his next move. He grabbed a few bottles of whisky and a pack of cigarettes, his essentials for the night. Heading straight to the ITC hotel, the venue for the extravagant celebration, Garv knew this was going to be a wedding unlike any other. The place was royal, and Garv's crew had been allocated three suits. He walked into his suite, the party vibe already in full swing.

The next two days were a blur of drinks, dancing, and pure joy, all in celebration of their friend getting married. It was one of those rare moments when life felt perfect—where nothing else mattered but the fun, the laughter, and the bond between friends. Garv and his friends partied like there was no tomorrow. They drank, they danced, they celebrated the wedding like it was their own.

As soon as the wedding came to an end, reality hit. Garv caught his 4 a.m. flight back to Vadodara, because, well, it was month-end and he had work to do. The high of the party still fresh in his mind, he knew the grind awaited him.

But just when it seemed like everything was starting to fall into place, life threw a curveball. You think everything is finally under control, but life, as it always does, reminded Garv that the real challenges were still ahead.

Chapter 26

Stars Are Really Farther Than They Appear

Finally, Garv's month-end chaos was behind him, and he had shifted his focus to a new goal: losing weight through diet and exercise. As the days went by, he found himself immersing in his studies. February came around, and Garv headed to Surat to celebrate his parents' 26th anniversary. It was during this time that Anshika told her mother about Garv and her relationship over the phone, and that evening turned into a rollercoaster of emotions for Garv. He had been anxiously waiting to talk to Anshika, wondering what the future would hold for them. The uncertainty weighed heavily on his mind.

He had quit smoking, and now, Garv found himself pacing the streets of Surat, sipping tea at a small shop, unable to calm his nerves. He made calls to his friends, each of them knowing how much this conversation meant to him. Over the years, they had witnessed Garv's loyalty—he had never flirted with anyone, never even looked at anyone else. His friends understood this about him, and they knew that if there was one thing he feared more than anything, it was losing Anshika.

For Garv, career success was important, but it was Anshika who truly held his heart. The thought of losing her seemed unbearable. He had never cared for material success or power. His goal had always been simple: to marry the love of his life. Even though his career wasn't progressing as fast as he hoped, he was willing to wait for the right time. But without Anshika by his side, life would lose its meaning.

His friends, too, were feeling the tension. Garv was unpredictable in moments like these, and no one could guess what his next move would be. On the other side, Anshika and her mother were talking about Garv. Anshika had sent her mother pictures from the wedding Garv had recently attended, and they discussed his career, his appearance, and many other things. In the end, they came to a conclusion: Garv would clear his CA exams this attempt and move to Bangalore, and they were willing to accept him.

When Garv heard this, he felt a rush of relief. Anshika reassured him that they were okay with him, and he promised her that he would give his best to clear his exams. But there was more at stake—his performance in the final quarter of the financial year. If he wanted to move to Bangalore with Anshika, he needed to perform well. Garv, deeply committed to his dream, promised himself that he would do whatever it took to make his life with Anshika a reality.

For Garv, his life had one singular goal: to marry Anshika. He never thought beyond that, never considered what might come after. All he knew was that once they were together, he would follow her wherever life took them, even if it meant moving to a new city or shifting his career. The only material goal he had was to own a Hummer before his life came to an end, and he was determined to reach it.

A few days later, on February 20th, Garv celebrated his mother's birthday in Surat. He gifted her a pair of parrots, as she had always wanted them. Her happiness warmed his heart, knowing that she often felt lonely when both of her sons were away. But soon, things took a dark turn.

Garv was in a meeting when his father called. He initially ignored it, but when his father called again, he knew something was wrong. He picked up the phone, and his father's sad tone made his heart sink. Garv's maternal uncle, his Mama, had passed away unexpectedly after suffering a heart attack. The news hit him like a ton of bricks. In every child's life, their Mama is someone special, always there with love and care. Garv couldn't believe it. He was devastated.

Overwhelmed by grief, Garv immediately ended his meeting and called his aunt in Surat to inform her. Then, without a second thought, he grabbed his two-wheeler and set off for Surat. He had to be with his mother. He told Anshika about the news, but even her comforting words couldn't ease his pain. He kept his sunglasses on while driving, knowing that once he reached Surat, he would break down.

He managed to reach Surat in just 2 hours and 30 minutes, making it to the airport just in time to meet his parents. He hugged his mother tightly, offering her the only comfort he could. Did Garv cry? No, he never did in front of anyone, except for Anshika. He never let his vulnerability show to the world.

After seeing his mother off to Delhi, Garv canceled all his meetings for the week and stayed in Surat, helping his Dadi, who was alone at home. A week later, he returned to Vadodara, but his workload had piled up. The emotional toll had affected his efficiency, and Garv found himself struggling to keep up with his tasks.

Finally, Garv's month-end workload had subsided, and he began focusing on his health. He adopted a diet and exercise routine and dove into his studies. In February, Garv traveled to Surat to celebrate his parents' 26th anniversary. It was a joyous occasion, but little did he know that the next few days would bring a whirlwind of emotions.

That evening, Anshika told her mom about Garv, and their conversation sparked an intense curiosity in Garv. He anxiously awaited their talk, pacing around, his mind consumed with thoughts about what the future held for him and Anshika. His friends—six of them—knew how much this moment mattered. Garv, who had never been interested in anyone other than Anshika, was now facing his deepest insecurity: the fear of losing her. He believed that while hard work would eventually pay off in his career, nothing compared to the value of Anshika. She was his everything. Without her, his life would be aimless. Garv had always prided himself on his loyalty, never once flirting with anyone, and his friends knew this about him.

The tension hung in the air for those three hours as Garv's friends shared his anxiety. Garv's commitment was unwavering. He was ready to face anything, even if it meant confronting Anshika's father. His dream had always been to marry her, and everything else—his career, goals, and ego—seemed insignificant in comparison. On the other side, Anshika and her mom discussed Garv's career, his figure, and everything that mattered to Anshika's family. The final conclusion was that Garv would pass his CA exams and move to Bangalore, and they were okay with him.

When Anshika told Garv about this, he felt a wave of relief and happiness. They both shared a quiet confidence, knowing they were on the same path. Garv promised to give his best in his career, especially now that the financial year was drawing to a close. His dream was to marry Anshika, and he was willing to work hard to make it a reality. His personal goals had one aim: to marry Anshika and buy a Hummer car before he breathed his last. For Garv, everything was focused on her.

In mid-February, Garv traveled to Surat to be with his mother for her birthday. He gifted her a pair of parrots, knowing how much she loved them. She had longed for them, and Garv was happy to make her smile. But just as he was settling into life, he received devastating news: his uncle had passed away from a heart attack. The news hit Garv hard. His uncle had always been a source of love and care, and now he was gone. Garv immediately called his Bua and rushed to Surat to be with his mother.

Anshika comforted him, but Garv struggled to express his pain. As always, he kept his emotions hidden, but Anshika's support helped him through it. After a week, Garv returned to Vadodara to resume work, but the stress of the past few weeks had taken a toll. His workload had piled up, and he found it increasingly difficult to keep up.

March arrived, and with it came the anticipation of the 10th anniversary of Garv and Anshika's relationship. However, fate had other plans. While playing cricket, Garv injured his right leg. The pain was excruciating, but he managed to push through, consulting his friend Dr. Harsha, who reassured him it wasn't serious. However, on March 7th, the day of their anniversary, Garv faced another setback. His leg injury worsened when he met with an accident on his way to work. The pain was unbearable, but Garv was determined to keep his promise to Anshika. He knew he had to be there for their anniversary, no matter what.

Despite the pain, Garv took four painkillers and somehow made it to the train station. He called Anshika and reassured her that he would make it to Bangalore as planned. Anshika, concerned for his well-being, urged him to take care, but Garv was resolute. He rested for a while, and his friend Bhuvi picked him up, albeit reluctantly, to take him to the airport. Garv had one goal: to celebrate their 10th anniversary with Anshika, no matter the pain.

When he finally landed in Bangalore, the pain was unbearable. But Garv's determination kept him going. He took another painkiller before heading to Anshika's house. Upon arrival, he was greeted by the most beautiful sight: Anshika had decorated the room with red roses, candles, and their favorite whiskey bottles. She wore a stunning dress, and the moment Garv walked in, he was overwhelmed by the love she had put into this surprise.

She hugged him tightly and kissed his forehead, making all of Garv's pain vanish. They spent the evening in each other's arms, cutting the cake and enjoying a romantic night together, surrounded by the soft glow of candles. Garv forgot his pain completely in her presence. As they danced under the soft light, he knew that, no matter what challenges lay ahead, their love would always be the one thing that would keep him strong.

For Garv, Anshika was everything. And in her arms, no pain could ever be too much to bear.

Garv swept Anshika off her feet, lifting her into the air with a playful grin. "Baccha, you'll hurt yourself," Anshika teased, concerned about his leg. Garv, unbothered, gently placed her back on his feet, and they moved together, swaying in a tight embrace. Their favorite song, *"Tum Hi Ho"* from *Anshikaqui 2*, filled the room as they danced, their bodies pressed closer with each step. With every movement, their hug became tighter, the night growing more romantic with each passing moment. The whisky, too, made their desires more apparent, igniting a hunger for each other's love. The atmosphere turned spicy, their passion growing with every beat of the song, until finally, Anshika, overcome by the intensity of it all, held Garv tightly in her arms and drifted into a peaceful sleep.

The morning light came slowly, and when Garv awoke, he was greeted by Anshika's gentle kiss. The whole morning and afternoon were spent wrapped in each other's arms, talking about the ten years they had shared and dreaming about the years to come. They kissed, held each other, and even shed a few tears. The emotional connection between them was deeper than ever.

Around 4 PM, Garv suggested they head to the mall. Anshika hesitated, knowing his leg was still hurting, but Garv insisted. He wanted to buy her a special gift to celebrate their tenth anniversary. After some reluctance, Anshika agreed, and they set off. As they left, their roommate and her sister wished them a happy anniversary, and the couple made their way to the mall.

Garv struggled to walk, his leg still aching, but Anshika held his hand tightly, steadying him. They browsed through the stores, but nothing caught their eye, especially in the jewelry section. After two or three hours of searching with no luck, Garv sighed in frustration. "Come on, we have to get something, it's our anniversary," he said.

But Anshika, always understanding, smiled. "It's okay. Next time, you'll get me something. I'm not going to leave you worried over this. I'll pick my gift when you're ready to buy it."

They left the mall and decided to grab a drink at *Social*. As they sipped on their beers, Garv suggested, "Why don't you ask Sheru if she can join us?"

Anshika hesitated, then explained, "Sheru's on bedrest—she injured herself at the gym."

Without skipping a beat, Garv suggested, "We should go visit her then."

So, they made their way to Sheru's house. Sheru, Chetna, and Chetna's boyfriend were there, and the conversation turned to feminism. The boys, as expected, mostly nodded along, barely contributing to the discussion. Garv, amused by the whole situation, leaned in and said to Anshika, "You know what? I might just take your surname, it won't make a difference to me. Men who truly love don't care about those things. And one thing's for sure—whenever we get married, every friend of mine will be there, supporting us. Because guys, no matter what, need their friends—at their weddings, their funerals. We want them by our side through everything."

The conversation carried on for a couple of hours, filled with laughs and deep discussions. Eventually, Garv and Anshika made their way back home, feeling closer than ever, knowing that no matter the challenges they faced, they would always have each other.

They spent the next few hours at Sheru's place, talking and laughing, until it was nearly 2 AM. Garv and Anshika finally decided to head back home, their bodies tired but their hearts full. As soon as they entered their room, Garv wrapped his arms around Anshika from behind, pulling her close. She could feel his warmth, and with the scent of her perfume still lingering in the air, they fell asleep peacefully, their bodies tangled in each other's embrace.

The next day, they spent a quiet morning window shopping, taking in the sights but not really looking for anything. It was their last day together before Garv had to leave for Vadodara. That night was long and intense, filled with emotion and passion as they held each other tighter than ever, not wanting to let go. They promised one another that no matter what, they would always be there for each other.

The next morning, Garv boarded his train to Vadodara, and life resumed. He juggled his studies and work while trying to keep up with the distance between him and Anshika. But life had other plans. Garv's grandmother, Dadi, slipped and fell while walking, requiring surgery. A few days later, his grandfather, Nanaji, passed away, throwing the family into mourning. Garv felt like he was drowning in a sea of emotional turmoil—his mom had already been devastated by the loss of Garv Mama, and now she was faced with the grief of losing her father too.

Unable to make the trip to Delhi because of his year-end work deadlines, Garv sent his friend Tushar to be with his family until his parents could arrive. Life seemed to be falling apart, piece by piece, but Garv kept pushing forward, focusing on what he could control.

Then, Anshika told him that she would be going to the US for 15 days for work. Garv felt a pang of sadness. With his own year-end work pressure, he was already struggling to find time for their late-night conversations. The thought of a time zone gap between them made everything feel more distant, but Garv, ever the patient one, tried not to let it bother him. He simply told her, "Bring back some Jordan shoes for me." Anshika agreed, and the two parted ways.

Garv spent his time in Ahmedabad before heading to Bombay for the final five days of his trip. He was exhausted from all the travel, but he knew it was part of the grind. However, during this time, Anshika barely communicated with him. Her replies were sparse, and the few calls she made lasted no more than fifteen minutes. She avoided his texts for hours, and though Garv noticed it, he didn't let it get to him. He had too much on his plate with his work and preparations for his exams. But as the days wore on, a part of him began to grow frustrated. He just wanted to hear her voice, even for a few minutes every day.

Finally, the day came when Anshika was set to return from the US. Garv had already planned his leaves for his exams, starting from April 12th, and he couldn't wait to see her again. When she returned, he was hurt by the lack of communication, and for a moment, he felt anger rise inside him. She hadn't talked to him enough, and she hadn't brought back the Jordan shoes as promised. But Garv quickly let go of his frustration, understanding that life sometimes got in the way.

He shifted his focus back to his studies, preparing for his upcoming exams. Time passed quickly, and soon it was April 27th, 2024—Anshika's

26th birthday. Garv posted a story on Instagram to celebrate her, replying to all the well-wishes from his friends. But something was off. Anshika had been acting strangely for a few days, and Garv couldn't quite figure out what was going on. Yet, he chose to push it aside, focusing on his studies. But deep down, he couldn't ignore the nagging feeling that something wasn't right.

As the day of her birthday approached, Garv couldn't shake the sense that something was brewing, though he tried to focus on his preparation. After all, excess of anything, even love, could be overwhelming at times.

Chapter 27

Love sometimes make people extraordinary Blind

Anshika's birthday had passed, but Garv couldn't shake the feeling that something was wrong. The next evening, he decided to talk to her about it. He told Anshika, "I'm planning a special gift for you—not just for your birthday, but for our anniversary too. I was thinking of booking a weekend house near Bangalore."

But Anshika didn't respond as he expected. She resisted strongly, almost harshly, and Garv sensed something deeper was at play. Despite his confusion, he couldn't figure out what had changed between them. He tried to push the worry aside, focusing on the fact that his exams were just three days away.

Garv's first exam went well, and he took two days off afterward to prepare. However, he stayed at his friend Bhuvi's house instead of his own, seeking to escape the comfort zone of home. During exams, he would barely sleep—just three hours in a 24-hour period. Garv didn't want any distractions. He spent his time studying diligently, focusing solely on the subjects he needed to clear.

But that night, as he sat in Bhuvi's living room, his phone buzzed. It was Anshika. She called, but something felt off. She didn't want to do a video call, which was unusual for them. Garv didn't question her. He stayed calm, listening to her voice through the phone.

"Aapko pata hain na," Anshika began, her voice tinged with emotion, "Maine hamesha aapse bahut pyaar kiya hain. I always loved you so much, and you'll always remain in my heart."

Garv listened quietly, feeling a strange weight settle in his chest. Anshika had always told him, "Kabhi mat jaana muje chhod kar," but he had never expressed his fears in return. He simply loved her with all he had, without question. Something in her tone, though, told him that all was not well.

They talked for hours, but the conversation lingered in Garv's mind, affecting his concentration. The next day, he found himself reaching for cigarettes again, the stress of the situation getting to him. His only focus was clearing his exams—everything else seemed secondary.

Despite the tension, Garv threw himself into preparing for his second paper. He worked relentlessly to cover the material, trying to push the thoughts of their conversation from his mind. By the end of the day, he felt more confident. He had done his best and managed the second paper well.

By the time he finished, Garv was almost certain he would pass the exams. He shared this with Anshika, wanting to reassure her that everything was going to be okay. But the final hurdle remained: the dreaded audit theory paper. Garv threw himself into the preparation with all his might, determined to tackle it head-on.

He had two days off to study, and everything seemed to be falling into place. But the night before his final exam, Anshika's mood shifted dramatically. She became sentimental and melancholic, and Garv could sense her sadness even through the phone. She knew he had his exam the next day, but it seemed like something deeper was troubling her.

Garv stayed focused, but his heart was heavy. The weight of their unspoken words hung between them, making it difficult for him to shake the feeling that something was about to change.

The next day, Anshika didn't seem to care. She spoke a few words that confirmed Garv's worst fears—that something was terribly wrong. Desperate for reassurance, Garv told her, "I'm not going to give the last exam if you don't swear on me that everything will be fine, that nothing is wrong." Anshika, perhaps sensing his distress, reluctantly swore on him, trying to calm him down.

But the damage was done. Garv had already wasted three precious hours, ruminating over their conversation. His mind was a whirlwind of doubt and anxiety, and no words could settle him. To release the tension building up inside, Garv decided to take Bhuvi's Continental GT 650 out for a ride. He pushed the bike to its limits, speeding past 130 km/h for a full hour, hoping the wind and the speed would clear his head. It didn't.

By the time he returned, he was still on edge, so he asked Bhuvi to stay awake with him as he studied. Garv was terrified—not of the exam, but of losing the one thing that mattered most to him: Anshika. Bhuvi, ever the supportive friend, stayed awake with Garv through the night, but he could tell his friend was far from calm. Garv hadn't slept a minute and felt like he was falling apart. He took a shower, hoping it would refresh him, but it was no use—the stress and anxiety over Anshika, along with the lack of rest, were overwhelming.

Realizing that nothing was helping, Garv gave up trying to calm himself and headed to the exam center two hours earlier than usual. He sat there, waiting for the exam to start, feeling utterly drained. When the paper arrived, he knew he'd be lucky to scrape through with exactly 40 marks. He had left out a few chapters in his revision, and to his horror, questions from those chapters appeared in the exam. They were basic, easy questions that should've been obvious—but he had missed them. Garv regretted his impulsive decisions from the night before, but there was nothing he could do now. He gave it his best shot, hoping he'd manage to pass.

After the exam, Garv immediately called Anshika, and when she picked up, she told him that they needed to talk. "Agar aap free ho toh ghar jao, aram se baat karte hain," she said, her tone distant. Garv, unsure of what was coming, went straight to Bhuvi's home and told his mom that he'd be home later that night.

Once at Bhuvi's house, Garv took a moment to calm himself, but the tension in his chest only grew as Anshika called him on video. She looked different—distant, unreadable. They shared a brief kiss, but something was off. Then Anshika, with no emotion in her face, said the words Garv had been dreading to hear: "It's over. My parents aren't agreeing for our relationship."

Garv couldn't comprehend what she was saying. He had never expected this, not after everything they had been through. "What do you mean it's over?" he asked, his voice trembling. "I don't understand. We've fought for this."

Anshika's voice was steady but full of resignation. "I've tried for the last 15 days, but they just won't accept it. It's not working."

A wave of anger hit Garv, and he snapped, "I'm coming to Bangalore today. I'm coming to fix this."

But Anshika resisted. "Why do you want to come to Bangalore? We can't even meet at my house."

Garv's frustration bubbled over. "You're breaking up with me over a video call? I'm coming. You can't stop me."

Her words were a quiet plea: "Okay, come. But you won't be able to meet at my house."

As the conversation unfolded, Bhuvi arrived home from the office. He had been expecting a celebration for something, but upon seeing Garv's tense and agitated state, his mood shifted. He immediately called Anuj and Rathi over, sensing the impending chaos. The three of them gathered, and Bhuvi, concerned for his friend, instructed them to stop Garv from going to Bangalore. They couldn't let him make a decision in this emotional state, especially with everything unraveling so quickly.

Anuj, always the practical one, just shook his head when Bhuvi tried to stop Garv. "Let him go," Anuj said. "You won't be able to stop him. He won't listen to anyone, and he needs to fight this out on his own." Anuj understood Garv in ways that no one else did—he knew Garv's stubbornness, knew that he wouldn't give up without putting up a real fight.

And so, Garv booked his flight from Surat to Bangalore, the departure just an hour away. Bhuvi, knowing how intense Garv was, agreed to drive him to the airport. As they neared the terminal, Anshika called. Garv could hear the hesitation in her voice, and she told him, "I'm going to Sheru's house by myself. You can come directly to my place."

This irked Garv. "You don't trust me, do you? You think I'm going to do something?" he snapped. His tone left no room for argument, and after a brief silence, Anshika reluctantly agreed that Garv would pick her up in a cab, and then they would both head to Sheru's together.

With his mind still in a storm of frustration, Garv wandered into Kalamandir at the airport, not knowing what was ahead. He knew Anshika's ring size—he had asked, and he had remembered—and so, without a second thought, he bought a ring for her engagement finger. When he called her afterward, he told her about the ring, and her voice cracked with emotion. She knew, deep down, how far Garv would go to show his love, and it touched her. "Will you ever stop making me happy?" she asked, her voice soft with tenderness.

But Garv stayed silent, his heart full but conflicted, and the conversation drifted to the side. He boarded the flight, his body fatigued from the sleepless nights, but he didn't care—his mind was set, and his love for Anshika was stronger than any exhaustion.

When he arrived in Bangalore, the first thing he did was smoke a cigarette outside the airport, trying to calm his nerves. The flight had been turbulent, both physically and emotionally. Anshika called again, and as they discussed their next move, they considered booking a hotel instead of going to Sheru's house. But everything was booked, and there was no choice. He would go to Sheru's with Anshika.

Throughout the cab ride, Anshika kept her distance, her eyes either closed in exhaustion or looking out the window. Garv watched her, noting how distant she seemed, the weight of their strained situation hanging over them both. It was May 7th, 2024—a day neither of them would ever forget.

When they reached Sheru's house, it was empty. Sheru wasn't there. Anshika and Garv sat down in his room, and the air was thick with tension. Anshika, trying to break the silence, asked, "So, what now? You don't want to go home, do you?" Garv was silent for a moment before replying, his voice barely audible, "You gave up in just 15 days. How could you?"

Anshika sighed, her frustration evident. "I'm trying, but it's not working."

Garv didn't argue. Instead, he reached into his bag and pulled out the ring he had bought for her. Anshika's eyes widened as she recognized the design—the one she had wanted for so long. It fit her finger perfectly, just as Garv had hoped. He had made sure of it, working with the store's executives to find the exact size. She smiled, her heart fluttering.

"Please, take it back," Anshika said softly. "If things work out, then you can give it to me."

But Garv, determined, replied, "I bought this for you, Anshika. If you won't accept it, I'll throw it out of the balcony right now."

With a sigh, Anshika reluctantly wore the ring, and Garv rested his head in her lap, hoping to give her some comfort and strength. He knew she was struggling, but his heart ached seeing her like this. Nothing he said seemed to change her mind. She had already made it clear she was giving up.

Eventually, Anshika drifted to sleep, and Garv sat beside her, rubbing her feet gently. It was 5 a.m. by the time they left for Anshika's house. There, she slept for a few hours, while Garv simply watched her, unable to tear his eyes away from her peaceful face. He felt her cheek, trying to remember the softness of it before things became complicated.

When she woke up, Garv took her hand, standing in front of her. "Give me the ring back," he said. With a soft sigh, Anshika handed it to him. Then, Garv got down on one knee, kissed her finger, and slid the ring back onto her hand. Tears welled up in Anshika's eyes as she whispered, "Why do you have to do this? I've accepted your ring, but why this?"

Garv held her tightly, kissing her forehead. "I just want you to know that I'm not giving up on us," he murmured. Anshika wiped her tears, still unsure but holding onto his warmth. "I'll try," she whispered, her voice breaking. "But if my parents still don't agree in the next few days, there will be news of my engagement to someone else."

Garv's anger flared. "Try. I'll give you the best engagement gift when that day comes, but I'll never stop fighting for us."

After Garv left for Surat, Anshika tried her best to fight for their relationship, but within a week, the situation had grown unbearable. She finally told him that it wasn't working, that her family wasn't agreeing, and that they should stop talking. The heartbreak was too much for Garv to bear. Anshika blocked him from every possible contact, and in an instant, Garv felt his world collapse.

He sat at Bhuvi's house, broken and lost, trying to piece together what had just happened. It was Sunday, a day meant for rest, but nothing about this day felt peaceful. Anuj, sensing something was wrong, came straight to Bhuvi's house. He walked into the room where Garv was sitting in silence, his head heavy with the weight of everything that had just shattered around him. Without saying a word, Garv closed the door behind them, and in an instant, he broke down, collapsing into Anuj's arms, his sobs echoing through the room.

Anuj didn't know what to say. He had never seen Garv like this—vulnerable, completely defeated. The only thing he could do was hold him tight, offering silent comfort. "Go home," Anuj said quietly. "Cry in front of your mom. She'll know what to do."

Garv nodded wordlessly, and, with his heart heavy, he left for home. On his way back, Anuj had already informed Garv's mother of what had happened. The moment Garv stepped into the house, he rushed to his room, feeling the weight of the entire situation on his chest. His mother entered quietly, closing the door behind her. It was the first time Garv had ever broken down like this in front of her. He rested his head in her lap, his tears falling uncontrollably. His mother, unable to find the right words, just held him, her arms wrapped around him in a desperate attempt to comfort him.

"No one's ever seen you like this, Garv," she whispered softly. "Everything will be okay. You'll see."

Garv's father, too, reached out to him, sending an emotional message on WhatsApp, urging him to stay strong. "We're here for you, son. Everything will work out in the end."

With a heavy heart, Garv managed to calm down a little. He went for a ride, trying to clear his mind, to process everything that had happened. The emptiness inside him was still overwhelming, but he needed to keep moving, keep thinking. It was then that he decided to reach out again.

He asked Shreyansh and Pankaj to contact Anshika. When they did, Anshika's bitterness towards him came spilling out. She spoke badly of him, blaming him for everything that had gone wrong. What she didn't know was that Garv was listening to every word.

Half an hour later, Garv picked up the phone and called her. His voice, though calm, was filled with the weight of his pain. "Do you know what I've done to you, Anshika? Everything I've done, except love you? I've given you my heart. And no matter what happens, I'll always wait for you. Because I can't undo this. I can't undo my love for you."

Love doesn't end easily; even when one side calls it quits, the other remains, holding on to the hope that it's not truly over. But for Garv, the pain was unbearable. He had never felt such agony in his life. After leaving Surat, he went back to Vadodara, but instead of finding solace, he sunk deeper into despair. He stopped eating, letting his weight drop drastically, consumed by the desire to fix everything before his results came in.

When you're in love, you beg for anything that can bring you peace, even if it means losing yourself in the process. Garv had never been a spiritual person, but for her, he found himself standing at Ajmer Sharif's dargah for the first time in his life, offering a chadar and praying for the chance to turn things around. When he returned to Vadodara, he spent hours in the temple, before and after office hours, simply praying and seeking peace for his tortured mind. But weeks passed, and no change came.

He started to wonder if it was all worth it. Despite everything he did for her, despite every ounce of himself he gave, she never even bothered to text him, to ask how he was doing. She didn't care about his pain. It hit him like a cold wave: never give anyone that much importance, never sacrifice your self-respect for anyone. But Garv had done exactly that. He had given up his way of life, his happiness, his ego—all of it, for her.

One Saturday, Garv returned to Surat, hoping to escape his torment for a while. That night, he partied hard with friends, trying to drown his sorrow in noise and distraction. The next morning, he spent time with his family, having breakfast with his brother who was home on vacation. Afterward, he left them a note, telling them he'd be back, and went to the beach. There, he had already written goodbye messages for everyone in his life, including a long letter for Anshika. He then made his way to Vadodara, donned his Batman T-shirt, and rode his two-wheeler to Bharuch, standing on the Narmada bridge, contemplating the unimaginable.

But the pain of hearing Anshika's words to his friend cut deeper than any wound—she had said she didn't care what happened to him. In that moment, Garv's heart shattered. He finished his pack of cigarettes, and in a haze of emotion, he stood on the bridge, ready to end it all. But just as he was about to jump, the police intervened, catching him in time and taking him to the station.

His friends, who had been desperately trying to reach him, found him there. They saved him that day, but the damage was done. While sitting in the police station, Bhuvi and Rathi arrived. Anuj wasn't there—he was in the hospital with a back issue. They all tried to reach Anshika, but she blocked them one by one. That was the day Garv realized something was wrong—not with her family, but with her. Something had shifted inside her.

When Garv returned home, his heart shattered further. He saw the pain in his mother's eyes and the sadness in his father's face. They were witnessing their strong son break into pieces, and it tore him apart. In that moment, he made a promise to himself that he would never go down this path again.

He took a week off from work, trying to clear his mind and calm his emotions. He returned to Vadodara, continuing his spiritual journey, finding solace in the temple and by the riverside. Sleep eluded him; he could only manage three hours a night. But he kept praying, hoping for peace.

Then, on July 12th, his results arrived. He had failed the last subject, despite performing well in the others. The disappointment hit hard. Alone in Vadodara, with no one to comfort him, Garv spiraled further. He drank to numb the pain, then impulsively traveled to Goa that same night. There, he sought even more destructive ways to feel the pain—he punched walls, did reckless things while driving, and lost a large amount of money in poker.

Days later, after returning to Vadodara, the month of Sawan began on July 22nd. Garv made a promise to himself that he wouldn't touch food or alcohol for the entire month, using this time to cleanse himself, to heal. For a few days, it seemed like he was sticking to his resolution, but on July 28th, everything changed. He saw a status update from Anshika's mother, where Anshika was smiling, showing off her engagement ring to everyone, laughing, and celebrating with her fiancé.

That moment, more than anything else, confirmed the truth to Garv— his love, his pain, his sacrifices... they had all been in vain.

The news of Anshika's engagement hit Garv like a tidal wave, leaving him helpless and angry. It had only been two months, and yet she had moved on. She was engaged. He couldn't wrap his head around it. Her engagement was a slap in the face, and as he sat there, unable to find the right words, his school friends—Rajat, Ruchit, and Daga—tried to reach out. But Garv was lost in his own chaos, trying to make sense of the betrayal, the anger, the deep hurt. He didn't know what to say, what to feel.

In that moment of frustration and rage, Garv made a decision: he would leave Surat. He transferred, packing up his life and leaving behind the memories that tortured him. Anuj called, as he always did, telling him to stay strong. "I'm always here for you," Anuj reassured him. But the truth was, Garv couldn't stay. After a few days back home, the house felt suffocating, filled with memories of Anshika. The room where they had spent hours on video calls for almost nine years was now a ghost, haunting him with every corner. So, Garv made another decision: he moved into Bhuvi's place.

This was where the journey of his book began.

Writing was never easy—it was toxic. But Bhuvi, Anuj, Rathi, and Ruchit were there for him, offering support and encouragement as he poured his soul onto the pages. The book was his therapy, a way for him to channel the anger, the betrayal, and the heartbreak into something tangible. Through it all, Kajol gave him the perfect cover, adding a beautiful touch to his work. But the process wasn't smooth—his days were consumed by alcohol, weed, and cigarettes. These vices were the only ways Garv could numb his emotions, to stay strong enough to write about his journey.

It was during this time that Garv started learning more about the man who had taken Anshika away. His curiosity grew, and as her engagement anniversary approached, Anshika had blocked all of their school friends—everyone, except Garv. But he was determined to find out who the guy was, who had replaced him in her life. Eventually, he discovered the truth. The man was from the same company as Anshika, and they had both traveled to the US in April.

Garv, despite his soft nature, could never tolerate betrayal. His patience, though vast, had its limits, and Anshika had crossed them. He made a vow—a target that would stretch over years—that he would deliver the best hit of her life, one that would leave her with no room to grieve. But that was the problem with men, Garv realized. They couldn't hold grudges forever. His anger would simmer, but with her, every night he tried to sleep, her engagement picture would flash before his eyes. And in the morning, it was her cute face that haunted him, taunting him, reminding him of what he had lost.

Garv tried to move on. He tried to date, to find someone else, even paying for companionship, but nothing worked. His heart couldn't let go. And his anger, his anger that had been so tightly controlled, began to surface again. The issue wasn't that he didn't know how to control it—it was that when he was angry, it was a force of nature, something so destructive that it scared him. He started keeping quiet, suppressing his rage to avoid hurting anyone unintentionally. But even then, it had its outlets. When his anger flared, it was unleashed on strangers—on people who had nothing to do with his pain. A few months passed, and Garv found himself lashing out at random people on the streets, his eyes burning with fury. His voice became a weapon, and if someone tried to strong-arm him, a single punch was enough to knock them down.

He had changed. He wasn't the same Garv anymore. His anger had taken over, and the once-patient man now feared his own temper.

Garv had always been the kind of person who thrived in the company of his friends, but after the betrayal, he couldn't bear to talk to anyone. He became increasingly isolated, even though he was surrounded by people who cared about him. Loneliness wrapped itself around him, squeezing tighter each day. His work life offered a brief escape. He had already taken an early release from his company, and the future seemed to promise something new. He received an offer from an NBFC with an 80% hike for the same location, but what truly stung was that he had also pulled an offer from a Bangalore-based NBFC, a 120% hike, all because he had once hoped to be closer to her. That was before she had shattered him in the cruelest way possible.

The pain of being rejected by someone he had once loved so deeply was more intense than anything physical. It was as if the emotional injury was so deep that no amount of physical pain could compare. Garv tried to numb it. He burned cigarettes into his hands, punched walls when he was alone, and sometimes, he would sit on the window ledge of his seventh-floor apartment, legs dangling over the edge, daring fate. The thrill of danger—speeding to Ahmedabad without a helmet, riding at over 100 km/h—was the only thing that made him feel alive, the only way to stop thinking about her, to stop remembering how much he had wanted her.

But nothing worked. His friends and family kept telling him that he deserved better. They urged him to move on, to forget her. But Garv never wanted better. He wanted her. He wanted to love her, to build a life together, to raise a little girl like her, to care for both of them for the rest of his life. But destiny had other plans, and with it, he lost peace in a way that he couldn't regain.

Eventually, Garv's work routine began. He started traveling back and forth from Surat to Vadodara every day—leaving at 6 AM and returning by midnight. He found some solace in the exhaustion, as it left him no time to think about anything else. For a while, that seemed to help. But after 20 days, when he took leave for his exams, he didn't care much for them. He prepared for a single paper, just enough to get an exemption and attempt the exams again later.

But fate had different plans for him. On the day after his last exam, Garv was driving at full speed across a bridge, his mind lost in memories of Anshika—her voice, their talks, the moments they shared. And that was when disaster struck. The bike slipped on the curve, sending Garv plummeting off the bridge. I got the call shortly after.

Who am I? I'm Anuj, Garv's best friend, and his emergency contact. The irony—now my emergency contact is no longer here, and with him, a love story ended. Garv's love will always be remembered, as will the man he was. He had a kind of love in him that was beyond measure, a loyalty and compassion that were unlike anyone else's. But sometimes, even the strongest people break.

His birthday was just around the corner, in twenty days. Garv had left behind everyone he loved, all for one person, and she didn't even have the decency to attend his funeral. It was a painful truth to swallow: 11 years together, and yet, it meant nothing to her in the end.

But I will remember Garv for who he was. He was the kind of man who could take on the world if his friends were in pain, the kind of person who would cut his own suffering to ease someone else's. He had a fierce loyalty that no one could match. And if you were in his good books, you had a friend who would fight any battle for you, without thinking twice about the consequences. Garv was unpredictable, but that was part of what made him so special. He was loving, and yes, his anger could burn with a rage that could scar, but it came from a place of pain.

I believe that God ended Garv's suffering when He called him home. The pain he had carried for so long—emotional and physical—had taken its toll. But Garv will live on, in every part of our lives. We will remember him as a man who loved deeply, who suffered deeply, and who never, ever gave up on the ones he loved.

He will always be remembered.

www.ingramcontent.com/pod-product-compliance
Lightning Source LLC
LaVergne TN
LVHW091705070526
838199LV00050B/2287